AND SURROUNDING AREAS

MAPLE BAY TOWN

THE TREASURE HUNTERS CLUB

A MYSTERY

TOM RYAN

Atlantic Monthly Press

New York

FIRST EDITION

Printed in Canada

This book was designed by Norman E. Tuttle at Alpha Design & Composition.
This book was set in 11.5-pt. Scala Pro
by Alpha Design & Composition of Pittsfield, NH.

First Grove Atlantic hardcover edition: October 2024

Library of Congress Cataloging-in-Publication data is available for this title.

ISBN 978-0-8021-6363-9
eISBN 978-0-8021-6364-6

Atlantic Monthly Press
an imprint of Grove Atlantic
154 West 14th Street
New York, NY 10011

Distributed by Publishers Group West

groveatlantic.com

24 25 26 27   10 9 8 7 6 5 4 3 2 1

In loving memory of Wheeler, 2009–2021

This is the last book we started together,
and the first we didn't finish together.

I miss him every day.

We must go on, because we can't turn back.

Robert Louis Stevenson, *Treasure Island*

PROLOGUE

If you were to spot them from a distance, you might wonder for a moment if you'd stepped back in time, so closely did the scene resemble an antique painting or a faded sepia photograph. A stretch of rocky coastline, rough and unspoiled. The open sea beyond, sailboats dancing against the horizon. A big, bold, active sky, wind and clouds and time racing above overhead.

An old man made his way carefully along the beach, his gaze fixed on the ground, stopping every so often to crouch and sift through the sand and gravel with his fingers.

A little girl ran back and forth nearby, burning off steam. She skirted the edge of the surf, then raced across the beach to a huge driftwood log. She hopped along its length, stopping where its tapered end hovered above the ground to perch effortlessly, like a seagull.

"Look at me, Grandy!" she called down, and the old man turned and smiled at her, shaking his head in amazement.

"If I've said it once, I've said it a thousand times," he called up to her. "You're nothing if you're not nimble. Now come on down from there and see what I found."

She skipped back along the log and jumped off the end before running to her grandfather's side. "What is it?" she asked, peering down at the object he held in his palm.

"It's a penny," he said.

"A penny," she repeated, unimpressed. "Better luck next time, I guess."

He laughed and reached out with his free hand to ruffle her hair.

"It's not just any penny, Dandy," he said, handing it to her to examine. "This penny is more than a hundred years old."

She turned it over in her hand. It was wider than a normal penny, flat and smooth, with only the faintest trace of a ridge around the outside edge. When she tilted it just the right way, Dandy could make out the ghost of a stern woman's profile pressed into the copper. Above her crown, CANADA was printed in big, bold lettering, and, sure enough, below her stately neck there was a date, 1901.

"Wow," she said under her breath. "What do you think it's worth?"

Grandy reached down to pluck the penny from her, holding it up to the light and considering it carefully.

"Well, now, Dandy," he said finally, with a wink. "I'd say it's worth about one red cent."

The two of them laughed and continued along the beach. As they rounded a bend, approaching the tip of the Point, Dandy noticed another figure in the distance. A woman, about as old as Grandy himself, was standing at the water's edge, staring out to sea.

"Look," she said, pointing. "It's Mirabel."

"That it is," he said, raising a hand as the old woman noticed them.

She returned the gesture, but instead of approaching she turned and began to make her way back across the width of the beach. Moving briskly, if not hurriedly, she climbed a short set of wooden steps, then crossed a lawn to an imposing Victorian mansion that sat on the very tip of the Point.

"She must not want to talk to us," Dandy observed as she watched the woman disappear inside the house.

"She probably doesn't feel like talking to anyone," her grandfather said. "Some people like to keep to themselves, and that's okay."

"Not you," she said, and he laughed.

"You're right about that," he said. "I like company. Yours most of all."

Dandy beamed at this. Her grandfather seemed to know everybody in Maple Bay. When they were out in town together, it felt like he spent half of his time stopping to talk to his many friends and acquaintances. She had learned many interesting things by listening in on Grandy's conversations.

"What do you say we head back and start thinking about some lunch?" he asked.

As they turned and began to make their way back along the Point, the old lady remained in Dandy's mind.

"Has Mirabel always lived in Bellwoods?" she asked.

He nodded. "Yep. She was born there. First she lived there with her parents, and later she had a family of her own. She's been on her own since her husband died. That was years ago now."

Dandy considered this. "It's a big house for one person."

"It sure is."

"I'd like to see the inside of Bellwoods someday," she said. A question occurred to her. "Have *you* ever been inside Bellwoods?"

Grandy nodded. "Many times."

Dandy was shocked. "Really?"

"You bet," he said. "Mirabel and I have known each other for a very long time. Since we were kids, in fact. She's one of my oldest friends."

Dandy's mouth dropped. She wouldn't have been more surprised if he'd told her Mirabel kept a pet triceratops in the backyard and rode it to church on Sundays. "You're friends with Mirabel?"

"What's so weird about that?" he asked.

"I didn't think she had any friends," she said.

"She has a few," said Grandy. "I'm one of them."

"Maybe you can take me to visit her," said Dandy. "Since you're friends."

"Someday," he said, after a pause. "When you're older."

"Why not now?" she pressed.

For a long time, Grandy was silent as he considered his response. "The truth is," he said finally, "Mirabel doesn't like to spend time with children."

"She doesn't like kids?" asked Dandy.

"I think she probably likes kids just fine," he said. "But they bring up bad memories for her."

"What kind of memories?"

"It's a long story," he said. "I'll tell you when you're older."

Dandy had more questions, but before she could ask them, something distracted her. Running ahead, she knelt in the sand

and leaned forward, peering down at the ground. Grandy soon caught up.

"What have you found?" he asked, crouching beside her.

She reached down and pulled aside a tuft of dried-up seaweed, revealing a bit of glass sticking out of the sand.

"Looks like the neck of a bottle," he said. "How in the devil did you spot that?"

"It caught the sun," she explained.

Together, they worked carefully to brush and dig away sand, and as more and more of the bottle was unearthed, Dandy began to imagine wonderful things. A miniature ship. A genie. *A treasure map.* But when Grandy finally lifted it out of the sand, she realized the disappointing truth.

"It's empty," she said.

But Grandy didn't seem to be disappointed. In fact, he seemed delighted, excited even, marveling as he held it up to the sky and examined it.

"This is a very old bottle, Dandy," he said, bringing it in close so she could see. "Look at how the bottom is puckered in like that, and all these little bubbles in the glass. That means it's handblown, and from the way the glass is soft and weathered like this, it's been in the salt water for years and years and years. Not a crack or a chip in it. Remarkable."

She reached out to run her fingers along the raised letters on the bottle.

"What does it say?" she asked.

"Farlowe and McGrath Ltd.," he read. "Whiskey. Maybe rum, but probably whiskey. It almost certainly came off a ship, and bobbed around in the surf for a very long time before landing here, just in time for us to find it. Imagine that."

She took the bottle from him and looked at it carefully. "Just in time for us to find it," she repeated, under her breath.

He nodded. "The sea reveals all her secrets eventually, my girl. But she does it on her own time. There's no sense trying to rush her."

"Maybe it came from a pirate ship," she said.

He laughed. "It's probably not quite that old, but you never know. Maybe it came off the *Obelisk* herself. Whatever the case, this is a fine discovery. Once in a lifetime. It will make a pretty specimen on your bookshelf."

"No," she said. "You should have it."

He looked at her with surprise. "You found it, girl, fair and square."

She held the bottle and looked it over. "I think it should go in your sunporch," she said. "It will be happiest there."

Still, he hesitated. "Are you sure? This is a very special thing you've found."

"It will be special wherever it lives," she said, and handed him back the bottle.

He smiled. "I can't argue with that," he said. "I'll tell you what. I'll buy it from you. For a penny."

"Deal!" said Dandy.

She grinned as he handed over the coin, clutching it tight in her fist as he carefully tucked the bottle into his battered old leather satchel.

The exchange complete, they continued on.

"Some people will spend their lives combing beaches and not find anything half as good as that penny or that bottle, and we found both in one day," said Grandy as they walked. He reached out to put an arm around his little granddaughter and pulled her in for a squeeze. "How's that for teamwork, Dandy?"

Years later, when Dandy was an old woman herself, with grand-children of her own and a long life behind her, she would remember this moment more vividly than any other. After everything in between, even the murders and the chaos and her terrifying brush with death, had faded away into distant memory, and all the secrets beneath Bellwoods's roof had long since been brought to light and committed to record, she had only to close her eyes and she was back there on the beach with her grandfather, a single old penny clutched tight in her fist, more precious to her than a sack full of gold.

PART ONE

October 12, 2023

Police have confirmed reports that two more bodies have been discovered in the small town of Maple Bay, Nova Scotia. The developments come on the heels of an investigation into another suspicious death which occurred on Tuesday at Bellwoods, a historically prominent local residence. While officials have released few details, sources have indicated that the deaths appear to be connected, and foul play is suspected.

Maple Bay is perhaps best known as the purported location of the *Obelisk* Treasure, widely considered to be among the most well-documented and independently verified cases of hidden treasure from the Golden Age of Piracy. Captain Barnabas Dagger's hidden cache has long attracted thrill seekers and amateur treasure hunters to the area, although its location remains a mystery.

At a press conference this morning, police refused to comment on a rumoured connection between the deaths and the treasure.

A LETTER FOR PETER

"Peter, is that you?"

Who else would it be? I think, hanging my bag on the hook by the door and kicking off my shoes. I stare into the kitchen, which is predictably filthy even though I know Ricky didn't go to work today. He likely hasn't left the apartment, either. Just once I'd like to come home and find the dishes washed, the counter wiped down, the garbage emptied. It would be so nice to cook a meal without having to squint past the grime to hold on to my appetite.

But this is Ricky's apartment, his name is on the lease, and I'm just renting a room, so I can't say much, if anything. His house, his rules. I can imagine him saying *If you don't like it, feel free to leave.* God knows he'd have no problem finding someone else to take the room. Considering how expensive rent has become in Vancouver, my shitty room in this garbage apartment is about the best deal going, filthy kitchen and all.

"Yeah," I call back. "It's me."

"There's mail on the table for you."

I frown. I can't think of anybody who would ever send me mail. I pay my bills online, and I can't remember the last time I gave anyone my address. Then I remember Aunt Carol guilting me into sharing it with her during our last rare and abridged *Yes, I'm still alive* phone call. "In case of emergencies," she said, and I broke down and gave it to her despite my better judgement. It wasn't like Bryce and Carol were going to show up here.

But she must have shared it with someone because, sure enough, when I step into the kitchen and look at the table, there *is* mail for me. Not just mail, but a heavy, expensive-looking cream envelope, addressed in elegant script to *Peter Bellwood Barnett*. I pick it up and look at the return address sticker in the corner. The embossed gold label reads, simply:

Bellwoods
Maple Bay, Nova Scotia

My heart skips a beat. Bellwood was my mother's middle name, and although I don't know much about her childhood, I do know that she grew up in Nova Scotia, an only child, like me.

But . . . Bellwoods, plural?

"Peter?" Ricky's annoying voice screams at me from the living room, pulling me from my daze. "Will you grab me a beer while you're out there? Grab one for yourself if you want, I sold a bunch of shit online today."

Normally I refuse his offers of beer or takeout, because I don't like to be beholden to anyone, but after the day I had at work, and now this unexpected letter from my mother's past, I really could use a beer. I grab two cans from the fridge and carry them, along with the letter, into the living room.

I'm greeted by a stale funk of weed smoke and sweat. Ricky is in his usual position: slumped into the chair at his desk in the corner, surrounded by empty energy drink cans and takeout containers, his giant bong within easy reach. I crack the beers and hand one to him, then flop down onto an armchair with the letter.

"Fun day at the office?" he asks, still focused on whatever toxic 4chan board has caught his attention today.

I grunt in acknowledgment, and he doesn't press. Ricky and I have learned to communicate in surface terms, and this kind of question is a social nicety that doesn't warrant a response. After more than six months living with Ricky, I'm still not entirely sure how he makes a living. I get the sense that my sublet helps him subsidize his own rent, and he's alluded to making a killing on some crypto that he sold off before the crash. But other than some vague talk about buying and selling stuff online, he seems to spend most of his time trolling around on the web.

I guess when you get down to it, he's like me, scraping together an existence in the gig economy and slowly giving up on any chance of a stable middle-class income.

In less than a month, I'll turn forty. I've spent most of my life passively watching the years go by, but something about the upcoming milestone has sharpened my senses, forced me to begin taking stock of my life. I'm going to be *middle-aged*. I graduated high school more than half my life ago, and what do I have to show for the twenty-plus years since? A useless bachelor's degree. A series of shitty jobs. Two failed relationships and a dwindling string of empty hookups. Three cities in ten years, and no connection worth mentioning to the couple who raised me.

I've been back in Vancouver for the better part of a year, hoping this time might be different, that I might finally start to put down some roots, but all I'm able to show for myself is a dead-end job at yet another call centre, a nonexistent social life, and a room in an apartment that I can just barely afford. I'm on the cusp of middle age but I'm living the life of a twenty-five-year-old.

Granted, these days that's really not so unusual. I can't keep track of the number of fully grown adults I've met at my various jobs over the past few years who are just barely keeping their heads above water. Forget about ever owning a house. We're overeducated and drowning in debt, living in tiny apartments or, worse, still at home with aging parents. Then there are the real loose cannons, people like me and Ricky, sharing accommodations to make ends meet.

I look at him now, a couple of years older than me, hunched over his computer with his baseball cap on backward, like that gif of Steve Buscemi. *How do you do, fellow kids?* I'm struck with an awful realization: my roommate, who I barely know and don't like, has somehow become the most consistent presence in my life.

Fuck.

I turn my attention to the envelope, allowing myself just a tiny glimmer of hope that there's something exciting inside. I know it's probably something boring, like a death notice for a distant relative, or maybe a wedding invitation for some unknown cousin, but as long as it's closed, it could be anything. An inheritance. A map leading me to buried treasure.

The truth is closer to both than I ever would have imagined.

I rip open the envelope and read the letter that slips out. Then I read it again. I'm staring at it so intently, in such a daze, that it takes me a few moments to register that Ricky is saying my name.

"Huh?" I say, looking up to find him staring at me from across the room.

"What the fuck is going on, man?" he asks. "You look like you've seen a ghost."

In the six months since I started living with Ricky, I haven't shared anything personal with him other than the absolute must-know basics. I'm gay. I'm single. I hate my job. But without hesitating, I hold out the letter. Partly because I don't even know how to explain, but mostly because I really need to share this with someone.

Ricky gives me an odd look but takes the letter and, after glancing at it, begins to read out loud.

> Dearest Peter. It's been several years since I last attempted to make contact with you, but as I'll explain, it was imperative that I make yet another effort. I am not sure if your aunt or uncle have ever really spoken to you about me. I'm assuming not, since you and I have never met—your mother decided before you were even born that she wanted nothing to do with me, or our legacy.

Ricky looks up from the letter. "Legacy," he says. "What the hell does that mean? It sounds like something from *Downton Abbey*."

"It gets weirder," I say.

He turns back to the letter and keeps reading.

> It brings me great sadness that I've never met my only grandchild, but I respected your mother's wishes, such as they were. It wasn't until much later—very recently, in fact—that I came to understand her reasoning.... but I get ahead of myself.
> Whatever the circumstances, fate denied us any opportunity to reunite. I grieved deeply when she died, but by that point we

9

had been estranged for the better part of two years, and she had refused my requests to meet you.

I briefly allowed myself some hope that once you were re-homed, your father's brother and his wife would see some sense and allow me to come visit you, but sadly, it wasn't to be. If anything, they were even more adamant than your mother and father: I was to have nothing to do with you.

I never met your uncle and aunt, or anyone in your father's family for that matter, but for sixteen years, I dutifully sent money every single month, for your education, and for sixteen years I got not one letter, or thank you card, not even a photograph.

But the cheques were deposited, so at least I've had the small satisfaction of knowing the price of your education was tempered by the funds I provided, even if they never told you where the money came from.

Ricky looks up at me.

"That true?" he asks. "Did she pay for your degree?"

I grimace. "Nope. I paid my own way through school. They didn't give me a red cent. This is the first I've ever heard of that cash."

"Shit, man," he says. "They stole from you? That's cold."

"Put it this way," I tell him. "We aren't close."

An understatement. My uncle Bryce and his wife, Carol, took me in when my parents were killed in the car crash, but they never made any attempt to fill the void left after the accident. If anything, they made sure I knew how much of a burden I was. It would have been just like them to take the money my grandmother had intended for my education. They would have looked at it as a payment for services rendered.

Ricky has reached the last part of the letter, and he slows down as he reads.

> It took me many attempts to finally convince your aunt and uncle to speak with me, and when they did, they were reluctant to provide me with your contact information. Finally, they agreed to forward me your address, but let's just say that palms needed to be greased before that happened.
>
> I will cut to the chase. The reason I have been so anxious to reach you comes down to this: I recently turned 90 years old. If my memory serves, that means you're coming up on a 40th birthday of your own. I hope you have plans to celebrate it with many friends, perhaps even a romantic partner. In all of my discussions—negotiations—with your guardians, they neglected to tell me much about you, but I hope you're living a life that satisfies and fulfills you. A milestone such as mine causes one to examine things carefully—to look backwards with perspective and, one hopes, acquired wisdom.
>
> It is a great regret of mine that I did not have the opportunity to resolve things with your mother before she died. I don't know how much you know about our family, but in this corner of the world, the name Bellwood once meant something. Now there are none of us left. None but me, and you. Your aunt mentioned that you are gay, and I shouldn't "expect any more apples from that tree," but I can assure you I have no issues with your sexuality, and if indeed you are the last of the Bellwood

line, it's very important that you take the rest of what I say very seriously.

"I'm on the edge of my seat!" says Ricky. He flips the final page.

Recently, quite by accident, I came across some . . . information. Secrets that had been kept for a very long time. I won't relate the details in writing, but I will say that this discovery has shaken me to the core, and called into question everything I ever thought I knew about our family.

We are the last two Bellwoods, Peter, and the burden of what I've discovered is too great for me to carry alone. I am asking you to please come see me, and help me bear this weight and tie up some loose ends. I am still quite healthy, and my mind is sharp, but as we both know all too well, time runs out for all of us, and I would like to bridge this gap before time runs out for me.

There are years to make up for. There are debts to be paid. There is a legacy that by rights should pass from me to you.

My house is large and comfortable, and in some ways, at least by virtue of your family history, it is your home as much as mine. I have no idea what you're doing with your life, but you are welcome to stay as long as you like. Indefinitely. I am opening my door to you. Please come in.

My contact information is at the top of this letter. Please feel free to call or email me to make arrangements. If I don't hear from you, I will assume that my pleas have fallen on deaf ears.

I hope very much to hear from you.

Sincerely,
Mirabel Bellwood Johnson,
"Grandmother"

When Ricky finishes reading the letter, he holds it out in front of him, squinting, as if to see whether what he just read is truthful or not.

"Holy shit," he says finally. "This is intense, man."

"I know, right?"

"So what are you going to do?"

I just shake my head. "I have no idea."

"You've got to go," he says. "I mean, come on. This is some high-roller shit. If I was you I'd shove a rose in my lapel and grab the next stagecoach to the East Coast."

"You want me out of here that bad?" I ask.

He shrugs. "Nah, you're fine. Stay as long as you want. But I mean, do you want to live here in this apartment with me forever? Just because the rent is cheap? How often does an opportunity like this come along?"

I stare at him, wondering if he's always been this insightful.

"Who knows?" he says. "Maybe I'll finally give up this dive and go do something exciting with my life."

I know he won't. He's been in this apartment for ten years, he doesn't have any goals, and he seems cheerfully comfortable with his lot in life. I find myself suddenly curious about him for the first time.

"Where's your family, anyway, Ricky?"

He rolls his eyes. "Who knows and who cares? I haven't spoken to my family in more than twenty years."

"No shit?"

He shrugs again. "They're a bunch of assholes. The less said the better. I like it like this. No contacts, no connections. I dealt with their shit for long enough, and then one day I just made a clean break, and it was the best decision I ever made."

"I'm not exactly estranged from Carol and Bryce," I say. "But I might as well be. They've never given a shit about me. If I disappeared tomorrow, they'd never notice. And even if they did, they wouldn't care."

It terrifies me, suddenly, to realize that I am on the exact same path as Ricky. I am cut off from the entire world as I know it, and in a sudden flash of insight, I see it laid out in front of me. What if I *did* stay here? What if I'm still here when I'm fifty, sharing my apartment with whatever down-on-his-luck stranger needs a cheap room and a place to flop? Worse, what if I'm still living here with *Ricky*?

Maybe this letter is the opportunity I need to finally put down some roots.

"She said indefinitely," I say. "Do you think she means it?"

He shrugs. "I dunno. She sounds like someone who has decided that she wants something, and she's desperate enough to put a pretty big offer on the table. I'd say she means it."

"It's weird," I say, remembering the label on the front of the envelope. "My grandmother's name is Mirabel Bellwood Johnson, but the label on the front says Bell*woods*, plural."

"Typo?" he asks.

"I don't know," I say. "I kind of doubt it. It's hard to tell from a letter, but she seems fussy or something. Like she wouldn't let a detail like that pass unnoticed."

Ricky spins around in his chair and focuses on his computer for a few moments, typing and scrolling. Then he laughs. "Holy shit, dude," he says. "Check this out."

I move to stand behind him, staring over his shoulder. On the screen is an internet header for "The Historic Town of Maple Bay" and below it is a photo of a huge, ornate Victorian mansion. The kind with a square turret and a wraparound veranda studded with elaborate gingerbread trim. Beneath the photo is a caption that reads *Bellwoods: one of Maple Bay's most iconic and beautiful old mansions. Continuously occupied by the Bellwood family for three generations.*

"Your family is rich, man!" says Ricky.

"I don't know about that," I say. "Lots of families had old houses like this back in the day. Doesn't mean the money is still there."

"I don't know," he says. "That house is in pretty immaculate shape. Do you know how expensive upkeep would be on a big old house like that? And it's just one old lady living there? She must be loaded, and now she wants you to come home and sign up for your inheritance!"

It isn't about the money. The last thing I want to do is take advantage of some little old lady. It's the thought of discovering my family that appeals to me. And I'd be lying if I said I wasn't intrigued by her discovery. What has she learned, and how does it relate to me?

"Maybe I'll go," I say, more to myself than anything. "Maybe I'll just fucking go."

"That's the spirit!" Ricky lifts his beer in salute before downing the rest of the bottle.

"But how does this play out?" I ask. "Do I just pick up and plan to leave forever?"

"Sure," he says. "Why not? What have you got to lose?"

"Won't I be leaving you in a bad spot?"

He shrugs. "I can find someone else to take over the apartment. Don't take this the wrong way, man, you're a good guy, easy to live with, but I don't really give a shit who lives here as long as they pay me the rent on time. This apartment is cheap. I'll have my pick of new roommates. Besides, it's not like you'd miss that job, right? You're always bitching about it."

"I hate my job," I admit.

"There you go," he says. "Pack your things, tell your boss to shove it, and go home to Grandma."

"When?" I ask.

He thinks this over for a long time, and when he finally speaks, he looks like he's come up with some kind of brilliant idea.

"First you need to go see your aunt and uncle," he says. "They live up north, right?"

"Yeah," I say. "In Barton, the little logging town where I grew up. But they're the last people I want to see. After learning about this? They stole from me!"

"That's exactly it," he says. "You need to confront them. Tell them right to their faces that you know they fucked you over, and you're cutting them off forever. Take no prisoners. Go full scorched earth on them."

I make a face. "That's not really my style," I say. "I think I'd rather just ghost them. They won't even notice I'm gone."

Ricky leans forward across the coffee table. "Peter. Take my word on this. You need to go see them; you'll regret it forever if you don't. Go stand in their living room, look them in the eye, and tell them you know what they did with your fucking money and you never want to see them again. Cut those ties, buddy. Do it in person. That's what I did, and I haven't regretted it for a single second. In fact, it was the best thing I ever did."

I have to admit, the idea is appealing. After all these years, it *would* be really satisfying to just cut them off, but even if I did take that step, am I prepared to take the next one? Am I really willing to pick up my life and move it somewhere totally new, where I'm a complete stranger, with no bearings or context?

"Hang on a sec," says Ricky. He returns to his computer, and after a bit more typing he clicks on something and leans back in his chair.

"Good old Google image search," he says.

I stare at the photo on the screen; it's of an elderly lady, small and poised, with fine features, directing her crisp, serious expression into the middle distance. The caption reads: *Mirabel Bellwood Johnson, President Emeritus, Maple Bay Ladies Society.*

My grandmother.

It occurs to me in a vivid, shocking blast as I stare at the photo: I'm not a stranger to this woman, I'm her grandson. She's my mother's mother. I might never have stepped foot in Maple Bay, or on the East Coast for that matter, but my family, my history, will give me bearings. What greater context is there for a person than their family? I have roots in an unfamiliar place, and now it's time to travel there and dig them up, begin to understand where I come from.

A veil has been lifted, and everything is suddenly as clear as crystal: this is a crucial moment, the kind of moment that separates the *before* and *after* of a person's life. The Fresh Prince moving to Bel Air, Charlie Bucket finding the Golden Ticket, Dorothy getting caught in the cyclone. I know that after tonight, my reality will have a different colour, my world will take on a different shape, and the person I'm supposed to be will finally come into focus. It might be happening forty years late, but there's no time like the present.

Ricky heaves himself out of his chair. "Big decisions, my man, big decisions. I'm going to grab another beer. You want one?"

I nod and watch as he leaves the room.

Goodbye, Ricky, I think. Goodbye, shitty apartment. Goodbye, dead-end job. Goodbye, aimless West Coast life.

I stare at the envelope on the coffee table.

Hello, Bellwoods.

AN OPPORTUNITY
FOR CASS

Cass and Falia drift around the edge of Washington Square Park, hand in hand, floating on a haze of rum cocktails. They're laughing, and then Cass is crying, pulling away and dropping to sit next to some bird shit on the edge of a curved stone bench.

Falia stops and turns around.

"Cass."

Her friend doesn't respond. She fumbles through her purse and pulls out a balled-up tissue. She unfolds it, wiping it across her eyes before blowing her nose with loud, honking abandon.

"Cass," Falia repeats. She steps closer, and Cass has no choice but to look up at her.

"What?"

"Are you going to move past the self-pity stage soon?"

Cass narrows her eyes. "How dare you."

Falia laughs. "Okay, drama queen. This is supposed to be our fun day out together, and you have cried at every single stop. Over brunch. While we were shopping for shoes. During happy hour. At dinner."

Falia's plan for the day, which Cass really did appreciate, was for the two of them to go on a memory tour of the city she's called home for almost five years. The day has been fun, but also a blunt reminder of just how much she's about to lose.

"I'm sad, okay?" she says. "I came to take a bite out of the Big Apple, and the Big Apple took a bite out of me."

"Oh my god," says Falia, snorting. "Listen to yourself."

She reaches out a hand and Cass reluctantly allows herself to be pulled up and into a hug.

"Honey," Falia whispers into her ear, "your life is a gift. If you focus all your energy on the things you're losing, you won't have any energy left to recognize new possibilities when they appear."

Cass pulls away and turns to stare into the park, at the activity going on all around them. A small group of teens laughs raucously as one of them climbs a statue; a busker plays sax under a streetlight; an adorable older couple sits tucked into each other on a park bench a few yards away. It's impossible for Cass *not* to imagine herself at the centre of everything, to avoid the dreadful, sinking, growing certainty that by moving away from this big, bright, shining city, full of color and diversity and music and traffic and noise and excitement, she's leaving behind the life that was always supposed to be hers.

It's easy for Falia to talk about possibilities when she's staying right here in the thick of things. What possibilities could be waiting in the basement of Cass's mother's split-level in the Milwaukee suburbs? She can easily imagine how it's all going to play out. A communications job at her stepdad's office. A few years dating some nice guy and eventually getting married. A couple of kids. A house in the suburbs.

The only real possibility is predictability, and predictability—as satisfying and fulfilling and wonderful as it might turn out to be—is the opposite of what Cass has always wanted from her life.

"You're just going to have to trust in the universe to present you with options," Falia continues. "Keep your eyes peeled and your heart open, and life will present you with every opportunity you need, no matter where you live."

"Okay, Oprah."

Falia ignores this. "You're going to get your ass back in the saddle and start writing again."

Cass shakes her head. "I already tried that. I flopped."

"You did not flop!" says Falia. "You were a victim of bad luck! Don't you remember your book launch? Standing room only?"

Of course Cass remembers. She remembers stacks of glistening hardcovers with her name embossed on the cover above a quote proclaiming it 'a stunning debut.' She remembers throngs of would-be admirers, drawn in by months of online buzz and the sparkle of a Kirkus star. She remembers wittily responding to questions from her interviewer as her adoring agent beamed at her, and signing dozens and dozens of books, and wrapping the night on a rooftop terrace with a champagne toast to her bright, glittering future.

But she also remembers the aftermath.

A failure to land on the *New York Times* Best Sellers list, despite her team's confident expectations. Lukewarm sales. Meetings with film and TV producers cancelled due to 'last-minute conflicts.' Zero interest from foreign publishers.

She remembers how things went from bad to worse. Her imprint abruptly shuttered by the publisher, a victim of cuts and an oversaturated YA market. Her editor laid off. The sequel she'd spent months writing unceremoniously cancelled.

Finally, she remembers the royalty statement that made it abundantly clear she would never earn out her advance in a million years. And now that same advance, the one that had once seemed so shockingly huge that it convinced Cass to quit her day job and move to New York to chase her bestseller dreams, is gone, eaten up by insane rent, expensive restaurants, and countless overpriced cocktails.

"I blew my shot," she says miserably. "My writing days are over."

"Bullshit." Falia slings her arm around Cass's shoulder. "You're an incredible talent who caught some unlucky breaks. You just need a few weeks to lick your wounds and then you'll dive into your next masterpiece. I know this sucks, and I'm going to miss the fuck out of you, but I want you to think of this as the beginning of a big new adventure, okay? You're Emily in Paris!"

Cass rolls her eyes. "You mean Cass in Milwaukee. I'm sure Netflix will be clamoring for the rights."

Falia ignores this. "Come on, let's grab a nightcap. There's a cute little wine bar a few blocks from here that I want to check out."

"Wine bar," Cass echoes sadly. "Does Milwaukee even have wine bars?"

Falia gives Cass a gentle shove sideways.

"No more whining," she says. "I need you to listen to me. Are you listening?"

Cass sighs. "I'm listening."

"This is just the beginning," says Falia. "Every good thing that happens to you for the rest of your life wouldn't have happened if you hadn't found yourself here to begin with."

Cass has had enough. "Falia," she says. "I love you, and I know you're just trying to make me feel better, but right now I am having a really hard time believing that any of this is part of some grand design. Sometimes people fail, okay? Sometimes people come to the end of the road, and the universe isn't there waiting with some wonderful opportunity."

Her phone rings.

In a daze, she pulls it from her purse. She expects to see her mother's name, but there's no contact or even phone number on the screen, just a message reading INTNL/Canada. She answers.

"Hello?"

"Hi, Cass?" says an unfamiliar but cheerful man's voice. "How's it going?"

"Well," she says, "I'm homeless and unemployed. How are you?"

There's a pause on the other end of the line.

"Yeah," says the man finally. "Your mom said you'd been having a rough go of things."

"My mom?" Cass snaps back to reality. "Wait, who is this?"

There's an awkward pause and then the man says, "Did your mother not tell you I'd be calling?"

"No," she says, thinking of the three calls she ignored this morning. Her mother insists on phoning when a text would suffice, and, frankly, that's *her* problem.

The man laughs. "Okay, that explains it. Sorry for jumping in like this. I must sound crazy."

Cass drops onto the curb. "What is going on?" Falia mouths. Cass shrugs.

"Let me start over," says the man on the phone. "My name is Alan Trapper. Do you remember me at all?"

Cass squints, trying to remember the name. It's vaguely familiar, but she can't place it.

"Maybe?"

"Ah," he says, and does Cass detect a note of sadness in his voice? "Okay, well, your father and I were friends. To be honest, we were basically best friends. Back when we were in college, before he met your mom and I met my wife, Judith. But you were only, what, ten when he died?"

"Eight," Cass says, feeling the slow, sad glow that always accompanies thoughts of her father.

"Eight," he repeats. "Yeah, so of course you don't remember me. I only met you once when you were really small."

Something about his story pricks at her memory.

"Yeah," she says. "I think I remember hearing about you, back when I was a kid. Alan, sure." This isn't exactly true, but something about the vibe of this conversation makes her feel like she should let him think it is.

"Yeah!" he says, brightening. "That's me! Your father and I were really close, Cass. Then he met your mom and got married and moved to the States, and then you came along. Then Judith—my wife—and I moved around a bit. We were on the West Coast for a few years, then Boston . . . You're probably too young to realize what things were like back then, but it was a lot easier to lose touch. No internet. Anyway, we kind of lost touch after your dad died. How old are you now, Cass?"

"I'm thirty-two," she says. She has no idea where this is going, but now that she knows this man had a connection to her father, she wants to hear what he has to say.

He laughs. "Thirty-two. How the hell did that happen, right?"

"Right," she says.

"Sorry," he says. "I'm rambling." He laughs again, and she realizes that she likes his laugh. It's rich and deep and . . . authentic. The fact that this man laughed with her father gives her a kind of sweet, sad feeling.

"Let me cut to the chase," says Alan. "I've kept in touch with your mom a bit since your dad died, mostly emails and Facebook posts. But last week I was feeling a bit sentimental and I really felt like talking to her, so I emailed to get her number and gave her a call. We had a great catch-up. We spent a lot of time talking about you, actually."

"Me?" Cass is surprised.

"Yeah," he says. "You're my best friend's kid. This might sound strange since you don't remember me at all, but you're important to me. Important enough that I should have done a better job checking in on you over the years."

Maybe it's because somehow, at the lowest point in her adult life, when she could most use her father's advice, his memory—his ghost—has unexpectedly been conjured, but suddenly Cass has a lump in her chest.

"I've read *The Sweetest Conversation*," Alan continues. "Actually, Judith and I both did."

"Really?" asks Cass, genuinely surprised.

"Of course!" he says. "Your mother sent me an email when you signed the deal, and I kept on top of it. We're not really your target audience, but we both loved it. We were looking forward to the sequel, but your mom filled us in on the situation with your publisher. What a pain in the ass!"

"Yeah," says Cass. "I guess you could say things have gone sideways for me over the past little while." Falia looks up from her phone, raising an eyebrow, and Cass shifts her tone. "But as my good friend here keeps telling me, every door that closes, a window opens."

"Well," says Alan. "I don't know if we're a window, or a door, or what exactly we are, but I wanted to call you because there's been an unexpected development in our lives. Judith and I find ourselves in a bit of a bind. I was thinking about that conversation with your mom, and it occurred to me that maybe you might be able to help us out, and in return there might be an opportunity for you, too."

Opportunity. A shiver runs down her back.

"Okay," she says.

"We've been planning a trip for a long time," Alan says. "Years, to be honest. It's the big retirement trip we've talked about forever. Three months in Paris, six months traveling around Europe, and three months in Rome. We have all the details ironed out, and we're supposed to fly out in a couple of days."

"Wow," says Cass. "A year in Europe. Sounds amazing."

"It does," he says. "Except for one last-minute glitch. The house sitter we had lined up has some family emergency, and she had to bail on us."

"Bail on you," Cass repeats.

"Yes," he says. "At literally the last minute. So now we're stuck, and we aren't really sure what to do. I mean, we could just lock the house and ask someone to check in on it once in a while, but the truth is this is our home, and we don't like the thought of leaving it all alone like that for a whole year. And then, of course, there's Banjo. We definitely don't want to leave him in a kennel for that long. Do you like dogs?"

"Um, sure?" The truth is, Cass has never really known any dogs. Not closely, anyway.

"Great!" he says. "So will you consider it?"

It takes Cass a moment to pull the pieces together. "Are you asking me if *I* can house-sit for you?"

"That's what I'm asking," he says. "I know this is totally out of left field, and your mother mentioned that you are supposed to fly out to Milwaukee tomorrow, so this would be a total shift of plans, but maybe it's the kind of change you're looking for? It's a paid gig, and obviously you get room and board."

"Um, I don't really know what to say," she tells him. "Where do you live?"

He laughs. "That would help, right? We live in Nova Scotia. Do you know Nova Scotia?"

"Not really," Cass admits. "I mean, Dad was Canadian, but we only ever went back to Toronto a couple of times when I was a kid. Is it near Toronto?"

He laughs again. "Not at all. It's on the East Coast. Think Maine, but Canada. It's beautiful here. Rugged coastline, beaches and sailboats, that kind of thing. We live outside a small town on the South Shore called Maple Bay. It's a fantastic little spot; there are some great cafes and restaurants, some nice shops, a decent library, and a great little bookstore. And you'd love our house. It's a modern build right on the water, with a hell of a view. Looks out onto a gorgeous old Victorian mansion, quite famous around here. It would be a wonderful spot to work on your next book."

"My next book," she repeats. And even as she says it, she can picture herself sitting in a window, staring out at the ocean and chewing on a pencil as she considers a turn of phrase.

"Maybe this isn't your thing," he says. "And that's totally fine. I called your mom again tonight to get your number, and when I explained the situation, she said that your stepdad has a job lined up for you at his company. That sounds like an excellent opportunity, and we don't want to be in the way, so please don't feel any pressure. We just wanted to make the offer, on the off chance you'd be interested."

As it always does when Cass thinks about the office job at Wilbur's medical supplies company, her heart sinks into her stomach and a little piece of her soul breaks off and dissolves into thin air.

"The thing is," he continues, "we'll need to know soon, because we're supposed to fly out the day after tomorrow. We'd pay you for the missed flight to Milwaukee, of course, and we'd cover your ticket to Halifax. It's a quick flight. Just a few hours, door-to-door."

Cass's mind races as she tries to take it all in. She's vaguely aware of Falia looking at her, of Alan waiting on the other end of the line.

Alan clears his throat.

"We don't need an answer right this second, of course," he says. "Why don't you take the night to think about it, and I'll call you in the—"

"Fuck it," she says.

"Fuck it?" he repeats.

Cass laughs. This is crazy. "Sorry. Yes. Fuck it. I mean, I'd love to. Thank you for thinking of me. Seriously."

"That's great!" he says. He tells her he'll look into flights, and after planning to chat again in the morning to finalize details, they end the call.

"So?" asks Falia. "Who was that?"

For a moment Cass just stares at the blank screen of her phone, then she turns to look at her friend, slightly dazed.

"Opportunity," she says.

A MISSION
FOR DANDY

After school, Dandy heads to the inlet for the first time in weeks, following the walking path that snakes along the wooded hillside behind Maple Bay Academy, where she's in ninth grade. Eventually, the path emerges from the trees onto a high, grassy field, and she stops to take in her surroundings.

The old town is behind her now, several streets of colourful wooden buildings clustered together around the eastern edge of Maple Bay. Across the bay, cutting inland for about a kilometre, is the inlet, with Dagger Woods sprawling west along the coast beyond it. Stretched out beyond everything, the sea: a vast quilt, churning with subtle colours, broken by rippling whitecaps and studded with islands and sailboats.

Grandy loved nothing better than to talk about the sea. He taught Dandy to read cloud formations and respect the tides and currents. He regaled her with stories of nautical adventures and tragedies. He rhapsodized about the promise of the open water.

As it always does when she thinks of her grandfather, Dandy's heart drops into her stomach. He's only been dead for a few weeks, but in some ways his absence is so huge that it almost feels like he never existed. One day sick with a flu, the next day wheeled into a hospital room, and within a week dead of stomach cancer. How could something like that happen so quickly? How can a person so vital just disappear?

The path descends quickly until it spits Dandy onto the gravel road that runs along the Point, the hilly spit of land that divides the inlet from the greater bay. There are only a few houses along the Point: Bill Jinx's crusty little trailer compound down on the shore, a newer contemporary home set high up on the hill, and, perched imposingly at the tip, Bellwoods, staring back across the bay at town, like a jilted lover.

Grandy's house sits on the inner curve of the inlet, where it begins to turn back on itself. It's a little cottage, with a fairy-tale feel to it: weathered grey shingles and bright red trim, a knobby stone chimney clinging to the side of the house, and tacked onto the back, staring straight down along the inlet, the sunroom where Grandy spent much of his time, reading and listening to old-time music on his antique wooden case radio.

The driveway is empty, which tells Dandy her mother hasn't arrived yet, and she finds herself slowing her approach. She hasn't been back here since the funeral, avoiding this visit for as long as she was able.

Dandy figured it would look the way it always has, cheerful and inviting. Instead it's dark: slumped and defeated and *empty*. The curtains are drawn and the lights are turned off, and the roof even looks like it's sagging, as if it's given up entirely.

She crouches to reach under the front step, pulling out the spare key and letting herself into the house. A familiar smell hits her as she crosses the threshold: apples and incense, black tea, and the mildewy foul-weather gear hanging on hooks inside the door. She closes the door and stops for a moment in the small entryway as a heavy weight presses down on her shoulders.

Gathering herself, Dandy slowly moves through the house, stopping for a moment in each of the rooms that she knows so well. The cozy living room, full of overstuffed furniture and woollen lap blankets, a half-burned log still sitting in the cold fireplace. The tiny den with books lining the walls around his enormous wooden roll-top desk. The kitchen with its ancient propane stove and rugged wooden shelves heaped with a random assortment of mismatched dishes, and the round wooden table in the corner.

Finally, she steps through the glass door at the back of the kitchen and down into the sunroom at the back of the house, full of plants and records and more piles of books, all nestled in around a mishmash of comfortable, well-worn furniture. The window ledge is lined with treasures Grandy collected over the years: wooden ships, brass nautical instruments, and bits and pieces of flotsam and jetsam from countless beachcombing adventures.

An old bottle catches some light from the sun that's making its way down over the western horizon. Dandy picks it up and runs her hands over the impossibly smooth glass. She remembers the day they found this bottle, how proud she was to pull it out of the sand and hand it to Grandy.

She might as well have found the *Obelisk* Treasure, by the way his eyes gleamed as he turned it over in his hands, marvelling at the bottle's condition.

Dandy places the bottle back on the shelf and turns around to scan the rest of the room. Along the back wall, a built-in bookcase dominates the space, filled with old books and record albums and stacks of *National Geographic*. There's one particular shelf in the middle on the far-right corner, butted up against the exterior wall, that catches her attention.

Moving closer confirms her suspicions. The little green wooden sailboat that has always occupied this shelf is facing left, Grandy's code that he's left something here for her.

She removes the sailboat and places it carefully on a nearby end table, then she kneels and reaches into the shelf. With two fists, she places her knuckles against two specific spots against the back panel, pressing firmly. Immediately, with a soft click, the panel pops open on an invisible hinge.

Grandy first showed Dandy the secret cabinet when she was about five. It's a small space, about the size of four shoeboxes stacked two by two. He would often leave little treasures inside for her to find: a sun-bleached bird's skull, a book of nautical knots, a bar of chocolate. When the sailboat faced north, she'd know to look.

Now, peering inside the secret cabinet, Dandy inhales sharply before reaching in and pulling out a familiar leather satchel, old and worn and battered. Grandy never left the house without this bag, which would be filled at any given time with all manner of things: the book he was reading, a wedge of cheese and some bread, fishing tackle, you name it. Clipped to the flap is a small piece of yellow paper, and written on it in Grandy's neat cursive is *Dandy*.

Dandy takes the bag out of the cabinet, then closes it carefully and replaces the sailboat, so that it once again faces south. As she drops into Grandy's beat-up old armchair, she registers how heavy it is. There are several pockets and compartments hidden throughout, and she makes her way through them one at a time. Inside each one is an offering. A small hardbound sketchbook and a collection of sketching pencils, bound with a rubber band; a brass compass; a knife for cutting mushrooms or shucking oysters; binoculars; Grandy's big, solid old flashlight.

Dandy smiles, remembering how Grandy used to call himself a well-prepared son of a gun. But as she returns each of the objects carefully back into its place, a grim and devastating realization hits her.

He knew.

He knew he was dying, and he left this bag, and all of these things, for her to find after he was gone. She thinks back to the month before he died, how he had gone out of his way to spend even more time with her than usual.

It had all seemed a bit strange at the time, but now it makes perfect sense. He knew.

She looks inside the main compartment last. Grandy's old green cardigan is neatly folded up and tucked inside, and she pulls it out and holds it up to her face, inhaling deeply to catch some of his scent. She pushes back her tears and is about to shove the sweater back into the bag when she notices something else slipped into a flap at the back.

It's a manila envelope, with her name written on it once again. The first thing she pulls out is a folded piece of a nautical chart, grimy with age and gridded with creases, but still tough and intact thanks to the heavy waterproof paper. The chart shows the coast around Maple Bay, including a basic map of the town. A curlicued legend in the lower corner reads *Maple Bay Harbour and Surrounding Approach; 1934.* She peers closer and is able to identify a rectangle marking this very cottage. At the other end of the spit, a much larger rectangle has been granted a caption, *Bellwoods*. Between them is a circle drawn faintly in pencil, marking what looks like another building, this one much smaller.

There's something else in the envelope, and even before she pulls it out, she knows what it is. She holds the letter in her hand for a long time before finally unfolding it.

Dear old Dandy,

It might seem strange to get a letter when you weren't expecting one, especially considering the letter writer has bit the biscuit, but I was always a master of surprise and spectacle, as you well know, so here I am with a surprise missive from (queue the Vincent Price voiceover) BEYOND. THE. GRAVE.

I wish more than anything, sweet, tough Dandy, that at the moment you're reading this, I was able to apparate behind you, a miracle, or a prank, or a comforting ghost, but I'm afraid that's beyond my abilities, my friend.

Dandy looks up and squints, hoping he'll prove her wrong and appear in the corner of her eye. But all she sees is dust motes floating through a shaft of light, the inlet, and in the sunroom window, a small, reflected slice of herself, a weird, pale girl, hunched over a letter and holding back tears.

This letter is all I can give you, and I hope it will serve as a decent substitute. Right here, right now, I want you to do me a favour. Close your eyes and remember my voice. Remember me speaking to you. Remember my side of our conversations. My own dear mother died many years before you were born, before your own mother was born, as a matter of fact, yet even as her face faded in my mind, her voice remained, a clear and precious gift. A voice is a magical thing, it echoes after death, as long as there's someone there to hear it.

Dandy, remember this: I am with you always, speaking to you in the back of your mind. Feel free to ignore or listen as you see fit.

I'm leaving you with a few things. First, the various items that you may have already pulled out of the bag. They all came in handy to me over the years, and you might find them equally useful. It's like I always said, it pays to be a well-prepared son of a gun.

This next part is more important, Dandy, so pay attention and don't get distracted.

For many years, I've been a member of . . . well, I guess you could say it's a genealogical society of sorts. On the surface, we're just a bunch of old farts who meet once a month at the public library to discuss the past and our family trees, but the truth is . . . well, I'll let them fill you in on the truth. The society meets at 7 p.m. sharp on the third Thursday of every month.

I want you to go to the next meeting of the genealogical society, and tell them it was my express wish that you should take over my spot in the group. They might be reluctant to share their secrets, but I expect they'll take my request seriously once you tell them I left behind a clue.

You'll notice that I've included a section of nautical chart with this letter. If they offer you admission, and I truly hope they will, I want you to join and then I want you to share the chart with them.

I know this must all be a bit confusing, so I'll give you a bit of vague clarity. I'm leaving you with one final thing: a mystery. I can't tell you what that is. That much is up to you. But I have faith that you'll find your way, both to the mystery, and to the solution. It's my hope that you'll get a bit of help from my friends, in the immortal words of John Lennon.

My time is coming to a close, my Dandy little pal. Don't let the bullshit stand in the way of the good shit. I've lived a long life, and I can tell you this: the good shit always outweighs the bullshit.

> With all my love,
> Reginald Alistair Feltzen
> "Grandy"

Before she has time to really consider the letter, Dandy hears the front door open.

"Hello? Danielle?" her mother calls from the entryway.

"I'm back here!" Dandy calls back, already tucking the letter back into the envelope.

"I've got some cleaning supplies in the car. Can you come help me unload them?"

On her way out of the sunroom, Dandy glances at the old paper calendar on the wall.

The third Thursday of the month is the day after tomorrow.

WELCOME TO
MAPLE BAY

Cass spends most of her flight daydreaming about her new life in Nova Scotia. She pictures herself bicycling along the remote seacoast, cozying up in the corner of a local pub with some brilliant and inspiring new friends, dedicating herself to daily vigorous sessions of yoga, and all the while, making progress on her next book.

Not that she has any idea what her next book will be about. One thing she *does* know is that it won't be another YA novel. She's been down that road already, and she doesn't have the stomach to risk that kind of disappointment again. Besides, after the fiasco that was *The Sweetest Conversation*, she's not sure she *could* get another young adult novel published. She's ready to try something completely different, and decides she'll just have to track down the inspiration once she gets there.

The pilot announces their descent, and through the window she watches a rocky coastline come into focus. They swoop over Halifax, a smallish seaside city, before touching down. Just like that, Cass has landed in her new life.

After navigating customs, she picks up Alan and Judith's Subaru, and finds her way onto the highway that skirts Halifax. After an hour or so of driving, she crests a hill and passes a quaintly painted billboard that announces, HISTORIC MAPLE BAY: *SEA IT ALL!*

Cass's phone guides her directly through the centre of town, past a series of colourful old buildings, a kaleidoscope of gingerbread trim and wooden shingles and huge, elaborate doors as impressive as fine furniture. She takes note of several places she wants to check out, including a couple of cafes and restaurants and, on one corner, a charming little bookstore that must be the one Alan mentioned. She drives past a busy waterfront bustling with tourists taking photos of the big old schooners that are tied up to the docks. Outside a pub that announces itself as THE SHIVERING TIMBERS, a lineup of people chat and laugh as they wait to be seated on a large patio.

Leaving the town centre behind, she drives to the far side of the bay, where her iPhone directs her to turn left onto a gravel road, Point Drive. She follows this to the tip of a narrow peninsula of land until she finally arrives at her destination, someplace called Bellwoods.

At the end of a tree-lined driveway sits a massive Victorian house: three impeccably maintained stories with a wrap-around veranda and a bell tower. Cass parks beside a vintage Jaguar and climbs out of the car, taking a moment to soak in the view. The house is built on the point of a small peninsula, and the ocean surrounds it on three sides. Back across the bay, Cass spots the town of Maple Bay looking like a postcard.

She climbs the wide steps and crosses to a set of huge double doors and presses the bell.

Immediately, she hears barking inside, and when the door opens a moment later, a scruffy little dog leaps out of the door at her. Caught off guard, Cass takes a step back, almost tripping in the process.

"Banjo!" says a sharp voice. "Down!" A small, elderly woman yanks on the dog's leash, just barely holding it back.

"It's okay," says Cass. She holds out her hand and the dog stops jumping long enough to sniff. He sits, his tail going a mile a minute, and Cass reaches down to scratch him on the head. "Good dog. Stay."

"You'd better come in," says the woman, in a less-than-friendly voice. "I have keys and the dog's things."

She turns and disappears down a long hallway, dragging Banjo along with her. While Cass waits for them to return, she takes in her surroundings. She's standing in a large, stately entrance foyer lined with wooden panelling, artwork in heavy frames, and expensive-looking furniture. Arched doorways on either side of the hallway reveal ornately appointed, grimly formal rooms that sit in the gloom beyond heavy drapes, drawn almost shut. It feels more like a museum than a residence.

Dominating the hallway is a massive wooden staircase climbing steeply to an upper level that peers down on Cass from the shadows behind a gallery railing. Every inch of the staircase, from the risers to the polished circular banister, is carved with an elaborate design, leaves and vines and birds, intricately interwoven and hauntingly beautiful.

Two portraits hang above the stairs. The higher of the two is a very formal painting of a distinguished elderly-looking man with a swoop of white hair and a thick matching moustache. His expression is severe, even angry, especially when compared to the other painting. This one, in a slightly more modern style, shows a younger man, perhaps in his early fifties. There's a clear resemblance between the two, but while this man's expression is also serious, it's more sad than angry, with a hint of gentle resignation in the eyes.

A door at the end of the hallway swings open for a moment, revealing the woman. From beyond her, Cass catches a quick glimpse of a large, bright kitchen before it swings shut and the old woman clip-clops efficiently back down the hallway, a leash in one hand, a clear plastic bin full of dog kibble in the other.

She hands the kibble to Cass as she crouches to clip Banjo to his leash, then stands and hands that over as well.

"There's a list of instructions inside the food bin," she says. "Best of luck to you."

It's clearly a dismissal, but Cass doesn't move, a bit surprised that the woman hasn't even attempted to make some kind of neighbourly overture.

"I'm Cass," she says.

The woman pinches her lips into a reluctant smile. "Mirabel Bellwood Johnson."

"Your house is beautiful." Cass looks around as if to emphasize her point.

"Thank you," says Mirabel. Then, almost as if she can't help herself, she offers: "Bellwoods. It was designed and built by a very well-known architect of the time. Jeremiah Buckland."

Cass tries to sound suitably impressed. "Wow. Cool. Do you live here all by yourself?"

Mirabel's eyes narrow in suspicion, and Cass realizes that she's said the wrong thing.

"I've lived here by myself for almost twenty-five years," she says coldly. "Since my husband passed away. I assume you're commenting on my age, and it's true that I'm ninety years old, but I manage quite well. My father lived to be a hundred, and this was his home until the very end. Besides, the house is secure, and I keep a gun in my bedroom."

Cass manages to stifle a snort. Does this woman think she's going to try to rob her? "Oh no," she explains. "I wasn't commenting on your age. I just mean, it's such an enormous house. It must be a ton of work to keep it up."

Mirabel sniffs. "I have help. It's very important that this house remain in my family. A Bellwood has lived here ever since it was built, over a hundred and twenty-five years ago."

"That's really nice," says Cass. "The whole family connection and all that." She realizes that she's babbling, and the woman wants her to leave, but her curiosity gets the better of her and she points at the portraits over the stairs. "Are those two men Bellwoods?"

Without turning around, Mirabel nods curtly.

"My grandfather and my father," she says. "Respected men, both."

Cass squints at the paintings and the resemblance comes into focus. Mirabel has the sharp, shrewd expression of her grandfather. But despite her imperious attitude, there's a hint of softness around her eyes that's reminiscent of the younger man.

"I guess your painting will be up there with them someday," says Cass cheerfully.

Any softness in Mirabel's eyes evaporates.

"Unlikely," she says, in a tight, clipped tone. "You know how to get to the Trappers' house?" It's another obvious invitation to leave, and this time Cass takes the hint.

"I have it plugged into my phone," she says. "I'm sure it will be easy to find."

"Let me show you."

Mirabel leads Cass out onto the veranda and points back along the road to a hill in the near distance.

"You can't quite see their house through my trees, but it's impossible to miss," she says. "Just take the first driveway on the left and follow it to the top of the hill. Their property used to be an original part of the Bellwood estate, and if I'd had my way, nobody would have ever bought that piece of land. The entire Point once belonged to the Bellwoods."

"The Point?" asks Cass.

"This peninsula," Mirabel explains. "My great-grandfather first settled on this land over a hundred and fifty years ago." She gestures to a wooded thicket behind the house. "He built the original house farther back, through those woods. His son, my grandfather, built this house. At some point he sold off most of the Point, including the hill where Alan and Judith built. Lord knows why he sold it, but it's out of my control now. I can't imagine what the Trappers paid for their land. Frank Oakley would have expected a pretty penny to part with even that much land. And don't get me started on that monstrosity of a house that they built."

"You know them well?" Cass asks.

"The Trappers? I barely know them at all," Mirabel sniffs. "I try to avoid them, to be honest. Judith is all right, but Alan has no concept of social nuance. I'm an old woman and I don't much care to socialize, especially with people I don't particularly like."

Cass knows she should leave, but curiosity gets the better of her. "If you barely know them, and you don't really like them, why did you offer to take Banjo?"

Mirabel sniffs. "I didn't offer. Alan arrived on my doorstep yesterday with the dog in town and some convoluted story about travel arrangements, and he had the audacity to ask me to my face. He totally put me on the spot; didn't even have the decency to leave a phone message I could ignore."

"But you said yes," says Cass.

"I could hardly say no," says Mirabel. "You see, there was a storm last year, and one of the old maples at the foot of the driveway was badly damaged. Alan took it upon himself to bring his chain saw and little tractor down to cut it up and clear it away. I'll admit that it was helpful of him, and kind." She says the last word almost distastefully. "But to be honest I'd have been just as happy to pay someone to come take care of it, because I ended up in his debt. I couldn't very well say no when he asked me to take the dog for the night, even though I don't like dogs. Not one bit. But now, at least, the debt is paid."

Cass nods and smiles as if this isn't one of the most insane transactional things she's ever heard.

"We'll get out of your hair," she says. "Thanks again. Perhaps I'll see you around."

With a crisp goodbye, Mirabel turns around and walks back into the house, and Cass leads Banjo down the steps and into the Subaru.

"Okay, dog," she says. "Let's break you out of this joint."

* * *

It isn't hard to tell why Mirabel doesn't approve of the Trappers' house. It couldn't be more different from Bellwoods if it tried. It's sleek and angular, wood and steel framing lots and lots of glass— like something straight out of a *Black Mirror* episode.

Banjo leads the way to the front door. There's no key, just a code. When Cass punches it in, there's a substantial, audible *click* and the door swings open smoothly despite its obvious heft.

The entryway is small and understated. A wooden bench sits beneath a row of heavy iron hooks, and an antique console is home to a stack of mail and a heavy pottery bowl full of keys and dog bags and chewed-up rubber balls. Above it hangs a large painted skyscape, greys and blues mingling to imply an imminent storm. Banjo disappears around a corner and Cass drops her bags and follows him, gasping out loud as she enters the next room.

She's in a large, modern kitchen, all walnut and industrial steel and black slate countertops. A massive kitchen island is surrounded by a half dozen wooden stools. Next to a small glass vase holding a single dahlia blossom, there's a card with her name on it. Lying flat on the counter next to it, several printed pages, labelled *House, Banjo,* et cetera. Cass doesn't have the energy to read through the document right now, so she leaves it for later and continues through the kitchen and down a couple of steps into the living space.

Floor-to-ceiling windows run the full length of the longest wall, turning a corner and continuing until they stop at a wood-burning fireplace with four huge leather armchairs sitting around it. Although the house is contemporary, it isn't cold—the Trappers have filled it with an eclectic mix of comfortable, well-worn furniture. There are books stacked everywhere, and artwork, area rugs, and cushions provide the airy, open space with splashes of colour. Across from the large sectional sofa, a wall of windows reveals the spectacular view of the water and the undulating coastline. Across the bay, the town looks like a postcard. Closer, at the bottom of the hill, Cass can see the Bellwoods tower peeking over the treetops.

Cass stands, taking it in for a moment. "Holy shit, Banjo," she muses. "I don't think I'm in Kansas anymore."

She wanders through the rest of the house, stopping when she enters a study, tucked into a corner behind the bedrooms. A desk is centred underneath a picture window with a full view down the hill to the water. On the wall opposite, floor-to-ceiling shelves are crammed with books and framed photographs. A snapshot catches her eye, and she picks it up by the frame and peers closer. It's her father, back when he was still a late-eighties rocker type, tall and lanky, with long black hair and a leather jacket. He's standing with his arm around another guy, shorter and stockier, with a full beard, who Cass assumes must be Alan. They're both grinning wildly, as if someone off camera just told them a hilarious joke.

For the first time, it begins to sink in that this isn't just some stranger's house; it belongs to someone who knew Cass's father better, in so many ways, than she ever did.

She replaces the photo and turns to look back at the desk, a wide expanse of reddish-gold wood, gleaming in the sunlight. She pulls out the chair and sits, which Banjo takes as his cue to settle onto a cushion in the corner, curling up and letting out a contented little sigh.

Cass raps her fingers on the desk, staring out the window at the ocean. For one whole glorious year, this house, complete with the view, the desk, and the connection to her father, is hers. She has to hand it to Falia, the universe really did rise to the challenge. If ever there was a perfect place to write another book, this is it.

The only problem is, what the hell is she going to write about?

PETER'S GRANDMOTHER

There are a lot of words I could use to describe Bellwoods—"stately," "impressive," "dominant"—but "intimidating" tops the list. Standing at the bottom of the front steps, I have to crane my neck almost all the way back to stare up, beyond the rows of gingerbread trim and decorative shingles, to the top of the bell tower.

It has a fucking *bell tower*. What the hell am I getting myself into?

I don't belong here.

When I drop my gaze, I realize that the front door is wide-open, and there's a small, dignified-looking woman standing on the threshold, her hands clasped neatly in front of her.

Mirabel Bellwood Johnson looks just like her photo from the internet, with none of the usual disconnect that usually exists between a professionally taken shot and the real thing. Her hair is twisted into a neat chignon, her makeup expertly applied, her grey pantsuit starched and pressed. A large amethyst pendant is settled into a fold of her white silk blouse. If I didn't know better, I'd think she had dressed up for my arrival.

Suddenly the weight of my decision, the implications of what this will mean—blowing up my world and heading to a new part of the world where I know *nobody*, leaning into this massive kind of gamble, all of it . . . come into crisp, clear focus.

This is the right thing for me. It is. I need to believe it.

"Hello!" I call out. I raise my hand. "I'm Peter."

As I climb the stairs, she unclasps her hands and takes a few steps forward, attempting a smile. "I didn't expect you for several more days," she says, the faintest trace of admonition in her voice.

"I'm sorry," I say. "I began to worry that I was on the verge of losing my nerve, so I just . . . I just came. I should have emailed to tell you I'd changed my plan, but I was worried that you might discourage me, and I worried that would make things worse. I—this is just a lot to deal with right now, and I'm not sure if I'm making the right decision . . ."

She seems to shift her perspective and her expression softens. "I'm sorry," she says. "You're right, of course. It's a lot for both of us to absorb." She takes a deep breath and looks up into my eyes. "I'm very happy to finally meet you. I'm glad you came early; that just means we have more time together."

Her voice cracks slightly and I can see that she's trembling. I freeze, wondering what I should do next. This woman is supposed to be my grandmother; shouldn't we hug? And so, without overthinking it, I lean forward and pull her into an embrace. She's tiny in my arms, frail, but with perfect posture and a pronounced sturdiness at the core of her slight frame.

She pulls back from me and we smile at each other, the awkwardness broken.

She reaches up with a thin hand to cup my chin, pushing my head from side to side as she examines my face.

"Your mother was a Bellwood through and through, with her fine, pale features," she says, scrutinizing me. "You must take after your father's people, or perhaps your grandfather's. My husband liked to play the devout Anglican, but there was some Irish Catholic in the mix back down the line, muddying the pot."

I have to force myself not to laugh. Is she for real?

"We'll have plenty of time to discuss genealogy later," she says, releasing me. "Please, come in. Let's have some tea and get acquainted."

I follow her into the house, kicking off my shoes inside the front door. I gaze around in awe.

"Holy shit," I say, before I remember to catch my language. "This place is amazing."

It's a mansion, clear and simple. Beyond high archways I spot beautifully appointed rooms full of expensive-looking artwork and furniture. In front of me, the most impressive staircase I've ever seen, polished wood, ornately carved, climbs steeply into the upper depths of the house.

"This is your family home," she says. "I only wish you'd seen it as a child. Children always found the house magical. I know I did as a child."

"I don't know," I say, my eyes darting from one expensive piece of artwork to the next. "I'm no spring chicken, but I still think it's pretty magical."

I can tell I've pleased her, and her face begins to break into a smile, but she turns away before I have a chance to see it, and leads me down a hallway past the impressive staircase. Beyond a swinging door, we enter a kitchen. While it's big, in keeping with the scale of the rest of the house, it's also much cozier and more welcoming than the museum-worthy rooms out front.

"Please," she says, "have a seat. Can I get you some tea?" I nod as she gestures to a table in a windowed nook, and as she begins to busy herself at the stove, I slide into the upholstered bench and peer out the windows at the simple but elegant gardens that surround the house. Several hydrangeas, sheltered from the weather by a stone wall, are still in full bloom even this late in the season. Between a couple of trees I catch a glimpse of ocean, a distant sailboat sliding quickly through the scene before disappearing out of sight behind a screen of maple leaves.

"I'm sorry again about surprising you," I say. "I know I should have let you know. I had planned to go see my aunt and uncle for a few days, but I changed my mind. Like I said, I started to feel as if I needed to get here as quickly as possible, or I'd lose my nerve."

"Bryce and Carol," she says, and there's undisguised contempt in her voice. "Do they know that you've come to see me?"

"No," I say.

"Why not? Aren't you close with them?" She rummages in a cupboard and pulls out two elegant china cups and saucers.

"Not really," I say. "We've barely been in touch for a few years. Whatever the opposite of close is, that's us. Distant, I guess."

She stops what she's doing and pauses for a long time. I get the sense she is being careful to tread lightly. Without looking at me, she clears her throat, then resumes making the tea as she speaks again.

"I'm surprised," she says. "Since they raised you, I've always imagined you out there on the West Coast, wholly absorbed into a perfect little family."

I laugh. "As a matter of fact, I emailed them after I got your letter to say I was cutting off ties completely. I don't want anything more to do with them."

At this, she does look at me, snapping her head sharply to examine me with those cold blue eyes.

"That's a bit extreme, isn't it?"

I shake my head. "They ruined my childhood. I lost both of my parents when I was so young, and they made me feel like I was a burden for the entire time I lived with them. Your letter is what really sealed the deal, though."

I know her interest is piqued now, and I wait until she's carried the tea tray over to the table and taken a seat across from me to continue. The teapot sits between us, forgotten, as she leans forward, eager for me to explain.

"In your letter you mentioned that you sent me money every month," I say.

She nods. "Every single month after your parents were killed," she says. "Five hundred dollars a month, like clockwork. I never missed a payment."

I quickly do the math. That's six thousand a year. More than eighty thousand over fourteen years. Back in the nineties, that would have been more than enough to pay for tuition at a decent school, but if Bryce and Carol had the foresight to invest it, there could have been quite a bit more than that.

"I never saw a penny of that money," I say. "They stole it from me. I paid for my university degree by myself, with loans and part-time jobs. They never gave me a cent. Until I got your letter, I didn't know that money even existed."

Her face is a mask of shock. She recoils from me, a mixture of horror and sorrow and regret flickering across her features. Her expression settles into rage.

"How dare they!" she says, her voice almost quivering with anger. "I made it abundantly clear to your aunt and uncle that my contributions were an investment in your education, full stop. I wanted you to have a head start with your future! I also made sure they knew that if you needed additional assistance for your education, I was prepared to help out."

"I'm sorry," I say.

"It clearly isn't your fault," she says. "But I'll admit that I always hoped that in time you'd find your way back to Maple Bay, if only to see where your mother came from. I took care to apply no conditions to that money, but I assumed you would someday reach out to say thank you. When you turned eighteen, I thought maybe I'd hear from you, and then when I didn't, I told myself you were busy with your studies, and that you'd reach out once you'd finished that stage of your life. When you turned twenty-five, I began to think I was waiting for a ghost to appear, and after thirty, my hope dwindled more and more. For the past several years, I've forced myself to put you out of my head entirely. I'm ashamed to say now that I thought you were simply ungrateful, but to think that this whole time you were entirely unaware of the whole thing . . ."

"I'm really sorry," I say again. "I have to be honest, I didn't even know you existed."

At this, to my dismay, she bursts into tears.

"Oh shit," I say, totally out of my element. "Shit. Okay. Listen, there's no reason to freak out."

But her tears continue to flow unabated, as if they've been held in for years and now they're being unloaded all at once. In a flush of desperation, I reach for the teapot and hurriedly pour her a cup.

"Milk, no sugar," she says through tears, and I quickly prepare it and pass it across the table to her.

"Listen," I say. "You found me. You found me despite everything."

Working to compose herself, she grabs a tissue from a box on the windowsill and wipes at her face. She takes a deep breath and then sips at her tea before speaking. "Yes. Yes, I found you."

"And I'm here."

"Yes, you're here." She takes another slurp of tea, and I'm relieved that she's calming down. She puts down her cup. "We'll sue them," she says. "I sent letters telling them exactly what that money was for. We'll make them pay back every last cent."

I hesitate for a moment before reaching across the table to take her hand. It's balled up tight, but I squeeze gently and she allows it to relax.

"I don't want to do that," I say. "I don't want to think about those people ever again. I want to start over and forget about those assholes. Let's put all those hard feelings and tears away. The money doesn't matter. What matters is what happens from here on out. What matters is that we've found each other."

She stares at me for a long time, and her reserved, challenging eyes soften in front of me. I know that I've struck a chord, that I've found my way to the centre of what matters to her more than anything.

"Quite right," she says finally. "The only thing that matters is that our family, small as it is, has found its way back together. We won't concern ourselves with those grifters. Besides, I'm hardly destitute. There's plenty of money left."

She picks up a napkin, using it to dab at her eyes, then raps on the table and stands up. "We have forty years of catching up to do, and a lot to fill you in on. I might be old, but I'm not dead yet."

As she gives me a tour of the house, she fills me in on the Bellwood family history.

"Your great-great-grandfather, Alexander Bellwood, was a very successful businessman," she says, stopping in the entrance hallway in front of a portrait of a stern man with a thick white moustache and eyebrows to match. "He went on to become a mayor of Maple Bay. When he died, the town erected a prominent monument over his grave, which you can see if you visit the old town graveyard."

"He's a pretty serious-looking dude," I say.

She nods. "Grandfather was a man of ambition and vision."

"He must have been important if this house is any indication," I say.

She nods, but there's something in her expression that makes me question what she really thought of the old man.

"He commissioned an architect to build the house," she continues. "A very famous man by the name of Jeremiah Buckland. Buckland came all the way from London with a full complement of craftsmen, artisans, and builders, and they worked for a year to build Bellwoods."

She caresses the huge carved newel post at the bottom of the stairs.

"There was no expense spared with this house," she says. "Every stone in the foundation, every marble tile in the kitchen and bathrooms, all of them were chosen carefully in consultation with Buckland. And this staircase was the crowning jewel, English walnut, quarter-sawn white oak from Hungary, and of course red maple from right here in Maple Bay."

I reach out and caress the intricately carved design that weaves its way up the stairs. Looking at it closely, I realize that the wood has been carved into a forest motif. The heavy newel post is a stylized tree trunk, with roots curling around from the bottom to merge seamlessly with the panels that make up its side. Along the base, spindles lift like branches from a base of pine cones and moss, and along the gleaming banister, clusters of leaves and berries sit smoothly in the spaces between elegantly twisting vines.

"It's a work of art," I say.

"It was carved by two brothers," she says. "Bavarian sculptors. In fact, this entire house was built by foreign workmen and artisans, originally here to work on the Academy building. Italian plasterers, French woodworkers, British masons. The very best builders in the world worked together on this house. It was supposed to be my grandmother's castle, but she died before it was completed."

She points at the other portrait, hanging just below Alexander's.

"My father, Henry, was old enough to remember when the house was being built," she says. "Some of his fondest memories were of spending time with the builders and craftsmen. He was very young when his mother died, and his older sisters were shipped away to boarding school. His own father was a brilliant man, but hard and distant, often away on business. He had no time for my father, and so Henry was left to be raised, essentially, by a local woman who came in to do the cooking and cleaning. Some of the builders, no doubt missing their own families back in Europe, also took the boy under their wing. He loved this house."

"Who wouldn't?" I ask.

She nods. "My father was a very good man, gentle and soft-spoken, but very well liked. He had a kind word for everyone, and he liked best of all to talk to the craftsmen in town. I believe, under different circumstances, he would have become a carpenter himself."

She pauses and stares at the floor for a moment.

"He was still alive when you were born," she says. "He didn't die until you were about a year old. He was very close to your mother, and would have loved nothing more than to meet you." Her voice becomes formal again as she turns and continues to climb the stairs. "Your mother had other plans, unfortunately. I know she had her reasons. She was an idealist, like so many young people back then. At the time, those of us in the older generations found those attitudes irritating and naive, but now I wonder if we couldn't use a bit more of that kind of attitude these days." Her face falls. "The bottom line is that Susan was always uncomfortable with our privilege, and I suppose at a certain point she decided that she couldn't reconcile her own morals with her family history." She pauses, suddenly looking very tired and old. "I didn't know the whole story back then."

I wonder if this is what she meant in her letter, about discovering new information. I'm about to ask when she reaches out and puts a hand on my arm, silencing me.

"There will be plenty of time to discuss that," she says. "But not today. Today is about you."

Without giving me the chance to respond, she turns, grabs the banister, and begins to climb.

As I follow her up the stairs, it strikes me how steep they are, and how impressive that a woman of her age manages to climb them with so little effort. When we reach the landing, she turns, and smiles at me.

"Thirty-three steps," she says, as if reading my mind. "And more to go."

I follow her up another, smaller flight of stairs to the third floor, where she opens a small door revealing yet another set of steps, little more than a ladder.

"If you wouldn't mind going first, Peter," she says. "There's a hatch at the top that's a bit difficult for me to open."

I climb the narrow steps, reaching up to pull back on the heavy iron bolt that's holding the hatch closed, and shoving upward. I'm immediately hit by a rush of wind to the face. I take the final few steps and emerge on the bell tower, a small, open-sided square room with ornate woodwork railings making a balcony out of each of the four sides.

The railing is a bit too low for comfort, and I keep a tight grip as I peer out over the surrounding countryside. Far below, the colours and shapes of the garden are blurred and abstract, Bellwoods's grounds somehow diminished from this new height and perspective. By contrast, the ocean stretched out in front of me appears much bigger than it did on the ground, the horizon suddenly so far away that I find myself getting dizzy.

I have a strong urge to climb back down through the hatch and never come up here again. But Mirabel has moved to stand comfortably against the east-facing railing, and so I steel myself and move to stand next to her.

From here, we have a clear view of the little town across the bay. Below us, the tip of the Point sweeps around us. I can see the road to my left, ending as it reaches the Bellwoods driveway. On the other side, a thick mat of forest borders the back gardens and then continues across to the far side of the Point.

Mirabel gestures in that direction.

"The original Bellwood home was on the other side of the Point," she says. "The house where my father was born was back there. Long gone, of course, along with the land, thanks to my grandfather."

She turns back to stare at Maple Bay in the distance. For a long time she doesn't say anything. The wind seems to come to a complete and unnatural pause, and a strange stillness falls on us as I wait for her to continue.

"But none of that matters now, Peter," she says finally. "Now that you've finally made your way home."

THE CLUB

Bonnie Brickland looks up as Dandy approaches the checkout desk.

"Hi, Danielle," says the librarian. "I haven't seen you in here for a while."

Dandy shrugs. "It's been a weird couple of months."

"I'm sure it has," says Bonnie, giving her the kind of warm and sympathetic expression Dandy has seen a lot lately. "I want to tell you how sad I was to hear about your grandfather. Reg was one of a kind."

Dandy is in no mood for a pity party, so she gets right to the point. "That's actually why I'm here," she says. "Grandy told me he belonged to some kind of group that meets here on the third Thursday of every month to talk about local history and genealogy and stuff like that."

"That's right," says Bonnie. "Like clockwork." She glances at a closed door in the back corner of the library. "They're in there now, but good luck if you're planning to speak to them. They run a pretty tight ship."

"What do you mean?" asks Dandy.

"Well, in almost twenty years working here, I've never seen anyone other than the core group invited into those meetings. I actually asked to join when I first moved to town, and they shut me down before the words were even out of my mouth. You can try, but I wouldn't get my hopes up."

Dandy approaches the door, but before she can knock, it flies open, revealing a short, slender man wearing a tidy wool blazer over a buttoned black cardigan, his thick white hair combed back into a neat coif. Dandy has known Dr. Oakley since she was born, literally. He delivered her, along with most other babies in Maple Bay. Even though he must be well into his eighties, he still runs a practice out of an old building on Central Street.

He's half turned so Dandy can see into the room. At the far end of a long library table, she sees Mirabel Bellwood sitting across from an elderly Black woman, Rose French.

"We're sorry you feel this way, Frank," Mirabel is saying. "Are you completely sure?"

"I think we all know this has run its course, Mirabel," he says. "You can consider this my official resignation. Good day, ladies."

He turns to leave and is caught off guard when he notices her standing there.

"Danielle," he says, peering at her over a pair of wire-framed glasses.

She smiles awkwardly. "Hi, Dr. Oakley."

"Let me guess," he says. "This is your grandfather's doing."

"Yeah," she says. "He left me a letter."

"Can't say I'm surprised," he says wryly. He catches himself and reaches out to give her a pat on the arm. "I'm very sorry for your loss, Danielle. Reg was a good man. He wore rose-coloured glasses, but it's hard to fault that in a person." He turns to glance back into the room and then he steps aside and gestures her in with a free hand. "In any case, enjoy the wild goose chase."

Dandy steps into the room. Glancing back, she notices Bonnie Brickland observing the exchange over the top of her glasses. Then Oakley shuts the door and she turns her attention to the table, where the two women are watching her with interest.

"Danielle," says Mrs. French. "How're you doing?" Rose French owns the bakery-cafe on Main Street, and Dandy has known her since she was a little kid, when Grandy would take her in for a croissant and a hot chocolate every Saturday. Mrs. French has always struck Dandy as someone who enjoys her life. She wears bright clothes and big jewelry, and she's rarely without a smile. Her cheerful, easygoing nature is highlighted against grim, serious Mirabel, who remains silent beside her.

"Hi," says Dandy, speaking quickly. "I'm here because of Grandy. He wrote me a letter before he died and told me to come see you. It was kind of his dying wish, I guess."

She pulls the letter out of her pocket and steps forward, holding it out so they can confirm her story, but Mirabel waves it away.

"That's a private letter," she says. "Why don't you just tell us what it says."

Dandy tells them about finding the letter in Grandy's bag, and then reads the most relevant section aloud. "Tell them it was my express wish that you should take over my spot in the group."

There's a long pause as the two women consider this new information. Finally, Mirabel speaks.

"I'll be honest, Danielle," she says. "We haven't had to deal with this kind of situation before. Our group has always consisted of the same members, and we have never entertained bringing anyone new into the fold."

Dandy nods. "I understand," she says.

"But it's not quite that simple," she continues, turning to Mrs. French, who picks up the thread.

"The thing is, Dandy, there really isn't much of a society anymore. We've just lost our third member in as many months. From the beginning, there were five of us: myself, Mirabel, Frank Oakley, your grandfather, and Bill Jinx."

"Bill Jinx?" asks Dandy, surprised.

"Yes," says Mirabel. "He stormed off ranting and raving about some conspiracy theory or another. The man's not right in his head."

"He's troubled," says Mrs. French, diplomatically. "And now that Frank has chosen to leave the group as well, that just leaves the two of us."

"Why did Dr. Oakley quit?" asks Dandy.

Mirabel rolls her eyes dismissively. "Frank has an overblown sense of his own importance. He claims he has more important things going on, but that's just a bunch of bluster, if you ask me."

"I think it all boils down to your grandfather," says Mrs. French. "Things haven't been the same since we lost him, Dandy. He was the heart and soul of this group."

Mirabel nods. "Reg had a way of making us all feel like this was an adventure, and we were on the cusp of a great discovery. I think Frank only stuck with us this long because he didn't want to miss out on anything, and now the magic is gone . . ." She trails off and shakes her head sadly.

Dandy is confused. Magic? "What do you mean, adventure?" she asks. "What kind of discovery?"

There's a long pause and the two women regard one another.

"Did your grandfather's letter not explain what this is all about?" asks Mirabel, finally.

Dandy shakes her head. "The letter says it would be up to the society to decide if they wanted to share their secrets."

The two women nod approvingly. "Reg took our story very seriously," says Mrs. French.

"We all did," says Mirabel. "In forty years, none of us has broken this confidence, but I think under these circumstances it might be time to share what we know with Danielle here."

"I agree," says Mrs. French. "Pull up a chair, Dandy."

As Dandy takes a seat at the table, her heart begins to race. She has the strong feeling that whatever these women are about to tell her is going to change everything. She leans forward in her chair, waiting to be enlightened.

"You've heard of the *Obelisk* Treasure?" says Mirabel.

Dandy blinks. She wasn't expecting this. "Yeah. Of course."

Every kid in Maple Bay grows up dreaming about the lost treasure of the pirate ship *Obelisk*. It's not just a local legend—the *Obelisk* Treasure is one of the most famous buried treasure stories in the world.

"Tell us what you know," says Mrs. French.

Dandy tries to piece together what she remembers. "I think the story goes that the treasure was hidden in the 1700s, when the pirate ship the *Obelisk* was chased into Maple Bay during a battle at sea. Two men were sent ashore to hide a cache of stolen gold and jewels, by order of the *Obelisk*'s captain."

Rose French nods. "Barnabas Dagger, one of the most notorious and bloodthirsty pirates to ever sail the seven seas."

"That's more or less the gist," says Mirabel. "The reason the *Obelisk* Treasure has had such staying power over the years is because its provenance is well documented."

"Historians and researchers believe there really was a treasure," says Mrs. French. "There are plenty of differing perspectives on what happened to it, but nobody denies that it probably existed."

"And people have been looking for it ever since," says Dandy, finishing the story as she knows it.

"That's putting it lightly," says Mirabel. "For over a hundred years, archaeologists and amateur adventurers alike have scoured the countryside with all manner of theories and plans. Metal detectors have gone over every corner of Dagger Woods. Several dive teams have explored the wreckage of the *Obelisk*. Books have been written."

"There's even been a TV show, Dandy," says Mrs. French.

"In short," says Mirabel, "the *Obelisk* Treasure has hooked itself into many imaginations."

"And it's never been found," says Dandy.

The room goes very silent.

"Well, that's the thing, Danielle," says Mrs. French. "What if it *was* found?"

Dandy leans forward in her chair. "Somebody found it?"

Mirabel sits forward and crosses her arms on the table. "Forty years ago this month, each of us, along with Bill Jinx, Frank Oakley, and your grandfather, received a typewritten letter. The letters were all the same. They told us that in 1920 five boys discovered the *Obelisk* Treasure. The boys were my father, Henry Bellwood; Rose's father, Junior French; Frank's father, Fred Oakley; Bill Jinx's father, Archie Jinx; and Elmer Feltzen, who would have been Reg's father."

Dandy thinks of the small sepia photograph of her great-grandfather on the wall in Grandy's study. For a man who was willing to talk about anything and everything, Grandy had little to say when it came to his father. Dandy knows the basics, namely that he got drunk and drowned in the bay when Grandy was a very small child, but beyond that it's a mystery. She wishes now that she'd asked more questions while that was still possible.

Mirabel continues. "The letter claimed that the boys decided to hide their find until each of them had turned eighteen, when they could legally claim their portions without any worry about family interference. But then the treasure went missing again."

Dandy's eyes are wide. "Someone took it?"

"Nobody knows," says Mirabel.

"But . . . what about the boys? What happened to them?"

Mirabel looks at Mrs. French, who smiles sadly at Dandy. "We only know so much about what happened between those boys," she says. "But, understandably, suspicions and accusations were thrown in all directions. To make a very long story short, the group of friends splintered, and by the time the letters reached us, each of them was dead."

Dandy's mind is spinning. Did Grandy really receive one of these letters, years before she was born?

Mirabel continues the story. "The letter claimed that the treasure was still hidden, and instructed the five of us—the closest living relatives of those five original boys—to take on the mission of finding it and completing the circle."

"Do you know who sent the letters?" asks Dandy.

"They were sent a few weeks after my father died," says Mirabel. "So the implication is that the letters were pre-positioned somewhere, and the death of the final boy triggered their mailing."

"There were no other clues?"

Mrs. French shakes her head. "No, not really, but the story was compelling enough that we came together to discuss the situation, and that's how we started to have these regular meetings."

"We've been comparing notes and throwing around theories ever since," says Mirabel.

"We've combed every inch of the coastline," says Mrs. French. "We've wandered through Dagger Woods with metal detectors. We've pored over any old documents we could get our hands on. We have devoted four decades of our lives to this, and now it seems as if we've reached the end."

"Let's not be hasty," says Mirabel. "It's not like Frank added much to the proceedings. He's always been a bit of a thorn in our side."

"I'm old, Mirabel," says Mrs. French. "I don't have the energy for it anymore. My days of climbing and hiking and digging are behind me."

"I think Reg knew that," says Mirabel. "Which is why he sent Danielle our way."

"I would have no problem with bringing Dandy into the fold," says Mrs. French, giving her a warm smile. "Lord knows we could have used some young blood a long time ago. But there's not much point in it, is there? Our trail ran cold a long time ago."

"I might have a clue," says Dandy.

"Come again?" says Mirabel.

Dandy places Grandy's satchel on the table and opens it, pulling out the chart.

"Grandy left this along with his letter," she says. "He said to share it with you."

Mirabel reaches for the chart and scans it. "This is very interesting," she murmurs.

"What is it?" asks Mrs. French.

Mirabel reaches across the table to the big pile of documents in the middle, and rifles through them until she finds another, similar chart. She places them next to each other.

"These are old nautical charts," she says. "And unlike a regular map, charts would sometimes indicate prominent buildings or structures that might aid in navigation. You can see here on your grandfather's chart from 1934, he's circled some sort of small building, but here"—she points at the same spot on the other chart—"the exact same spot is empty, just two years later."

"That land is on the Point below Bellwoods," says Mrs. French. Mirabel nods distractedly, and Dandy notices that she seems to be lost in thought.

Dandy stares at the two charts. Except for the tiny circled building, they're almost identical. "So you think there might be something where this little building used to stand?" she asks.

"It seems your grandfather might have thought so," says Mrs. French. "It might very well be another dead end, but maybe it's worth looking into. Especially now that we have someone as young and spry as yourself to help us."

"I know every corner of the inlet," says Dandy. "Grandy and I used to go beachcombing along the shore."

"Well," says Mrs. French. "It sounds like you're the girl for the job. What do you think, Mirabel?"

The other woman is still staring at the nautical chart with a look of deep concentration. With some effort, she pulls herself back to the conversation.

"I suppose it can't hurt," she says. "Although I daresay I know that coastline as well as you do, Danielle, and I highly doubt you'll find anything in that spot. But Reg seemed to think it was worth exploring, so check it out and see what you can find." She pauses, considering something, before she continues. "When you're done, why don't you pay me a visit? There's someone I'd like you to meet, and some things to discuss."

Mirabel lives alone, so Dandy can't imagine who that could be, but for now it hardly matters.

She's finally going to see the inside of Bellwoods.

THREE STRANGERS

Cass wakes while it's still dark. It takes her a moment to remember where she is, and another moment to realize that Banjo is beside the bed, his face just a few inches away from hers. The moment her eyes open, he snorts excitedly and does a little twirl.

She shrugs into some clothes and drags her ass outside. The sun is beginning to rise over the eastern horizon, throwing up a red flush that catches the undersides of the clouds, and she finds herself staring, almost hypnotized, at the shifting light.

A large-winged bird—a heron? an eagle?—glides through the mist and alights on a rock, forming a perfect graceful silhouette in the smooth red water.

It's a stunning moment, rare and hushed, and Cass feels like the world is revealing itself to her alone. It's the perfect way to start her first morning in her new life.

"Okay, Banjo," she calls. "Let's go back inside."

There's no answer. She whistles and yells out again, and then circles the house, peering into the surrounding brush and fields, but there's no sign of him. Her heart sinks as she stares at the expanse of fields stretching in all directions. He could have run anywhere.

She remembers the information package Alan and Judith left, still sitting unread on the kitchen island. Leaving the door open in case he returns, she goes back inside and skims through it until she finds the section on Banjo. After reading more than she'd ever expected to about another creature's pooping habits, she finds something that might be useful.

Banjo loves the beach more than anything, and we hope you come to love it too. Whenever he's acting restless, a quick stroll along the inlet will always set him right.

Cass walks down to the road muttering to herself.

"Lost her job, lost her apartment, lost her boyfriend, lost a stranger's dog. What a loser."

The beach is mostly hidden from view by a low line of scrubby trees, but she soon comes to a break and follows a narrow gravel lane through the trees until it opens up suddenly to a view of the water. It's low tide, and seaweed and large granite boulders are fully exposed on a wide beach of wet pebbles. Nearby, on a sparse patch of seagrass, is Banjo.

Cass is so relieved to see him that it takes her a moment to realize she's in somebody's yard. Not far from the tideline, a rusty old pickup truck is pulled up outside a low weather-beaten shack, sitting up from the ground on low concrete pilings. Banjo is sitting just a stone's throw away, staring resolutely at the front door with his head cocked.

As Cass watches, the door flies open and an old man steps out and throws a shovel, an actual rusty, dirt-encrusted shovel, directly at Banjo. Unruffled, the dog easily bounds out of the way and cheerfully takes a new seat just a few feet away.

The man is clearly enraged and, from the looks of him, slightly unhinged. A wild tangle of white hair dangles out from a knitted blue cap to hang below his shoulders, at about the same length as a wispy, erratic twist of white beard. He's wearing an old plaid shirt smeared with dirt, ratty old trousers, and a pair of rubber boots. As he storms down from the step, Cass takes an instinctive step backward, but Banjo isn't fazed. He simply hops out of the way as the man takes a lunge in his direction.

The action is so aggressive and unexpected that Cass lets out a small yelp. The man and the dog both turn, noticing her for the first time.

"Who the hell are you?" asks the man. He points a finger and jabs at something behind Cass. "Didn't you see the fuckin' sign?"

Cass turns and, for the first time, spots the sign tacked to a tree along the driveway.

It looks new. Garish orange spray paint announces:

THIS AIN'T THE BEACH GET THE FUCK OF MY PROPERTY SO HELP ME GOD I'LL SHOOT YOU IN THE ARSE!

Cass turns back to the dog with a new urgency. "Banjo! Come on!"

The dog refuses to move, so she runs across the yard, gratified when Banjo doesn't try to get away as she grabs his collar. Only then does she realize that she's forgotten to bring his leash. She swears under her breath.

"I'm really sorry," she says, turning back to the man, "but is there any chance you have a length of rope I can borrow? I can return it. I just . . . I'm only dog-sitting for a little while and I don't know if he'll follow me."

Without saying anything, the man disappears inside the shack and comes back a moment later, tossing Cass a frayed length of nylon cord. As she ties a makeshift loop around Banjo's neck, the man stands with his arms crossed over his chest and glares at them.

Banjo secured, Cass turns to the man. "Thank you, I'll bring back your rope!"

"Keep the damn rope, woman," he growls. "And from now on try to do a better job of keeping this repugnant little shit from sneaking onto my property and using it as his personal toilet."

"Totally," says Cass. "I won't let him out of my sight. It won't happen again, I promise!"

"Good," says the man, and then he spits on the ground and steps back inside his shack, letting the door slam behind him.

Cass needs a break from Banjo, so after a quick shower and bowl of yogurt and granola, she drives into town to explore. It's a lovely day, and the streets are already full of people bustling about with coffees and shopping bags.

She wanders for a while before finding herself outside the bookstore she noticed on her drive into town, called Word of Mouth. As she steps inside, a bell jingles, and a woman glances up from behind the checkout.

"Morning!" she says cheerfully. "Let me know if you need any help."

"Thanks," says Cass. "This is your shop?"

"You bet." The woman steps out from behind the counter. "These are the words," she says, turning to sweep her hands around the space in a grand gesture, then flips her hands and points her index fingers at her face. "And this is the mouth. I'm Bree, your friendly neighbourhood bitter-divorcée shopkeeper."

Cass extends a hand. "I'm Cass. I'm new to town."

"Oh wow!" The woman's face widens into a grin. "You're the writer who's staying in Alan and Judith's place down the inlet!"

Cass is surprised. "How did you guess that?"

She smiles knowingly and taps a finger against her temple. "I grew up here, darling. I know everyone and everything. Alan's a regular customer, so we're buddies. He stopped by last week to tell me you'd be house-sitting and asked me to keep an eye out for you. Of course, I already knew about you because of your book."

"Really?" Cass's eyes widen.

"Of course," says Bree. She walks to a shelf in the corner and, to Cass's surprise, pulls down a copy of *The Sweetest Conversation.* "Alan and Judith had me order a copy when it came out, so I brought in a couple, and I've kept it in stock ever since. I've hand-sold a bunch of them this summer, actually. It's a great beach read."

Cass blinks. "You've actually read it?"

Bree laughs. "You sound so surprised. I am a bookseller after all. I thought it was great."

Cass is at a loss for words. Something about this exchange, and the fact that her big fat flop of a novel has a spot in this bookstore, and is being *hand-sold,* no less, seems to mean something. Before she can respond, the bell on the door jingles and an elderly woman comes in.

"Hello, Frances," says Bree, moving to greet her. "Your special order is in, I've got it over here behind the counter." She points at Cass. "Don't go anywhere, I want you to sign this copy before you leave."

While she waits, Cass browses the shop. In the corner, near a window, is a display dedicated to local-interest titles. Along with the usual photography books and regional history, there are several books about sea lore and pirates. A small green paperback, *Legends of Maple Bay*, catches her eye and she pulls it off the shelf.

All of Maple Bay's mysteries, ghost stories and unbelievable tales together in print for the first time! Do ghost ships haunt our waters? Did a UFO crash land in the bay in the 1940s? Where is the Obelisk *Treasure?*

The other customer leaves, and Cass brings the book to the checkout. As she signs the copy of her novel, Bree rings it in.

"You going to take a crack at finding the treasure?" asks Bree as she slips the book into a bag.

"Is that really a thing?" Cass asks. "The *Obelisk* Treasure?"

Bree rolls her eyes. "Are you kidding me? Did you see all the pirate books I keep in stock? That stupid treasure story keeps the lights on. Tourists come in droves to play Indiana Jones."

"Seriously?" says Cass, holding out her credit card.

Bree nods. "There's even a Pirate Festival in the summer. Start paying attention to the business names around here, you'll see what I mean. The Shivering Timbers and the Yo Ho Hotel and shit like that."

"That's kind of cool," says Cass. "A buried treasure."

Bree shrugs. "I guess if that's your thing." She puts the book and a receipt in a bag, and as she hands it across the counter, her eyes narrow as she considers something.

"I don't suppose you're looking for a job?" she asks. "I need to hire someone part-time. I had a student working here all summer, but she's gone back to school in the city, and I'm finding it a bit much to handle the place by myself."

Cass shakes her head. "Right now I'm just giving myself some time to figure out my next steps. Sorry."

"Don't sweat it," says Bree. "I've got an ad in this week's paper, I'll find someone eventually. I bet that house is a great place to do some soul-searching. All those windows! It's so beautiful down by the inlet."

Cass smiles. "It *is* beautiful, but I'm not sure how I feel about the neighbourhood."

Bree smiles knowingly. "Let me guess, you've met Mirabel."

"You know her?"

"I told you," she says, "I know everyone. But seriously, everybody knows Mirabel. She's a bit of an institution around here." She adopts a haughty British accent. "Very important, yes, yes. Bellwoods, you see. Old money, pip pip, cheerio."

"I did meet Mirabel," Cass admits. "She was definitely standoffish, but I'm talking about the old guy in the trailer farther back along the road." She describes the morning's awkward encounter.

"Oh, that was Bill Jinx," says Bree. "Town hermit. He's like a hundred years old and spends most of his time wandering around drunk, yelling about crazy shit."

"What kind of crazy shit?"

She shrugs. "You name it. He's nuts. Screams at the birds for trying to read his thoughts. Stops random tourists on the street and accuses them of being Russian spies, like it's still the Cold War. A few weeks ago he went on a real bender and started stomping about town, telling anyone who would listen that there was a plot to steal his land."

"Okay," says Cass. "That makes me feel a bit better."

"This town is full of whackos," says Bree. "My mom would have said it's a real cast of characters. Don't worry about Bill, though, he's harmless. I'd be a lot more scared of Mirabel."

Cass realizes suddenly how much fun she's having talking to Bree. It feels natural, like she's making a connection.

"This might be weird," she says, "but should we be friends?"

"Obviously," says Bree. "I thought you'd never ask. I'll be your doorway into Maple Bay's glittering and dramatic social scene. Just so long as you're not some clingy weirdo."

Cass isn't sure how to respond to that, but she laughs. "I'm just joking, girl. *I'm* the clingy weirdo, how'm'ever, I know all the single men in town, so I can definitely help you get laid, although if you're looking for something serious, you might want to manage your expectations. The guys around here aren't really the marrying type, if you catch my drift."

Cass laughs. "Trust me, I'm coming off a bad breakup. Dating, serious or otherwise, is not on my agenda."

Bree nods approvingly. "We'll have a platonic romance. You like to eat good food and drink boxed wine?"

"Absolutely," says Cass.

"Perfect. I'm going to have you over for dinner."

They exchange numbers, and when another group of customers comes into the store, Cass takes her leave, waving to Bree as they promise to connect soon.

* * *

Cass is driving home, thinking about the interesting day she's had, when she takes the turn onto Inlet Drive a bit faster than she should. The Subaru beeps furiously as it slides on a patch of gravel and fishtails through the intersection. She yanks the wheel, trying instinctively to straighten out, but it's no use. She might as well have driven onto a field of marbles.

Everything happens super quickly. Cass slams on the brakes, which only serves to whip the Subaru's rear end around, the momentum throwing it into a 360-degree spin toward the ditch.

It's at this moment that the runner appears, as if from thin air.

He turns to stare in horror at the massive SUV sailing directly at him, and time seems to slow. Cass throws her hands in the air and shuts her eyes tight.

"Jesus, take the wheel!" she screams.

With a dramatic *thunk* the Subaru slams heavily into something and comes to a sudden, juddering stop.

"Oh my god, oh my god," Cass says. "Oh my god." Her heart is pounding, and an anxiety attack is racing at her over the horizon, but she knows she needs to get control of herself. Somebody has to see if the guy is still alive and keep him stable until an ambulance arrives, and she's the only person here. She also knows she's responsible for whatever's happened.

"Oh my god."

With a trembling hand, she manages to put the car in park. She sits for a moment, catching her breath, before opening her eyes.

The running man is standing right next to her, smiling through the driver's-side window.

"Oh my god!" she shouts.

He jumps back on two feet, throwing both hands in the air. "Don't shoot!" he yells. From his cheeky grin and the twinkle in his eyes, Cass can tell that he's joking around, and even though *she* was the one who almost ran *him* off the road, she kind of resents it. Can't he tell she's on the verge of a nervous breakdown?

As he steps forward again, lifting a hand, Cass's irritation dissolves and she almost forgets about the last few minutes, because this guy? This guy is hot, hot, hot. Tall and lean, with a tousled shock of dirty-blond hair, a couple of days' worth of scruff, and an easy, comfortable slouch.

"Are you okay?" he asks through the closed window.

She rolls down her window. "I should be the one asking you that," she says.

He waves this off. "I'm fine. You didn't even come close."

"What did I hit?" she asks.

He points around to the rear end of the Subie. "Come and see," he says. "I'll help you check for damage."

He moves away, and even though every muscle in her body is still vibrating with residual fear, she manages to climb out of the car and follow him.

"Check it out," he says, pointing. Both passenger-side wheels are pressed snugly up against a small embankment that divides the road from the ditch.

"Looks like you're not the only person to lose control here," he says. "That bank is there for a reason."

"I'm so embarrassed," she says. "Obviously I was driving too fast."

"Hey," he says. "Don't sweat it. We've all driven too fast at one time or another." He crouches and checks out the back of the car. "And it looks like you got off without even a scratch, so it's all good, right?"

She gives him a weak smile. "Right," she says. "All's well that ends well."

Without warning, she turns sideways, bends over, and barfs all over the road.

"Are you okay?" the man asks, reaching forward to put a hand on her back. Mortified, Cass straightens up.

"Just nerves," she says, her face burning with embarrassment. "Listen, I think I really want to get home and have a nap. I'm sorry again. I'll be more careful driving next time."

"You're okay to drive?" he asks.

"Oh yeah, I'll be fine." Cass turns back to the car, desperate to get away from the hot man she just barfed in front of.

"All right, then," he says. "Hope the nap helps." With a slap of his hand on the side of the Subaru, he pivots and breaks into an easy jog. A few yards away, he twists around to shoot a peace sign. "Maybe I'll see you around, lead foot," he calls out with a wink before continuing on his way in the direction of town, leaving Cass wondering who the hell that was.

EXPECTATIONS

It's as if I've stepped into something written by Edgar Allan Poe, complete with an ancestral seaside castle, a mysterious old woman, and a collection of dark family secrets. A week ago, I'd never heard of this house, this woman, or this family, but now I'm suddenly the most important character in the story.

I find myself scrambling to fill this strange new role: Peter Bellwood Barnett, last living heir to the Bellwood name and all the baggage that encompasses. The prodigal grandson making a triumphant return.

On my first night in Bellwoods, I lie awake late into the night wondering if I've made a terrible mistake. The ceilings in my large, cold bedroom are so high that they disappear into the gloom, and I imagine them gone entirely, revealing an endless chasm of sky, an empty, lonely universe staring down at me, judging me for the life I've lived so far. I close my eyes against the darkness, and my thoughts emerge, spinning, to fill the void. Can I rise to this challenge? Can I become a completely different person? Can I live up to Mirabel's expectations?

More to the point, what *are* her expectations?

For all her talk of trust and secrets, the next day doesn't do much to enlighten me. Mirabel's anxiety has returned, and she takes me from room to room, filling me in on trivial information about the house—*This was Grandmother's wedding china! My parents bought the armoire on their honeymoon in Montreal!*—and a mind-numbingly detailed series of genealogy lessons that all stop with her own birth. If she *is* inclined to talk about her only child—the daughter who left before her only grandchild was born—she doesn't show it. Instead my presence seems to give her license to pretend that the intervening forty years never happened.

The roses need to be pruned aggressively every other October. My father's two sisters were childless spinsters who resented my birthright. The Bellwoods have always shopped at MacIntosh Grocery, never the garish supermarket outside of town.

There's no room to breathe, and by the time we sit down to a simple supper, complete with a detailed explanation of every real estate development her father oversaw, I feel completely suffocated. When she stands from the table and announces that she'll be heading out for the evening to attend some sort of meeting—*my genealogical society*—my relief at the unexpected development is intense.

The next morning, she's up ahead of me, but she's not at her usual spot in the breakfast nook, hovering over a newspaper, waiting for my arrival. I pour myself a cup of coffee and go looking for her. I find her in her study and knock on the half-open door.

"Come in," she says.

I enter, leaning against the doorframe and looking down at her as she goes through papers at her large roll-top desk.

"I was wondering if I could borrow your car?" I ask.

"Certainly," she says, looking up from her paperwork and peering at me over the top of her reading glasses. "May I ask where you plan to go?"

"I have a job interview in an hour or so," I say.

"You have a job interview?" she asks, as if I've just told her I've adopted a panda bear.

"Last night while you were out, I did some poking around online," I say. "There's an opening at a bookstore in town," I say. "I thought that could be kind of cool. I like books. I called and I'm going to meet the owner in an hour. It's called Word of Mouth. Do you know it?"

She sniffs. "Yes, of course. I suppose you could do worse than work at a bookshop, although the owner is a bit much." She lowers her voice, as if discussing a dirty secret. "She isn't from here, you know."

I laugh. "Neither am I."

"That's a very different situation."

"I can't just live here mooching off you," I say.

Her face twitches, and I get the feeling she's working hard to hold back a smile. "So you're thinking of staying for a while?"

"If that's okay with you," I say.

"Of course," she says, working hard to keep her enthusiasm under wraps. "Stay as long as you see fit. But please, my dear, don't feel you need to get a job on my account. There's plenty of money to keep us both afloat."

I smile at her. "I appreciate that, but if I'm going to stay, I'll need to feel like I'm contributing. Besides, it might be a good way to meet some people."

She sighs. "Fair enough. Life in this house with an old lady is bound to get boring pretty quickly." She points at a chair across the table. "But if you can bear with me for just a little while, why don't you take a seat. There are a few things I want to walk through with you."

"Okay," I say, pulling the chair over to sit next to the desk.

"If you had to guess," she asks, "why do you suspect I went to the trouble of tracking you down?"

I think about this. "I guess I'd say it was painful for you to know that you still had family out in the world, and you decided you couldn't live without trying one last time to attempt a reunion."

She looks at me and smiles. "That's a lovely sentiment," she says. "And part of me wishes that was true, but I'm not a sentimental person. I never have been. The truth is that I'm old, Peter. Old enough that I'm worried about how many things might disappear if I die before I have a chance to pass them along to someone."

"What kind of things are you talking about?" I ask.

She doesn't answer. Instead, her gaze turns to the upper edge of her desk, where a small collection of framed photographs shares space with a classic brass-and-green-glass desk lamp.

She reaches up and takes one of the photos down. It's a man, bald and slightly portly, with a gentle smile. He's wearing a white lab coat open over a three-piece suit and leaning against a tree in a comfortable slouch.

"Your grandfather," she says, using the cuff of her sleeve to gently rub dust off the glass, suddenly lost in a reverie. "He was a very good man," she says. "A very good man indeed. You know, everyone in town knows me as Mirabel Bellwood, even though I was married to John Johnson for forty years. He was a come-from-away, you see, and as well liked and respected as he was, many in this town saw him as some kind of appendage to the Bellwood family. He was one of the finest men I ever met, cheerful until the day he died."

"I wish I'd met him," I say.

She places the picture back on the desk. "Yes, well," she says, her voice tightening. "He thought about you every day until he died."

She reaches up and takes down another photo, this one a snapshot of a pretty girl in her teens. Tall and tan, with an easy, elegant lankiness, her blond hair is pulled into a ponytail, and she's wearing a pale blue sundress and a cheerful, natural smile.

"My mother," I say, taking the photograph from her and staring intently at the stranger behind the glass. What a tragedy, I think, to be taken from your child before he even has the chance to form a memory of you.

"You don't look like her," she says, stating the obvious. "I guess it's a particularly cruel twist of fate that you took so completely after your father's side of the family. A resemblance to people we never met, people who kept you from us."

"Did you know my father?" I ask.

"Oh yes," she says. "He came from British Columbia to spend a summer working on a boat and experiencing the East Coast. He was very handsome—it was no surprise why your mother fell for him—but we thought it would be a summer fling and that would be it. Then she went and got herself pregnant."

I stare at her, unable to wrap my head around the old-fashioned sentiment.

"I know what you're thinking," she says. "These days a young unmarried couple having a baby is nothing at all, but at the time it wasn't done. Perhaps out in the wider world, but not here. For a family like the Bellwoods, it was an unbearable scandal. John saw it all differently. A blessing, he called it, and of course I should have listened to him. But I went in the opposite direction. We warred. She was a young, pregnant girl who could have used her mother more than ever, and I let her down."

I know better than to say anything as Mirabel works through these emotions. It's almost as if I'm not in the room and she's musing to a therapist, or a room full of ghosts.

"She was a happy, loving daughter," she says, "the light of our lives, and then she was gone. I like to believe that she would have found her way back to us, but fate intervened. And so, here we are."

"But it all happened in the end," I say. "Our family found our way back together again, despite everything."

She nods approvingly, and then her eyes drift off to the middle distance, and she seems to consider something for a long moment.

"I've beaten around the bush long enough," she says finally.

She slides open a drawer in her desk and pulls something out. It's a book, leather bound, with gilt edges. She places it on the desk and puts her hand on top of it.

"This journal belonged to my father," she says. "He died almost forty years ago, but I only found it recently, hidden beneath a loose floorboard in his bedroom. I don't know if he intended for it to stay hidden."

"What does it say?" I ask.

She clears her throat, and then she tells me.

She speaks for a very long time. She stops from time to time to read a relevant passage from the journal, but most of what she tells me is her interpretation, in her words. This isn't the tight, controlled historical tour guide presentation from earlier. This is an unburdening, a raw, honest description of her father's deepest secrets, his disappointments and tragedies, and the dark, twisted history of Bellwoods.

Through the entire tale, I sit and I listen with genuine fascination, completely absorbed by the story, until she stops and I realize that she's come to the end.

"But . . . that's it?" I ask.

She nods, her mouth a grim line. "Yes."

"So what do we do now?" I ask her. She's just told me one of the wildest stories I've ever heard, but the end result is clear: despite everything this journal lays bare, it leaves one crucial question unanswered.

She shakes her head. "I don't know. That's what I'm hoping you can help me figure out. You understand what all of this means, don't you, Peter?"

I nod slowly. I want to ask her a million questions, but when I glance at the small clock on the desk, I realize that I'm expected at the bookstore in ten minutes.

"Maybe I should cancel this interview," I say.

"No," she says firmly. "You should go. You're right that it would make sense for you to find something to do for as long as you're staying here. Besides, you probably need some time to process this. We can continue this conversation later. We have all the time in the world."

On an instinct, I reach across the table and take her hand in mine. "I want you to know that we're going to figure this out together."

"Good," she says, giving my hand a gentle squeeze. "That's what I had hoped for when I went looking for you. Now I think I need to take a nap. I haven't spoken that much in years!" She laughs weakly and pulls away from my grip. She replaces the journal in her desk drawer and then stands. She appears older, somehow, and I realize just how much of a toll this has taken, the divulgence of a lifetime of family secrets.

I stand to follow her out of the room, taking one last look at the photographs on the desk. It strikes me suddenly that despite all the family pictures in the house, the looming formal portraits and dreamlike black-and-white photographs from a distant era, these are the only ones that gesture at Mirabel's own personal life. One small photograph of her husband. One small photograph of her daughter. A tiny bit of space carved out of a house that stands as a testament to something much bigger than her own place in the story.

She seems to guess what I'm thinking. "I would have kept a photograph of you up there with them," she says. "But nobody ever sent me one."

We stand together quietly for a moment, this saddest of thoughts hanging between us, until I break the spell.

"I really need to go or I'll be late," I say.

She follows me to the landing and puts her hand on my arm.

"Whatever you do, it's a huge relief to my old bones that I have someone here to confide in. There are things in this journal that change everything, things I can only trust with family."

I smile at her. "I understand. There's no way I'd ever consider sharing any of what you just told me."

"Good," she says. "Now go knock 'em dead."

* * *

The bookstore, Word of Mouth, is on a corner in the middle of town, the main floor of a classic old building, white clapboard with large glass windows featuring attractive displays of bestsellers. When I push through the door, it jingles, just like something from an old-time sitcom.

The owner, Bree, is at least a couple of years younger than me, but she has an earthy quality that gives her an impression of being kind of a den mother. She has thick tangles of reddish-brown curls, and she's wearing a loose linen top over jeans, with several tangled strings of large, colourful beads dangling down over her chest.

It turns out that I'm the only person who answered the ad, and she barely glances at my resume. She doesn't seem too concerned about my qualifications. "Listen, darling," she explains. "If you suck, I'll fire you. But I doubt you'll suck, because you're a grown adult, and the job isn't that hard. So let's keep things simple and start with a two-week probation, I'll show you the ropes, and at the end of that we'll have a chat and see how we both feel about it. Sound good?"

"Sounds great," I tell her, amazed at how simple this was.

We make plans for me to begin in a few days, and I leave the shop. I step out onto the bustling main street of Maple Bay, marvelling at the colours, the architecture, the *rightness* of it all.

I turn my face up to the sky and close my eyes for just a second, letting my face feel the sun and the crisp fall air. I have a job, and a fresh start, and maybe if I play my cards right, I have a home right here in this quirky little town.

I run a few more errands, stop at a cute little bakery to linger over a quick cappuccino and a croissant, and finally I climb into

Mirabel's old but beautifully maintained Jaguar and meander back along the coast.

As I arrive back at Bellwoods, I'm in a better mood than I can remember being in a very long time. Things are finally coming together, and I skip up the steps feeling cheerful and alive.

I unlock the front door and step inside, noticing right away that the house is cold and dark and silent. I stand and stare across the foyer.

Mirabel is lying motionless on the floor at the bottom of the stairs.

Even from a distance, I know that she's dead.

EXPLORATIONS

The coastline below Bellwoods has changed a lot over the years, and a thick tangle of vegetation now covers the low bluff where the unknown outbuilding supposedly stood. It makes for slow going, and Dandy is forced to take her time as she searches the area.

Moving deliberately, she maneuvers her way through the brush, kicking aside bushes and pushing aside rocks. After more than an hour, she's found a ton of driftwood, a few weathered bricks, and some battered remains of Styrofoam buoys, but no signs of a foundation or anything obvious that would indicate a building was ever in this place.

Dr. Oakley's insistence that the society has reached a dead end is starting to feel accurate.

She's about to call it a day when she hears someone yelling at her. Quickly, she folds up the chart and shoves it into Grandy's bag, looking up just in time to see Bill Jinx striding across the beach, waving a stick in her direction.

"You!" he yells. "Girl!"

Dandy forces her face into an innocent smile and heads to meet him.

"How's it going, Bill?"

He drops the stick as he gets closer, but his face retains the angry scowl as he squints to make out who she is.

"Dandy Feltzen," he says. "What the hell are you doing down here?" He appears to be on a bit of a bender. His eyes are glassy and there's a distinct scent of rum wafting from him.

Dandy tries to adopt a neutral, childish expression. "I'm just poking around."

He rolls his eyes. "You don't fool me, girl. I know those old farts have you tight in their grip. They've got you down here doing their grunt work for them."

"What makes you think I'm caught up in anybody's grip?"

"You can cut the bullshit, Dandy," he says. "Your grandfather was a good man, but he had too much faith in people. He told me himself that he was going to send you to the society if anything ever happened to him. Wouldn't listen to reason when I tried to talk him out of it."

"When did he say all of this?" asks Dandy.

"I went to see him in the hospital before he died," says Bill. "We had things to discuss. Your grandfather was no fool, Dandy. He had theories of his own, and the old bugger was willing to share them with me. But he was also willing to share with the rest of them. And they *are* fools."

He stops to cough, working for a few moments to dislodge something that he spits off to the side, where it sits yellow and glistening on a rock.

"Anyway, you can save your time and your breath. There's nothing here, and there never was anything here. You can take that back to the next meeting, and let them know I told you so myself."

"Why don't you trust the rest of them?" she asks.

He laughs, as if it's obvious. "Frank Oakley is a scrounger. He doesn't care about treasure, the only thing he cares about is money. Mirabel only cares about her family name. Mind you, the Bellwoods weren't all bad. Her father was a good man. After my father died, he made sure me and my mother had a place to live. If anyone knew where the treasure was, he did."

This surprises Dandy. "What makes you say that?"

Bill looks like he's said more than he intended. "I'll tell you this much," he says. "Those letters came right after he died. I think he wrote them himself and arranged to have his lawyer's office send them."

Dandy considers this. "If he knew where the treasure was hidden, why don't you think he told Mirabel?"

Bill shakes his head. "I think he must have had his own reasons for keeping it secret until after he died." He turns to stare at the big house looming over them. "Bellwoods is full of secrets."

Dandy absorbs this. "What about Mrs. French?"

His face darkens. "I wouldn't trust that woman if she was the last person on earth."

This catches Dandy off guard. It's hard to imagine anyone disliking Rose French, but from the look on Bill's face, she knows better than to pry.

"The point is," he continues, "if there *is* a treasure out there, the likes of them aren't going to let the likes of me get his hands on it. But the joke's on them, because I'm a few steps ahead, and soon there won't be any reason for the society to meet at all."

He reaches inside his jacket and pulls something out from the inside pocket, holds it out in front of him so she can see. It's a small red notebook, wrapped in elastic bands, with folded pieces of yellow paper sticking out of it from the sides.

Dandy stares at the notebook. "What is that?"

"These are the fruits of my own, private investigation," he says, the gleam in his eyes intensifying. "And let's just say that it won't be long before the pieces finally fit into place and those other three can give up the ghost."

He shoves the notebook back into his pocket and takes a step closer to Dandy, jabbing a finger into her chest. "If you know what's good for you, you'll stay away from them. But if you are going to ignore my advice, you tell those old bags of bones to stay the hell away from my property." He considers her with a shrewd eye, then spits on the ground. "And I'd better not catch you sniffing around, either."

Dandy pulls back. "I'm not going anywhere near your house, Bill."

He waves this away, irritated, and then appears to lose interest in the conversation. His confrontational demeanour slips away, and his eyes, rheumy and faded, shift to stare out at the horizon.

Dandy is about to take her leave when she hears the first siren. Bill turns at the sound, and together they watch as an ambulance, followed closely by a police cruiser, rushes past on the inlet road and takes a hard turn into the driveway at Bellwoods.

THE STAIRCASE

I hover nearby as the cop on duty, Officer Cherton, surveys the scene, taking photos and notes, before finally giving the paramedics the okay to cover Mirabel's body in a sheet. Then he turns his attention to me. I'm in the middle of answering his basic questions— what was my relation to the victim, when had I last seen her alive, had I moved or touched the body—when an elderly man carrying a leather bag bustles his way up the steps and into the house.

Without acknowledging us, he moves quickly to the body, crouching down to pull back the cloth.

"Oh, Mirabel," he says sadly.

"We wanted to wait for your official opinion, Doctor," says the officer. "But it's pretty clear what happened here. We've looked upstairs and it appears that there was a fold in the rug on the upper landing. Mrs. Bellwood Johnson must have caught her foot and then taken a tumble down to the bottom. The wood is slippery, and the pitch of the stairs is pretty steep."

After a brief but thorough examination, the doctor draws the sheet back over Mirabel's face and stands to face us.

"Her injuries are certainly consistent with a fall," he says. "I've been telling her for years that she needed to move out of this house, but the woman was stubborn. She wouldn't consider saying goodbye to her precious Bellwoods. At the very least she could have stopped using this monstrous staircase. There must be at least a couple of dozen steps."

"Thirty-three," I say. They both turn to look at me and I smile ruefully. "She mentioned it when I arrived."

The doctor seems to notice me for the first time. "Who are you?" he demands.

"I'm Mirabel's grandson," I explain.

The blood seems to drain from his face. "Susan's son? But . . . but how?"

As I explain how Mirabel's letter found its way to me, the doctor shakes his head in amazement.

"This is unbelievable," he mutters, almost to himself.

"You're telling me," I say. "A few weeks ago, I didn't know I had a grandmother. Then we reunited, and now . . ."

The doctor's face softens as I trail off, and he reaches out to shake my hand. "I knew your grandmother very well. She looked for you for many years, and I am sure she was very, very happy to have you home. Where were you, Peter?"

"Here and there. I've been a bit of a nomad, to tell you the truth. Vancouver. The Alberta oil fields. Spent a couple of years in Seattle. Haven't really stuck anywhere long enough to call it home. Then I got Mirabel's letter." I shrug. "I guess it was time for a change."

Dr. Oakley gives me a funny look that I can't quite interpret, but before he can ask me anything else, the police officer interjects. "I'm sorry to break this up, but I have a few more questions for you,

Peter. Do you remember if your grandmother was upstairs when you left the house this morning?"

I nod. "Yeah, she was in her study."

At this, the doctor's expression shifts, for just a moment, and his eyes flicker very briefly to the top of the stairs. What about the study has caught his attention?

"Can I stay here?" I ask, turning to Cherton. "I don't really have anywhere else to go."

The cop looks a bit unsure, so I'm grateful when the doctor speaks up.

"Officer," he says, "I knew Mirabel Bellwood very well, for many years. I know that she would have wanted her grandson to stay here as long as he wanted." He turns to me. "Am I to understand you were to have moved into Bellwoods on a permanent basis?"

I nod. "She invited me, so I gave up my apartment in Vancouver and . . . well, I took her up on it and moved here."

Oakley nods and turns back to Cherton. "There you have it. For all intents and purposes, this is the young man's home. I'm sure his grandmother would have seen it the same way."

Cherton seems satisfied with this.

"I think under the circumstances that would be okay, at least for now. Mrs. Bellwoods had no other family?"

"I'm the end of the line, apparently," I say.

"Well, we'll have to deal with lawyers and so on and find out what her intentions were with the property, but for now I don't see any reason you can't continue to stay here."

He shuts his notebook and steps outside to speak to the paramedics, and then Dr. Oakley and I watch as they put Mirabel's body on a stretcher and wheel her out of the house.

Cherton gives me a card and tells me to call if I have any questions. Then he climbs into his cruiser and follows the ambulance as it pulls away from Bellwoods.

Dr. Oakley and I watch them leave from the veranda. He seems in no hurry to leave.

"You know, Peter," he says, "your grandmother and I were very close friends. I knew her background almost as well as I know my own. If you need any help interpreting anything that she may have said, or that you may find in the house. In the study, for instance . . ."

I squint at him. "I'm not sure what you mean."

He coughs and then laughs awkwardly. "Please don't hesitate to call on me if you need anything. Maple Bay can be a rather difficult place to fit in, but you've certainly arrived with the bona fides to give it a go."

I get the sense he wants me to invite him back inside, but I'm not in the mood for company. I smile blankly at him until he finally takes the hint and leaves.

Something in his tone has unsettled me: an eagerness, a thirst for information that doesn't sit right. As soon as he's gone, I head straight back up the stairs to the study and open the drawer in Mirabel's desk.

The journal is still sitting there, staring up at me. As I'm pulling it out of the drawer, I realize that I'm relieved, although I'm not sure why. It's not as if anyone was going to enter her office and take it.

In our last conversation, Mirabel told me in her own words what Henry wrote in this journal. Now it's time to hear the story in his own words.

I sit at the desk, open the journal, and begin to read.

THE CONFESSIONS OF HENRY BELLWOOD

As remembered in October of 1983

I was a small boy, just a few years younger
than my sisters, when our mother died of a
sudden illness. Only a few fragmented memories remain, and all of them are tied up with
the old house. A gentle breeze rustling a
curtain. The scent of lilacs drifting in
through the kitchen door. The low stone wall
in the front garden. Mother's living face is
a mystery to me, a blur in the corner of my
eye, but I remember her voice whispering in
my ear like the soft, clear echo of a ringing
bell, and I remember the scent of sea breeze
through spruce, and I remember how I felt:
loved and safe and comfortable.

The house is long since fallen; we only
lived there until the new house was finished. Father had been building it for her,
but she died a year before it was completed,
and after we moved he wanted nothing to do
with the old place and its sad memories.
He let the trees and shrubs take over the
property, and soon animals began to make
their way into the walls and water into the
roof and it wasn't long before the house
began to collapse under the weight of its

abandonment. By the time I was twenty, it
had buckled under its own weight, and now
the house is gone entirely, eaten by nature,
a fate that awaits us all.

Father was never the same after Mother died.
He felt unqualified to raise girls, and so
my sisters, Anna and Catherine, were sent
away to boarding school and we rarely saw
them. For some reason, perhaps because I was
so small, and perhaps because I was a boy,
he opted to keep me at home. A cousin of my
mother's came to live with us, a sad woman
in her fifties who cleaned and cooked and
made sure I was clothed and bathed. Beyond
that, she basically ignored me, and since my
father had thrown himself into his work, and
often left town on long business trips, I
was essentially left to my own devices.

I occupied myself at the new house. Until
Mother died, the house had been Father's
driving passion. He had hand picked the
architect, Jeremiah Buckland, and spared no
expense in paying for a full complement of
talented craftsmen to come from Europe to
build Bellwoods, a monument to his industry
and a gift for my mother. It was to be their
castle, but after she died, Father turned
away from the project. He still paid the
bills, likely because he was in too deep at
this point to quit, but he rarely visited
the site.

The men were kind to me. They must have seen
me for what I was: a lonely boy, orphaned of
his mother, neglected by his father, quiet
and observant and desperate for some form
of attention. It is a curious thing about
aging: we reach a point where we can see our

younger selves as different people, and we come to consider those versions of ourselves as long-lost acquaintances. I have complicated feelings about the person I became later, the things he saw and did, the things he neglected to do, the evils he facilitated, but I still think of that young boy with fondness and compassion.

The builders and craftsmen took me under their wing and treated me like a sort of mascot, a cat on their ship. They would invite me to have lunch with them, or show off the work they had done that day. I was smart enough to stay out of the way and avoid becoming a nuisance, and I would spend many happy quiet hours perched on a wooden box, watching as a plasterer smoothed fresh white compound onto lathe, or a tiler assembled gleaming squares of porcelain into a perfect mosaic. In this way I gradually learned about the building trade, and a seed was planted that would one day grow into my career as a land developer.

My favourites among the men were a pair of woodworkers, brothers from Hungary. I am sad to say that their names are lost to me now, but their faces are clearer in my memory than my own dear mother's, and I can still hear their laughter and cheerful chatter when I stop and squint into the past. The brothers were cheerful, boisterous men who could do magical things with wood. They were responsible for all of the trim work and cabinetry in the house, but it was the staircase that took pride of place. Father had requested a work of art, and the brothers spent weeks carving and shaping and fitting the various components.

Their chisels danced over dozens of maple
dowels as lightly and deftly as paintbrushes,
and branches and twists of vine emerged.
Wide planks of hard walnut were carved with
intricate designs, leaves and twigs and various fruits and pine cones. A huge length of
chestnut was designated the banister, and,
working from opposite ends, they transformed
it into a massive bough that gradually
divided into two, and finally at the end
into a spray of fine, leaf-covered branches.

No two pieces of the staircase were the
same, but they all fit together as part of
a grand vision that the brothers seemed to
share, almost telepathically. If there were
sketches, I never saw them, and most of
the communication about this grand project
involved the two men standing next to one
another, scratching their chins and staring
intently across the foyer at the gradually
evolving structure, until they silently came
to an agreement on one detail or another and
went back to work.

I was there to watch the entire beautiful
masterpiece emerge, and I was there when
Father arrived home from a long work trip
overseas to see the finished product. On
every other occasion I'd witnessed Father
visit the building site, he had been gruff
and businesslike, unwilling to spare any
compliment beyond a slight nod. But when he
stepped through the front door and saw the
finished staircase, an expression crossed
his face like I'd never seen before, a combination of grief and wonder, and he gripped
my shoulder for a moment almost as if willing me to help him stand.

"Well done," he said to the brothers, who stood with their hats in their hands, awaiting his assessment. "Very well done indeed."

The next morning, Father was late to rise and leave for his office, and when I trotted along the path to the new house—now almost complete—I spotted one of the brothers bent over the bushes, clearly ill. It wasn't until a little while later when one of the local teenagers who was apprenticing on the site told me that my father had brought two bottles of fine scotch to the brothers, and that the three of them had proceeded to get very drunk together until late into the night. It was a scenario in which I had never glimpsed my father before, and never would again.

Eventually the house was completed and my friends on the building site returned to their homes in Europe. To my surprise, once we moved into Bellwoods, Mother's cousin returned to her home in the city, and Father hired Iris French, a young widow from a nearby community, to keep house and watch after me.

Mrs. French was a breath of fresh air after the dark, grim year following my mother's death. She treated me well and brought light and cheerful chatter into our home. Best of all, she had a son around my own age who she would sometimes bring with her. Benjamin French, known to everyone as Junior, had lost his father a year or so before we met, and, without ever speaking of our losses, we bonded in part due to our shared grief. Before long we were fast friends.

It wasn't until I was older that I realized that Junior only came to the spit with
his mother on days when my father was away
on business, or otherwise preoccupied. The
French family was black, descendants of the
Empire Loyalists who had settled in the
area over a hundred years before the Bellwoods arrived. My father, among his many
other forms of bigotry, would have believed
that qualified them for housework, but not
friendship. But Mrs. French was a wise
woman, and, like the builders, she recognized my loneliness and saw that I needed
a friend. In her calm, unruffled way, she
found a solution.

Junior was as kind and cheerful as his mother,
and at heart, he was an adventurer. He would
orchestrate exciting missions and outings, in
which I was always a willing participant. We
launched countless toy boats into the inlet,
we built forts and hunted for salamanders and
combed the beaches along the coast for as far
as we could travel on foot, and always, always,
we were looking for the *Obelisk* treasure.

Junior was obsessed with the treasure. From
the cliffs he would gesture dramatically out
at the open Atlantic, describing the great
battle between the *Obelisk* and the *Renegade*
in such detail that I could almost imagine
it happening. Wandering the fields and forests and coastline, Junior always had his
eyes peeled. He would regularly point at suspicious lumps or hollows in the ground, or
oddly shaped root formations beneath trees,
and pronounce them worthy of further explora-
tion. We made countless firm plans to return
with spades, but we rarely followed through.
Despite this, Junior's enthusiasm for the

treasure never waned, and he seemed genuinely
convinced that someday he would be the one to
find it. For my part, I was just happy to be
along for the ride. After the loneliest year
of my life, this adventurous new friend was a
gift.

The new house was big and beautiful, and
Junior's mother made sure it was kept clean
and that there was always good food at hand. I
was growing quickly and as much as the thought
pained me, my mother was becoming a more distant memory with every day. I missed her terribly, of course, but the pang of loss was
fading as the world grew wider around me.

I wasn't forbidden to visit the old house,
but I knew that Father wouldn't approve, and
somehow I was able to avoid thinking of it.
Junior occasionally pestered me to visit the
old homestead and search the surrounding woods
for the treasure, but I pretended it was forbidden, and he knew better on that note than
to press the issue. Besides, there were many
other places to search.

One day, when my sisters were home on a rare
visit from school, Catherine mentioned something that took me by surprise.

"Mother would have hated Bellwoods," she
said with a sniff. "She never wanted to
leave the old house. She loved it there."

"It's true," said Anna, noticing the look
on my face. "This house is Father's folly.
Bellwoods indeed: What possible reason is
there for us to have a bell tower?"

I knew they didn't really feel this way
about the house. They were understandably

envious of me for living in the mansion
while they were stuck away in boarding
school, but the rest of their comments had
the ring of truth, and I felt a pang of
guilt. I felt illogically as if I had abandoned Mother and left the house to fall into
disrepair, as if I could have done anything
to stop it.

Whatever the truth of the situation, I began
to visit my old home. I would slip into the
trees and walk through the forest to sit
on the old stone wall outside the house,
where I would talk to Mother. This place
soon became a refuge for me, a place where
I could escape from the pressures of the
world, and for years I would visit faith-
fully every few days, grateful for the
opportunity to spend this time in the woods
with my thoughts.

Later, after everything that happened, I
stopped my visits. Perhaps I was ashamed, or
perhaps I was simply overwhelmed. Whatever the
reason, without anyone to watch over it, the
house was taken over by nature, and over
the years it dissolved into the earth.

In time, Junior and I made other friends.

The house at the tip of the inlet had been
built to house the workers, but once they
finished their jobs and went back to their
home countries, it sat empty for a while,
until Father hired a caretaker who moved
in with his family. Elmer Feltzen was a
year older than us, an intelligent and
good-natured boy, always ready to join in

our shenanigans. He was skilled at building things, and admirably capable of taking
Junior's wildest plans and making them a
reality. Under Elmer's guidance, a driftwood
raft would become seaworthy, or a tree fort
sturdy and elaborate.

The next to join our group was Archie Jinx,
the son of a fisherman who lived with his
parents and three younger siblings in a
small weathered shack on the inlet. Archie
was rough and coarse, with a foul mouth and
a terrible temper, but he was a loyal and
capable friend who knew the ins and outs of
the ocean better than anyone I've ever met.

At some point, my father looked up long
enough from his work to decide that the company I was keeping was too rough, and that
I needed to spend time with boys who were
closer to my social standing. With this in
mind, he arranged for me to play with the
youngest son of the local doctor. Freddie
Oakley, known by the rest of us as Red, was
younger than the rest of us by a couple of
years and a whiner by nature, but shrewd in
his own way. The rest of us found his company tedious, but there was no point in com-
plaining about it, since Father had decreed
it a condition of my freedom to include Red
in our games. Besides, the boy was willing
enough to follow along with the rest of us,
so we grudgingly accepted his presence, and
soon he was a fixture of the group.

Our days were full of adventure, and our
adventures had a focus: the *Obelisk* Treasure. Like everyone in the area, we'd grown
up hearing the stories of Captain Dagger's
magnificent cache, and together we resolved
to find it. We certainly weren't the first

to look for the treasure, but I doubt anyone
else had devoted quite so much energy to the
search before we took up the task.

From the cliffs that edged Dagger Woods we
would stare down at the open Atlantic, talking at such length about the great battle
between the *Obelisk* and the *Renegade* that I
could almost imagine it happening in front
of us. Armed with spades and pickaxes, we
wandered the fields and forests, our eyes
peeled for suspicious lumps or hollows in
the ground, or oddly shaped root formations
beneath trees. We'd dig with abandon in any
spot that seemed worthy of further examination, and although we always came up empty,
our enthusiasm never waned.

Crucially, Archie had a small dory that he'd
salvaged and fixed after a storm tossed it
onto shore. The little boat gave us access
to points unreachable by foot, and we would
take it up and down the coast, searching for
new spots to look for Dagger's treasure and
enjoying our freedom from the shackles of
dry land.

I'm not sure who first began to call us the
Treasure Hunters Club, but once the name was
spoken aloud, it stuck. We were five boys
straddling the divide between childhood and
the mysterious realm of adults, quite different in so many ways but united by a common mission.

There have been many moments in my adult life
when I have been truly happy—the day I married my wife, the birth of my daughter Mirabel and then my granddaughter Susan—but all
of them have been tinged with a pall of shame
and guilt, a sense that I didn't deserve them

because of everything that came before. I also
knew that I owed it to those three women to
let myself live my life out from the shadow,
if only for their sakes.

But there were no shadows hanging over the long
summer days I spent with the Treasure Hunters
Club. They were the happiest of my life, full
of adventure and innocence and the promise of
youth, and we were unbothered and blissfully
unaware of the terrible fate in store for each
of us.

We found it on an overcast day in late
August. Rain was threatening, but for the
moment it seemed to be holding off. The wind
was warm but with the tiniest hint of chill
mixed in, a warning of what would soon come.

Archie wanted to take the dory out for a
row around the far point below Dagger Woods
to explore the rugged coastline beyond.
On another day, the rest of us might have
resisted, with the weather as uncertain as
it was. But school was only a week away, and
every day was an opportunity slipping past,
and so we climbed into the small yellow boat
and set off.

The weather began to pick up shortly
after we rounded the point, and the swell
rose more quickly than we ever would have
expected. The dory was thrown around in the
waves, and in a matter of moments it became
clear that we were in trouble. Bounded in by
the jagged rocks at the base of the cliffs,
there was no natural place to set in, and

our best efforts to work the oars were
futile.

Red began to cry, and I had the terrible
sinking certainty that we were going to die
like this, bashed against the rocks. But
Archie and Elmer managed to stay collected,
and before I knew what was happening, Elmer
had jumped off the side and Archie was
throwing him a line. Elmer was the strongest
swimmer among us, but he was hardly a match
for the sea in this state. We watched, our
hearts in our chests, as he was tossed about
in the waves like a rag doll. Every time
he slipped under, I was sure he would never
surface again, but somehow he managed to
make his way to a rocky ledge in the cleft
of two cliffs, with the line still in tow.

He tied off the boat to a dangling spruce,
and then one after the other, we jumped over
and followed the line to shore. Dripping and
exhausted, we climbed onto the rocks just
as the storm landed in full force, and the
water that had been merely rough just minutes before became a churning maelstrom.

The dory was no match for the force of the
storm, and we watched as it was lifted and
battered onto the rocks, each of us imagining, no doubt, our own fates had we still
been in the little rowboat. Together, we
cowered under the shelter of a small outcropping as the wild squall of wind and rain
passed over us.

It was over almost as soon as it began. The
sky opened and we stepped out from our hiding place to dry in the hot sun, almost giddy
from our close call. We all knew that Archie

would face a beating for losing the dory, but he shrugged it off. Considering how bad things could have been, he was willing to face his punishment.

We were now faced with the dilemma of how to get home. The cliff above us was steep and ragged, its peak jutting out beyond its base, so that climbing wasn't an option. A bit farther down the coast the cliff dipped to a tiny rocky beach. If we could make it that far, we could clamber up onto the headland and then make our way home through Dagger Woods, but the rocks separating us from that haven were impassable. The water had calmed significantly, and we decided to swim.

We were almost at our destination when I chanced to glance down through the water. If I had waited only a few seconds, or if the sun hadn't been hitting the surface of the water at exactly the right angle, I would have missed it entirely. But I didn't miss it. It was right there beneath me on the floor of the ocean, wedged between two huge boulders. About 6 feet down, clear as day, lay an iron chest.

I called for the others, and they collected around me. Treading water, we all stared down at the unbelievable find.

Junior was never a great swimmer, but on this day he must have been guided by some outside force. He dove to the chest and we watched as he put all of his strength into pulling on the corner, dislodging it from the rock. After what seemed like hours, but must have been seconds, he surfaced, gasping for air but shining with excitement.

"We've found it!" he exclaimed.

It took us almost three hours to move the
chest the last few feet along the ocean floor.
Taking turns, we would dive to the heavy chest
and push it with all our might, managing to
nudge it only a few inches at a time.

But in this way, we managed to move it
around the outcropping to the shallower
waters below the beach, and finally Junior
and Elmer and Archie and I took hold of a
corner each, and with Red hovering excitedly
nearby, we staggered onto shore. Laughing
and panting, giddy at the audaciousness of
our accomplishment, we dropped to the ground
and took a closer look at our discovery.

The chest was encrusted with barnacles and
thick clumps of bright red seaweed, but generally in excellent condition, especially if
it really *was* over two hundred years old.
There was a latch, and two heavy hinges,
but the rim of the lid was so misshapen
with corrosion and age that it was clear the
chest would not open easily.

"We need to open it!" yelled Red, and I
couldn't help noticing that his childlike
enthusiasm was tinged with something else.
Greed? Hunger?

Our hands were raw and our energy was spent,
but we set to work, using stones to batter
away the corrosion on the lid.

Evening was fast approaching by the time we
finally broke the seal. The sun, low on the
horizon, illuminated the top of the chest
with a rich golden glow as we carefully
pried it open.

We were all struck silent as the contents
were revealed. The only sound was the low
rush of the waves dragging at the rocky
beach below us, and the endlessly whispering
wind.

Gold doesn't tarnish. After two hundred
years hidden by the sea, the pile of gleaming coins were as bright as if they had been
polished that morning. Mixed in with the
coins was jewelry: chains and brooches and
rings studded with multiple colours of glittering gemstones. It was a proper treasure,
the kind from a storybook.

And it was ours.

FAMILY DINNER

Dandy's aunt Margot lives with her husband, Chet, and their two kids in Bayview, a fancy new subdivision just outside of town. Their house is large and new and "decked to the nines," as Grandy would say.

As Dandy's mom pulls into the driveway, Margot is standing at the door to greet them like she's the manager at a White Lotus.

Margot is a Realtor, and it's very important to her that her own home exude a certain image. She and Chet were among the first buyers in Bayview, and probably expected the neighbourhood to quickly fill up with Maple Bay's hoi polloi. Instead, most of the other houses in the development were bought by investors, and so now she's surrounded by Airbnbs and spends a lot of time calling the cops on house parties.

"Hi, Mary!" she says, waving excitedly as they climb out of the car. "Hi, Dandy! Have you heard the news?"

Mary hands her sister a bottle of white wine. "Hasn't everyone? Danielle was on the beach below Bellwoods when the emergency vehicles arrived."

"No!" says Margot, her eyes widening. "What did you see?"

Dandy shrugs. "Not much. I just heard sirens and then a cop car and an ambulance showed up." She leaves out the part about being with Bill Jinx.

Margot ushers them into the house. In the kitchen, Uncle Chet is at the counter, cheerfully chopping away at something, a beer within easy reach.

"Hi, guys," he says. "Wild news about Mirabel, hey? I kind of thought she'd live forever."

Mary takes a seat at the counter. "Apparently she fell down the stairs."

"She should never have been in that big old house all by herself," says Margot. She slides a glass of wine across the counter to Mary, then takes a long sip from her own. "I wonder what will happen to the old place. There's so much value in the land, let alone the house."

"Atta girl," says Chet. "Always working an angle."

Margot shrugs. "Real estate is my business, Chet," she says. "Someone is going to swoop in and buy it up. Why not me?"

"I wouldn't be so sure," says Chet, pulling a roast from the oven. "The word around town is that Mirabel has a grandson, and he just moved into Bellwoods a few days ago."

Margot purses her lips with her glass lifted halfway to her mouth. "What?" she asks, and her voice is especially sharp. "Where did you hear that?"

"When I had the boys at hockey practice yesterday," says Chet.

"I wonder if he discovered the body," Mary muses.

"A grandson," Margot repeats, almost to herself.

Dandy wonders if this grandson is the person Mirabel was planning to introduce her to. "I didn't know Mirabel had kids," she says.

"Just the one," says her mother. "Susan. She left town right after she had the baby and never came back. She and her husband died in an accident out west. Car crash, I think. That was years ago now. I can't have been much older than you, Dandy."

"Anyway, the baby's back," says Chet. He lowers his voice conspiratorially. "Apparently he's gay."

Dandy's mom laughs. "You hockey dads always have the best gossip."

Dandy wants to hear more, but she's sent to the basement to fetch her cousins for dinner. Mason and Simon, moon-faced dullards with no skills or attributes other than an ability to fart on demand, are sitting about three feet from the TV, playing some screamy-shooty video game.

She announces dinner and they clomp past her without acknowledgment. By the time she follows them upstairs, the food is being brought into the dining room and the conversation has moved on from Mirabel.

"I'm so happy we could do this today," says Margot as they sit. "I've missed our Sunday family dinners."

"This is the first one since the old fella died," says Chet, holding up his glass in tribute before tossing back a healthy gulp.

"Poor Dad," says Margot, reaching over to scratch the back of Mason's head. "The boys miss him so much. Don't you boys?"

The boys grunt their agreement through mouths of roast beef and Dandy glares at them from across the table. She knows damn well that Mason and Simon didn't appreciate Grandy half as much as she did.

"Dandy and I were at the house the other day," says Mary.

This catches Margot's attention. "Is that so? Why?"

Dandy catches an edge in Margot's voice, but Mary either doesn't notice or chooses to ignore it.

"We were just tidying up," she says. "Cleaning out a few things. Opening the windows to air the place out."

Margot makes a big show of cutting a piece of beef. "Hopefully you didn't accidentally take off with anything valuable," she says.

Mary lays down her cutlery and stares across the table at her sister. "Of course I didn't, Margot," she says, after a cool pause. "Do you really think I'd go in there and steal stuff out of the house?"

Margot hastens to backpedal. "Oh my gosh, no, that's not what I was suggesting. It's just such a big job. He was basically a hoarder."

"He wasn't a hoarder," says Dandy. "He was a collector."

Margot ignores this. "It would be so easy to accidentally toss something of value into the trash," she says.

"You don't need to worry, Margot," says Mom. "Dandy and I were doing a cleanout. It's been over a month since Dad died, and to be honest I got tired of seeing the place just sit there with no one paying it any attention."

"To be honest," says Margot, "I don't know why you're even bothering. It's not your problem, sis."

She sounds magnanimous, but Dandy knows this is Margot's way of reminding Mom who inherited Grandy's house. Not that anyone needs reminding.

"C'mon, hon," says Uncle Chet. "You know you don't have any time to clean out the house. You're doing us a favour, Mary, and as far as I'm concerned, we should be paying you."

"Oh, you don't have to worry about that, Chet," Mary says quickly. She pauses and then, as if sensing an opening, she goes on. "I was actually hoping to talk to you both about this." She takes a breath and then smiles. "I was just wondering if you would be open to renting Dad's house to us."

Margot's eyes shift away. She reaches out to pick up her wine glass and takes a long sip before answering.

"You know how much money we could make by renting that house out, Mary," she says. "The vacation rental market is so lucrative, and it's only growing. If we rent it out by the week, we can make an unbelievable return on the place."

"But the tourist season is only really in full swing from June through October," says Mary. "It would be really tough to rent it out for the rest of the year, and if you balance it all out, maybe it would come out even. And we'd be taking care of it, shovelling the driveway, cleaning . . . You wouldn't have to worry about any upkeep at all."

"I'm sorry but it's not that simple," says Margot. "I've run the numbers, and even if we don't rent for a single week from November to May, we'll make twice as much by renting to tourists the rest of the year. And that includes paying for housekeeping and property maintenance. It's a total no-brainer. Hang on, I'll grab my laptop and show you some spreadsheets."

"I don't want to see your spreadsheets, Margot," says Mary. "I'm trying to talk to you as a sister here. This is our family home we're talking about."

"It *was* our family home," says Margot. "Now it belongs to me."

"I realize that," says Mary. "I'm not asking for a handout, I'm asking to rent the place. What if I took care of upkeep as well? The gardens, the gutters. There are some rooms that could really use painting."

"You know what will happen if we do that," says Margot, her voice dripping with phony regret. "You and Dandy will get nice and comfortable, and all of a sudden you'll have renter's rights."

"That would be terrible," says Dandy. "If we got rights, we might start to think of ourselves as human beings."

Margot puts her hands up. "I'm sorry, Mary, but I can't afford to rent it out at a loss for the sake of charity."

Dandy and her mother turn to look at each other, something unspoken passing between them. Together, they push back their chairs.

"Oh, for Pete's sake," says Margot. "Are you really going to make a big dramatic fuss about this?"

"I'm not making a fuss," says Mary, standing. "We need to run a few errands before we go home, so we're going to head out now. Dinner was lovely, thank you, Chet."

Margot clearly doesn't buy it. "Mary, it would be a real shame for this to evolve into an estrangement. My hands are tied! I know Dad wouldn't have taken this kind of decision lightly."

In this moment, Dandy hates her aunt so much that she has to squeeze her eyes shut just to contain it. But her mother just smiles, even though Dandy knows it takes every single ounce of energy she has.

"No estrangement," she says. "Dad wouldn't want us to part ways over his decision."

Margot sits back in her chair, relieved and satisfied. "Exactly," she says. "Now, are you sure you don't want to stay for dessert?"

They do not stay for dessert. On the ride home, Mary is quiet, in a defeated, weary way Dandy hasn't seen since the period after her father left.

She reaches out to put a hand on her mother's arm. "It'll be okay."

"I know it will. It's just . . . I wish Dad had thought through this decision a bit more."

It's something Dandy has been struggling with since Grandy died: Margot might be the oldest, but after Granny died Mary was the one who took care of Grandy, bringing him meals, making sure to stop by at every free opportunity. After Dandy's father flew the coop shortly after her fourth birthday, he stepped in and more than filled in the gap. More than anyone, Grandy would have known how much that house would have meant to them.

"Why do you think he did it?" Dandy asks.

Her mother sighs. "I've asked myself that question a thousand times, and the only explanation I can come up with is that your grandfather gave the house to Margot because she's a real estate agent. He knew Margot and Chet didn't want to live there, and it would have been just like him to think she could sell it for a good price and then divide the profits with us."

"I guess he didn't know Margot very well," says Dandy.

"I think he probably knew her as well as anyone," she says, "but he didn't want to admit it. Family was the most important thing to your grandfather, Danielle. He was determined to be a good father to us, and a good grandfather to you and your cousins. I think a lot of that was because he didn't have much of a relationship with his own father."

"Did Grandy ever tell you much about his father?" Dandy asks.

She shakes her head. "Not really. The story goes that he was drinking and drowned in the inlet when Dad was just a kid. They never found a body, so they couldn't even have a proper burial. It was a terrible accident."

Dandy struggles to wrap her mind around it. Grandy's father, her *great*-grandfather. One of the five boys who found the treasure. This shadowy person, and every choice he ever made, lead directly to her.

Mary continues. "I think Dad grew up feeling abandoned by his own father, whether that was warranted or not, and that had a big impact on how he lived his own life. He never touched a drop of alcohol, and he went out of his way to be there for anyone who needed him. Maybe that's why he gave people—like Margot—more credit than they necessarily deserved, but if that's the worst thing you can say about a person after they're gone, they lived a hell of a good life."

Dandy remembers what Bill said about Grandy just that morning. *Your grandfather was a good man, but he had too much faith in people.* She resolves to imitate her mother's brave face. She had the perfect grandfather for fourteen years, and one questionable decision doesn't change that even a little bit. They'll figure it out. They always do.

As they come around the bend, Bellwoods comes into sight in the distance, and Mary lets out a deep sigh. "All the old-timers are disappearing," she says. "Dad, now Mirabel. To think of all the knowledge of this town that goes with them."

Dandy nods, and something occurs to her for the first time. Two members have died in two months. What will happen to the society now?

Beneath this, there's a second question, a more troubling one. Can this really be a coincidence?

ARE YOU OKAY?

"So this is how you've been spending your days," says Falia. "Swanning about like a Real Housewife. Nice work if you can get it."

Cass laughs and flops into one of the big living room armchairs. She's just given a FaceTime tour of the Trappers' house to Falia, who was suitably impressed.

"I have to admit," she says to her phone screen. "I feel like I've won the lottery."

It's true that her lifestyle has been pretty satisfying over the past couple of weeks. She gets to live in this beautiful house, with its world-class view. She sleeps in expensive linen sheets and cooks elaborate meals in the gourmet kitchen. She starts her days with a long hike with Banjo, and often drops into town to buy groceries and talk to Bree at the bookstore. There's a sweet little cafe just down the street, French's Bakery, that makes a killer cappuccino and the best brownies she's ever eaten, and she's taken to hanging out there a couple of times a week, with her notebook.

Her *still-empty* notebook.

She sighs. "I just wish I could figure out how to take advantage of it and actually get something done. This year is going to fly by, and I'm going to have nothing to show for it."

"So the writing isn't going well?"

Cass shakes her head. "I just can't seem to settle on an idea."

"Okay," says Falia. "Let's brainstorm. What kind of book do you want to write?"

Cass sits up straighter, ready to be guided. "The only thing I know for sure is that I don't want to write another YA novel. I was thinking maybe a thriller, and I started toying around with the idea of a woman who takes a house-sitting gig in a small town on the coast and people start turning up dead."

"I like that!" says Falia. "You're halfway there already, right?"

"Yeah," says Cass, "but then the first person I met in town *did* turn up dead."

"Wait, what?"

"You remember that old lady I told you about? The one who had the dog and the keys? She fell down the stairs in her big old house and died."

"Jesus," says Falia. "That's grim."

"Right? Anyway, it's not like it was a murder, but it put a bad taste in my mouth and turned me off the idea."

"What about something historical?" asks Falia. "You know those World War II books that are so popular? About women who become spies or foreign correspondents and have to parachute into places? Something like that, maybe."

"That's not really my thing," says Cass. She stands up and walks to the huge picture window that looks down the hill and over the inlet. She turns the camera to share the view with Falia.

"I thought if I stared out at the water long enough, I'd be struck by inspiration. Turns out it isn't that simple."

"It is beautiful," admits Falia.

Cass ignores this. "Do you want to hear something crazy? Apparently there's a hidden treasure somewhere down there."

"A treasure?"

Cass turns the phone back toward her and crouches to scratch Banjo's belly.

"It's a big deal around here, the *Obelisk* Treasure. Way back in the day there was a pirate battle offshore and the captain sent some of his guys ashore to hide his treasure. It's historically documented and everything."

"That's pretty cool," says Falia. "So people still think the treasure might be out there?"

Cass nods. "It's a whole thing. Apparently people have been searching for it ever since. There's a whole tourist economy built around it. Back in the sixties, an investor from Louisiana even went bankrupt trying to find it."

"Maybe you should take a crack at it," says Falia.

Cass laughs. "It might be easier than trying to land on an idea for a book." She stops suddenly and stares past the phone at the water.

"What's going on?" asks Falia.

"What if that's the book?" says Cass, almost to herself. "What if *I* search for the treasure and write about it?"

Falia raises an eyebrow. "You just told me people have been searching for two hundred years. What are the chances you're going to find it?"

Cass shakes her head. "Finding the treasure isn't the point. *Looking* for the treasure is the point. Do you remember *Julie & Julia*?"

"Yeah," says Falia. "Meryl Streep and Amy Adams."

"That's the movie," says Cass. "But it started with a book. Actually it was a blog first, one of the first blogs to blow up. This woman, Julie, decided to cook every recipe in *Mastering the Art of French Cooking*, and she blogged about it, and then she got a book deal."

"Because people love cooking," says Falia. "And Julia Child."

"No," says Cass. "Because people like to hear about someone relatable doing something interesting. Julie was a bit of a mess. She was dealing with job stuff, relationship stuff, family stuff, and just basically being a human in the world. Like me."

"Okay," says Falia. "I'm listening."

"Think about it. My life explodes and at the last minute I'm given a golden ticket to this storybook town. I'm at loose ends, and so I decide to hunt for the legendary hidden treasure. I take the *Obelisk* Treasure and give it the *Julie & Julia* treatment."

"I'm not going to lie," says Falia, nodding slowly. "I would read that."

"So would I," says Cass. Her mind is suddenly spinning with possibilities, and the more she thinks about it the more she sees just how much this makes sense. This is an incredible story, and she's *here right now*.

How can she not write this book?

In the afternoon, Cass drags Judith's bicycle out of the garage, and soon she's gliding along Inlet Drive with the wind in her face and the smell of salt air in her nose.

Dagger Woods is on the other side of the Spit from Maple Bay, more than a hundred acres of forest perched on a bluff over the ocean. The terrain is hillier and more heavily wooded, and Cass is forced to dig deep as she begins to climb. Through the trees she catches glimpses of water, and here and there a house appears, tucked into the rugged terrain. Finally she comes to a sign announcing the Dagger Woods Recreational Trail. The trail meanders along through the woods, and the rich scent of pine needles and leaf mulch fills the air.

After a short distance, the woods open up to a wide bluff high over the ocean. An elderly couple is taking photographs of the view while a young family enjoys lunch at one of the picnic tables nearby. Cass leans her bike up against a tree and walks to the edge. Below her, huge, ragged boulders step into the churning surf, waves breaking against them with thick walls of spray.

She peers back along the coast. From here Maple Bay is a tiny speck of buildings in the distance. Much closer, the tower at Bellwoods climbs above the treeline. Her stomach drops as she thinks about poor Mirabel. What a terrible way to go. She knows it's a bit crass, but she can't help wishing she had a chance to interview her for the book. She has a feeling that the old woman might have had some interesting insights into the *Obelisk* Treasure.

She turns her attention back to the ocean, which is sparkling in the sun. She begins to paint a picture in her mind of an epic sea battle. Two hulking ships slowly circling one another in a ghostly moonlit fogbank. Muskets and cannon fire illuminating the night sky with erratic, staccato bursts of light. A rowboat slipping surreptitiously through the mist, low in the water thanks to a cargo of unimaginable riches. She pulls her phone out of her pocket and steps a bit closer to the edge to take some shots.

"Be careful," says a voice. Cass spins on her heels and realizes that someone has come up behind her. It's a runner, in athletic shorts and a hoodie, his face glowing with a sheen of sweat. It takes her a moment to make the connection: it's the guy she almost ran off the road the other day. He pulls back his hood, running his fingers through his hair and grinning at her.

"Sorry," he says. "Didn't mean to scare you."

Cass smiles back. "I guess this makes us even."

He raises an eyebrow. "I startled you," he says. "I didn't almost kill you."

"Hey!" she says. "What happened to 'All's well that ends well'?"

He laughs and puts out a hand. "Fair enough. Let's call it even, lead foot."

"Lead foot?" says Cass.

"What am I supposed to call you?" he asks, his eyes twinkling. "I don't know your real name. I'm Bryson, by the way."

He's flirting, and Cass realizes to her surprise that she kind of likes it.

She reaches out to take his hand. It's a basic handshake, nothing sexy or seductive about it, but when their palms connect, an unexpected shiver runs through her.

"Cass," she says.

Maybe it's her imagination, but the handshake seems to last just a split second longer than necessary before he releases his grip.

"Why were you telling me to be careful, anyway?" she asks. "Was it just a general suggestion after I almost ran you off the road?"

He laughs. "As a matter of fact, I was talking about the rocks down there." Together they turn and stare down the edge of the cliff at the huge, jagged boulders below. "A few years ago, a tourist climbed down to get some shots and got swept out to sea."

"Jesus," says Cass. "Really?"

He shrugs. "That's the story I've heard. I'm not from here, though."

"Are *you* a tourist?" she asks.

"Nah," he says. "I'm just in town for a few weeks doing some contract work. What about you?"

"I'm not from around here either," she tells him. "But I'm here for a year. House-sitting."

"A year," he says, his eyebrows lifting. "That's quite the house-sitting gig."

Cass nods. "No kidding. It all kind of fell into place kind of quickly. Let's just say the timing was right. I've only been here for a few days, so I figured I'd explore the area a bit."

He nods. "Did you know that this forest gets its name from the infamous pirate Barnabas Dagger?"

Cass hopes her face doesn't betray her. "Yeah, I've heard about the *Obelisk* Treasure."

He laughs. "Hard to avoid it around here." He turns and points out at the water, to a spot in the middle distance. "It all started with a battle somewhere just about there," he tells her, "when the HMS *Renegade* managed to corner the *Obelisk* about two and a half kilometers from the entrance to Maple Bay."

Cass's eyes widen. "Wow, you know a lot about it."

He grins. "When I was growing up, my family spent a lot of time on our sailboat down here in Maple Bay. I was obsessed with the legend. What could be more exciting to a little kid than a pirate treasure?"

"Captain Dagger and the missing gold," says Cass. "It sounds like something out of a Disney movie from the sixties."

"It does, doesn't it?" says Bryson, his face taking on an almost dreamy quality. "I'd be lying if I said I didn't still imagine finding the treasure every once in a while."

Cass considers telling him about her own plans, but she doesn't know this guy at all.

"Where do you think the treasure is hidden?" she asks.

"Your guess is as good as mine. The men who rowed it ashore were caught right here in Dagger Woods, and according to most theories it's buried here somewhere. But I doubt anyone will ever find it, to be honest."

"You don't think so?" she asks.

He shrugs. "Nobody has managed to find it in over two hundred years. I think it's lost to history at this point."

"You're probably right," says Cass. "It's a cool story, though."

"That it is." He drops his eyes and grinds his toe into the dirt. "So, if you're new to the area, I guess you don't know many people around here yet," he says.

"I've made a few friends," says Cass. She's pretty sure she knows where he's going with this, and she's not sure how to feel about it.

"Well," he goes on, "I don't really know anyone around here, either. Maybe we can get together sometime and grab a drink or something to eat?"

Cass hesitates, and Bryson smiles.

"It's totally cool if you're not feeling it," he says.

"It's not that," she says. "It's just . . . I guess you could say I'm in a period of transition, and I don't know if I'm up for dating at the moment."

"I totally get that," he says. "Listen, I don't want to put you on the spot, so don't feel any pressure at all, but if you change your mind and feel like grabbing a drink at the Shivering Timbers with another Maple Bay newbie, the offer stands. We don't even have to call it a date. We can call it a hang." He gestures at her phone. "I could give you my number, and if you decide you're bored someday, you can drop me a text."

She smiles, appreciative that he isn't trying to give her a hard sell. "Why not?"

She hands him her phone, and he plugs in his details. They stand smiling awkwardly at each other for a moment, and then he points over his shoulder. "Well, I think I'll try to wrap up my run while it's still nice out," he says. "You know what they say about the weather around here: if you don't like it, just wait five minutes."

"I should head back too," says Cass. "The dog who comes with my house-sit is bound to be wondering where the hell I went."

After he's gone, Cass walks back to the water and takes a few photos, doing her best to frame the area where Bryson indicated the battle took place. It occurs to her that she's stumbled across her first lead, and when she replays the order of events—almost hitting Bryson with her car, unexpectedly running into him here in the park, the fact that he just happens to be a fount of knowledge about the history of the treasure—she realizes how much texture this whole episode would add to her narrative.

She pulls a notebook out of her jacket and jots down a few quick thoughts. At the bottom, she poses a question in block letters and underlines it three times.

Do I follow through and meet with him?

The answer is obvious. Of course she has to follow through. Doesn't she owe that much to the book? To her readers? To herself?

She skims through her contacts and finds that he's entered himself as simply *Bryson*. No last name means she can't investigate him online. As she climbs back on her bicycle, she thinks back to his tall, lean frame, his tousled hair, his impish grin, and decides that investigating him in person, the old-fashioned way, might just be preferable.

WORK

I open my eyes in the deepest depths of night, and Bellwoods is already awake. Perhaps it didn't go to sleep. Perhaps it never does. I climb out of bed, my feet searching the floor for my slippers in the dark, and step out of my bedroom and into the hallway. All around me, the house crouches into its own shadows, still and ready.

I wander from room to room, pushing open doors into dusty, unused bedrooms, half expecting to stumble into a meeting of diaphanous ghosts, glowing transparent faces turning to recognize me as an intruder in their home.

I wonder if this is how Mirabel spent the last quarter century of her life. Did the house feel as empty to her as it does to me now, or did the ghosts and memories of her family—her father, her husband, her child, years of lives lived—give structure to the space, filling the rooms with remnant energy?

Whatever spirits were here for Mirabel, it appears they have not stayed for me. When I stop and listen, the only heartbeat I hear is my own, the only other presence the house itself. It remains stubbornly silent, refusing to answer my unspoken questions.

At the top of the stairs, I stop and stare down the chasm of steps into the inky shadows below. I shut my eyes against a vivid image of Mirabel tumbling, crashing, to her death. When I open them, the light has shifted. Somewhere the sun is crawling back to the surface of my new world.

I make a coffee and take it into the study. Once more, I flip through Henry's journal, trying to pull together the threads of this wild and sordid tale, but despite all the questions it answers, the most important one is left unresolved.

Maybe Mirabel could have helped me make sense of it all, but she's gone.

I have no choice but to figure things out on my own.

Bree is surprised to see me when I arrive at the store for my first shift.

"Um, hi," she says. "I'm sorry, I would have called, but I realized after you left your interview that I didn't have your number. You totally don't have to be here today, under the circumstances."

"No," I say. "I wanted to come in."

"Are you sure?" she asks. "I mean, the job's yours, man. I'll hold it for you. Take as long as you need."

"If it's all the same to you," I tell her, "I'd like to start right away. I could use the distraction."

She nods. "Fair enough. I've got a few boxes in the back that need unpacking. Let's start there so I can give you a rundown on our inventory system."

The next few hours fly by, and I find that Bree is really funny and smart and interesting to hang out with. Within an hour of my shift beginning, she's clearly decided to take me under her wing.

"I was really sorry to hear about your grandmother," she says as we sort through a newly delivered box of books behind the counter. "I know you only really moved here to be near her, so it must come as a big shock."

"It *was* shocking," I tell her, "but if you want the truth, I didn't really know her, so it's kind of weird. I'm not really grieving her as much as I'm grieving what we should have had. Does that make sense?"

She nods. "I totally get that."

"What I'm really dreading is the funeral," I say. "Do you know you're literally the only person I know in the whole town? I'm really not looking forward to sitting by myself in church while several hundred strangers stare at me."

Her expression goes serious. "Wow, that didn't even occur to me. I'll just have to come with you."

I stare at her. "Are you serious?"

"Of course I am," she says. "It will still suck, but I'm sure it will be easier with someone at your side. Besides, how could I pass up a front-row seat to the biggest show in town? Sorry if that sounds crass, but the best thing about living here is the characters. And Mirabel Bellwood was a hell of a character."

"Wow," I say. "I hardly know what to say. Thank you so much."

She waves this away. "Don't give it a second thought. I'll just close up the shop for a couple of hours. Honestly, I know this town can be hard on newcomers." Her face brightens as something occurs to her. "That reminds me! I made another new friend this week. She's house-sitting on the inlet, pretty close to you, actually. Cass. She's really cool and she doesn't know anyone, either. Since I've decided to make both of you my projects, I think we should all hang out together. Maybe we can all have cocktails!"

I nod slowly, not sure how keen I am at making so many new friends so fast, but Bree is clearly enthusiastic about the idea, and after her offer about the funeral, I can't really turn her down.

There's a bit of a rush over the lunch hour. I sell the new Louise Penny, a stack of picture books, and a copy of *Bluenose Ghosts* to some tourists. After that, things quiet down a great deal and Bree tells me she's going to run out to do some errands.

"You'll be okay here on your own?" she asks.

I take an overt glance around the entirely empty shop and give her a thumbs up. "I think I can handle it."

She scurries out the door, and I come out from behind the counter to wander around and get acquainted with the different areas of the store. In a section labelled LOCAL INTEREST, I spot a book called *Legends of Maple Bay* and take it back to my seat at the counter to peruse.

It's no surprise that there's an entire chapter on the *Obelisk* Treasure, but it's just a recap of the standoff between the *Obelisk* and HMS *Renegade*, along with a bunch of vague speculation that the treasure is deeply buried somewhere in Dagger Woods.

One thing that's conspicuously absent is any mention of the Treasure Hunters Club—confirming that, as far as the public is concerned, the treasure has never been found. I wonder if Mirabel and I are the only people alive who know the secrets inside Henry Bellwood's journal.

The bell on the door jingles and I put the book aside as a woman enters the store. She's around my age, short and plump, and she appears dressed for the weather of the future, rather than the weather of today. She's tucked into a wool coat, with a colourful tapestry scarf and a green wool cap and mittens. She doesn't glance around like a typical browser, and instead walks right up to me at the counter.

"Hello," she says, with a cheerful smile. "Bree phoned yesterday to say that my special order had arrived. Bonnie Brickland."

"Just give me a second," I tell her. "I'll check in the back."

When I arrive back with her order, she's flipping through *Legends of Maple Bay*. "I'm going to guess you're new to town if you're catching up on this stuff," she says, smiling again.

"Guilty," I tell her. "I haven't even been here a week. My family goes way back around these parts, and I figured I should do a bit of research into my family tree."

"Who's your family?" she asks, sliding the book back to me.

I cough, suddenly feeling a bit awkward at the direction this conversation is taking. "My grandmother was Mirabel Bellwood."

Her face goes white. "Oh," she says. "Oh my goodness. You're the grandson."

I smile, awkwardly. "Yep, that's me."

Bonnie Brickland looks like she's about to cry. "I am so, so sorry for your tragic loss."

"It's okay," I say. "I mean, it's not okay, obviously, it's awful, but I barely knew her, to tell you the truth. We'd only just reconnected. I was actually in town because she found me after all these years, so it's all a bit strange . . ."

I turn to the cash register and begin to ring in her books, mainly to avoid her pitying expression. We make the exchange and I slide the books into a bag, and when I hand them across to her, she takes them but stays at the counter, looking at me and considering something.

"I was helping her with a bit of research," she says, abruptly. "I admired her so much. She was a woman of the old school. Dignified and elegant, with a backbone of steel. She didn't suffer fools, and she didn't waste time on insincere displays of emotion. But she and I had much in common, and I learned over time that there was a great deal of kindness underneath that gruff exterior. I'm very sorry for your loss. She was a great lady, and I'm sorry the opportunity to get to know her better was taken from you."

"Thanks," I say, unsure of how else to respond to her little speech.

"Listen," she continues. "I work at the library, and I know the town archives inside out. If you find yourself looking for information about the Bellwood family, or Bellwoods, or anything else, why don't you come see me?" She rummages in her purse and hands me a business card. "That book you're reading might be fun, but it barely scratches the surface of this area's history."

"Thanks," I say. "I might actually take you up on that after, you know, the funeral and all the other stuff . . ."

She nods quickly to let me know she totally understands. "Any time at all," she says. "Consider it an open-ended offer."

I smile, expecting that she'll finally turn and leave, but she doesn't. Instead she catches me off guard by reaching across the table and grabbing my hand, squeezing it firmly.

"Your grandmother and I were very close friends," she says, in a low, earnest voice. "She must have mentioned me."

I shake my head. "I don't think so . . . but I didn't really know her for all that long."

She releases her grip. "Of course." Clutching her package, she takes a step back. "Well, it was very nice to meet you."

With that, she turns and exits into the early evening.

I take another long look at the business card before sliding it into my wallet. Bonnie Brickland is clearly a bit strange, but she might end up being more help than she even realizes.

THE FUNERAL

Mirabel's funeral is a whole town affair. Everyone turns out, partly to pay respects to the grande dame of Maple Bay, and partly to catch a glimpse of her long-lost grandson, recently arrived from afar.

From her seat near the back of the church, Dandy observes Peter Bellwood. He's in a pew at the front with Bree Vonnegut, who is turned around in her seat, chatting with Mrs. French and Bonnie Brickland, the librarian. Peter seems oblivious to their conversation. He just sits there staring straight ahead at the casket.

"He's handsome," her mother whispers.

"I guess so," says Dandy. It's not the word she would have used. *She* would have said average: average height, average build, sandy brown hair cut to an average length. She wonders whether he'll choose to stay in Maple Bay, now that his grandmother is dead. Word on the street is that he's taken a job at the bookstore, which would explain why he's sitting with Bree. Does he plan to stay in Bellwoods?

She thinks again of what Mirabel told her when she visited the library: *There's someone I'd like you to meet.*

Obviously it was Peter, but why? What possible reason would Mirabel have had to introduce them?

The minister steps through the door at the back of the church and the congregation stands for the first hymn, but the organist has only made it through one bar of the intro when the door flies open and someone stomps loudly into the church.

"What a bunch of bullshit!"

Gasps ripple through the crowd and heads swivel to see Bill Jinx standing at the back of the room, his knitted cap pulled down low on his forehead, his dirty canvas coat buttoned up to his neck against the cold.

Bill is swaying on his feet, clearly drunk. The organ goes silent, and the only sound is the whirring of the huge ceiling fans hanging overhead, gently circulating air.

"You're all a bunch of damn hypocrites," Bill goes on. "Singing Mirabel's praises when you all know as well as I do that the Bellwood family never did a goddamn thing for this town except crush it under their boot."

Dandy steals a glance at Peter, who is watching Bill with an expression of stunned fascination.

"Call the police!" someone yells out.

"There's no need for that," says another voice, and Dandy turns to see Dr. Oakley standing from a seat on the other side of the church. He walks calmly down the aisle to stand in front of Bill.

"Let's take this conversation outside," he says. He reaches for Bill's arm, but Bill jerks away and squares up, eyes flashing. There's a tense moment when it looks like things might escalate, but then the fire goes out of him and he drops his fists, his shoulders slumping.

Oakley steps forward and puts a placating hand on Bill's shoulder. Without warning, Bill bursts into loud, sloppy tears.

For a few awful moments, the church is full of the sound of the old man's sobs. Nobody seems to know what to do. Dr. Oakley releases his grip and awkwardly steps back, and even the minister seems frozen on the pulpit.

Finally Bill gets himself under control, and when he speaks again, his voice, still wet with tears, is loud and defiant. "You all think I'm crazy anyway, so I'm just going to say it. Last night the ghost of my old man came to me. I opened my eyes, and as sure as I'm standing here, Archie Jinx was at the foot of my bed, staring right at me."

It's a preposterous thing to say, but Bill's voice is firm with conviction, and nobody so much as cracks a grin. Every single person in the church is hanging on his every word.

"I never met the old man," Bill continues. "He died when I was just a wee little thing, but some of you already know that. Isn't that right, Rose?" He's staring directly at Mrs. French, and Dandy remembers what he said at the beach about not trusting her.

The old woman calmly meets his accusing glare. "I do know that, Bill. I'm sorry."

He laughs, a harsh, unkind sound, and then waves her off like a pesky mosquito as his head swivels to scan the rest of the crowd.

"I heard there was another Bellwood in town. Where is he?"

Peter lifts a hand. "That's me," he says, tentatively. "I'm Mirabel's grandson. Peter."

"I'm sorry for your loss," says Bill. He reaches up to pull off his cap, holding it in front of him, and suddenly the weeping, drunken mess of just a few moments ago is gone, replaced by a man who has suddenly gained control of a situation. "Your grandmother and I knew each other for a very long time. I respected her, but I didn't trust her. Do you know what my father told me, Peter?"

Peter just shakes his head.

"He told me the Bellwood family carries an unsettled debt. Now that Mirabel's gone, I guess that means you're going to have to settle up."

"Okay," says Dr. Oakley, finally moving to put a hand on Bill's arm. "That's enough."

Oakley begins to guide Bill outside, but in the entryway Bill pulls away. "You can only bury the truth for so long," he says, jabbing his finger at the gobsmacked crowd. "Sooner or later, it always finds its way to the surface." Finally, Oakley manages to get Bill through the heavy church door, which slams shut behind them.

Somehow, the minister manages to get things under control, and the rest of the service goes off without any other shocking interruptions. Finally, Mirabel's coffin is pushed back down the aisle to a parting hymn, followed by the awkward, self-conscious figure of her grandson making the mourner's procession all on his own.

After church, Dandy's mother has to head to the hospital to start her shift, which means Dandy has the rest of the afternoon to herself. She considers going home to watch TV, but she decides there's someplace she'd rather be. She's about to start walking when someone calls her name, and she turns to see Rose French approaching, a hand raised.

"Hi, Mrs. French."

"I was hoping to catch you," says the old lady. She gives a wry smile. "That was quite the memorable funeral, wouldn't you say?"

"Yeah," says Dandy. "I think Bill must have been pretty drunk. Why do you think he said those things about Mirabel?"

Mrs. French considers this. "I'll be honest, Dandy, I don't rightly know. If I had to guess, I'd say Mirabel's death churned up some emotions and he lost the script. He's had these kinds of public breakdowns before."

Dandy hesitates before asking her next question. "Why did Bill single you out?"

Mrs. French sighs. "It's very sad," she says. "Our fathers were friends a very long time ago, but there was some kind of altercation. Bill's father, Archie, ended up dead, and my father, Junior, ended up in prison."

Dandy stares. She isn't sure what she expected, but it definitely wasn't this.

"That's awful," she manages to say.

Mrs. French nods. "Daddy never talked about it, except to insist it was an accident. It's a story with no winners, but Bill doesn't see it that way. My father lost almost a quarter century of his life in prison, but when he got out he immediately opened the bakery, met my mother, and started a family. Better late than never, he always said. Bill's father didn't get that second chance, and Bill spent his whole life living in that shack with his mother, who was a sad, sick woman, until she died. I'm sure he looks at my life and thinks he got the raw end of the stick. He's had a rough life, and I can't begrudge him his grievances."

"What will happen to the society?" Dandy asks. "Now that Mirabel is dead, I mean."

"That's why I wanted to talk to you, Danielle," says Mrs. French. "I think this likely means the end of the society. We probably should have thrown in the towel years ago, but your grandfather had real enthusiasm, and Mirabel was also deeply invested. Bill only ever had one foot in at best, and Frank Oakley insisted there was nothing to it. I think he only stayed involved because he didn't want to miss out if something ever *did* come of the search. After your grandfather died, he dropped out."

"But what about you?" asks Dandy.

Mrs. French smiles kindly. "I'm old, Danielle. It was fun when I was a younger woman, but I just don't have the energy left to keep it up. I'm sure that's a bit disappointing to you, considering you just joined, but we've been spinning our wheels for forty years, and every single lead has gone up in smoke."

"But what about the chart that Grandy left?" asks Dandy. "I went to the inlet to explore it just a few days ago!"

She raises an interested eyebrow. "Did you find anything?"

"No," Dandy admits. "But I saw Bill, and I really think he knows something."

Having hoped this would intrigue the old woman enough to renew her interest, Dandy is disappointed.

"If Bill really is onto something, I'm happy for him to see it through. I've got everything I need. Let Bill find the treasure." She regards Dandy with a twinkle in her eye. "Or better yet, why don't *you* find it?"

Dandy leaves the churchyard feeling deflated. After Grandy's death, she fell into a deep, grey funk. Nothing seemed capable of brightening her days or sparking her interest. She's smart enough to know that part of this is just moving through the grieving process, but it's impossible to ignore that the part of her life that kept things bright and sparkly and interesting is gone.

In the years after her father left, Grandy kept Dandy afloat. She was a five-year-old who missed her father and couldn't understand why he wasn't coming home. Grandy filled in the gaps, helping Mary with school pickups and grocery shopping, lending his car and keeping an eye on things, but most of all, he spent time with Dandy, teaching her about life and pointing out the magic all around her.

Then suddenly her interpreter and guide was gone, and she learned that trying to replicate Grandy's enthusiasm and joy on her own was next to impossible.

Until she found the letter.

Joining the society was the first thing since Grandy's death to get her genuinely excited about something. It was a final, unexpected, thrilling connection between them. Now, just like that, it's gone.

She wishes more than anything that he were here to discuss all of this with. He would have had questions and theories, and he would have paced around his sunroom, working through the events and possibilities aloud, as Dandy sat and watched him, feeling the thrill of adventure dancing up and down the sides of her arms.

Perhaps that's why, without even really making a decision to head in that direction, Dandy finds herself at the inlet, standing at the front door of Grandy's little cottage. For a moment, she lets herself imagine that the door isn't locked, that she can just push her way in and call out, that Grandy's voice will call back from the sunroom or maybe the kitchen. *Come on in, girl!*

But she knows the door is locked, so she pulls the key out of her bag and lets herself in.

It's quiet inside. So quiet that she's immediately hit by a deep and overwhelming sense of sadness that makes her second-guess her decision to come back. The cottage feels like it's been asleep for a long time. It's chilly and dim, and the only sound is the hum of the refrigerator.

At least the sunroom is slightly warmer, and she drops into Grandy's chair, and pulls his soft old quilt around her, and stares out the window at the tip of the inlet. Grandy used to say that this was where the *Obelisk*'s men landed in their rowboat. She knew it was impossible to know that for sure, but he was able to describe it so clearly that she could picture the men as if they were in front of her, pulling the rowboat out of the water in the mist, heaving the trunk full of treasure out and then . . . disappearing.

The memory draws her thoughts back to the society. Dandy feels almost silly even admitting it to herself, but she'd allowed herself to get excited about the possibility of finding the *Obelisk* Treasure.

Maybe Mrs. French had the right idea. Maybe she *should* keep looking for the treasure on her own. Grandy wanted her to join for a reason. Doesn't she at least owe him some effort?

She works through what she knows.

When Dandy spoke to Bill on the beach, he implied that there was something in his little red notebook that he was keeping from the rest of the society, something relating to the location of the treasure.

His outburst in church was different. It wasn't about the treasure; it was about Mirabel, or more specifically the Bellwood family.

Dandy is pretty sure she doesn't believe in ghosts, and she knows that alcoholics can sometimes descend into madness and hallucination. But regardless of whether Bill hallucinated or not, he seemed to really believe what his "ghost father" had told him. What possible insight could have led him to make such a scene at church? At a funeral, no less.

Dandy thinks back to Mirabel's grandson. Does he have the first clue what he's got himself into?

Over the past few weeks Dandy has lost track of how many times she wished she could speak to Grandy, but she's never felt it as keenly as right now. If anyone could pull these threads together and make sense of what's happening, he could.

Dandy is yanked from her thoughts by noise from the opposite end of the house. She sits upright as a bolt slides in the front door, and a moment later Aunt Margot's voice fills the house.

"You need to listen to me," she says, her brash voice carrying clearly down the hallway. "It might be harsh to say this out loud, but this is the best thing that could have happened to us. It was a terrible accident, but now the biggest obstacle is out of the way, don't you get that?"

She pauses, and Dandy wonders if maybe she's with someone else, but then Margot speaks up again and it's clear that she's on the phone.

"It's true," she says, her voice dimming slightly as she moves out of the hallway, presumably into the den.

Dandy has a snap second to make her decision. She can choose either to unlock the back door in the sunroom and sneak out through the yard, leaving it unlocked, or to hide in the house. With no real time to decide, she turns around and darts back up the steps into the kitchen and very quickly slides into the pantry, closing the door behind her right as Margot's footsteps come down the hallway and stop just a couple of feet from where she's hiding.

"I don't know why you're getting cold feet *now*," Margot says. She sounds irritated, almost angry. "A couple of more pieces just need to fall into place and we'll be ready to roll. My father left his affairs in a bit of a muddle, so I still need to track down some paperwork. But there's nothing to worry about, and all you have to do is keep your mouth shut and let me handle things until the deal is done."

There's a long pause as Margot presumably listens to whoever is on the other end of the line. Dandy remains as still and quiet as possible, straining to listen.

Margot laughs, but she doesn't sound happy. "You need to stop overthinking this! Just leave them both to me. You think the grandson wants to be tied to a giant mansion and all the upkeep that comes along with it? No way. He'll take the money and run."

Margot's voice drops off as footsteps move away and into the sunroom.

Dandy sits back against the pantry wall, trying to catch her thoughts. Margot is clearly talking about Bellwoods and Mirabel's grandson, but she also said *leave them both to me.* Who else was she talking about? And who was she talking *to?*

More to the point, what did she mean about Grandy's affairs being in a muddle?

There's no time to mull it over in detail, because the screen door inside the sunroom slams shut. Margot has stepped into the backyard, and Dandy doesn't take time to second-guess herself. Staying low, she shuffles out of the pantry, then hurries back down the hallway, and slips out of the house through the front door.

BILL JINX

Cass waves a metal detector over a small pile of rocks but comes up empty, yet again. She tracked the machine down on Facebook Marketplace and bought it for a hundred bucks and she's spent the morning wandering the coastline at the tip of the spit, figuring out how to use it. It's kind of fun, but so far she's found nothing but a few coins and beer tabs.

She scans the beach. Banjo is down at the water's edge, scampering in and out of the waves. The inlet and Maple Bay are separated by a few miles of craggy, erratic coastline, and acre upon acre of fields and farmland stretching inland from the shore. She turns and looks in the other direction, past Bellwoods, and can just glimpse the edge of Dagger Woods sitting atop its cliffside perch, another vast territory to consider.

If there is a treasure around here, it's the proverbial needle in a haystack. The thought prompts her to pull her phone from her coat pocket and create a new voice memo.

"There is a lot of terrain around Maple Bay," she dictates to the phone. "If there *is* a treasure here, it's no wonder it hasn't been found."

She shoves the phone back in her pocket and begins scanning the sand again. A moment later, the dial on the detector beeps, and she crouches to dig. To her surprise, she doesn't pull another quarter or rusted bottle cap from the sand, but something more substantial. It's about the size and shape of a cigarette lighter and appears to be made of brass, pockmarked and weather-worn, satisfyingly hefty.

She turns it around, examining the threads on one end and the loop on the other, just big enough to put her little finger through. She suspects this is something from a sailboat or even a ship. It's obviously nothing of value, but she is surprised at the rush of excitement she feels. If this modest discovery gives her so much satisfaction, it's easy to understand how the *Obelisk* Treasure has captured so many imaginations over the years.

She tucks the object into her pocket and stands, just in time to see Banjo jerk his head up and bark at something. A moment later, he breaks into a run and disappears around the tip of the spit.

Cursing the dog, she picks up her pace and follows him around the bend, stopping when she catches sight of a familiar figure sitting on a driftwood log. Bill Jinx.

She feels a rush of irritation. She took great care to stay far away from his little patch of property. What is he doing all the way down here at the head of the spit?

Banjo has stopped and is staring at Bill from several yards away, but the old man doesn't seem to have noticed. He's staring intently up the bank at Bellwoods, seemingly oblivious to everything else around him.

Banjo glances back at her, and she silently gestures for him to come back and retreat with her before Bill clocks them, but the dog has other plans. After a split second of debate, he lets out another loud bark and closes the distance to the old man.

"Shit," she mutters as Jinx turns at the sound, noticing them. She expects him to stand and kick Banjo away, or at least toss a rock, but to her surprise he reaches out a hand, inviting the dog in for a scratch on the head, before returning his gaze to the mansion.

Reluctantly, she walks toward them.

"Come on, Banjo," she says. "Let's leave him alone."

Banjo shows no interest in leaving. He's curled up next to Bill, who is running his hand over the dog's head. She notices a half-empty bottle of rum in the sand next to him. As she gets closer, he twists around to look up at her again, and she can see that his face is flat and dull, no sign of the rage and harsh energy from their first meeting. There's something else, too. His eyes are red rimmed and puffy, and she could swear he's been crying. She's hit with an unexpected pang of sympathy for the old-timer.

"I'm sorry to interrupt," she says. "Come on, Banjo."

But Banjo is clearly content to stay where he is, and Jinx doesn't appear to mind. He continues to absentmindedly scratch the dog.

"What's that thing?" he asks abruptly. It's the first thing he's said to her and it takes her a moment to realize what he means.

"It's a metal detector," she says.

He grunts. "You lose something?"

She shakes her head, unsure how to explain herself, but Jinx quickly comes to his own conclusion.

"Holy shit," he says. "You're looking for the treasure, aren't you?"

Cass doesn't answer, but she can feel her face reddening as the old man begins to chuckle. This quickly evolves into a series of deep-throated guffaws, and before she knows what's happening, he has fallen onto his side, literally rolling on the ground with laughter as tears run down his face.

"What is so funny?" she demands, her sheepishness replaced with irritation.

It takes him a minute to stop laughing, and she stands there with her hands on her hips.

"You're drunk," she says.

He looks up at her from the ground. "I may be drunk, but that's not why I'm laughing. I'm laughing because I've got about as good a chance of finding a diamond necklace up my arse as you've got finding the *Obelisk* Treasure with that contraption."

"I don't really think I'm going to find it," she says. "I'm not a moron."

He picks himself up and brushes the sand from his coat and pants, his giddiness suddenly gone. He grabs at his forehead and sighs. "Don't pay me any mind, girl," he says. "I'm an arsehole. I can't help myself. Ask anyone around here, 'Who's the biggest arsehole in Maple Bay?' and they'll point at me." His face darkens, and he stares out at the water with grim, silent intensity. "Especially after yesterday, but that's another story."

A cloud has fallen over him, and Cass gets the sense that he wants to talk to someone. She hesitates, then takes a chance.

"What happened yesterday?"

He turns back to her and narrows his eyes at her. "You don't want to hear about my troubles, girl."

"Sure I do."

He shrugs and sits back down on his driftwood log, reaching over to grab the bottle of rum. "I'll need a drink if I'm going to talk about it."

He opens the bottle and takes a hearty swig, then points up at Bellwoods.

"You ever meet Mirabel?" he asks.

Cass nods. "Just once. She seemed like a force of nature."

"That's a nice way of putting it," he says. "She was hard as nails, that's for sure. I take it you weren't at her funeral?"

Cass shakes her head.

"Well, I was," he says. "If you must know, I got drunk and made a big scene in the church." He sinks into his seat, clearly embarrassed, but then he chuckles ruefully. "You should have seen the looks on some of those faces."

Cass doesn't know what to think. "Why would you do that?"

"You won't believe me if I tell you," he says.

"Try me," she says.

"Okay, then," he says, taking another big swig from the bottle. "The night before the funeral, I saw my father's ghost."

"Your father's ghost," Cass repeats slowly.

"I told you you wouldn't believe me," he snarls.

"I'm just trying to keep up," she tells him. "Go on. Please."

He pulls a pack of cigarettes out of his jacket and holds it out, offering her one, but she waves it away. He lights one and continues his story.

"Here's the thing," he says. "I might be a drunk and a shithead, but I'm not stupid. I know the whole thing was probably a hallu-cination, or a drunken dream, something like that. But it *felt* real, and every time I go back to it, I *remember* it as real. I woke up, and it was just like I said, the old man was standing at the foot of my bed, as sure as you're sitting there. I don't remember my father, but I'm almost certain that's who it was. For a long time we just stared at each other, and then he pointed a finger at me and he said, 'The secrets remain unspoken, and the Bellwood debt remains unpaid.' And then he disappeared."

"That's pretty creepy," says Cass.

"You're telling me," he says. "My old man was murdered, did you know that?"

Cass shakes her head. This story has already taken several wild turns.

He nods, his expression darkening. "Junior French spent twenty-five years in prison for it." He pauses to take another swig from his bottle. "Anyway, as you can imagine I had a hard time falling asleep after the old man disappeared. There was a bottle on the floor next to me, and I started drinking right there in bed. By the time the morning rolled around, I was well and truly pickled, and something possessed me to take my drunken, sleep-deprived arse down to the church and heckle a dead woman's funeral." He chuckles mirthlessly. "And that's why everyone in town hates me."

"I don't hate you."

He gives her a skeptical look. "Yeah, well, you don't know me well enough to hate me."

Cass places the metal detector on the ground and moves to sit on the other end of the driftwood log.

"You're right," she says. "But I know what it's like to feel like the whole world is against you."

She finds herself telling him about her disastrous final weeks in New York, and Bill listens intently. When she's done he points at the metal detector.

"So after your book went kerplunk, you decided to quit writing and look for buried treasure instead?"

"Actually," she says, "I'm going to write another book. About the treasure. I'm going to research the history of Maple Bay, and Captain Dagger and the *Obelisk*, and all the attempts to find the treasure over the years. And I'm going to weave my own attempts to find it into the narrative."

He listens to this with an eyebrow raised. "Well, it sounds like you've got a plan, but I can tell you you won't find the treasure."

Cass is irritated at this. "That's not the point of the book. I already told you I know I won't find it. There's too much ground to cover. The story will be the *attempt*."

"That's not what I mean, girl," he says. He takes another long swig from the bottle and then he stares at her for a long time. Cass gets the distinct impression that he is deciding whether or not to tell her something very important.

"You're really writing a book about the treasure?" he asks finally.

Cass is aware of something significant hovering in the air between them, crackling and electric. Falia's voice whispers in her ear: *Opportunity*. She can't explain it, but suddenly it feels as if everything that's happened over the past few weeks—the catastrophic implosion of her life in New York, the unexpected phone call from the Trappers, stumbling across the story of the *Obelisk* Treasure—has led her precisely to this moment.

She nods slowly. "Yes," she says.

"I know the truth about that treasure," he says, "and it's the likes you've never heard."

Cass finds herself leaning toward him, her mind tingling with expectation.

"Tell me," she says.

So he does. He tells her one of the wildest stories she's ever heard, about pirates and an epic battle at sea; about a group of friends who make an unbelievable discovery; about family secrets and unforgivable grudges; about a secret society, nautical charts, and cryptic clues; and, at the heart of it all, a fabulous treasure: buried, discovered, and then lost again in the mists of time.

It would all be totally unbelievable except for the expression on his face as he tells it. There is no question in Cass's mind that Bill completely believes everything he's told her.

When he's finished, he lets out a long breath. He looks calm, almost at peace, and she gets the strong sense that he's been dying to tell this story for a very long time.

Cass's mind is reeling from everything she's just heard, and she has questions. "Do you really think the treasure is still out there?" she asks.

He nods. "I do. When I received the anonymous letter, my first thought was that Junior French must have stolen it after he killed my father. That was as good an explanation for the murder as anything, and besides, how else could the man have left prison and opened a business the next day? But that didn't hold up to scrutiny. Why work your arse off baking bread every day for decades if you were sitting on a pile of gold? Rose French still lives in the same little apartment above the bakery that she was raised in, so if she's somehow concealing a fortune, she's a hell of a good actor."

"So you decided to join the rest of them," says Cass.

"I did," he concedes. "But I wasn't keen on the idea. If it wasn't for Reg Feltzen, I wouldn't have touched the rest of that crew with a ten-foot pole, but Reg was one of the few people in this town who I liked and trusted. He convinced me that there was something to the story, and so I went along with it, on and off, for years. When Reg died, I quit once and for all."

"But you didn't stop looking," Cass guesses.

He points at her, his eyes gleaming. "You're a smart one." He reaches into an inner pocket of his jacket and pulls out a battered little red notebook. It's the kind that has a coil on the top edge, and its grimy cover is tightly clasped, thanks to a little cluster of elastic bands around its middle. He holds it out in front of him, gripping it so tightly that his knuckles go white.

"Let's just say I've learned things," he says. "I haven't quite deciphered everything yet, but I'm getting close, and when I do . . ." He whistles and makes a vague gesture with his hands that seems to imply *big things that must not be spoken*.

Cass stares at the notebook, wondering what exactly he has written inside it. "So you're telling me you're close to finding the *Obelisk* Treasure?"

"I think I'm closer than anyone has been since it went missing the second time," he says, shoving the book back into his pocket. "But I'm not about to share all my secrets."

"Do you think that your father's ghost was referring to the treasure?" she asks.

His expression falters, and he slips the notebook back into his pocket. "I can't say for sure," he admits. "But the Bellwood family was hiding something. I'm sure of it."

He reaches for the bottle and takes another long draw and then points up at the mansion.

"Alexander Bellwood, who built that house, was a mean old bastard, but his son Henry, Mirabel's father, was as soft as his old man was hard. I think if Alexander got wind of the discovery, he'd have been able to beat or humiliate it out of his son. But I don't think that's what happened."

"Why not?" Cass asks.

He shakes his head. "Alexander Bellwood fell on hard times not long after all of this went down. He even had to sell off half of the spit. The land my house stands on used to be Bellwoods property, and old man Bellwood never would have sold off this land if he hadn't needed the money."

Cass remembers what Mirabel said about Alan and Judith buying property that used to belong to Bellwoods.

Bill tips the bottle back and drains the last of the rum, then tosses the bottle into the sand. "The only thing I regret more than causing a scene at Mirabel's funeral is that I didn't get a chance to talk this through with her." He registers Cass's expression and laughs. "I'm sure that's a surprise, after everything I've just told you. Mirabel and I were friends of a sort. She was a tough old bird, and lord knows I'm no picnic, but we knew each other when we were young and that goes a long way when you're as old as I am."

They sit in silence for a while, staring out at the water as Banjo dances in and out of the surf.

Finally, Cass turns to look Bill in the eye. "Why are you telling me all of this?"

"I'm not going to be around forever," he says. "I want to make sure that my story doesn't get lost when I'm gone."

"So you want me to write it down and put it in my book," she says, just to make sure she's getting it straight.

He nods. "I think that I'm going to find the treasure soon. *Very* soon, and I want it well documented, because I don't trust a single person in this town. That makes me vulnerable."

"You mean you're worried that someone is going to try to get to the treasure before you?"

"Or worse." He narrows his eyes. "There are people in the world who'd be willing to do just about anything to get their hands on this kind of loot. With someone like you following me around and keeping an eye on things, there's less chance of something bad happening to me."

Cass remembers what Bree told her about Bill yelling at tourists in the street. She realizes that these are probably the paranoid delusions of a madman, but his story is so well considered and so thoughtfully laid out that she can't help feeling like there's something here. Maybe it's wishful thinking on her part, but there is no question that this would make for one hell of a story.

"Okay," she says. "So how do you propose we do this?"

When Cass gets home, she makes some tea and immediately writes down every last detail while it's fresh in her head.

Her mind is spinning. Bill's story has everything. A solid hook. A completely unexpected twist on a familiar story. A lineup of fascinating characters. Best of all, *himself.* Bill Jinx is one of the most unique people she's ever met, a central casting dream, and he's just handed her the scoop of a lifetime.

She wants to talk to someone about this. She considers phoning Falia, but she's too removed from the action. It would be like explaining a book you've just read to someone. Bree has the context and would eat it up, but Cass is pretty sure that if she filled her new friend in, the whole world would know about it within a few hours.

She pulls out her phone and before she has a chance to second-guess herself, she sends a text.

Is this the mysterious Bryson?

A reply comes almost right away.

That depends - is this the mysterious Lead Foot?

She responds.

I'm pretty sure I told you to stop calling me that!

Her phone rings.

"I'm sorry," says the cheerful voice on the other end of the line. "But it's such a cute nickname, it's hard to resist."

"I don't go out for drinks with people who call me Lead Foot," she says.

"Oh wow," he says. "She plays tough. Okay, I promise to be on my best behaviour, Cass."

"That's better." Cass finds herself smiling like a fool and tries to rein in the flirting a bit. "Listen, I know this is kind of out of the blue, but I was wondering if I can take you up on your offer of a beer at the Shivering Timbers. Just as friends," she hastens to add. "I could use your insights into something."

"Shit," he says. "I'd love to, but I'm in the city on business for a couple of days. Can it wait till I get back?"

"Sure," she says, surprised at how disappointed she is. "You've got my number now. Drop me a text when you're back in Maple Bay."

"Will do," he says. "Only now you've got me curious. What kind of insights are we talking about?"

She hesitates, wondering how to even begin. "Well," she says, "I don't think I mentioned this, but I'm a writer, and I'm working on a book about the *Obelisk* Treasure."

"You most definitely did not tell me that," he says.

"So I learned some very interesting background information the other day," she says. "It's kind of a long story."

"I've got time right now," he says. "You can't leave me hanging after you've piqued my interest like this."

Cass picks up her tea, carries it into the living room, and drops into one of the big leather chairs by the fire. "Okay," she says. "Well, you should probably prepare yourself for one hell of a yarn."

A NEW ROUTINE

In the days after the funeral, I sink into a purgatory of routine as I await news of my fate.

I go to work and meet locals, many of them curious about Mirabel's long-lost grandson. I buy coffee and pastries at the little bakery around the corner from the bookstore. Bree convinces me to come with her to the Shivering Timbers for beer and wings, and I meet more locals. Maple Bay is starting to become familiar to me. It's starting to feel like home.

In the evenings, I wander Bellwoods. It's like being in a dream where I've been picked up out of my life and dropped into someone else's. And I suppose that's what's happened. In a strange way, I've replaced Mirabel.

In her kitchen, I make myself dinner. In the evenings I sit in her armchair by the fire and make my way through decades' worth of paperwork. From the window of her study, I stare out at the sea, and at a season of change. October is almost here, and the last days of summer are pushing back against the first signs of fall. Bright September sun blazes hot through leaves that are rapidly turning to orange and red and bronze, and the warm breeze that twists through the open windows during the day chills and quickens by nightfall, shaking the house as I try, in vain, to sleep.

An email arrives, and I read it over and over until the date and time are burned into my mind.

I wait.

I wait.

I wait.

Until finally, it's happening, the most fateful meeting of my life. Someone pulls into the driveway and a car door opens. I step to the front door; through the stained-glass window I see a blur of motion, the vague figure of a man approaching the house and climbing the steps.

He's here, and I'm finally reaching for the door, preparing for the most important encounter of my life.

"You're killing me here," says Bree, leaning forward to fill my wine glass. "Are you going to tell us what he said?"

She turns to fill Cass's glass, explaining. "Peter finally met with the lawyer today to discuss the will."

We're at Bree's charming little farmhouse for drinks. Outside, wind rattles at the windows, but inside the scene is warm and cozy. We're settled around the fire, candles are lit, and old jazz is playing on a vintage turntable. Bree arranged the evening as a chance for her "two new besties" to meet each other. Cass is easy to like, and there's something reassuring about hanging out with someone who is kind of an outsider like me.

I inhale, realizing this is the first time I've spoken about it aloud, and Bree and Cass are the first people I'm going to tell my big news to.

"It's mine," I say, the words feeling strange as I say them aloud for the first time. "Bellwoods is mine. Or at least, it will be once I figure out some paperwork and sign a few forms."

"Unbelievable," says Bree.

I nod. "You said it."

"Are you going to sell it?" asks Cass. "That's a big house."

I shake my head. "There's a real estate agent who has been pestering me to sell to her, but I'm not ready for that yet. It's a lot to wrap my head around and I'm still trying to figure things out. In Vancouver I could barely afford my apartment, and now I live in a mansion."

Cass smiles. "That's kind of my situation. I loved my apartment in New York, but it was so tiny. Now I'm in that giant house on the hill, and I keep pinching myself that it's real."

I smile. "My grandmother hated that house. Apparently the land used to belong to my family."

"Don't worry, she told me," says Cass. "I met her when I stopped to get Banjo and the keys, and she didn't seem too impressed with the Trappers."

"She was a hell of a woman," I say. "I keep expecting her to walk through the door."

Cass gives me a sympathetic smile. "I was really sorry to hear about her accident. I was actually hoping to talk to her for a book I'm working on."

"I thought you were writing a novel," says Bree.

"I *was* writing a novel," says Cass. "But then I changed course a bit. Peter, you've heard about the *Obelisk* Treasure, right?"

I nod. "I know the basics. Mirabel filled me in, actually."

"I've decided to write a nonfiction book about the treasure. The history of piracy in the area, the legend of the missing gold, all of that stuff. And I'm kind of weaving myself into it."

"Love that for you," says Bree. "Hot pirates and buried gem-stones. Sign me the fuck up."

"I doubt they were hot," says Cass. "They were probably stinky and unwashed, with missing teeth and scurvy."

"Don't knock my type till you've tried it, sweetheart," says Bree with a wink.

"Why did you want to speak to Mirabel?" I ask.

Cass shrugs. "I got the sense that she took local history very seriously. And Bellwoods is kind of ground zero for the mystery."

"Maybe you can help her, Peter," says Bree.

"I doubt it," I say. "I barely had a minute to get to know Mirabel, let alone hear her theories on the mystery."

In the back of my mind, Henry's journal screams for attention. I ignore it. There is no way I'm going to share anything about that here.

"No worries," says Cass. "That's what I figured." She seems happy to let it drop, but I get the feeling there's something she isn't saying.

At the end of the night, I offer to give her a ride home, since she's had a few glasses of wine. She gratefully accepts, and we run through the rain to Mirabel's Jaguar.

Once we're in the car, I look at her.

"Were you holding something back?" I ask. "When you asked about Mirabel."

She gives me a sheepish grin. "Was I that obvious? Yeah, I was. Sorry. I love Bree, but she knows everyone in town, and she has a big mouth. I've learned a few things that I want to keep quiet for now. But I think you're safe. You know who Bill Jinx is, right?"

"You mean the guy who cursed me at my grandmother's funeral?" I laugh. "Yeah, I remember him."

She winces. "He told me about that. I think he feels pretty shitty about it."

"You know him well?" I ask her, surprised.

"Not really," she says. "Except maybe? It's complicated. Either way, he told me a pretty crazy story."

"What kind of story?" I ask.

"Did you know that Mirabel and Bill were part of a secret society dedicated to finding the *Obelisk* Treasure?"

She misinterprets my surprise as being focused on the treasure, but it's the secret society part that really catches me off guard.

"Can you explain?" I ask.

She breaks down Bill's story, and suddenly a lot of the questions I've been asking about Mirabel since she died begin to come into focus.

"So what do you think?" she asks, fixing me with an intense stare. "You're closer to the heart of it."

I pause, trying to put my thoughts into words. "I mean, it sounds kind of implausible," I say finally. "But if you'd told me a month ago I was going to inherit a giant mansion on the East Coast, I would have thought it was equally unbelievable. So who knows?"

"Well, Bill sure believes it," she says. "He thinks he's close."

"To the treasure?" I ask, surprised.

She shrugs. "I know he's a crazy old man, but he sure sounds convinced. He's going to let me interview him soon and find out more. But I was hoping you could help me out too."

"Me? I don't really know all that much."

"You're directly connected," she says. "I want to learn more about the five boys who were involved, and that includes your great-grandfather. I bet you anything there's information somewhere inside Bellwoods."

"Maybe," I say. "I mean, there's a ton of paperwork in the house. I could take a look around and see what I dig up."

"Nice!" she says. "Thank you!"

Once again I think about the journal, imagining Mirabel's reaction if I shared it with anyone, let alone someone who's writing a book. But maybe I can find another way to help Cass, and she can help me figure out a few things in return.

"Shit," she says. "Act casual."

Up ahead, red and blue lights flash, a traffic stop. A couple of police officers are milling about, chatting with one another, and one puts his hand up indicating where we should stop, then approaches the vehicle.

Beside me, Cass gasps. "No way," she says. "Peter, that's Officer What-a-waste!"

"Who?"

"He's a cop Bree is kind of obsessed with," she says. "He's hot and single, but he's also gay so she calls him Officer What-a-waste."

Before I have a chance to absorb this, he's knocking on the window. I roll it down.

"Evening, folks." The cop bends down to peer in at us and I realize it's the same officer who managed the scene at Bellwoods when Mirabel died. He recognizes me as well. "Hello again. Peter, right?"

I nod. "That's right. Good to see you. Everything okay out here?"

He nods. "Just a routine traffic stop. Do you mind if I take a look at your license and registration?"

"Sure thing," I say, reaching inside my jacket for my wallet, happy that I had a Nova Scotia driver's license printed just this afternoon.

Cass leans across to squint up at the cop. "Hi, Officer," she says. "Do you guys know each other?"

He takes my license, not bothering to respond to her, and squints at it before handing it back. "Looks like you're sticking around at Bellwoods," he says.

"Yeah," I say. "Starting to look that way."

He hands the card back. "You been doing any drinking tonight?"

"I had one glass of wine at a friend's house," I say, "several hours ago."

Cass leans over from her seat. "He's the DD!" she says. "I'm the boozy one."

He smiles at her as he hands back my license.

"Glad to hear it," he says. "You folks head straight home."

"Just to be clear, we're not going home *together*," announces Cass. "We're just friends. Peter's gay."

The police officer gives her an indulgent smile, but I'm almost certain that he gives me a quick blink-and-you'll-miss-it double take, as if he's subtly checking me out. "Either way, don't stay out on the roads longer than you need to. The weather is really picking up, and there might be some localized flooding. That's always a possibility down on the inlet."

"Thanks, Officer," I say.

"Have a good night," he says. "Don't go causing trouble. And happy birthday, by the way." There's a twinkle in his eye, and do I imagine it, or does he keep his hand on the roof of the car for a hair longer than necessary?

He pulls away and taps the roof of the car, and as he moves to the vehicle stopped behind us, the other officer waves us through the checkpoint.

"Birthday?" asks Cass. "Today is your birthday?" Before I can stop her, she snatches my wallet from the centre console and flips it open. "Peter!" she says. "It's your fortieth birthday and you didn't even tell us?"

I grimace and shrug. "I don't love the idea of aging, especially under the circumstances."

She scoffs. "You look great. If you don't believe me, ask Officer What-a-waste. He was totally checking you out. You *have* to follow up on this."

"You're imagining it," I say, but I'm thinking about the look on his face when she told him I was gay, and I think she might be right.

"Someone has a crush on you," she says in a singsong voice. "Bree is going to lose her shit when she hears about this."

I laugh. "Oh, come on, you can't tell Bree. She'll never get off my case!"

She just smiles coyly, and I know there's no way she's going to refrain from telling Bree. I go quiet as my mind spins forward, playing out the implications.

By the time I drop Cass off at home, the storm has picked up even more, the surf racing dramatically into the inlet, waves churning over the shoreline and obliterating the beach. The rain is falling heavily, running in thick sheets over the windscreen, and as I head back down the long driveway, I'm forced to navigate slowly to avoid going into the ditch.

Bill Jinx told Cass that he'd discovered something that would solve this mystery. Are there pieces of information there that would complement the revelations in Henry's journal, the final crucial pieces of the puzzle?

I decide that I need to go see him, ask him to his face.

Finally I pull into my driveway and turn off the engine. I stare up at the darkened mansion looming above me, shuddering as my mind returns to Bill's outburst in the church. Is his father's ghost now lurking inside Bellwoods, waiting for his debt to be paid? Does he lurk in the shadows with Mirabel?

Will other ghosts join them someday, maybe even my own?

I close my eyes and push against the thought. *Ghosts don't exist.*

I take a deep breath and open my eyes, then I get out of the car and run through the rain and up the steps and across the porch until finally I'm reaching for the heavy front door and pushing it open and stepping back inside the dark embrace of this strange new life.

I remove my wet clothes and crawl into bed. Preparing for another long, sleepless night, I reach for Henry's journal on the bedside table and crack it open, revisiting the flush of discovery I felt when I first turned its pages.

THE CONFESSIONS OF HENRY BELLWOOD

As remembered in October of 1983

Junior was the first to react. He reached
into the chest and ran his hands through the
coins, lifting them and letting them drop
with a gentle, mesmerizing clatter. He began
to laugh, and the noise seemed to break
something up within us, and soon we were all
hooting and hollering and screaming out loud
with our good fortune, five boys who had
stumbled across what was surely one of the
greatest finds in history.

Through my giddiness, I glanced at the horizon and realized with a start just how low
the sun had sunk. If we didn't begin to make
our way home now, we'd be forced to navigate
through Dagger Woods in the dark.

"We need to go home," I said. "They'll be
worried about us."

Red pulled a pile of coins from the chest
and began stuffing them into his pockets,
but Archie reached out and grabbed his arm,
stopping him.

"What the devil are you doing?" he asked.

He was two years older and a great deal bigger than Red, but the younger boy bristled and pulled back with surprising force.

"I'm taking my share," he said, his eyes flashing. "We all found it, so we all divide it. Don't try to pull a fast one on me just because I'm younger."

"Nobody is pulling a fast one," said Elmer, as always the voice of reason. "You're entitled to your piece, just the same as the rest of us. But we need to think this through. Archie is the oldest, and he's not yet fourteen. You're only a kid, Red. What do you think is going to happen to this gold if we return home with it now? You think your father is going to let you keep it?" He turned to look at the rest of us. "What about you, Archie? Junior? Henry? You think you'll have freedom to do with this money as you see fit?"

I considered this. I knew that my father would never allow money like this to slip past him unnoticed. But there was another complication: for the past several months, he'd been spending more time in his office, up late at night with one hand pinching his brow as he stared at papers, frowning. I'd overheard short snippets of his conversations as well, with lawyers and bankers who came to the house to confer. There was tension in the air, and I had an uncomfortable feeling that something had gone wrong with Father's business.

I shook my head. "No," I said.

"I don't care," said Junior. "I'll be sharing mine with my family."

At this I felt a shameful, selfish twist in my gut. With this kind of fortune, Mrs. French would surely leave Bellwoods, and Junior along with her.

But Archie was shaking his head. "No," he said. "Elmer is right. We found this treasure, fair and square, but if we own up to it now, there's no way we'll be able to use it the way we like. Your mother is a good woman, Junior, but my father is a bad man. He'll claw away every last bit of this gold from me and use it to turn rum into piss."

"So what is the solution?" I asked.

"It's simple," said Elmer. "We hide the treasure again, and we wait until each of us is eighteen before digging it up again. When's your birthday, Red?"

"June sixth," said the boy.

Elmer considered this. "So we wait until your eighteenth birthday. June sixth, 1927."

"Seven years!" exclaimed Archie.

"You'll only be twenty-two," said Elmer. "I'll be twenty-one, Junior and Henry will be twenty. We'll be young men, and we'll be able to decide on our own what to do with the money, without the risk of it being taken from us."

Junior looked skeptical. "I don't like that my mother will have to work for seven more years," he said. "With money like this, she could leave now and we could build a house of our own."

"I understand that," said Elmer. "I'd like
to do the same for my family, but this seems
like the only fair way to do it. Besides,
Junior, your mother is still a young woman.
Not even forty. She likes working at Bellwoods, doesn't she?"

Reluctantly, Junior nodded. "She does." He
looked at me. "She'd have a hard time leaving you to fend for yourself."

I felt a flush of pleasure at this, and I
would have gladly thrown the treasure back
into the ocean to hold on to that feeling,
to the confirmation that someone cared about
me that much.

"Well, Red?" asked Elmer. "Does that seem
fair to you?"

The younger boy nodded firmly. "Yes."

"It's settled, then," said Elmer. "We'll
come back together here at noon on June
fifth, 1927. But we'll have to promise,
each of us, to not breathe a word of this
to anyone. Not our parents. Not our sisters
or brothers. Seven years, and then we can
divide the spoils and do with our portions
what we wish, but until then it's only to be
spoken about among ourselves."

We were standing over the treasure in a
loose circle. Junior was the first to put
his hand out, and one at a time—Elmer,
Archie, me, and then Red—we reached forward
and clasped our hands together. In this way,
we sealed our bond.

We dragged the chest away from the tideline
and covered it with driftwood and seaweed,

although there was no chance of anyone else
finding it in such a remote and desolate
spot. Then we climbed onto the headland and
entered the dim confines of Dagger Woods. We
made our way home with plans to return the
next day and bury the treasure properly.

In the morning, we congregated on the beach
as planned. Only Red was missing, which
wasn't unusual. His mother often kept him
home for various reasons. After waiting an
obligatory amount of time to confirm he
wasn't coming, we set off through the woods,
shovels and spades in tow.

The chest was just where we'd left it. We
spent a few minutes marvelling at the contents, and then we got to work. On our way
home the night before we'd passed a large
maple, prominently situated at the edge of
Dagger Woods, and decided it would be a good
signpost for a hiding spot.

Now we proceeded to dig a hole in the soft,
loamy soil under the tree's canopy, and when
we'd decided it was deep enough, we returned
to the chest. Elmer had been smart enough
to take some pillowcases with him, and we
filled them with gold and jewels, carrying
them up the hill and depositing them in the
hole.

By the time we'd filled it back in and used
a spruce bough to sweep needles back over
it, our hiding spot was indistinguishable
from the forest floor. But I knew none of
us would ever forget where we'd left it.
This secret was emblazoned on our minds. We
dragged the chest back to the water's edge
and pushed it back into the surf, to let the

sea take care of it, and then we headed for home.

"Seven years isn't that long to wait, when you think about it," said Elmer, ever the optimist, as we walked back through the forest.

"A lot can happen in seven years," said Junior.

"We'll be men by then," said Archie. "In charge of ourselves. It's worth the wait."

I didn't say anything. I could only hope he was right.

Even now, even all these years later, I grow angry with myself when I think about how easily we could have avoided everything. I have no doubt that the four of us would have kept the secret for seven years, but we let ourselves forget about the fifth.

Red was younger and weaker. He needed our assurances. He needed to feel like he was part of the equation. If only he'd been with us, we could have made sure he knew he was a member of the team, but he wasn't there, and we didn't spare him an extra thought. We would have told him, of course, the next moment we saw him. We would have explained the situation. We would have put him at ease.

Our mistake was in waiting.

How easy it would have been for me to find a way to go to him that day. I could have

taken half an hour to walk to his house and
tell him where we'd hidden the treasure, to
explain to him that we would take him there
at the first opportunity. But I was tired
and dazed after two days of strenuous activity, and the weight of this new development.
Red didn't cross my mind.

It was three days before I saw him again,
and in that time I'm not sure I thought
about him at all. I was preoccupied with
our sacks of gold. The promise of what they
offered us in seven long years. I floated
through my days, imagining what life would
look like once I'd put my hands on my share.
I would travel the world, I decided, making
it a point to have at least one adventure in
every country on earth.

I was lying on my bed after dinner, lost
in one of my reveries, imagining myself
on a safari, perhaps, or an Egyptian dig,
when there was a knock on my bedroom door.
Before I had a chance to respond, it
opened, and Father was standing there, his
face clouded.

"I need you in the study," he said.

As I entered the book-lined room behind him,
my heart sank into my stomach. Red Oakley
was sitting on a sofa, and his father, Dr.
Philip Oakley, was standing in the window
with his arms crossed in front of his chest.
When he turned to look at me, his expression
was dark and indignant. I looked at Red, and
he avoided my eyes. Something was wrong.

"Henry," said my father, "young Oakley here
has told his father a wild tale about what
you boys got up to a few days back."

"He woke us in the night," interjected
Dr. Oakley, "claiming the five of you discovered the *Obelisk* treasure, and you were
going to hide it until you turned eighteen.
Convinced you were keeping him in the dark.
The story is hard to believe, I'll agree,
but Freddie is a serious boy and I've never
seen him so worked up about anything."

"It is a rather fanciful tale," agreed my
father. "Henry, do you care to shed some
light on the matter?"

I know now, in retrospect, that this was my
final chance. I could have feigned ignorance
or even amusement. Red was only eleven years
old. I could have made him sound a fool. *We
were playing a game. We played a trick on
him. We let him believe he'd found a hidden
treasure. I'm sorry, Father. We should never
have been so cruel. Please forgive me, Red,
we let ourselves get carried away.*

I have no doubt that's what Junior would
have done, or Archie, or even kind, good-
hearted Elmer. But I was a guileless boy,
and as I stood there struggling to find
words, my face confirmed everything. I
glanced at Father, looking for support, and
saw his expression shift as the truth dawned
on him. Red's story was true.

Dr. Oakley had clearly come to the same
realization. "It's true," he said, striding across the room. "You little bas-
tards planned to cut Frederick out of this
entirely."

"No!" I protested. "We didn't! We were going
to—"

"That's enough, Henry," said my father. He turned to Oakley. "What do you propose we do next?"

The doctor looked surprised. "Well, I'm not quite sure," he said. "I suppose we should gather the other boys and their families and discuss a fair approach to this dilemma."

"You want to bring my housemaid and grounds-keeper, and an illiterate, drunken fisher-man, into the study and work out an appropriate arrangement?" asked Father.

"Well, when you put it that way," said Oakley, "perhaps you and I can make the decisions about how to proceed."

"No," said Father.

Oakley looked taken aback. "I beg your pardon?"

Father didn't answer, he went to his filing cabinet in the corner of the room and rummaged inside until he found a document that he brought to his desk. As the rest of us watched, wondering what he was doing, he sat and made some notes on the paperwork. Finally he stood and walked over to Oakley, handing him the papers.

"What is this?" asked the doctor, confused.

"That is a deed of ownership for almost a hundred prime acres of land on the Point," said Father.

Oakley scoffed. "Are you trying to pay me off?"

"It's simple, Philip," said Father. "You will take this offer or I will ruin you. I will

begin by suggesting that you were negligent
in the death of my wife, and I will use the
full weight of my status in this community to make everyone believe that you are
incompetent and a menace. I will call on my
many contacts to make sure that your license
to practice medicine is revoked. Your family will be left penniless and destroyed by
scandal."

Dr. Oakley stared at Father in amazement.
"You wouldn't dare," he blustered.

"Of course I would," said Father. "And I
could easily accomplish all of it. Alter-
natively, you could leave this office with
your reputation intact, along with ownership
of a piece of the most beautiful real estate
in the county. Forget your son's story,
Philip. Forget that this conversation ever
took place, and you'll leave Bellwoods a
richer man than when you entered."

Oakley considered this for a long moment.
Finally, he snatched the paper from Father's
hands and turned to Red, who had been
watching this whole scene unfold with wide
eyes.

"Frederick," he said. "Time to go home."

But before Red had a chance to stand, Father
knelt before him and put his hands on the
boy's knees, pinning him to his seat.

"Don't touch my boy, Bellwood," said Dr.
Oakley.

Father ignored him and leaned forward so his
face was only inches from Red's, who was
clearly terrified.

"If you breathe so much as a word of this to anyone," he said, in a low and menacing voice, "I will come to you in the night and rip out your throat. Believe that."

"How dare you!" blustered Oakley, but Father had made his point, and as he stood, he pointed dismissively at the door.

"Get out of my house," he said.

Oakley looked like he wanted to argue, but instead he gripped the papers in his fist and indicated for Red to stand and follow him. As they left the room, Red turned and gave me one last look, a mixture of regret and anger and self-pity. Father and I stood and listened as their steps descended the enormous wooden staircase, and then the front door opened and slammed shut again, and they were gone.

Father turned to me once Oakley's automobile had pulled out of the driveway. "Tell me it's true, boy. Tell me I didn't just hand over some of my choicest real estate for the sake of a fairy tale."

I nodded. "It's true. We found the *Obelisk* treasure."

"Let's go," said Father. "We have no time to waste."

In a daze, I followed him as we stepped outside into the late afternoon. In the few short days since we had discovered the treasure, autumn had landed in full force. In the distance I could hear the crash of heavy waves, and it occurred to me that as the season had changed, so too had the direction of my fortunes.

Father grabbed two spades from the garden
shed, and we set off. Neither of us spoke
as I led the way to our destination, but he
didn't seem angry. If anything, there was
a charged, intense energy about him that
I couldn't quite decipher. At the tree, I
stopped and stared at the ground where we'd
buried the treasure. There was no way that
anyone would ever be able to tell just from
looking at it that there was something buried there.

I jabbed my spade into the ground and we
began to dig.

It was much easier going than when we had
buried it in the first place. The earth had
already been loosened, and so it came away
easily, and soon the pillowcases were poking
up from the dirt, and we pulled them up like
giant, lumpy potatoes.

There were three pillowcases. Father knelt
beside them and untied the top of one. He
stared down, and then, to my amazement, he
began to laugh, and laugh, and laugh. The
sound was unmoored and manic, like nothing
I'd ever heard from my father before, and I
took an instinctive step backward.

Finally he collected himself. "Do you see
what you've done?" he said, lifting a hand
full of coins and letting them rain back
down into the bag. "You've saved us. You've
saved our family. You've saved Bellwoods.
This money will protect us for generations.
There's enough here to build ten more mansions. You and your sisters can go to the
best schools. And of course, if we invest it
wisely, we can turn it into much, much more

than this. But we'll have to do it slowly,
over years, you see." He was beginning
to mutter to himself, running through the
options and implications in his head.

"But . . ." I ventured. "What about the
others?"

He looked up at me quizzically. "Others?"

"Yes, Father," I said. "Junior and Elmer and
Archie."

He shook his head firmly. "No. You'll put
all of that out of your head at once. This
land belongs to our family, did you know
that?"

I had not. I knew that we owned a great deal
of property in the area, but the state of
our family's wealth and landholdings were
unknown to me.

"But we didn't find the treasure here," I
said. "We found it in the ocean and hid it
here. We were going to divide it equally
when we were all eighteen."

He was barely listening to me. "You'll soon
realize, Henry, that there are two kinds
of people in this world: the doers and the
scroungers. Your friends are scroungers,
looking to get rich from another man's treasure. Unwilling to work for their own fortune, they seek it out in others."

None of what he was saying made any sense.
It wasn't another man's treasure; it wasn't
his treasure; it was a shared treasure. We'd
found it together. Quite aside from this,
my friends were the furthest things from

scroungers I could imagine. Junior was as
hardworking as his mother, and dedicated to
his community and extended family, always
concerned about preparing for the future.
Elmer was enterprising and crafty, with an
engineer's mind and a plan for every situation. Even rough, foulmouthed Archie was
more adept on the water than any man I'd
ever known, with an instinctive understanding of tides and currents and an encyclo-
paedic knowledge of the intricacies of the
local coastline, not to mention a fierce
loyalty to his friends that hinted at just
how unpleasant his home situation was.

Only Red Oakley came close to Father's
description. I'd seen the greed in his eyes
when he saw the treasure, a greed that
had bred impatience and ruined our plan
before even a week had ended. I cursed him
silently.

"Why did you give Dr. Oakley land?" I asked.

Father was too preoccupied with his newly
claimed spoils to notice the defiance in my
voice. "Philip Oakley is sniveling and weak-
spined, just like his son," he explained as
he tied off the bag. "But he's no fool. He's
an educated man, and he could complicate
things for us. I needed to get ahead of the
game, so I called his bluff. He knew as well
as I did that we had the upper hand."

"How did you know that?"

"The boy was panicking like a rat," he said.
"If his story was true, it was clear that he
didn't know what you'd done with the treasure and worried that you'd cut him out.
That gave us a leg up over them."

"How did you know that the story was true?"
I asked.

Father smiled. "It was a bit of a risk, I'll
admit. But I know you well, son. I know your
face better than you know it yourself. Until
I asked you if the story was true, I would
have bet anything that the boy was just
caught up in a fabrication. But then I saw
your expression . . ."

He trailed off and looked back down at
the heavy, lumpy sacks lying on the ground
beside us.

"It was a gamble," he said. "But it paid
off. Now let's get moving: we have a lot of
work to do before the night is over."

Over the next few days Father took me into
his confidence in a way that I would never
have expected. He explained to me that
the house had run up costs at an alarming
rate, and he'd taken to gambling to pay the
bills, bringing us to the brink of ruin.
By the time my friends and I had come upon
the treasure, we were hanging on by just a
thread.

There was a true fortune in those three
sacks. The money Father needed to pay off
his debts barely made a dent in them. The
rest he placed inside the large safe inside
his office. After some internal debate, he
shared the combination with me.

"If anything happens to me," he said sol-
emnly, "this money is the lifeblood of the
family. You need to keep it safe. Gold will

keep its value and grow. No investment is
more stable."

I had access to that money from the very
beginning, and that thought has haunted me
every day since. I could have waited until
Father was away on business, opened the
safe, and distributed the money among the
five of us. There would have been plenty
left for me and my father and my sisters,
for the Bellwood family.

But I knew in my heart it was impossible.
Not at my age. Not with the risk it would
bring to the others.

So I came up with a different plan.

PART TWO

INVESTIGATIONS

Bill Jinx is dead.

The news makes its way through town as quickly as a sea mist pushed by a southerly wind. Someone walking their dog found his body washed up on the beach early this morning. By all indications, the old man went out in his boat after dark and drowned. It was a rough night. He must have been drunk.

By the time Dandy gets to school, stories are already flying around: how Bill would drunkenly wander around town yelling at tourists; the way he'd come out in a rage, waving people away if they so much as wandered along the beach below his shack; and, of course, the shocking scene he caused at Mirabel's funeral, ranting and raving about being visited by his father's ghost.

"It was just a matter of time," Dandy hears as she passes two teachers gossiping in the hallway. "The man was his own worst enemy."

But Dandy isn't so sure.

The more she thinks about it, the more convinced she becomes that something stinks. It couldn't have been an accident; that just doesn't make sense. Why on earth would Bill Jinx, who knew this coastline better than anyone, have taken a boat out into that water after dark in rough weather?

Did he do it on purpose? Did he find himself at the brink of despair and decide to take that last, biggest leap? But that doesn't fit for Dandy, either.

There's no question that Bill acted pretty unhinged in church, but he also looked angry, like he had something to prove. Because he *did* have something to prove. When she ran into him at the beach, he was adamant that he was close to finding the treasure. He was also worried that someone was after his secrets.

The secrets he kept inside his little red journal.

As soon as school is over, she heads in the direction of the inlet, but this time, instead of letting herself into Grandy's house, she continues along the road to Bill's driveway. Bill always had a reputation for being a crotchety old monster who didn't like visitors, but now she notices that he recently nailed prominent NO TRESPASSING signs to the trees along the length of the driveway, underscoring the point.

She isn't sure what she expected to find at Bill's shack—maybe police cars and a cluster of nosy locals—but whatever follow-up there was has already ended and the authorities have moved on, because there's nobody around.

The little shack looks especially weary today, slumped and defeated, like a dog waiting for its master. Even as Dandy is telling herself to turn around and go back to Grandy's house, she's walking up to the door, and even as she's telling herself that this is a terrible idea, she's checking the handle. It's unlocked. She pushes it open and steps inside.

The shanty is even more depressing on the inside, and Dandy is immediately struck by just how uncomfortable it must have been to live here. A damp, mildewy odor floats above everything. There's a thick, dirty old rug on the floor, but it barely contains the biting sting of sea air and ground chill that whistles up through the floorboards beneath it.

She steps into the middle of the main room and slowly turns, trying to take in everything with a detective's eye. A tiny kitchenette takes up one corner. The sink is full of unwashed dishes, and on the counter several beer cans and a couple of mostly empty liquor bottles are lined up near a half-eaten plate of congealing baked beans.

In the opposite corner, a stained, lumpy old mattress lies on the floor, covered with a tangle of tattered blankets and bedsheets. Her eyes move to the foot of the bed, and she shudders as she remembers what Bill said about his father's ghost appearing there. Dandy pauses and stares at the space, half expecting the grizzled spectre to appear in front of her, pointing a finger and commanding her to leave. But other than a gentle drift of dust motes through a slanted crack of light, everything is perfectly still.

A battered armchair covered in dirty laundry sits next to a window, in front of a bookshelf. She walks over and runs her finger along the spines. There's a surprisingly eclectic collection of fiction, everything from Stephen King to Donna Tartt, along with a whole shelf dedicated to local history, but there's no red notebook.

She turns her attention to a small desk squeezed into a corner behind the TV. A small stack of unreturned library books and an old tin can full of pens and pencils flank an empty spot right in the middle of the smooth wooden surface.

It's based solely on instinct, but in sudden, vivid Technicolor, Dandy has a vision of Bill sitting at the desk, writing furiously into the notebook, splayed open in that exact spot.

So where is it now?

Maybe he took it with him out on his rowboat that night. Or maybe, just maybe, someone came looking for it.

She thinks back to her talk with Bill on the beach. *These are the fruits of my own private investigation.* Did someone take Bill's journal? Who? And if so, what were they willing to do to get it?

She takes a final, careful look around the shack for the notebook, but comes up empty-handed.

She turns back to the door, about to leave, when something jumps out at her. Propped up in a corner, just inside the door, are a shovel and a pickaxe. They're both crusted with dirt, as if they've been recently used. Where was Bill digging? What did he find?

She takes a photo of the tools and then leaves and walks down to the shore. The surf is lively, waves scratching at the beach, but there's nothing ominous about it. The sun shines down through a crisp autumn sky, setting the surface sparkling and brightening the sea foam. Like Grandy, Bill loved the sea, but he took it further than most, choosing to live his life right on the tideline, literally on the boundary between water and land.

It makes Dandy sad to think of him spending his last moments alone on the wrong side of that divide. Cold and wet and scared.

Her thoughts inevitably drift to the hospital, where Grandy spent his own final moments all alone.

Less than one month ago, all five of the original members of the society were still alive. Now there are only two left. Grandy's death was sudden, but it wasn't suspicious. He was sick, plain and simple, and he even took the time to prepare things for her. There's no room in his story for foul play or devious deeds, so she has to chalk it up to the cruel finger of fate.

But Bill's death is a different matter. She can't prove anything just yet, but there's a weird feeling in her gut telling her there's more than meets the eye when it comes to what happened to the old man.

And what about Mirabel? Like Bill, her death was chalked up to an accident, but is there any chance that *her* demise was misinterpreted as well?

She squints, trying to remember the conversation on the beach. What exactly had Bill said? She turns to look down the stretch of beach at the bell tower rising above the tree line, and his words come back to her as clearly as if he's just whispered them into her ear. *Bellwoods is full of secrets.*

Maybe he was right, and maybe someone was willing to go to great lengths to uncover what Mirabel and Bill *both* knew.

Dandy thought she was looking for a treasure. What if she's actually looking for a murderer?

She presses the doorbell with a firm, confident finger, and immediately hears the dim chime of bells from the other side of the huge wooden door.

She waits for a long while, and is just considering whether it's too early to ring the bell again, when the door is thrust open and Mirabel's grandson is standing on the threshold. His hair is wild and unkempt, and he's wearing a ratty, grease-stained t-shirt and old jeans. He blinks out into the sunlight as he takes her in.

"Peter Bellwood, there's mischief afoot," says Dandy. There's no point in beating around the bush. She needs an ally, and she needs one fast.

He blinks at her. "Excuse me?"

She tries to lay things out more clearly. "My name is Danielle Feltzen, but you can call me Dandy. I was an associate of your grandmother's. She was planning to introduce us; did she mention that?" She glances past him into the house, hoping he'll invite her inside, but instead he steps out onto the veranda with her.

"An associate?" he repeats, bewildered. "No, she didn't mention you."

Dandy is disappointed. She was hoping Peter would be able to shed some light on Mirabel's intentions, but there's not much she can do about that now, so she presses on.

"Did you know that Bill Jinx died last night?"

"I heard," he says. "It's awful."

She nods. "You don't know the half of it. Now, listen, I don't have anything to go on here except my gut, but my gut is telling me that something about it stinks."

Peter raises an eyebrow at this, but before she can continue, an erratic, metallic clanking judders from somewhere deep in the house, and he throws his hands up in frustration.

"Goddammit. Listen, I have to run down to the basement to deal with something. Just hang here for a minute, okay?"

She nods and he disappears back inside, leaving the door open a crack. She debates letting herself in but settles instead for stepping closer and peering inside.

She's able to catch a glimpse of the legendary staircase, enough to confirm that it's as beautiful as she's heard. She can't help thinking of its grim new association, and her eyes are drawn to the hard marble floor at the bottom.

Did Mirabel fall or was she pushed?

Peter appears suddenly in the doorway, forcing her to jump back. "Sorry," she says. "I was snooping."

"No worries." He steps outside again, closing the door and giving her an exasperated smile. "I don't suppose you know anything about giant ancient oil furnaces, do you? This one keeps me up at night, and I can't figure out why."

Grandy would have had some useful advice, but Dandy is no handyman. "I hear home ownership can be a real bitch," she says with a shrug.

He laughs at this. "I can confirm that. Anyway, you were saying?"

"I'll cut right to the chase," she says. "I don't want you to panic, but I think we need to consider the possibility that Bill was murdered, and also, possibly, your grandmother."

His eyes go wide. "Wait, what?" he asks. "Mirabel? Murdered?"

She rushes ahead. "For one thing, the police think Bill got drunk and took his rowboat out in a storm, but I don't buy that for a hot second. Bill Jinx might have been a boozer, but he knew the ocean better than anyone, and he was no fool, no sir, no way."

"Okay," he says. "But what about Mirabel?"

She takes a deep breath. There's a lot to explain and she needs to keep Peter focused so he'll understand how serious this is.

"Okay," she says. "Before he died, Bill told me that Mirabel was holding on to secrets. Actually, he said *Bellwoods* was full of secrets."

"I didn't really know the guy," says Peter, "but I do know he showed up at my grandmother's funeral ranting and raving and talking about a ghost who had a grudge against my family. Frankly, he sounded completely delusional."

"He might have had a screw loose," she admits. "But that doesn't mean he was wrong about everything. He had a little red notebook that he carried around with him everywhere. He showed it to me and told me that it was full of clues and information, and I believed him. I really believe he had started to figure things out."

Peter squints at her. "Figure *what* out? What kind of secrets are you talking about?"

He stares at her, waiting for her to respond, and Dandy's confidence begins to diminish. She has the sinking feeling that she hasn't thought this explanation through as well as she could have.

"Before she died," she says, "did Mirabel ever talk to you about the *Obelisk* Treasure?"

He barks out a laugh. "Is that what this is about?" he asks. "You think somebody killed Bill and Mirabel because of a buried treasure?"

Dandy flares. "There's a lot more to this story than you know, Peter, and you're tied up in it too, whether you like it or not."

"Okay," he says. "So fill me in."

Dandy had hoped to keep things simple, but she finds herself telling Peter almost everything she knows. About the five boys, and the anonymous letters, and how Grandy's death led her to the historical society in the first place. He listens with interest, and when she's done, she feels like maybe she's convinced him that there's more to this story than he knows.

"Okay," he says. "If you really believe all of this, and that my grandmother and Bill Jinx were murdered, why don't you just go to the police?"

She rolls her eyes. "Are you kidding me? Listen, I know how this sounds. It sounds nuts. I can't go to them until I have concrete evidence or they'll laugh me out of the room. That's why I came to you. You're an adult with skin in the game, and I thought you might be willing to help."

Peter gives Dandy the kind of indulgent, patronizing smile that she's been getting from adults—other than Grandy—since she was a kid. "I wish I could help you, Danielle," he says. "Really, I do. Mirabel tracked me down because she wanted me to help her tie up some loose ends, but she died before we could get very far into it, and as much as I wish she'd told me where to find the location of the *Obelisk* Treasure, she didn't. I can also tell you with certainty that she wasn't murdered. The doctor who examined her backed up the police theory that she tripped on a fold in the rug at the top of the stairs."

"Wait a minute," she says. "Which doctor?"

He thinks about it. "I think his name was Oakley. He said he was a friend of hers."

"Very interesting," Dandy muses.

"Why?" he asks.

"Frank Oakley is one of the last two people from the society who are still alive," she says. "It's just kind of a strange coincidence that he was the one to determine Mirabel's cause of death."

"You don't honestly think he had something to do with her death, do you?" he asks. "He seems like a nice little old man."

She shakes her head. "No, probably not. But there's just something about him that doesn't quite sit right. I can't put my finger on it. I also know that Bill didn't trust him."

"Danielle," he says, smiling kindly. "I'm just going to come out and say this. I think your imagination is getting the best of you. I don't think anyone has been murdered."

He glances back at the door, and Dandy can tell she's being dismissed. She nods and forces a smile.

"Okay," she says. "I guess it was worth a shot. But be careful, okay? If someone *did* have it in for them, we might be next on the list."

Peter looks momentarily taken aback, like he hasn't considered this. Then he collects himself and smiles.

"I'll keep it in mind," he says. "Thanks for the heads-up."

It isn't until she's walking back along the inlet that she realizes something. Peter said Mirabel didn't tell him where the treasure was buried.

He didn't say anything about secrets.

WHAT A MAN

The Shivering Timbers is exactly the kind of place it sounds like. Dark, wood-panelled walls liberally sprinkled with nautical artwork and portholes to nowhere; yacht rock blasting from the speakers; driftwood signs marking the BUOYS and GULLS rooms.

A teenage waiter dressed like a pirate greets Cass as she steps through the front door. "G'day, you scurvy dog!" he chirps. "I'm Chad, and I'll be your server. How many will ye be today?"

"Two," she says, scanning the dining room. "I'm meeting someone, but I don't think he's here yet."

Chad grabs a couple of menus and leads her across the dining room to a booth in the corner. She slides in under a painting of a kraken, orders a shandy, and stares into the distance, preoccupied by the events of the past couple of days.

"You look like you're waiting to walk the plank."

She turns, momentarily startled. She's been so lost in thought that she didn't hear Bryson approach, and suddenly she feels uncharacteristically shy. This is the first time she's seen him wearing anything other than workout gear, and he's even handsomer now that he's cleaned up. His thick blond hair is pushed back by a pair of sunglasses, his beard is trimmed close, and he's wearing a navy blue polo top over khaki shorts.

"Sorry," she says, managing a smile as he slides into the booth across from her. "I was just . . . Do you remember that guy I told you about, the one who brought back Banjo and told me that crazy story about the *Obelisk* Treasure?"

"Well, yeah," says Bryson. "Half the reason I wanted to meet you for a drink was to hear if you learned anything more from him."

She smiles faintly, then looks down at her hands. "Okay, so, he drowned."

Bryson's eyes widen. "What? Are you serious?"

She nods and then forces herself to tell him the worst part. "I found his body."

"Holy shit," he says, reaching out to put a hand on her arm. "I am so sorry. That's awful."

The feeling of someone touching her almost pushes Cass over the edge, and she squeezes her eyes shut tight to ward off tears. After a moment, she gathers herself and tells him the story.

"I was walking Banjo on the beach yesterday morning, and he saw something in the distance and raced ahead. By the time I caught up, Banjo was sitting next to the body and whining. I could tell right away that he was dead," she says. "He'd obviously been in the water for a while. You know, he was . . . it was . . ." She trails off and shakes her head, unwilling to put her impression of Bill's ghastly, bloated remains into words.

Bryson squeezes her forearm gently. "I can imagine," he says gently. "I'm sure it was awful. I'm so sorry that you had to go through that. With a friend, especially."

"He wasn't really my friend," she says. "I only met him twice." But even as she's saying it, she's thinking that Bill chose to trust her with his huge secret. Did he think of *her* as a friend? It occurs to her now that she might have overstepped her bounds by telling Bryson the story in the first place. But Bill *did* tell her to use it for a book, right? How private did he want her to keep things? A nagging tickle at the back of her mind asks if maybe he meant for her to keep it secret until he had solved the mystery. Bill said he was giving her a head start. Did she jeopardize his confidence?

It's all really weird and uncomfortable, but she guesses it doesn't matter now.

"Anyway," she says. "I called 911 and waited with the body until an ambulance came, and then I stayed around to talk to the police."

She doesn't tell him that while she waited, she sat on the sand next to Bill, crying and holding one of his cold, bloated hands in hers. She doubts she'll ever tell anyone about that. She feels as if she owes Bill the respect of keeping those final, intimate moments to herself.

"What did the police say?" asks Bryson.

"They said it was pretty cut-and-dry," she says. "He was a heavy drinker, and his rowboat was missing. They called me today to tell me they'd found the boat washed up somewhere along the coast. I expect they'll find alcohol in his system, if they even bother to do a toxicology test."

She gives her head a shake, pulling herself out of the rabbit hole. "I'm sorry. This is a terrible subject of conversation for a first date."

"Is that what this is?" he asks, raising an eyebrow appraisingly.

She's saved from answering by the dread pirate Chad, who appears at the table with her drink. "Oh, hey, man," he says to Bryson. "What can I get you?"

"You're not going to call him a scurvy dog?" Cass asks.

Chad shrugs. "He's a regular."

Bryson orders a beer, and Chad departs.

"A regular, eh?" she asks. "I thought you weren't a local."

"I've eaten here every day since I got to town," he says. "I guess that does make me a regular."

She wants to ask more, but before she has the chance, he leans in.

"So do you think it's real?" he asks. "The stuff about the treasure? You think he was actually onto something?"

"I don't know," she says, shaking her head. "Probably not. He was a delusional old man. I mean, he hallucinated his dead father. But the story was really compelling and exciting, and *he* definitely believed it."

Bryson nods. "You can convince yourself of pretty much anything if you're desperate enough," he says. "If you want my opinion, I don't really think there is a treasure."

This surprises her. "I thought finding that treasure is your lifelong dream."

"My childhood dream," he corrects. "Look at it this way: How many of the things that sparked your imagination when you were a kid turned out to be true? I bet you thought you'd live with your pony and your best friend in a Barbie Dream Home, right?"

She laughs. "Something like that."

"And it all went bust as soon as you were old enough to pay a bill, am I right?"

She nods, already seeing where he's going with this.

"That's me and the treasure," he says. "When I was a kid I was obsessed. A real-life pirate treasure in the same place my family went on vacation every year? Bring it on. That shit was tailor-made for an imaginative kid like me. But now that I'm grown up, I'm pretty convinced that treasure will never be found. Even without Bill's story, it's pretty hard to swallow."

"And with it?" she asks.

"Let's say everything he said is true," he goes on. "Let's say a group of boys found that treasure way back in the 1920s, hid it, and then when they went back to dig it up, it was missing again. What's the simplest conclusion to that story?"

"One of the boys got there ahead of the rest of them," she says.

He points at me. "Nailed it. Someone took that money and ran. If anything, this whole story kills the dream even a little bit more for me."

"Well, that's cheerful," she says.

Bryson laughs. "You were right. Shitty conversation for a first date."

His drink arrives and they clink glasses, and the conversation shifts in a new direction. Before Cass knows it, they've been sitting there for almost two hours. Bryson is funny, and smart. He also doesn't like to talk much about himself, which she finds refreshing, but also a bit frustrating. She manages to find out that he's an only child, his parents are dead, and he works as a nautical surveyor, just like his dad, but most of the time he keeps steering the conversation back to her. She doesn't really mind that, though, and by the time they're standing up from the table and getting ready to leave, she realizes that she's opened up to him about practically everything, including her publishing disaster. It feels good to talk about it.

As they step out into the slightly cool early September evening air, she realizes just how much fun this has been.

"So your place is nearby?" she asks as they stroll along the waterfront.

He nods. "Care to check it out?"

Maybe it's the three shandies, or the nice evening, or just how goddamn handsome the guy is, but she finds herself agreeing. She expects him to lead her up the hill to an Airbnb or a room in one of the quaint Victorian inns that are sprinkled throughout the old town, but instead he continues along the boardwalk and then takes a hard right down onto a wharf. She follows him almost to the end, where he stops in front of a sleek, well-kept sailboat.

"This is your boat?" she asks.

"That she is," he says. "You sail?"

"Not really," she admits. "But I was obsessed with sea shanty TikTok, so I feel like I'm halfway there. It's very pretty."

"Thank you," he says. "She's my baby."

"You keep calling her 'she,'" says Cass. "How do you know? Was there a gender reveal party?"

He laughs. "Boats are shes. It's a thing." He hops over the side and then reaches across to give me a hand. "Come on over."

She takes his hand and steps over the railing, and he continues to hold it for a moment until she finds her footing. As she looks around the boat, he moves across to a cooler on the other side, pulling out two Heinekens, popping them on an opener attached to the wood frame around the door, and handing her one.

"Cheers," she says, clinking her bottle against his and taking a sip.

"You've got a wheely thing," she says, pointing.

He laughs. "Yep. That's how we steer her."

"Just like a car," she says.

"Not exactly," he says, "but kind of. I'll spare you the boring boat talk. Once you start talking to a boat person about boats, they never stop talking about boats. For now, all you need to know is that this is the cockpit, and this"—he reaches to pull a wooden door up and off the hatch—"leads down to the cabin."

She leans over the side to peer down into a cozy space belowdecks.

"It's really cute," she says. "Do you live here?"

"I have an actual apartment in the city," he says, "but sometimes I stay on the boat when I'm on a contract." He moves some stuff off one of the benches and gestures for her to sit.

"It's great," she says. "Romantic." He raises an eyebrow and her face goes hot. "Not that kind of romantic. I mean, like, old-style romantic. The loner on the high seas, reading books by the light of the oil lamp, nothing but the sound of the waves and gulls for company."

He laughs. "You're not that far off," he says. "Although I wouldn't call myself a loner. I just happen to be alone a lot of the time, at least lately."

She smiles and takes a sip of her beer, trying not to look like she's finding this as interesting as she actually is finding it, which is to say *very* interesting.

"So what are you going to do now?" he asks. "About your book, I mean."

She thinks about it. "I want to keep going with it," she says. "Even though I think you're right and I'm not going to find the *Obelisk* Treasure. But even without that, the story is kind of amazing.

What happens when a group of friends finds a fabled treasure, and the treasure goes missing again? Who were these characters? It's even more interesting to me than plundered gold."

He nods. "Fair enough. So where do you begin?"

"For one thing," she says, "I'm going to have to find some background on those five kids. Bill told me that there were originally five members of the society, but one died a while back, and so now that he and Mirabel are dead, there are only two left. One of them owns the bakery in town, and the other one is a local doctor. And I also want to build in some deep background, so I'm going to have to learn as much as I can about Dagger and Pynchon and their ships."

"Well, I can't help you with the first thing," he says. "But I can definitely help you with the second. Would you like to take a trip out to see where the sea battle actually took place?"

"Are you serious?" she asks.

He grins. "Absolutely. I have a couple of free days later this week, and I could take you on a little tour along the coast. We could bring a lunch."

Cass considers this. "Just to be clear, are you proposing a research trip or a second date?"

Bryson's eyes twinkle and he shrugs. "Can't we mix business and pleasure?"

"I don't see why not," she says, meeting his smile and realizing that the book has suddenly taken a back seat to another new interest.

OVERDUE

I'm in the basement when I hear the old-fashioned chime of the doorbell echo through the house. I swear under my breath and drop my wrench on the small worktable I have set up next to the massive old furnace.

I wipe my hands on a rag and slap the side of the furnace.

"Don't go anywhere," I say. "I'm not done with you yet."

Chuckling at my own absurdity, I head upstairs to answer the door.

To my surprise, it's the lawyer who delivered the news of Mirabel's will.

"Mr. Reid," I say, surprised.

"Is this a bad time?" he asks. He's in his work attire, a blazer and slacks, and he's holding a file folder.

I'm suddenly hit with a wave of anxiety, as if the rug is about to be pulled out from under me.

"No, it's cool," I say. "Come on in. Is everything okay?"

He follows me into the house. "Everything's fine," he says. "I just have some information you might find interesting. Is there somewhere we can sit down?"

I lead him into the kitchen and direct him to the breakfast table. "Sorry about the mess," I say, suddenly conscious of the dirty dishes and food wrappers piled up all over the counters. "I've never lived anywhere even a tenth of this size and I'm finding the housekeeping to be a bit overwhelming."

Reid smiles. "Understandable. Have you thought about selling the house? I know Margot Feltzen would kill to have this place on her roster."

I chuckle. "She's stopped by more than once. I made the mistake of telling her I'm not sure what I'm going to do with the place and I think she saw that as an opening. But the truth is, I don't know yet if I'll stay here at Bellwoods. But I'm not sure where else I'd live."

Reid puts the folder on the table and smiles. "That's kind of the reason I'm here," he says. "You do have another option, of a sort."

"Really?" I ask, surprised.

"Well," he says with a wry smile, "it's unlikely that you'd actually want to live there. You've likely heard that your neighbour, William Jinx, recently passed away?"

I nod. "Drowned. Terrible way to go."

"Yes, well," says Reid. "Jinx was a sorry character, a victim of his own demons. You saw a bit of that at your grandmother's funeral, I'm afraid. But he was a fixture in Maple Bay. It's very sad."

I nod, not sure what this has to do with me.

Reid slides the folder across the table to me. I open it and find a stack of yellowing papers held together with a paper clip. They appear to be legal documents.

"What is this?" I ask.

"This is a contract between Jinx's mother and your great-grandfather," says Reid. "It appears that many years ago, in the 1930s in fact, Henry Bellwood—Mirabel's father—had a small cottage built on the shore and gave official rights to Bill's mother and her children and descendants to live there until such time as they chose to leave or the final person in the line died."

"And Bill was the final person in the line?" I ask, rifling through the pages.

Reid nods. "He was. To tell you the truth, I don't know if Bill ever knew he was living on Bellwoods property," he says. "Did your grandmother mention it to you?"

I shake my head. "We barely scratched the surface of estate business before her accident," I say.

"She may very well have been unaware of the arrangement herself," says Reid. "As I understand it, his mother moved in when he was just a baby, after his father had been murdered, and he continued to live there after her death. That's a very long time—long enough that she might have just assumed Bill owned the land. It was only flagged upon his death because our firm has been handling Bellwoods for so many years."

"So where does this all leave it?" I ask.

"You're the proud owner of a run-down shack," he says. "Congratulations."

My curiosity gets the better of me. As soon as Reid leaves, I wrap up my work in the basement, throw on some clean clothes, and head out into the misty afternoon to check out the new addition to my portfolio of properties.

There's something particularly mysterious about the inlet in this weather. There's a chill in the air and a blanket of fog hovers over everything, obscuring the horizon. I turn into Bill's narrow driveway and navigate carefully along the potholes until his ragged shack comes into view through the haze.

It's hard to imagine a dwelling as far removed from Bellwoods as the slanted, weather-beaten shanty in front of me. It sits in a tangle of beach weeds just a few yards from the barely visible shoreline. Seabirds, invisible in the mist, circle and cry somewhere overhead, and small waves scratch helplessly at the shore. I almost expect a shrouded boatman to emerge from the void, beckoning for me to join him on a journey into purgatory.

The front door isn't locked, and I push my way into the small house. My first reaction is that it feels colder inside than it does outside. The interior of the miserable little space is damp, and drafts swirl up from the floor. I wonder if the cottage is built on anything more than a few stones.

The place should probably be knocked down, but I already know I won't go to the trouble. I assume it would also be easy to sell the property, but I'm not interested in that plan, either. I'll just let the weather deal with it, and from the looks of things, that won't take long.

The truth is, there's only one reason I'm here. Ever since I was visited by that strange girl, Dandy Feltzen, her frantic accusations and warnings have been spinning through my mind. She strikes me as the kind of oddball who people don't really take seriously, and I probably don't have anything to worry about. On the other hand, she seems pretty convinced. Does she really believe that Mirabel and Bill were murdered?

Bill told Dandy and Cass that he was hot on the trail of the treasure, but I assumed that whatever he knew—or thought he did—had died with him. Then Dandy mentioned his little red notebook, and suddenly a new question appeared: What did Bill Jinx have written down that would have been worth murdering for?

I move around the dilapidated space, but there's no notebook of any kind in plain sight. I begin to look more carefully, slowly at first, but with a building intensity as I open cupboards and rifle through stacks of books.

There's no way I was going to tell Cass or Dandy about Henry Bellwood's confessions. His journal might not point to where the treasure is hidden, but it reveals so much more. Bill was right—Bellwoods *is* full of secrets—but considering the implications of what I've learned, I'm not about to spill the beans.

Henry explained a lot, but he also left some big questions unanswered. If Mirabel was still here, maybe she and I would be figuring things out together, but she's no help now.

Could Bill's notes help fill in some of the gaps?

I begin to search more aggressively. I pull the cushions off the sofa and yank out drawers, dumping their contents on the floor. As the debris of Bill's depressing life begins to accumulate in piles, I'm hit with a tidal wave of recognition: this could be me someday. A lifelong bachelor becoming more and more reclusive by the day, surrounded by a collection of worthless, useless shit.

I drop into the armchair in the corner and catch my breath. I'm done. I've torn the place inside out, but to no avail. If there was a red notebook here, it's gone, and its secrets are lost to me.

I know there's a good chance Bill had it with him when he drowned, but Dandy's accusation sticks out. Could someone really have taken it?

Dandy seemed to really believe that Bill and Mirabel were targeted because of what they knew. But she neglected to consider another crucial point: Who *else* might have information that would be worth killing for?

My eyes move across the wrecked room and land on a stack of library books sitting on the little wooden desk in the corner, and suddenly I've answered my own question.

Bonnie Brickland is busy at her computer and doesn't look up when I drop the stack of library books with a thud.

"I'd like to return these," I say.

"You can just drop them in the slot on the other end of the counter," she says. "Thank you."

When I don't move, she turns around in her chair to look at me, and recognition immediately crosses her face.

"Peter!" she exclaims. She pushes back her chair and stands, pulling off her reading glasses as she comes to greet me. "I'm sorry I didn't recognize you at first. It's acquisitions day, so I'm hypnotized by data entry."

"No problem at all," I say. "I'm just dropping these books off because the, um . . . the borrower has passed away."

"Oh my," she says, putting a hand on the stack to pull them toward her. "I don't remember your grandmother checking anything out recently."

"Not her," I say. "It was actually Bill Jinx." She looks at me curiously and I briefly explain the situation with Jinx's shack.

"Well, I appreciate you bringing them back," she says. "They could have been lost to the dust heap."

"To be totally honest," I say, "I wanted to talk to you about something else, and finding the books just reminded me. But if you're busy . . ."

"Not at all," she says. "How can I help?"

"You mentioned that you were helping my grandmother with some research, and I'm wondering what exactly she was researching."

A funny expression crosses Bonnie's face. It's just a flicker, but enough to tell me that she's carefully considering what to say next.

"Well, Peter, your grandmother was a friend of mine, and she asked me to keep everything she was working on confidential. I take that kind of relationship seriously."

"Yes," I say hastily. "Of course you do. I totally understand."

She doesn't respond, just continues to smile fixedly at me.

I hesitate for a moment, deciding whether I should ask my next question or not, then decide to dive in. "Mirabel told me that she was part of a . . . group of sorts. I think she referred to it as a historical society."

Bonnie nods. "The historical society met here once a month."

"Do you know what they discussed?" I ask.

"Mirabel didn't fill you in?"

"I know there was a lot more she intended to tell me," I say. "But we never got the chance."

"Of course," she says. "Well, I hate to disappoint, but I wasn't privy to their conversations."

"You don't know if they were meeting to discuss the *Obelisk Treasure?*"

"Who told you that?" she asks sharply.

"Nobody," I lie. "I just . . . I've been reading about local history, and that treasure story kind of dominates. I guess I just let my imagination run away with me."

Bonnie considers this. "That group met here once a month," she says. "But they kept the door shut tight and they didn't welcome new members. If they were looking for the *Obelisk* Treasure, they kept it to themselves."

"Got it," I say. "This is all a bit of a stretch anyway. I mean, a buried treasure. What is this, a Disney movie?"

"Indeed," she says. Her smile is tight, and her eyes examine me with shrewd interest. Suddenly I just want to get out of the library.

"Well, listen," I say. "I'll get out of your hair and let you get back to work now. Thanks so much for your time."

I push through the double doors and step out into the afternoon, suddenly anxious to get away from the library as fast as I can. By the time I've crossed the parking lot to the car, I'm convinced: there's something Bonnie Brickland isn't telling me.

THE FRENCH BAKERY

The French Bakery takes up the main floor of one of the classic old buildings on Main Street. As Dandy pushes through the heavy wooden door, she's greeted by the rich scent of freshly ground coffee mingled with a sweet, warm fragrance of baking coming from the kitchen in the back. The place is quiet, the only customers a couple of young mothers chatting at a table in the window, their sleeping babies settled into strollers beside them.

Mrs. French is behind the counter, looking through some paperwork. She glances up and smiles widely as Dandy enters.

"Hello, Dandy," she says. "You're a sight for sore eyes."

"Hi, Mrs. French, how's it going?"

She holds up some paper. "I'm just getting caught up on bills. I had to put a new roof on this place in the spring and I'm still paying for it."

"Do you own the building?" Dandy asks, surprised.

"I do," she says, nodding. "Would you believe I've lived in the apartment upstairs since the day I was born? Not too many people can say that, especially at my age. But my daddy was smart enough to buy the building back when he started the bakery. Lucky too,

I suppose. Mr. Bellwood gave my father a break when he most needed it."

"Alexander Bellwood?" I ask.

"No," she says. "Alexander was Mirabel's grandfather, and from everything I've heard about him, he wouldn't have helped a pregnant lady out of a ditch. I'm talking about her father, Henry. You see, my father didn't have a lot of prospects when he was released. In those days there weren't many people looking to hire a Black man who'd been in prison. But he'd worked in the kitchen at the prison in Halifax, and eventually became the head baker. Mr. Bellwood helped him get the business off the ground, rented him the space, and let him pay a percentage of every month's profits until he owned the place outright."

"So this building belonged to the Bellwood family too?"

Mrs. French laughs. "Along with almost every other building in town," she says. "And plenty of land, to boot. Sometimes it felt like old man Bellwood spent his life trying to hoard as much as he could, only for his son to turn around and give most of it away as soon as he died. Did you know that your grandfather's house used to belong to the Bellwood family?"

"No way," says Dandy. "Really?"

She nods. "I don't know the whole story, but when Reg was just a small boy, his father disappeared. The family had been living in the house at the time, and Henry Bellwood gave it to them."

"Gave it to them," Dandy repeats, almost to herself.

"Something like that," she says. "Henry Bellwood was a well-loved man. He had a good heart, and I know Mirabel thought the world of him. She was some proud of the Bellwood name, I'll tell you that."

Something occurs to Dandy. "Don't you think it's kind of weird? I mean that all three of them were from the original group that found the treasure."

"Well, they were friends," says Mrs. French. "Henry Bellwood was certainly blessed with his share of good fortune, and it would have been in character for him to help his friends."

Dandy considers this. "Did your father ever talk about the treasure?" she asks.

Mrs. French's expression turns serious. "Never," she says. "Not even once. My father was into his forties by the time he got out of prison. He bought this building and opened the bakery, and then he met my mother and they had me, and I think he deliberately closed the door on the first half of his life. It was very rare for him to talk about his younger days, and when he did mention his childhood, the treasure wasn't part of the story."

"If he never talked about it," Dandy asks, "why did you decide to get involved when you received that letter?"

She smiles wistfully. "My father had died a few years before that," she says. "I missed him terribly, and to be honest, I'd regretted not asking him more about his youth when he was alive. Then suddenly this letter arrived, out of the blue, telling me that he'd been part of this crazy adventure, and it felt . . . I don't know, Dandy, I guess it felt like an opportunity to reach back into the past and get to know him a bit better."

"Didn't the whole thing sound kind of unbelievable?"

She laughs. "Oh yes, of course. The entire scenario was completely outlandish, just as wild and bizarre as it gets. But it also kind of had a ring of truth to it. *Someone* took the time to send that letter to the five of us, and it would have been a very complicated practical joke to orchestrate. All the boys involved were dead at that point, so they couldn't back up the story, but it was plausible that they'd all been hanging out together down on the shore. Daddy's mother used to work for the Bellwood family, helping take care of Mirabel's father after his own mother died. He would have been about the same age as Henry, so it wouldn't be all that surprising if he had spent time down on the inlet."

"With Henry Bellwood and the other three," says Dandy.

She nods. "Your grandfather was one of the most enthusiastic. He believed to his core that the treasure was out there, and his enthusiasm rubbed off on the rest of us. When Reg was around, you felt like you were part of a big adventure, and this was a once-in-a-lifetime opportunity to be part of something big and exciting. It was fun, and if my father *had* been involved way back in the day, I liked to think that part of his story deserved to be completed."

"Why do you think Grandy was so enthusiastic about it?" Dandy asks.

Mrs. French smiles. "You knew Reg better than anyone," she says. "He was a dreamer, through and through. But I always thought there was more to it than that."

"What do you mean?"

"Well," she says, her expression growing thoughtful. "After Reg's father disappeared, the general assumption was that he drowned."

Dandy nods. That's the story her mother has told her.

"But people around here like to talk," Mrs. French continues, "and there were some who thought he'd flown the coop. There was never a body, you see. Early on, one of the theories brought up at the society was that he took the money and ran. But Reg was adamant.

He insisted that his mother told him there was no way on earth that her husband would have left them in the lurch like that, hungry and penniless. He was convinced his father had died, and that the treasure was still hidden out there. The letter backed him up, too. The note didn't say the treasure *might* still be around here; it was very clear that the treasure *was* still around."

"Bill Jinx thought Henry Bellwood wrote those letters," Dandy says.

The old lady nods. "I think he was probably right," she says. "Although Mirabel refused to entertain the idea. She was close with her father, and she insisted he never would have kept her in the dark about such a thing, but who else could it have been?"

Dandy bikes across town, the details of Mrs. French's story swirling in her brain. As she tries to wrap her head around the countless relationships that have played out here over the years, and the interactions and conversations and arguments and love affairs that spiralled out from them, it almost makes her dizzy.

All of these stories, lost to history. A few months ago, Grandy was alive and available, and it was as simple as asking him to tell her about his childhood or family history. Now she's left shaking trees, turning over rocks, hoping some little piece of information will emerge to help her understand the big picture. And it doesn't stop with Grandy, either. Mirabel and Bill are both gone as well, along with their own stories and perspectives.

Did someone want their stories to disappear so badly that they were willing to kill them? If so, does anybody but Dandy even care?

She focuses on pulling together what she knows. The Bellwood family built their mansion at the tip of the Point, at the opening to the inlet. Grandy's grandfather was the caretaker at Bellwoods, and they lived in the cottage that Margot now owns. Bill Jinx said that his family lived and fished along the inlet long before the Bellwood family arrived. Mrs. French said her grandmother worked for the Bellwoods, and her father would have been around the property as a boy. So that explains why four of the boys would have been there the day the treasure was found.

That leaves one thread to follow.

Dr. Frank Oakley lives in a small, neat bungalow on a private, nicely landscaped lot at the end of a cul-de-sac. His little green hatchback is parked in the driveway, and when Dandy glances at the picture window, she sees a figure pass in front of the window. He's home.

She drops her bike into some bushes next to the curb and then walks up the driveway and onto the porch. She's about to ring the doorbell when something gives her pause. Is it safe to be here by herself?

She pulls out her phone and sends herself a text.

IF I GO MISSING, DOCTOR OAKLEY DID IT.

If she feels uncomfortable or threatened at any point, she can show him this text as an insurance policy. These days, police always go straight to the cell phone records.

She lifts her finger and is about to press the bell when the sound of a vehicle slowing catches her attention. Without giving it any extra thought, she hops off the side of the porch and ducks behind a large rhododendron just as a car pulls into Oakley's driveway.

From her hiding spot, she stares in amazement as her aunt Margot gets out of her Lexus and marches determinedly up the steps and onto the porch, pressing the doorbell and holding it down, then immediately rapping on the door with a firm, insistent fist.

"Are you in there, Oakley?" she calls, loud enough to be heard through the closed door. "We were supposed to meet an hour ago. Did you forget?"

She waits briefly, then bangs on the door again, louder this time.

"I did not go to all this trouble just to be blown off," she calls. "If you're having cold feet, we are going to have a problem!"

When the door still doesn't open, she lets out an exasperated sigh. As Dandy watches through the foliage, Margot rummages in her bag and pulls out a large envelope and a pen. She scrawls something on the back of the envelope and then props it up against the door. With an air of irritated determination, she turns and leaves. A few moments later, her Lexus squeals out of Oakley's driveway and disappears.

She knows she should get on her bike and follow Margot, but Dandy finds herself fixated on the manila envelope on the doorstep. She waits for a long time for the door to open and an elderly hand to reach out and snatch it from the doormat, but it doesn't happen. The envelope just sits there, staring back at her.

The curiosity gets the better of her. Against her better judgement, she creeps back up onto the step, crouching below the window, and snatches the envelope, pulling it toward her and sliding back down into her hiding place.

A message is scrawled across the front, Margot's big, loopy script instantly recognizable from fifteen years of bland birthday card greetings. *Frank, we need to get a move on. Take a look at these and get back to me ASAP. M.*

The envelope isn't glued shut, just folded in on itself. Dandy pulls out a sheaf of papers and unfolds the top page. It takes her only a moment to recognize that it's a map of the inlet and the Point. Peering closer, however, she realizes that something isn't quite right. Small blocks indicate buildings, and while she can easily make out Bellwoods, and the Trapper house up on the hill, there are a lot of new structures marked where she knows full well that nothing currently stands. They're clustered together in a few spots, small rectangles that appear to look like cottages.

It's when she looks for Grandy's cottage that Dandy's heart really starts to race. It's gone, replaced with a much larger structure. What is Margot up to?

She gets her answer when she turns her attention to the other pages in the package. It's a glossy document, with an image of the inlet on the cover, under the caption *Maple Bay Spa and Resort: Retirement and Time Share Investment Opportunities.*

As Dandy quickly flips through the brochure, everything begins to come into focus. Architecturally designed images of sleek, contemporary buildings are superimposed against actual photographs of the spit. Clusters of cottages, all glass and wood shingles; a marina; and worst of all, where Grandy's cottage currently sits, a large contemporary building with a caption that reads: *Nordic-style spa, complete with saltwater treatments.*

Margot and Oakley are working together to develop the inlet, complete with removing Grandy's beloved cottage.

Once this information has sunk in, an inevitable question arises: How far were they willing to go to cobble together all of this land?

NOVEL ADVICE

"The secrets remain unspoken, and the Bellwood debt remains unpaid."

Bill Jinx stared down the length of his bed to where his father's ghost pointed at him from the gloom. Within moments, the ghost—his message delivered—was gone. Within hours, Bill was crashing the funeral of a prominent local woman and making a violent drunken scene that would soon be the buzz of tiny Maple Bay, Nova Scotia. Within days, Bill was dead, the victim of a tragic accident on the water, just offshore from the place he had called home his whole life.

But if his final days were marked with drama, that was nothing compared to the decades that preceded them. Bill had dedicated the second half of his life to solving the greatest mystery his little town had ever known: the location of the Obelisk Treasure. The Treasure is one of the best-known and most well documented in the world, and over the years countless treasure hunters have scoured the woods and coastline around Maple Bay, searching for its hiding place. What none of them realized was that Bill Jinx, along with a few select others, was in possession of a startling secret that cast a surprising new light on what is known about Captain Barnabas Dagger's legendary missing treasure.

A secret he shared with me before he died.

Cass reads over the passage twice and then saves it. Satisfied, she sits back in the desk chair and stretches her arms over her head.

"That's a solid prologue, Banjo," she says, turning to look at the dog, who is flipped upside down on the armchair in the corner, snoring softly, his paws paddling the air as he chases a squirrel through his dreams.

She stands up and walks to the blank wall where she's stuck a few dozen index cards, all marked with an idea for a scene, character, or question she wants to explore. Along one side, five cards, neatly arranged one above the other, spell out the names of the boys who purportedly found the treasure.

HENRY BELLWOOD
ARCHIE JINX
BENJAMIN "JUNIOR" FRENCH
FRED "RED" OAKLEY
ELMER FELTZEN

She stares at the names, recapping what Bill told her. Mirabel's father, Henry Bellwood, was the last of the boys to die, forty years ago, shortly before the anonymous letters arrived and prompted the formation of the historical society. Archie Jinx, Bill's father, was murdered by Junior French in Dagger Woods. Buddy's daughter Rose, who owns the Rose Café and Bakery, was in the historical society with Bill and Mirabel, as was Dr. Frank Oakley, son of Dr. Fred Oakley.

Something about the name is trying to jog something in Cass's memory. *Frank Oakley.* She squints, trying to retrieve it, and then she remembers: Mirabel! When she stopped to pick up Banjo, the old lady mentioned that the Trappers bought their land, the land that this house sits on, from Frank Oakley. Land that used to be part of the Bellwoods estate before her father sold it.

How exactly had Mirabel put it? *The entire Point once belonged to Bellwoods.*

The final man, Elmer Feltzen, was the caretaker's son, and then the caretaker himself. He disappeared several years after the treasure and was presumed drowned. *His* son, Reg Feltzen, died a few months back, of cancer.

Cass considers this. Three out of five of the members of the historical society have died within the past little while. What a strange coincidence.

She jots something onto a new sticky note—*CONTACT ROSE FRENCH AND DR. OAKLEY. INTERVIEWS??*—and sticks it to the wall near the list of names. Then she stands and moves to the window and stares backward along the Point to the head of the inlet. She can just make out the edge of a roof through the colouring leaves.

"Come on, Banjo," she says. "We're going for a walk."

Even though she's driven or biked past the Feltzens' little cottage dozens of times, she hasn't paid a lot of attention to it. It's only now, standing on the road and peering down at it, that she realizes just how unoccupied it appears. There's no car in the driveway, the curtains are all drawn, and the lawn hasn't been mowed in weeks.

After a quick glance around to confirm that there's nobody nearby, she leads Banjo down the driveway to get a closer look. Despite its abandoned air, the cottage still manages to be charming. It's cute and unassuming, clad in weathered wooden shingles with a low-slung sunporch along the front, and tangles of wild roses pressed up against it from all angles.

When she walks around to the front yard, she realizes that the cottage has a clear view down the inlet, with the mansion perfectly framed at the end. It almost feels like the houses were situated this way deliberately.

She's wondering what, if anything, this connection implies, when a noise catches her ear. Glancing up, she notices that one of the windows in the sunroom is open a crack. As she steps closer, someone passes in front of it, and the noise comes into focus. Someone is crying.

Cass is suddenly very aware that she's trespassing. She yanks on Banjo's leash, hoping to slink away without being noticed, but the dog has other plans. He refuses to budge, and lets out a loud, indignant bark to tell her he isn't going anywhere.

The crying stops, and a second later a voice calls out from the sunporch. "Who's out there?"

Cass debates whether she should make a run for it, but it's too late for that. Besides, she thinks, maybe this is another opportunity.

"Hello!" she calls out cheerfully. "I'm just a neighbour stopping to introduce myself!"

A moment later the door to the sunporch flings open and a girl, around fourteen or fifteen, sticks her head out. She's an odd-looking character, with wild, tangly hair pushed down beneath an old sailor's cap and a ratty green cardigan hanging loose over her shoulders. A battered leather bag is draped over her shoulder.

She stares at Cass. She's clearly suspicious, but also very unhappy. Her face is pale and blotchy, and her eyes are bright red, as if she's been crying for a while.

"Who are you?" she demands.

"I'm Cass," she says. "I'm house-sitting for Alan and Judith Trapper, up on the hill."

The girl continues to stare, wary. Cass deliberates something and then decides to continue.

"I'm writing a book," she says. "About the *Obelisk* Treasure, and . . . the historical society."

She wonders if this will register with the girl. Sure enough, her eyes widen in surprise.

"How do you know about the historical society?" she asks, clearly not pleased.

"Bill Jinx told me the story," says Cass. "Or most of it, anyway."

"Bill?" she asks, incredulously. "Bill hated everyone! You're telling me he spilled his guts to you?"

"More or less," says Cass. "I think maybe he just needed someone to talk to."

"And now you're writing a book about it?"

Cass nods. She wasn't expecting this kind of reaction.

The girl throws her hands in the air in exasperation. "For the love of Christ. It took a lot to piss off Grandy, but this would have."

Cass is confused. "Grandy?"

"My grandfather," says the girl. "Reg Feltzen. This was his house."

Finally, things are starting to come into focus. "He was in the society," says Cass.

The girl nods. "I'm Danielle," she offers. "Most people call me Dandy. Grandy and I were really close, and we started calling each other that when I was really little. Grandy and Dandy. It kind of stuck. It's stupid, I know."

"It's not stupid," says Cass. "It's sweet." She begins to sense an opportunity. "Would it be okay if I came in and we had a chat?" she asks, gesturing at the door.

Dandy is taken aback. "Why?" she asks.

"There are parts of the story I'm having trouble with," she admits. "Maybe you could help me by answering a few questions."

After a brief moment of consideration, Dandy shrugs and steps back inside, leaving the door swinging open. Banjo is sitting contentedly on the ground, chewing on a stick, so Cass ties him to a tree and follows her inside.

The sunporch is a lovely room. The walls and ceilings are lined with wood, rich with patina, and built-in shelves, full of books and framed photographs, take up the entire back wall. There are plants everywhere, and interesting objects—stones and old bottles and the weathered skull of a seabird—line the windowsills. Mismatched but comfortable-looking furniture fills the space, and Cass instantly feels like this is a place where she'd be happy to spend lots of time.

The girl unslings her bag and drops it on the floor before flopping into a huge old armchair in the corner. "Have a seat," she says, pointing at a love seat beneath the window across from her. Cass sits and Dandy leans forward in her chair, fixing her guest with a scrutinizing glare.

"This is a really nice house," says Cass.

"It's my favourite place in the world," says Dandy. "I've been stopping by every once in a while to make sure everything is okay, because I know Grandy would have appreciated it." Her face crumples, and she looks like she's about to cry, but she steels herself and manages to hold it in. "What did you want to ask me about?" she says briskly.

"I'm trying to learn more about the five boys who supposedly found the treasure," says Cass. "I know a little bit about Mirabel and the Bellwood family, and Bill told me about his father being murdered, and the other boy going to jail for it. But I don't know anything about Elmer Feltzen. He would have been your great-grandfather?"

"Yeah," says Dandy. "Grandy's father. He grew up in this house, and then after his father died he stayed on as the caretaker. Grandy didn't like to talk about him, because he died when Grandy was just a little kid. Just another on the long list of things I wish I'd asked him about."

"What about Grandy?" asks Cass. "Your grandfather, I mean. Did he also become the caretaker?"

She shakes her head. "No, he worked for the county. Got his fifty years of service and was some proud of it. But he lived here; it was the family home. Not that that means much anymore."

"What do you mean?" asks Cass.

"Grandy left my aunt Margot the house in his will, and she's got plans for it." She reaches inside her leather bag and pulls out a manila envelope, which she hands to Cass before slumping back in her chair with a deep sigh.

Cass pulls out a stack of paper from the envelope and begins to flip through. "It looks like a land development plan," she says, looking up.

Dandy nods. "My aunt inherited Grandy's house. She's a real estate agent, and it looks like she's going to have it bulldozed so she can build some kind of resort here on the Point."

Cass looks at an artist's rendering of the development. The cottage they're sitting in has been swapped out by a spa, and Bellwoods has been altered to include a sizeable modern addition, marked

BELLWOODS HERITAGE LUXURY HOTEL. Bill's shack is also gone, replaced by one of a series of charming little cottages that run along the inlet, connected by a boardwalk.

The Trappers' house is about the only structure along the Point that's been spared.

"Wow," she says finally, the understatement of the year. Dandy's face crumples, and for a moment Cass is worried that she's going to start to cry again, but the girl pulls herself together.

"I don't think Peter is in any rush to sell Bellwoods," says Cass.

Dandy isn't buying it. "I overheard Margot talking about it. She has a plan to wear him down."

"Talking about it to who?" asks Cass.

"I think it was Dr. Oakley," says Dandy. "She was on the phone. It was after Mirabel's funeral."

Cass is surprised at this. "Dr. Oakley from the society?"

Dandy nods. "I'm pretty sure he's Margot's partner in all of this, although I'm not sure how or why."

Cass ponders this. "When I first arrived in town, I had to stop at Bellwoods to pick up the keys and the dog from Mirabel. It's the only time I met her, but she said something that stuck with me . . ."

Dandy perks up and sits forward in her chair.

"What did she say?"

"She said that the entire Point used to belong to the Bellwood family."

Dandy drops back in her seat, disappointed. "Yeah, I knew that already. Grandy said that this cottage was part of the estate. The crew built it first and lived here while Bellwoods was going up, then it became the caretaker's cottage."

Cass closes her eyes, trying to remember exactly how the old lady put it. "But she also said that her father—no, her *grandfather*—sold off almost all of the Point before she was born. Then she mentioned that the Trappers would have paid a lot for their plot, and that 'Frank Oakley would have expected a pretty penny' for it. That's how she put it, 'a pretty penny.'"

"That makes so much sense all of a sudden," says Dandy, her eyes widening. "If Oakley owns most of the land on the Point, of course he'd be in cahoots with Margot."

Her expression suddenly goes distant as if she's made some connection.

"What is it?" Cass asks.

But Dandy clams up. She shakes her head. "It was nothing," she says. She jumps up from the chair, adjusting her bag to hang over her shoulder. "I need to get home before my mom finishes her shift. Listen, will you do me a big favour?"

Cass stands reluctantly. She feels like she's missing out on some important insight, but she can also tell that this girl is not the type to fold easily.

"What kind of favour?" she asks.

"Don't talk to anyone about this stuff for a few days, okay? Like, don't mention anything about this development stuff. Whatever you do, don't talk to Dr. Oakley. If you can just look the other way for a few days, I'll make it worth your while, I promise."

"That's no problem," says Cass, eager to keep this new connection open. "I have other stuff to work on, anyway. Tomorrow I'm going out on this guy's sailboat and we're going to check out the spot where the sea battle took place."

"Some guy?" she asks.

"Yeah," says Cass, smiling. "This guy in town doing contract work. I guess you could say we're kind of dating? Or maybe not dating exactly, but in that weird stage before you start dating where you're trying to decide if you actually want to start dating. But I think we will. Anyway, he lives on his sailboat, and I've always been afraid of the water, and—"

"Lady," says Dandy, "I don't have time for relationship chatter. Just don't talk to anyone about what I've told you for a few days and I'll be in touch."

"Okay," says Cass. "You know where I'm staying."

There's so much more she wants to ask this strange girl, but it's clear this conversation has come to a close. Reluctantly, Cass leaves.

She unties Banjo, and as they walk home something occurs to Cass: she wouldn't have expected this, but she thinks she's discovered a character even more interesting than Bill Jinx, and she's right at the centre of the story.

BINGO

When I arrive at work for my shift, Bree hands me a small white envelope with my name written on it in neat block letters.

"Someone slipped this through the mail slot," she says. "I found it when I opened this morning."

I know she's dying to know what it is, but I wait until she runs out to grab coffee before I open it. Inside, a single sheet of loose-leaf paper reads: *Meet me at the docks after your shift ends. I've discovered crucial information. Dandy Feltzen, Teen Detective.*

At seven o'clock, I lock up the bookshop and stroll in the direction of the harbour. It's twilight by the time I walk down onto the docks, and there's nobody around except a pair of tourists walking in the opposite direction. For a moment, I wonder if I've been stood up, but then I notice a figure sitting on a bench at the far end of the dock, their face shoved down into a book.

I approach and, after confirming that it's Dandy, I take a seat on the opposite end of the bench.

"Is anyone watching us?" she whispers, without looking up.

"No," I say. "There's nobody around. Besides, it's almost dark."

"Good," she says, closing the book and sliding it inside her big leather bag.

"That's quite the outfit," I say. She's wearing black from head to toe, complete with a voluminous trench coat.

She turns to peer at me over the top of large vintage sunglasses. "I'm trying to remain incognito."

"Right," I say. "You'll really blend into the crowd in that beret."

"Listen," she says, "I didn't come here for fashion advice. I have information."

"So I gathered from your note. What's up?"

"I'm just going to cut right to the chase," she says. "What if there was *another* reason for someone to kill Mirabel and Bill?"

"Another reason," I repeat.

"This might be a bit confusing to explain," she says.

"I'm all ears," I tell her.

"Okay," she says. "So my aunt Margot has joined forces with Frank Oakley to turn the Point into some kind of tourist development."

"Really?" I ask. "This is the first I've heard of it."

"They're keeping it a secret," she says.

"So how do you know about it?" I ask.

Instead of answering, she reaches into her bag and tosses me a glossy brochure.

"Maple Bay Spa and Resort," I read. I look up at her. "Where did you get this?"

She looks sheepish. "I went to Oakley's house to ask him some questions, but then Margot showed up to drop those plans off, and I hid in the bushes."

"You're really into lurking, aren't you?"

"That's not the point," says Dandy. "The point is the Point. They can't go forward with their plan until they own *all* of the land on the Point, including Bellwoods."

"Which belonged to Mirabel," I say, picking up the thread.

She nods. "Then there's Bill's shack, and his prime little patch of shoreline. There wasn't a snowball's chance in hell that either Mirabel or Bill would have parted with their land."

Finally, I see where she's going with this.

"If Mirabel and Bill were no longer the only issue, that would clear the path for their development," I say.

She nods. "Bingo."

"But then I showed up and complicated things," I say, following the thread. "Which explains why your aunt has started approaching me about buying Bellwoods."

"You catch on quick," she says.

"This all sounds a bit far-fetched," I say. "Your aunt Margot is pushy, but she doesn't seem dangerous."

"It's not Margot I'm worried about," she says. "She's an asshole, but I don't think she's a killer. I think this all comes back to Oakley."

"Frank Oakley is a tiny, ancient man," I point out.

"Hear me out," she says. She begins to hold up fingers. "One: Frank Oakley quit the historical society because he supposedly had something more important going on. Two: he showed up right after Mirabel died and pronounced her death an accident."

I think back to Oakley's face after he examined Mirabel's body, the way he glanced surreptitiously at Mirabel's office. Was there something he was hoping to learn?

Dandy continues. "Three: when Bill lost his shit at Mirabel's funeral, it was Oakley who calmed him down and managed to get him outside."

She stares at me intently. "Four. Less than two hours after the funeral, I overheard Margot on the phone with someone. She was angry, and she accused whoever was on the other end of the line of getting cold feet."

"Oakley," I say.

She points a finger at me. "Bingo. And he's been avoiding her ever since. He was home when she dropped off those plans, but he wouldn't answer the door."

"Which you witnessed while you were lurking in the bushes," I say.

"Peter!" she says. "You're missing the point! Don't you think it's suspicious that he changed his mind right after the funeral? Right after he had a private conversation with Bill Jinx?"

I shrug. "I guess so."

She groans and then begins to spell it out for me. "Bill Jinx was convinced he knew where the treasure was hidden," she says. "He told me so himself. Most people thought he was nuts, but I believed him. What if he let something slip that made Oakley change his mind about the development?"

She drops back onto the bench as she begins to excitedly lay out a possible chain of events.

"Okay," she says. "So Margot and Oakley decide to get together on this development. Together they own most of the land on the Point. They just need Bellwoods, but Margot thinks Mirabel is old and they can wait her out. But Oakley is too old for that, and he knows Mirabel is in good health. He takes matters into his own hands and pushes her down the stairs, then makes sure *he's* the one to officially pronounce that her death was an accident."

"That sounds pretty grim," I say. I don't tell her that it all sounds completely implausible because, despite myself, I'm caught up in her theory and keen to hear the rest.

Dandy's brain is working overtime as she pulls together the threads. "But Bill is a different story. Oakley thinks that maybe he can convince him to give up his land, but before he has a chance to try, Bill has his breakdown at the funeral and tells Oakley what he's learned about the treasure. He implies that he's getting close and tells Oakley it's all inside his notebook. He loved to show off that notebook."

I pick up on her speculation. "So Oakley decides to kill Bill and steal the notebook? Oakley isn't exactly a big guy, not to mention he's in his late eighties."

"I think he could have managed it with booze and persuasion," says Dandy. "He gets Bill drunk enough that he's able to get him into that rowboat and pushes him out to sea. Then he goes back for the notebook. He figures, either way, getting Bill out of the picture is good news. If the notebook doesn't prove anything, at least he can get that land for the development. But then the notebook *does* prove something," says Dandy.

"But what, exactly?" I ask.

She shakes her head, clearly frustrated. "I don't know, but it's enough to get him to bail on Margot and the development."

"Maybe we should go see Oakley," I say. "We can ask him straight up."

She gapes at me, aghast. "Are you out of your mind? The guy might have killed two people!"

"Surely he can't overpower both of us at once," I suggest.

She shakes her head firmly. "If he's crazy enough to push someone down the stairs and send someone out to sea to drown, he's crazy enough to pull out a gun when he's cornered like a rat."

"Didn't you already go to see him on your own?" I ask.

"I did," she admits, "but I didn't end up talking to him, and at that point I hadn't pulled all these pieces together. Besides, I sent myself a text message saying that if anything happened to me, Oakley was responsible. I was ready to show it to him if he let me into the house, but it didn't come to that."

"You've really thought this through," I say.

She shrugs. "There's a lot at stake."

"I don't understand," I say. "Why are you telling *me* all of this?"

"Don't you get it yet?" she says. "You're the only other person who's directly connected to this. You told me yourself that your grandmother called you home to help you untangle some family business, and my grandfather asked me to try to finish solving this mystery. These were their final wishes, Peter. Doesn't that mean anything to you?"

I consider this. I can tell that Dandy Feltzen is not going to give up on this mission, whether I decide to join her or not.

"Okay," I say. "So what do you suggest? What's your plan?"

She pushes her sunglasses up onto her beret.

"We need to figure out what Bill had learned," she says. "If we can't have the journal, we have to somehow retrace his steps."

"And how do you propose we do that?" I ask. "No notebook, two dead contacts, and no leads."

"I have one lead," she says. She pulls her phone out of her pocket, and scrolls until she finds what she's looking for, then holds it out to me. I peer at the screen, trying to make out what she's showing me.

"It looks like garden tools," I say.

She takes the phone back. "I saw them in Bill's shack after he died."

"Jesus, Dandy," I say. "You broke into his shack?"

"I didn't break in; the door was open," she says. "I know it was wrong, but I needed to see if the notebook was there. It wasn't, but these were." She holds the photo up and points at it.

"So he had a garden shovel," I say. "Big deal."

"Did you see a garden down there by his shack?" she asks. "These are digging implements. Bill was digging for something, and it must have been somewhere on the Point. Otherwise, why would Oakley have pulled the plug on the development?"

"Even if that's true," I ask, "how are we supposed to know where, exactly?"

She sits back down on the bench and grabs the envelope of documents, riffling through until she finds the one she's looking for. It's an artistic rendering of the Point, drawn from above, with all the structures for the proposed development sketched out. She points at the tip of the Point, the wooded area behind Bellwoods. In the rendering, the trees have been cleared, and a collection of buildings have been arranged to take advantage of the freshly cleared view.

"I think it's in there," she says. "It's the only section of the Point that's still forested, and it would have been easy for Bill to sneak onto that piece of land and start digging. At least it's a good place to start looking."

I think this over. Dandy might be young and she's definitely weird, but there's no question that she's smart, with sharp instincts. A possibility begins to form in my mind.

"These woods are where the original Bellwood homestead used to be," I say. "But Mirabel told me it hadn't belonged to the family in a really long time. Do you think maybe it belongs to Oakley?"

Dandy looks excited. "I think it must," she says. "We have to check it out!"

"That would be trespassing," I point out.

"Peter, come on! There's a time to follow the rules and a time to break the rules, and this is definitely a time to break the rules. It backs onto your property, so it would be easy to sneak onto it without being noticed. We need to check it out right away, before he has a chance to hide his tracks. Like, tomorrow."

"I have to work tomorrow," I say. "But I'm off all day Sunday."

She looks disappointed. "Okay. We'll check it out together on Sunday."

"In the meantime," I say, "no more lurking. Stay away from Frank Oakley until we find out what he's up to."

She nods. "A hundred percent. We need to cover our asses, Peter. We're too close to the truth to afford a clumsy mistake." She stands and holds out a hand. "Are you with me?"

I reach out and shake. "I'm with you."

She looks satisfied. After pulling her trench coat close around her, she disappears into the night.

I watch her walk away, my mind spinning. There's no way I was going to spill the beans about Henry's journal with Dandy—the Bellwood family secrets are between me and Mirabel—but I'm starting to realize that it doesn't matter. Journal or not, Dandy seems to be on track to figure a lot of it out all on her own.

THE CONFESSIONS OF HENRY BELLWOOD

As remembered in October of 1983

I had time. None of the others knew of what
had transpired, except for Red, and his parents had promptly sent him away to boarding
school halfway across the country. As far as
Junior and Elmer and Archie knew, the treasure was still waiting for us beneath the
huge maple on the edge of Dagger Woods.

My plan was simple, I would wait until
the night of Red's eighteenth birthday and
meet the others at the hiding spot, having
spirited the treasure from Father's safe,
and re-bury it. There were some holes in
my plan—whether or not to involve Red, how
exactly I would keep Father from noticing—
but I had time to sort those details out.

So much time.

Seven years to pretend in front of my
friends as if nothing was wrong. Father
made the job slightly easier: he separated
me from my friends. He began by letting
Mrs. French go, suddenly and without warning, explaining that I was old enough to
manage without a nanny, although she had

never been a nanny, and he immediately hired a new housekeeper, a mean, pinched woman from town. He had Archie's family evicted from their shack on the inlet, and they were forced to relocate farther down the coast. Only Elmer's family remained in the caretaker's cottage. Having apparently decided that it would be difficult to find a capable replacement, Father warned me to keep my distance from Elmer.

"You're becoming a young man," he told me. "You need to begin moving in the proper circles."

Of course, the four of us continued to rendezvous, but only rarely, away from my father's gaze. It was easy enough to explain away the reason—I simply told them that my father didn't want me associating with them anymore, which they had no trouble believing. It was true, after all. The meetings were painful for me. All they wanted to talk about was the treasure, and the whole while I was keeping my terrible secret. Eventually, I began to make excuses, and gradually the meetings fell off entirely as the rest of them moved on with their lives, and soon it was only Elmer I saw, by virtue of our proximity.

The years rolled by. Every few weeks, I would slip into Father's study when he was away and examine the treasure. True to his word, Father had taken the discovery as a sign, and he had put his house in order, paid off his debts, and found his way back to the straight and narrow path. The gold and jewels remained, and were soon joined in turn by the fruits of his investments.

Stocks and bonds and stacks of cash were
added to the coffers, and I watched as my
tiny family grew richer and richer. I would
sit and stare at the treasure, imagine carrying it back to the forest, burying it
under the maple tree, and standing with
my friends as they finally uncovered their
fortune.

A year before our planned meeting, Elmer
told me that Archie had married a local girl
and they'd had a baby.

"A little boy," he said, smiling. "William."

Archie's family had moved on from the area a
couple of years earlier, in search of work
in the city. But Archie had remained behind,
taking on odd jobs by the harbour. It was
obvious to me why he'd chosen to stay. I
imagined that little baby growing up in
itinerant poverty, and my resolve to make
things right grew.

As the months dissolved into weeks, and the
weeks to days, I worked my plan over and
over, fine-tuning my approach. I took every
opportunity to enter Father's safe, checking and rechecking the status of the spoils
within. Father had long ago discarded the
moldy pillowcases in lieu of simple pine
boxes that stacked neatly inside the safe,
and I took great care to remove and replace
them in exactly the same order as I'd found
them. I carefully gauged the weight of the
contents and estimated that, carrying them
by myself, it would take me three trips back
and forth from the house to the maple tree.

I pilfered three pillowcases from the linen
closet, trying to find some that were as

close a match as possible to the ones we'd
originally used, although I wasn't especially worried about the detail. Enough time
had passed that nobody was likely to catch
the difference, especially in the excitement
of the unearthing. I was also relatively
confident that nobody would notice the dis-
parity in just *how much* treasure there was.
Despite my constant worries over the past
few years, father had been true to his word;
with a few exceptions here and there, he
had left the treasure relatively untouched,
and since we hadn't taken time to properly
count it back on that fateful day of discovery, I was sure nobody would notice the
difference.

The day before our meeting, I carried a
spade to the tree and dug a hole to save
myself time, then I went home and waited
to learn what Father's plans for the day
would be. Because this was the wild card,
had *always* been the wild card: if my father
found out what I had planned, there would be
terrible repercussions for all of us—most of
all, me.

Over a quiet dinner, he announced that he
would be leaving for the city in the morning
to check on some of his investments. When he
added that he would be away for two nights,
I had to use every ounce of restraint to
keep from laughing out loud with relief. I
would have free rein to carry out my plan
without worry of being caught. By the time
he returned from his business duties, the
deed would be done, and there would be no
turning back from that point. I had no doubt
that he would rage, and throw accusations,
and threaten and cajole, but once the horse

was out of the barn, there would be no putting it back.

Besides, I reasoned with myself, I would
hand my fifth of the fortune back to him.
I had no interest in making a claim for
myself—this was all to repay my friends for
what had been secretly taken from them.
Father could have what was left.

In the morning, I watched from my bedroom
window as Father packed his bags into his
automobile. When he returned to the house
and called for me, I came out to stand at
the top of the stairs, looking down at him.

He looked like he was trying to decide something. "Would you like to come with me?" he
asked finally.

I was surprised. Father had never invited
me on one of his business trips. I was left
stammering awkwardly. "Me? What for?"

He shook his head, clearly disappointed in
my answer. "You're almost twenty," he said.
"It's time you got to know the business, since
you'll be running it someday. But no matter.
We'll discuss your future when I'm back from
this trip. We need to begin making some plans
for you."

Without another word, he turned and left.
He didn't close the door behind him, and I
descended the steps in time to see his car
pull out of the driveway. I stood in the
doorway, watching as it departed along the
winding coastal lane and disappeared onto
the main road, headed toward town. When the
dust it kicked up had settled, I turned and
hurried to Father's study.

* * *

The first pillowcase was heavier than I'd
expected. It took me almost an hour, with
many stops and starts, to drag it through
Dagger Woods. When I came in sight of the
huge maple, I hid the bag in some bushes just
past the tree line, then I turned and hurried
back to the house.

Somehow, I managed to get into a rhythm, and
the second trip was much quicker than the
first. I returned back to Bellwoods for the
third and final load with a spring in my
step. I was almost there!

I was about to step through the front door
when I heard someone call my name, and I
dropped the remaining pillowcase out of
sight just in time to see Elmer strolling up
the driveway. He gave me a cheerful wave.

"Saw your old man driving away from town,"
he said as he climbed the steps of the
veranda. "Off for business, I imagine?"

I nodded. "He'll be gone for a couple of
nights."

He grinned. "Makes our job easier, doesn't
it? What do you think about all of this,
Henry. The day our lives change forever.
Almost worth the wait, wasn't it?"

I nodded and tried to smile, but I clearly
wasn't very convincing.

"Don't worry," he said, slapping me on the
shoulder. "Your old man will be happy when
he sees what you bring home. Have you heard
from Red?"

"Red?" I asked, alarmed.

Elmer looked surprised. "Yes, of course. It's the day, isn't it? His eighteenth birthday."

I scrambled for an explanation. "I just fig-ured, since he's away at boarding school and all, that he wouldn't be coming."

"Oh no," said Elmer. "He's back in town. My mother saw him out and about with his par-ents yesterday."

My pulse quickened, and an eerie chill spread over my entire body. In all of my plans and deliberations, it had never occurred to me that Red would return to Maple Bay, not after the way things had been resolved between our fathers seven long years ago.

I tried to rationalize; perhaps Red was sim-ply home for an unexpected visit. But in all the years he'd been gone, I had not heard of a single instance when he had come home. Then again, it was his eighteenth birthday. The day he officially became a man. Perhaps his parents had attached a degree of impor-tance to this. Whatever the reason, he was here, and there was no avoiding the fact.

"I haven't seen him," I said.

"Maybe I should go get him," said Elmer. "He wasn't with us when we buried the trea-sure. He'll need someone to bring him to the tree."

I froze as I realized I couldn't very well explain the true situation to Elmer.

"It's still early, isn't it?" he asked, mis-reading my expression. "We agreed on noon, didn't we? Junior and Archie likely won't be here for another couple of hours, so I've got plenty of time to walk back to town and fetch him, wouldn't you say?"

My heart sank. There was no way of avoid-ing it. But now that I was presented with the reality of things, I realized that it had always been meant to be this way. Why shouldn't Red receive his share of the pro-ceeds? Sure, he was ultimately responsible for the frantic situation I found myself in now; if he hadn't spoken to his father of his suspicions, the five of us would be gathering to unearth our destiny together, the way we had originally intended. But Red had only been a boy, and to be fair we *had* gone ahead and buried the treasure without him, and wasn't my role in this as bad as his? I had kept this enormous secret from our friends for seven long years. There was the matter of the land transaction between our fathers, but that was a negotiation that had played out beyond our control. We would have to find a way to deal with that later. This was just the way it had to be.

Besides, I still had a bag of loot to bring through the woods.

"That's a good idea," I said. "Why don't you go to his house and see if you can bring him with you?"

As soon as Elmer was gone, turning to head in the direction of town, I sprang into action. I grabbed the final sack of treasure and headed for the woods.

I glanced at my wristwatch as I approached the maple tree, relieved that it wasn't quite eleven. I had time to finish the task before my friends returned. But as I arrived at the space in the trees where I had stashed the other two bags, I heard voices raised in anger.

Peering through the bushes, I saw to my horror that Junior and Archie were standing over the hole I had dug, arguing.

"I'm telling you," Junior was saying, "I had nothing to do with this."

"Then why are you here by yourself an hour before everybody else, standing over an empty hole?" demanded Archie.

"I found it like this," said Junior, his voice growing heated. "And I could ask you the same question. What are you doing here so early?"

"I wanted to make sure I wasn't left out of the action," said Archie, almost spitting the words.

"You've lost your mind," said Junior. "Why would any of us possibly want to cut you out?"

As their argument escalated, I sat there in the bushes, wondering how to intervene. Should I simply step out and tell them *I* had dug up the bags? That I was anxious to get ahead of things? But they would see that the bags were perfectly clean. Should I just admit it all right now? Tell them the true story of what had happened here seven years ago?

"I don't know why you think I should let it
slide when I find you sneaking in here like
a snake," said Archie angrily.

He lunged at Junior, and the two men began
to scuffle, scrabbling at one another's
faces and trying to get in punches.

It was terrible to watch. I knew that their
conflict was driven by panic and desperation, Archie's paranoid fear that someone
was planning to steal away the one chance at
freedom for himself and his family. And the
sad truth was that his paranoia was justi-
fied, it was simply pointed in the wrong
direction.

Everything that had been building for the
past seven years seemed to fall into the
clearing then. All of the lies and the
secrets, the exhilaration and expectation
and the long march of anticipation that had
led us to this day, this moment that was
always supposed to separate the world before
and the world after. Archie somehow broke
free, and as he staggered back from Junior,
he accidentally stepped into the hole and
fell backward, landing with a heavy thud
that I could hear even from my hiding place
within the trees.

For a moment, Junior was stopped in his
tracks. The tension broken, he stepped forward, reaching down with a hand to help
Archie up.

Archie didn't reach back, and for a moment,
I thought he was simply being churlish. *At
least he's stopped yelling*, I thought. But
as I watched, I realized that Junior was
standing frozen in place, his arm still

outstretched. Time seemed to slow, and I
stifled a yell as Junior's facade finally
slipped, and his arm fell to his side.

"Archie?" Junior asked, his voice shaking.
He dropped hesitantly to his knees, attempting to lift Archie up by the shoulders, but
Archie's head lolled back, loose and limp. I
knew then that he was dead.

That was the moment to make my presence
known, my opportunity to step into the
clearing and explain to Junior that I'd seen
everything, heard everything, knew everything. Perhaps together we could have come up
with an explanation that worked, that exon-
erated him, that put us back on the right
path, but I stared at the bag of treasure
on the ground beside me and realized that it
was far too late for any of that. As Junior
began to weep, I hid the treasure in a thick
tangle of shrubs and ran back through the
forest to Bellwoods.

I made it back to the house in time to throw
cold water on my face when I once again heard
Elmer calling cheerfully up the driveway.

When I stepped through the front door, he
was approaching with a tall, thin young man
whom I didn't recognize. It wasn't until I
came down from the porch and got closer that
I recognized that this was indeed Red Oakley. He had grown a great deal in the years
since I'd last seen him, but his face was
the same.

"Red," I said, stepping forward to shake his
hand.

"It's Fred now," he said. "It's been a
while, Henry."

He raised an eyebrow and I knew we were both thinking of the last time we'd met. There was a look of cynical humour on his face, and I knew that he was looking forward to seeing how our long-planned unearthing would play out when both of us knew there was nothing left in the ground.

But he never had the chance, because as we stood there, an awkward trio, a noise drew our attention, and we turned to see Junior staggering out of the forest. There was blood on his hands and his shirt, and his eyes were wild as he regarded us.

"Archie is dead," he said. "I think he got to the treasure before we could."

Junior collapsed to his knees, and as Elmer rushed to him, Fred Oakley gave me a strange look. I knew he was asking me what was happening, but I could only shake my head. I didn't know what to say.

Junior confessed. He surrendered himself to the constabulary and told them that he and Archie had argued and begun to fight. During the scuffle, Archie had fallen and hit his head on a rock. Junior was whisked away to stand trial in the city. Everything happened very quickly, and before I knew what was happening, he had been sentenced to twenty years in prison for aggravated manslaughter.

Junior could give no rational explanation for why the two of them had been in the forest or the meaning behind the hole in the ground. Perhaps he knew that mentioning the

treasure would only make him sound crazy.
Perhaps he was simply trying to protect the
rest of us. Whatever the reason, rumour and
gossip rushed in to fill the vacuum, and
it soon became common understanding that
the two young men had been involved in some
illicit criminal activities, perhaps smug-
gling or theft.

I was wracked with guilt for not intervening,
but I could see no way around the conundrum.
However I dissected it, there was no way to
bring this situation to a fair conclusion.

Elmer was bewildered by what had happened.
The two of us knew that the treasure was
behind things, but I couldn't bring myself to
tell him the truth of the situation. He came
to believe that Archie had stolen the treasure and moved it before Junior arrived that
morning, and was confronted by Junior, and I
said nothing to undermine his theory.

"The thing that I still can't figure out,"
he said to me one day, a few weeks after
Junior went away to prison, "is what he
would have done with the money. His widow
and son are still living in a squalid apartment near the docks. He certainly didn't
share it with them before he died. Where do
you suppose it is, Henry?"

I could only shake my head. I had returned
to the forest late at night to retrieve the
treasure and it was once again tucked into
Father's safe, but I could hardly explain
that to Elmer.

But he had given me another idea, a way to
perhaps begin to make amends. I went to see

Archie's widow and their young son, and I told her she could make a home in the out-building on the shore, the same one the Jinx family had lived in before they had been pushed out by my father. She gratefully accepted the offer, and with Elmer's help I set to turning the shack into a home for the young woman and her baby. We repaired the roof and replaced the windows, and generally did our best to tighten the small building against the wind and cold. I found some old furniture in the basement at Bellwoods, and we furnished the house to the best of our ability.

Father did not protest. By now I was pretty sure he had figured out at least some of the truth of what had happened in the woods that day, and perhaps there was a small amount of guilt in his reaction. A young man was dead. He made no objection when I invited Jinx's widow and their small son to move to the inlet, to the same place where Archie had lived when we were boys. I would see the young Jinx boy running along the beach, and I would think to myself that at least Archie had left behind a piece of himself.

In time, life moved on. I met my wife and married her. We were very much in love, and for a time I thought that everything would be forgiven. When our daughter, Mirabel, was born, I felt as if I would never be so happy again.

Elmer also got married, and his son Reggie was born within six months of Mirabel. As the two of them grew up, they became fast friends, and I would often see them on the beach with the slightly older Bill Jinx, the three of them involved in one adventure or another.

Life continued. The world had fallen into a state of some equilibrium. The treasure was still locked up in Father's safe. Junior was locked up in Halifax.

I had not seen Red Oakley since the morning of his eighteenth birthday. He had gone away again, and as far as I could tell or imagine, he had no reason to return to Maple Bay.

DANDY THE SPY

It's not like Dandy is actually breaking a promise or anything. Peter told her *he* couldn't explore the woods until Sunday, and he suggested they should check it out together. Nobody said anything about her not checking it out on her own first. This is just a bit of practical recon, a chance to scope the scene and vet things before she comes back with Peter on Sunday and they do the *real* investigating together.

She doesn't want to risk being seen, so she leaves her bike in Grandy's little lean-to shed and then makes her way along the coast toward the Bellwood property. She feels a particular pang when she passes Bill's shack. He won't be charging down onto the beach to confront her ever again.

What did you learn, Bill? Where did it lead you?

When she gets close to Bellwoods, she clambers up the bank and through the backyard and then steps into the woods behind the house.

She was worried it would be hard to find her way once inside the forest—there are several acres of trees back here, a mix of pine and spruce and assorted hardwood—but she finds herself moving naturally in a particular direction. It's almost as if there's an invisible path through the trees, an intangible natural rhythm to the space that pulls her confidently forward.

The first thing she comes across is a low stone wall, mossy and partly disassembled. It's low enough to hop over, and then she sees them: the holes in the ground.

They're neatly spaced, not too deep but a roughly uniform shape and size, about three feet in diameter. It looks deliberate, like there is a grid laid out in the ground, as if somebody has been methodically working their way through the area, looking for something. It's obvious to Dandy what that is.

She imagines Bill back here, determinedly digging his way through the woods, looking for the treasure. What had made him decide that the treasure was here? What had been so convincing that he'd spent all this time digging these holes, a man of ninety-plus years? And has Frank Oakley taken up the challenge now that Bill is dead? Where did Bill's holes stop and Frank's begin?

She's so busy examining the holes, trying to determine whether there's some kind of grander pattern that she's not seeing, that she doesn't notice the ruins of the old house until she's almost upon them. The foundation is all that remains, a rectangle of boulders that must have been dragged up from the shoreline. Their hard edges are softened and obscured by moss and vines and a huge, tangled colony of brambles, but the vegetation only serves to highlight the footprint of the old house, masses of brilliant red leaves tracing an outline of the structure's ghost.

This was once the Bellwood estate, or, more accurately, the first house the Bellwood family built when they arrived here in Maple Bay. What did they look like back then? Did Mirabel's great-grandparents see themselves as bastions of the colony, triumphant newcomers with a well-defined mission, to take over, to dominate, to build? Or were they running from something?

There's no telling now. Mirabel might have known some of these things about her family, but Dandy doubts that Peter had time to learn many of those details. If it wasn't for the stones, there'd be no sign of that moment in the settler experiment.

And if it wasn't for the holes in the ground, there'd be no sign that anyone had ever tried to look for something in here.

She wanders around the outer edge, examining the area carefully for clues, but nothing obvious jumps out at her, so she moves on, deeper into a weedy, swampier area behind the house. Back here, it's impossible to move quickly. Dandy is forced to work hard to push through a dense, tangled screen of alders and spindly, tight-knit shrubs, some of them freckled with thorns. Her feet keep getting caught up in thick, sucking mud, and a couple of times she almost loses one of her boots.

She's about to turn back when something catches her eye. It's a burst of colour, bright orange, about a hundred yards farther ahead, but only faintly visible beyond the tangled screen of vegetation that reaches up like a mass of spindly fingers grasping at the dim light above. She presses on and finally the shrubs begin to thin, and the ground dries up a bit so that she is able to hop and step carefully from one dry area to the next.

As she gets closer to the pop of color, she begins to recognize letters, and then she steps around a tree and everything suddenly comes into focus. It's a sign, propped against a pile of rubble on a dry, raised area.

DANGER: STAY AWAY, the sign reads, and the connection comes to Dandy immediately. The orange spray paint, the ragged piece of old plywood, the warning: this sign looks just like the ones down by Bill's shack.

Why would Bill have written a sign? What was he trying to hide?

She jumps over a muddy, squelching patch of bog and lands on the dry hill. As she steps up to the sign, she realizes that it's not leaning against a pile of rubble after all, but a more defined structure: a circular ring of mortared stones with a wooden slab on top held in place with a stone. An old well.

It's creepy as heck. She remembers Bill Jinx yelling about his father's ghost, and she feels a shiver run down her spine as if she's being watched. She spins quickly on her heels to scan the area around her. She's alone. But instead of making her feel better, it only makes her more aware of the layers upon layers of shadow and darkness that circle her.

For a moment, she wants to turn and run, to squelch back through the swamp, and out of the woods, and along the coast, and even past Grandy's house. Back home to her apartment, and her mom, and her homework, and a life that doesn't include wild goose chases and crazy conspiracies.

A life where Grandy is a beautiful memory, and not standing right behind her just out of sight.

Get a grip, girl, she can almost hear him say, and she smiles as the words from his final letter come back to her. *I'd come back and haunt you, Dandy, but there's no such thing as ghosts.*

"But you're here now anyway," she says out loud. "Aren't you, you old bugger?"

The thought emboldens her. Grandy sent her on this mission for a reason: he knew she could handle it. If he *was* a ghost, lingering in the shadows around the edge of this strange space, he'd be embarrassed to see her turn and leave.

She steps up to the edge of the well and leans across to push the rock out of the way. The board on top is just a piece of old plywood, and she imagines Bill placing it here, over the hole. Maybe Bill had started off digging holes, but had something ultimately led him to this well?

"Let's find out, Grandy," she says as she picks up the edge of the plywood and flips it backward. It clatters away, revealing an opening about four feet in diameter. She peers down, squinting, but all that greets her is an inky black void.

She pulls her iPhone out of her pocket and turns on the flashlight. As she skims the beam down the rocky wall, she catches a glimpse of something scuttling across a rock and disappearing into a crevice. The well is deeper than she would have expected; when she trains the flashlight on the bottom, the light reflects against a small puddle and she realizes that it's basically dry and almost empty except for a lumpy bundle of *something*.

Her mind goes wild. From this distance the iPhone beam is very faint and weak, and she can't quite make it out. It could be anything, but she can't help imagining a heavy sack full of gold coins and silver chains and uncut gems. She shimmies forward on her stomach so that her upper body dangles farther over the edge. With her right hand, she guides the beam over the bottom of the well, while with her left she hooks on to get purchase.

Maybe it's the echo inside the well that distorts the noise, but she hears the sound behind her just a split second before she feels someone yank her feet up from the ground, tipping her forward, and just as she registers that she's falling, everything goes black.

I'M ON A BOAT

Bryson is late getting to the boat, and so Cass stands by the edge of the dock, trying to look like she belongs. She's wearing white shorts and a blue-and-white-striped shirt, with flip-flops and a visor to protect her from the sun. Bryson asked her to take care of lunch, so in a large canvas bag she has a baguette and some cheese, some cookies and apples, and a chilled bottle of wine that she grabbed from the fridge.

Tucked into a flap on the side is a notebook and a couple of pens. Wine notwithstanding, work is today's main priority.

Or at least one of them.

She spots Bryson at the end of the dock, striding toward her, his hand raised and his big smile gleaming.

"Sorry I'm late," he says as he approaches. "Got caught up with a couple of errands."

She wonders what kind of errands, since he isn't carrying any packages, but she doesn't want to pry. "No worries," she says. "I've just been taking in the sights."

He gestures at the boat. "You could have hung out on the boat," he says.

"It's okay," she says. "The people watching is better on the dock."

She doesn't want to tell him the truth, which is that she doesn't know how to climb aboard without slipping through the crack between the boat and the dock and being strangled by an octopus, but she suspects he guesses anyway. He gives her a sly, knowing smile.

"Trust me," he says. "You're going to have fun. You've just got first-timer jitters. Give me the bag."

She hands it to him, and he slides it over his shoulder and then takes her hand and helps her step smoothly over the side of the dock and onto the boat.

"See?" he says. "Nothing to worry about. Boats are easy."

"We're still tied up," she observes.

"Not for long," he says cheerfully. He reaches down into the cabin to deposit her bag on the galley counter, and then he sets to moving nimbly around the boat like a goat. A tall, hot, seafaring goat.

Before long, they've untied from the dock and Bryson is motoring them out into the bay.

This is fine, Cass tells herself, seated rigidly into a corner of the cockpit near the hatch, her arms clasped tightly around herself, *this is totally fine.*

From his place at the wheel, Bryson is chattering away, but over the roar of the engine she can only make out a few smatterings of words, including ". . . bring her out . . ." and ". . . below . . ." and ". . . untethered . . ."—this last with a grand sweep of his arms in all directions.

She considers throwing some relevant statements back at him, like ". . . landlubber . . ." and ". . . overboard . . ." and ". . . nautical disaster . . ." but she just plasters a smile on her face and nods furiously at everything he's saying, her eyes fixed on the little town that grows smaller, and smaller, and smaller the farther away they get.

Without warning, Bryson cuts the engine and suddenly the noise snaps from loud and aggressive to calm and natural and *oceany*. Waves slap softly against the bow, gulls cry overhead, and a soft breeze lightly rattles the lines against the mast.

"This is actually kind of nice," says Cass as the boat bobs gently in the waves.

"Right?" says Bryson. "We're lucky: this is late in the season for such nice weather. Here, come grab the wheel while I put up the sails."

"What?" she asks, but he's already moving across the deck, leaving the wheel untended.

"It's easy," he says over his shoulder as he hops up to the mast and begins unpacking the mainsail. "Just keep her on the right side of the centre line."

"What centre line?" she asks, panicked, as she scrambles to the wheel.

He laughs. "I'm messing with you. You see that green buoy out there?"

She squints. "Yes."

"Just hold on to the wheel and keep her pointed at that buoy. It's easier than driving a car."

Cass realizes she doesn't have a choice, so she grips the wheel at ten and two and clenches her jaw in concentration. To her surprise, however, it *is* easy, and after a bit of negotiating she soon feels in control.

"Great job," says Bryson as he crouches to toss the sail cover down into the hatch. "You're a natural!"

"Hell yeah," she says, pumping the air with her fist. "I'm driving a boat, motherfuckers!"

He laughs and jumps back down into the cockpit, where he unties a line from a metal cleat along the edge.

"Get ready!" he says.

"Get ready for what?" she asks, but he's already letting off the line.

The large mainsail unfurls from around the mast, and as it catches wind the boom flies with a dramatic snap from one side of the boat to the other, swinging over Bryson's head as he smoothly and expertly ducks to avoid it. Suddenly and without warning, the sail goes taut and the boat tips dramatically onto its side, messing with everything Cass has ever known about gravity.

She staggers sideways, losing her hold on the wheel, which spins as the boat circles aggressively into the wind.

"Mayday!" she screams as Bryson deftly hooks the line onto a cleat and jumps across the deck to grab the wheel. He quickly rights the boat, which is still tipped onto its side but at least moving in a consistent direction.

"You all right, sailor?" Bryson asks.

She glares at him. "This is not what you promised."

He grimaces apologetically. "We caught a little gust there," he says. "Should have warned you about the heeling. Just grab the wheel for one more second and I'll get us sorted out."

Reluctantly she takes the wheel again, and soon he has them on a gentler course, and the boat is gliding gently, if swiftly, out of the bay. Cass finally manages to get her legs sorted out beneath her and gradually begins to relax.

"Look," says Bryson, pointing over to the right. "There's the Point."

Sure enough, Bellwoods has appeared, standing prominently at the tip of the little peninsula. Beyond it, above the trees, Cass catches a glimpse of the Trapper house.

"Cool!" she says. "It's like seeing the world from the other side of the looking glass."

"That's what I love about sailing," he says. "You get a totally different perspective on things. Now let's get out of the mouth of the bay so you can see the big picture."

It isn't until they're completely out of the bay that the reality hits Cass: she's really enjoying this. It's undeniably beautiful out on the water, the sea cradling the boat and the sky spinning around them in a glorious 360 degrees. In an almost mystical way, she feels centred in the universe.

It's also impossible to ignore how romantic it is: just the two of them, out on the open sea. Occasionally they chat but mostly they remain silent, enjoying the experience of being together. Vaguely, Cass wonders what Jason would think if he were to see her like this with another guy, but the thought appears almost absentmindedly, without the expected sharp edges, and she doesn't even consider taking a photo for Instagram. Instead she lets the thought of Jason drop into the water and recede into the wake behind them, and she happily turns her attention back to Bryson.

At the wheel of the boat, he's utterly in his element. He's wearing a fleece jacket zipped up against the chill, and a grey woolen cap, and his face is serene against the wind, which has picked up quite a bit since they left the bay.

When they're a fair distance from shore, he lets the sails down so that they bob gently in place, and then sweeps his arms out to gesture to the sea around them. "This is the place," he says grandly.

"Where the ships battled?" she asks.

"More or less," he says. "It's hard to know the exact coordinates, but it would have been somewhere out here, just beyond the mouth of the bay."

She looks back at the shore. They've sailed far enough away that the town of Maple Bay is just a blur in the distance, and when she squints, she can pretend it isn't there at all, that the landscape still exists, clean and un-trampled, the way it was before settlers arrived and colonized it into something different. Cass can see miles of rocky coastline, interrupted by the occasional sandy beach, backing up against countless acres of fields and trees. From here, it really comes into focus just how many places there would be to hide something as small as an iron chest.

"Somewhere below us is the wreck of the *Obelisk*," says Bryson, and she joins him at the side of the boat and together they stare down through the inky, briny depths, as if they might somehow catch a glimpse of something all the way down on the ocean's floor.

"It's hard to imagine," says Cass as she pulls out her phone to take some reference photos.

"There have been several dives over the years," says Bryson. "There's even a little museum in town with some artifacts on display. Nothing too dramatic, but it's worth a visit. Maybe we can check it out sometime."

"I'd love to," says Cass as she moves about the deck, framing different perspectives of the shoreline. "The thing I can't get over is the men who left the ship. They were responsible for getting the treasure ashore *and* for hiding it. They're the most important people in the story, or at least that part of it, but they were shot on sight. We don't even know their names!"

Bryson shrugs. "I guess that's the plight of the minion," he says.

"It just pisses me off," she says. "I wish there was some way to learn more about them, but they're lost to the ether, while Dagger and Pynchon get all the glory. It isn't fair."

"History forgets most of us," says Bryson. "I think it's liberating."

"I don't know," she says. "I prefer to think that we all have a story that's worth preserving. That's why I'm so grateful for everything Bill told me. If I can figure out how to do my job, I'll be resurrecting those five boys and breathing life into their stories long after they're dead."

He smiles. "You sound really hyped when you talk about this book."

"I am!" she says. "This project is saving my life. I think I was floundering for a long time, and I didn't even realize it. I thought I was in the only place that mattered to me, until I found myself here and landed on this story. I thought I had a career, but I really just had a job. I thought my relationship was perfect, and it wasn't even close. This trip, this mystery . . . it's all given me purpose."

Cass realizes that he's staring at her with a funny smile on his face.

"What?" she asks.

"Nothing," he says. "I was just thinking about how beautiful you are when you get excited."

She blushes, despite herself. "Is that right?" she says. "Well, I have to admit you're not so hard on the eyes yourself."

Instinctively, she gets up from her seat and moves to stand next to him. With one hand still on the wheel, he reaches his other arm around her waist, pulling her in toward him.

"We'll have to remember this conversation later," he whispers. "When we're back on dry land."

"I'll remember," she whispers back.

He bends down and just like that they're kissing, soft and sweet and salty from the sea breeze.

He pulls back and smiles down at her. "I was wondering if that would happen."

"I suppose it was inevitable," she says.

"I think you're right," he says, "but it's getting a bit chilly out here, and I'm getting hungry. Let's head back to the inlet. It'll be less breezy, and we can tie up to a mooring and have lunch."

"That sounds perfectly civilized," says Cass.

This time when he asks her to take the wheel, she doesn't put up a fight. He sets her on course and then moves about the boat, pulling down sails and tying off lines. He turns the engine back on, and they begin to motor gently back toward the inlet.

They're coming at Bellwoods head-on. Cass pulls out her phone to get a few shots of the stately old mansion.

"Apparently there are some people trying to develop the Point," she says.

Bryson looks back at her from the wheel as he negotiates the boat through the mouth of the inlet. "Where did you hear that?"

"I met a strange girl the other day. Her grandfather was one of the members of that society Bill told me about." She points at the cottage in the distance. "That's his house up there at the head of the inlet. Anyway, she told me that her aunt and one of the other guys in the society are trying to snatch up all the land along here and build some kind of development. She was weird about it, like she thought there was some kind of conspiracy to rip people off or something."

The Trapper house suddenly comes into view on the top of the hill, and Cass clambers up onto the top of the boat to grab some more photos.

When she glances back at Bryson, his face is flat and impassive and he's staring directly ahead, carefully navigating the boat down the centre of the inlet. She could swear he looks bothered by something, but then he looks up at her and smiles.

"Come on down here and grab this wheel, will you?"

He cuts the engine and calls instructions over his shoulder for her to keep the boat in line as they approach a mooring buoy in the middle of the inlet. Working quickly, he crouches and uses a long hook to catch the rope on the mooring and hook them up.

"There we go," he says. "I have a few things to take care of up here. Do you want to pull together a lunch for us?"

"Aye aye, Captain," she says.

"Great. You should find everything you need in the galley."

As he steps up to the front of the boat and begins to fuss with the sails, Cass climbs down the little wooden ladder in the cabin. She's surprised at just how spacious it is down below. She can easily stand up, and everything is neatly designed to fit perfectly inside. The galley, basically a tiny kitchenette, is tucked into the space at the bottom of the stairs, and a desk, covered with navigational instruments and buttons and gauges, fits in on the other side. The centre of the cabin is taken up by a comfortable corner sofa surrounding a teak table covered with charts and papers.

There are shelves and pigeonholes and little brackets everywhere, all neatly organized. And underneath the bow, she sees a comfortable-looking bunk that she can't help thinking would easily be big enough for two people.

From the tousled pile of bed linens on the bunk, the French press half full of coffee in the kitchenette, and the small piles of clothes scattered around the space, it's clear that Bryson considers this his home.

She finds a cutting board and knife in the little galley cupboard and begins to slice the baguette. The boat has been creaking with the sounds of Bryson moving around overhead, but suddenly they stop and she hears him speaking. She freezes to listen, wondering if he's saying something down to her, but then she realizes that he's on his phone, speaking in a low, serious tone.

She knows it's tacky to eavesdrop, but she can't help it. She moves a bit closer to the hatch, straining to hear.

At first, all she can make out is a faint muttering, but then Bryson steps closer and stops right overhead, and now his voice is much clearer.

"I don't know," he's saying. "Why don't *you* tell *me*?"

There's a long pause, presumably as someone on the other end of the line speaks, and then he lets out an exasperated groan. "Do you know what?" he says. "I didn't sign up for this bullshit. You'd better clean this mess up quick."

"Sorry!" he calls down a moment later, and she figures he must have hung up. "I was just dealing with some work stuff up here. You okay down there?"

"I'm just fine!" she calls back. "I'll be up shortly!"

His head suddenly appears in the hatch, startling her. He grins down.

"Take your time," he says. "I still have to tie up these sails."

"Okey-dokey," she says.

He disappears, and Cass hears him moving around again, up above. Something about the phone call scratches at the back of her brain, but she pushes the thought aside. She's been listening to too many stories about secret societies and suspicious deaths. This is a date, goddammit. Time for cocktails.

She finds a couple of plastic tumblers and pulls out the white wine. She rummages through the drawers in the galley looking for a corkscrew, but comes up empty. She turns around, scanning the cabin, wondering where else she might find one, and notices more drawers underneath the desk. On a whim, she opens the top one, and freezes.

Sitting on top of a loose assembly of random papers is a battered red notebook.

BONNIE BRICKLAND
WANTS TO CHAT

I spend the first half of the morning running in about ten different directions, trying to check as much off my list as possible before I head to my shift at the bookshop. I'm in Mirabel's office, sending one final email before heading out, when the phone rings.

I pick up. I'm still not used to the heft of the clunky receiver against the side of my head.

"Yeah?"

"Hello," says a vaguely familiar voice. "Is this Bellwoods?"

"Yeah," I say. "This is Peter. Can I ask who's speaking?"

"It's Bonnie. Bonnie Brickland from the library. Do you have time to chat?"

"Sure," I say. "I've got a minute. How can I help you?"

"Well," she says, "there's something I want to talk to you about. Something I've . . . discovered. I wonder if you have a bit of time to come to see me today?"

"I'm kind of busy at the moment. Can you tell me what it's about?"

There's a long pause on the other end of the line. "I don't think it's a good idea to talk about it over the phone," she says finally.

Through the coiled line of this ancient telephone, her voice sounds like it could be coming from a distant past, from a moment before certain choices were made, when other outcomes were still possible.

"Okay," I say. "I'll come now. You're at the library?"

"No," she says. "I'm at home." She gives me directions and we end the call.

I glance at the clock on the upper edge of the desk. My shift starts in about half an hour, so I really need to move. But my eyes stick to one of the photographs. Susan, young and blond and beautiful. It's clearly the summer, and her hair is short, and her cheeks are glowing, and I can tell from the look on her face that she knows something, and for the first of the many times I've stared at this picture, I realize that what she knows is that she's pregnant.

Perhaps she even knows that someday she'll have a son.

Bonnie lives in a tiny bungalow at the end of a long lane, surrounded by trees and a small garden. I pull up next to a small shed, its door partially ajar.

Behind me, a screen door creaks open, and I turn to see Bonnie stepping outside to greet me.

"Come on in," she says. "I just made some tea."

I follow her through a small back porch into a warm, simple kitchen. Through a doorway, I spot a darkened living room, sheer curtains smothering the daylight so that the wallpaper, covered in large pastel roses, appears dull and lifeless. The house smells cloying, like cigarettes and mildew.

I look around the kitchen as Bonnie moves to the stove and pours from a chipped yellow teapot.

Everything in the room is neat and orderly, except for a pair of dirty leather gloves on the corner of the counter nearest the door. They stick out like a sore thumb.

She hands me a cup of tea and I take a sip. The gentle, fragrant warmth seems to immediately work its way down through me. "It's nice," I say.

"It's my own herbal blend," she says. "No caffeine, but everything in it came from my garden. Mint. Chamomile. Lavender."

I gesture at the gloves. "Looks like you were doing some gardening today."

She just nods, then gestures for me to follow her into the living room. I carry my tea with me, and when she takes a seat in an armchair beside the window, I take that as a cue to drop onto the couch.

"I inherited this house from my grandfather," she says. "I was living in Toronto, wondering when life was going to begin, and suddenly an opportunity was handed to me on a platter. A house, all my own. In a town I'd only ever visited once or twice as a kid."

"That sounds a lot like what happened to me," I say.

She just nods, smiling, as if she's already said everything she needs to say. In my awkwardness, I reach again for my tea, cupping the mug into my hands against a sudden chill that runs along my arms and the back of my neck. I wonder if a draft is coming from the window, but the curtains don't move, not even so much as the gentlest flutter.

When I look back at Bonnie, she's staring at me.

"Mirabel and I were good friends," she says. "We were very close. When I first moved to town, I didn't really know anybody.

I got the job at the library and that's where we met. She came in every month for one of her meetings. We began to talk about history and genealogy, and I think she saw that I was lonely and a bit adrift in this new town, and she kind of took me under her wing, inviting me to Bellwoods and making me feel like I belonged here in Maple Bay."

She turns away and for a long moment she stares into the middle distance before continuing. "Mirabel was a help and a comfort to me, and I like to think I was able to return the favour."

"I'm glad to hear that," I say, and my own voice sounds weak and faint, as if I'm hearing myself through a closed door, speaking softly in another room.

Bonnie carefully places her tea down on a side table and leans forward in her chair, fixing me with an intense stare.

"Then something happened," she says. "Mirabel pulled back. She didn't return my calls, and when she came to the library for her meetings, she was cordial, but distant. I wondered if I'd offended her. I wondered if she had come to decide that I wasn't worth her time. I almost rolled over and gave up on our friendship, but then I decided to give it one more chance."

She stares at me meaningfully, as if she expects me to understand what she's saying.

"What do you mean?" I ask.

"One night, when the rain was falling heavily outside, I drove to Bellwoods. I didn't think it through, I just put on my raincoat and got in my car and drove out to the inlet and ran up the veranda and I rang the doorbell. The house was dark and silent, and I stood there for a long time, wondering if she was home. I was about to give up, to turn around and leave, to put Mirabel behind me entirely, when the door opened and she was standing there, swaying on her feet, a highball glass in her hand."

"She was drinking?" I ask, surprised.

Bonnie nods. "She was in a bad state. In all the time I'd spent with Mirabel, I had only ever seen her immaculately presented. But her hair was a mess, and her clothes were disheveled, and her makeup had run. It was clear she'd been crying. The poor woman fell into my arms, and I led her inside and sat her down in the kitchen and made her some coffee, and then . . ." Here Bonnie pauses and spreads her arms out wide. "She told me everything."

I realize that I'm now leaning forward on the sofa, my mouth open, the tea hovering in the air in front of me, rapidly growing cold. I put down the cup and clear my throat.

"What?" I ask. "What did she tell you?"

"She told me about her father's journal, of course," she says.

I stare at her, struck dumb.

Bonnie stands. "There's something I want to show you," she says. Without waiting for me to respond, she turns and disappears around a corner. A moment later, I follow.

Something about this isn't right, and I realize that I'm dreading following her.

Go, says a voice inside me. *Go now while you still can.*

But I can't. Not now. Not until I know what she is going to show me.

"It's just in here," she says, and when I turn the corner, she's stepping into another room.

I move to stand in the doorway and stare into a small office. There's a single lamp lit on a desk against the far wall, casting a dim glow up and around the room. The desk is piled with books and documents, and the wall above it is blanketed with clippings and photographs and index cards, all surrounding a huge map of the Point.

One section of the map has been marked off clearly with a Sharpie and filled in with a yellow highlighter. Even across the room I can see that it indicates the wooded area behind Bellwoods. The original homestead.

"Mirabel learned a lot in those final months of her life," she says. "She discovered the truth about her family, for one thing. And I think, above all else, that's why she suddenly became so desperate, after all those years, to find her long-lost grandson. There were things she needed to tell someone who was connected to her in the most important way of all. By blood."

Bonnie turns away from me, but not before I see the look of hurt and betrayal the memory provokes.

"She told me she'd found him," she says, "and I knew in that instant that my role in her life was changing, and that's exactly what happened. She abandoned all interest in anything and everything that didn't have to do with the magnificent return of the prodigal grandson."

"I don't know if that's a fair description," I somehow manage to point out.

Bonnie bristles. "How would you characterize it?" she asks. "A young man who you basically bankrolled for his entire life, who couldn't be bothered to so much as send an old lady a Christmas card, or call her on her birthday, is suddenly hopping on a plane to come meet dear old Granny? It all stunk to high heaven."

"None of it was like that," I say. "None of it. My aunt and uncle stole the money. They kept me from her!"

She waves her hand at me, impatient. "*I* had been Mirabel's confidante. *I* had been the one helping her, guiding her, advising her, assisting her, only to have the rug pulled out from under my feet. If you had any idea how much legwork I did for that woman. I swear, it was like getting fired from a job with no notice, after you've helped the company turn record profits, all because of nepotism."

Suddenly I see where this is going.

"You were jealous," I say.

She laughs. "Oh, please. Of course I was jealous. But I'm a big girl, I know how the world works. I kept my chin high, and licked my wounds, and told myself that none of it belonged to me in the first place. Then she died, and there was nothing left but to let you finish her work for her."

I open my mouth to protest, but she holds up a hand, determined to finish.

"I tried to turn the other cheek and do the right thing," she says. "When I met you at the bookstore, I introduced myself and offered to help you. Who knows, I might have even told you what I knew, what we'd learned together, but before I had the chance, do you remember what you told me?"

I can only shake my head, slowly beginning to worry that I should never have come here.

"You said she didn't mention me," she almost spits. "Not even in passing. A fine thank-you for everything I did for her, but at least it showed me my place. So I smiled nicely, turned around, and decided to wash my hands of the whole thing."

"That's why you refused to help me when I came to see you at the library," I say.

"Why should I help you?" she asks, practically spitting the words at me. "Why should I involve myself where I clearly wasn't welcome?"

I am tired of this woman. I am tired of listening to her delusional, self-important rant.

"Oh, I see," I say. "You've clearly washed your hands of the whole thing, what with your insane conspiracy wall."

She glances at it and shakes her head, smiling. "You really have no idea, do you?" she asks.

"No idea about what?" I manage to ask.

"That I've figured out what nobody else in this town has been able to," she says, her lips curled into a hard, nasty grin.

I know now, as I stare into her wild eyes, that it was a terrible idea to come here.

WELL, WELL, WELL

Dandy isn't sure how long she's out cold, but when she does wake up, she wakes up fast, and it takes her only a couple of seconds to remember where she is.

She's flat on her back, and she can feel something soft beside her. Grandy's satchel. She wiggles her fingers and then her toes, and gradually tries out each of her limbs and extremities in succession, breathing a sigh of relief when she's verified that everything seems to work.

It isn't until she's managed to sit up that she realizes the satchel isn't the only thing that's broken the fall. She must have fallen directly onto the lumpy pile that she saw from above, and she can tell one thing for sure: whatever it is, it doesn't feel like a sack of treasure. She jerks up and moves away, pressing her back to the wall on the other side.

It's dark in the well, the only light a dim, ambient glow from the opening above. Dandy stares up and figures she must be about fifteen feet down. If she hadn't landed exactly the way she did, she doubts she'd still be alive.

She glances away from the opening so her eyes have a chance to adjust to the dark. Then she scans the floor until she spots her iPhone. She picks it up and realizes that the screen is cracked and the battery is either dead or broken. Either way, it's no use now.

"Okay, kid," she says, trying once more to channel Grandy, "what's the plan?"

She almost laughs out loud when the thought occurs to her. She opens the top flap of the satchel and rummages inside until she comes out with Grandy's big old flashlight. There's a long crack in the casing, likely from the fall. She snaps it on. Nothing. She's about to toss it to the ground in despair when she thinks to check back inside the pocket. Bingo. She slides an unopened package of batteries from where they were wedged beneath the flashlight.

"Grandy," she says, "you were a well-prepared son of a gun."

She replaces the batteries, snaps on the light, and suddenly the interior of the well is illuminated. She scans the walls and is happy to see that there are some substantial gaps between the stones. The height is definitely a challenge, but if Grandy said it once, he said it a thousand times: *You're nothing if you're not nimble, Dandy.*

She aims the flashlight at the bundle on the floor. It's bigger down here than it looked from above, long and misshapen and bulky, something wrapped in a blanket, and from the looks of things, it hasn't been down here all that long.

She wants to ignore it. To pretend it isn't there. To carefully step around it and begin climbing, send someone else back to make the grim confirmation. But Dandy is here, right now, and if that bundle is what she thinks it is, she needs to look and make sure there's nothing to be done.

She crouches by the bundle and examines it more closely. It *is* a blanket, tied loosely with rope. Her dread mounts as she holds the light over her head with her left hand and uses her right to pull back the rope and yank back the top corner of the blanket.

Frank Oakley's lifeless face stares up at her.

Dandy stifles a sob as she jerks back, landing on her butt and scrabbling away from the body.

The man was clearly beaten up. He has a busted lip and a black eye, and the hair above his forehead is matted with a thick crust of dried blood. From the greenish-grey colour of his skin, she guesses that decomposition is underway. Worst of all are his eyes, which are stretched wide with horror.

"Pardon my French, Grandy," she says, "but shit, shit, shit."

She pulls herself together. If being stuck in a well with a dead guy wrapped in a blanket is her fate, hysterics won't help. She knows she doesn't really need to check—Oakley is as dead as a doornail—but she forces herself to kneel and press two fingers to his neck. There is no pulse, just cold, leathery flesh.

"I'm sorry, Doc," she says as she pulls his eyelids down the way she's seen in the movies. "I'll make sure they come back for you."

She debates leaving Grandy's satchel behind, but she can't bear the thought of it sitting down here alone in this hole. She slings it over her neck and then stands and faces the opening high above.

Stretching her hands over her head, she cracks her knuckles and then jumps up and down in place a few times, getting the blood flowing. Then she steps up onto the ledge, reaches up to grasp a gap in the wall, and begins to climb.

* * *

A half hour later, scratched and bruised, with every muscle in her body aching, Dandy stumbles back through the trees in the general direction of Bellwoods. She's running scared, worried at every step that someone is about to jump out from behind a tree and ambush her. *Somebody* threw her down that well.

Her mind races. Whoever it was also killed Frank Oakley. Why? Did Frank Oakley reveal to the wrong person what Bill Jinx had told him, prompting them to follow him into the forest to kill him and steal the secret? None of it makes sense. There has to be someone else in the mix, but who?

Finally, she crashes through the edge of the woods and comes to a stop in the backyard at Bellwoods. Peter's car isn't there, but she runs up onto the veranda and tries the doorbell anyway, standing with her ear an inch from the glass, hoping to hear footsteps approaching from the back of the house. She shifts to the iron knocker, slamming it heavily four times and then waiting the respectable amount of time before gingerly taking the doorknob and wiggling it, checking to see if it's open.

Of course, it's locked. She knows she should probably keep running, but her mind is stuck on the old-fashioned landline telephone she heard when she first visited Peter. If she can just get to that phone, she can call for help.

The wind is howling down the inlet and slithering through the trees and pinching at the back of her neck as Dandy runs around to the rear of the house. On the back porch, there's a door with a window leading directly into the kitchen. It's locked, but Dandy can see the old-fashioned phone hanging on the wall.

Dandy stares at it and her mind races. There's a working telephone fewer than ten feet away, a dead man at the bottom of the well, and a killer who might be in the vicinity and getting closer to her as she wastes time overthinking it.

There's a garden rake leaning up against a tree. She runs down and grabs it, then returns to the back door and holds the blunt end of the rake in line with the window.

"I'm sorry, Peter," she mutters, before ramming the rake handle through the window.

It breaks more easily than she expected, a hail of shattered glass clattering into the kitchen. Carefully, so she doesn't cut herself, she reaches through and undoes the deadbolt, letting herself into the kitchen. Dandy has wanted to see the inside of Bellwoods since she was a little kid, but she never expected it would finally happen by breaking and entering.

She half expects the phone to be dead, the line cut by whoever has brought her to this desperate moment, but a monotonous hum greets her when she picks up the receiver. There's a phone book hanging by a hook on the wall next to the telephone, and she picks it up and quickly leafs through to the Maple Bay listings, silently grateful for old people and their archaic ways. She finds the number for the bookstore and dials.

It rings three times before she hears a click. "Word of Mouth," a woman says.

"Um, hello? Is Peter there?"

"No," the woman responds, and she sounds irritated. "Peter didn't show up for his shift today and he isn't answering his phone."

Dandy's heart skips a beat. "Do you know where he is?"

"All I know is that he's not here," she says. "And I'm not at the massage session I had booked. I would offer to take a message, but I'm annoyed at the little prick, to be honest."

"Listen," says Dandy, speaking quickly. "If he shows up, tell him Dandy Feltzen told him to stay there. Tell him it's not safe for him to come home. Not yet."

"Wait, what?" the woman asks.

"I have to go," says Dandy. "I have to call the police."

She begins to say something else, but Dandy hangs up before she has the chance. She lets up the cradle again, prepared to dial 911, when something catches her attention. She stands still and then she hears it again, a noise from somewhere else in the house. She pauses, listening carefully, and then it comes again, a banging sound.

Clank. Clank. Clank.

Pause.

Clank. Clank. Clank.

Carefully, Dandy hangs up the phone. She moves through the kitchen and steps into a darkened hallway. At the other end of the hallway, she can see the elaborate staircase, its carved expanse impressive even in the gloom. To her immediate right is a closed door. From somewhere behind it, the noise comes again.

Clank. Clank. Clank.

She stops at a closed door, remembering the first time she came to see Peter. There was a strange noise then as well. He mentioned that the furnace was acting up, and she's pretty sure he disappeared into this door to deal with it. Is that what she's hearing? A finicky furnace?

The noise comes again, this time much quicker, almost urgent. It sounds deliberate. Like someone is trying to get her attention.

clankclankclank

clankclankclank

clankclankclank

She turns the knob, and the door opens inward, revealing a rough wooden staircase. She gropes inside and finds a light switch, and when she flips it, a dim light illuminates the stairs and the narrow hallway below.

She pauses on the threshold. She knows she should go back and call the police right now, that she should find somewhere safe to hide and wait for them to arrive.

But something, either a hunch or a throbbing curiosity, overrides her concerns, and she finds herself stepping through the door and down the rickety wooden steps.

Bare lightbulbs dangle at intervals along the length of the corridor. The floor is gravel, and the walls are dusty, dirty brick. Many decades' worth of random detritus—bits and pieces of broken furniture, empty paint cans, cardboard boxes—are piled up against the wall, making the passage narrow in spots.

As she makes her way along the hallway, she passes a series of rooms, their doors ajar. In the first room she sees a few shelves of ancient, dusty jarred goods, in the next a worktable covered with rusty, outdated tools.

At the end of the hallway, a large wooden door is shut and locked from the outside with a rudimentary wooden bolt, basically a two-by-four and a sleeve. She slides the bolt back and pulls the door open, revealing a furnace room.

She almost laughs. No wonder Peter has been having problems with the furnace. This thing is enormous, a bona fide antique. Pipes come out from all directions, twisting up into the ceiling like a thick cluster of seaweed.

She turns and steps back out of the room, reaching to pull the door closed.

Clank.

This time the sound is faint, almost defeated, but there's no question it's coming from inside the furnace room. She steps back inside. This time she walks around to the back of the furnace, and as she does, every single inch of her body tenses, and her blood chills, and her mouth drops open to scream, although she can't seem to make a sound other than a thin, rasping, hollow yelp, the kind of sound she makes when she's waking from a nightmare.

There's a man in the corner of the room, staring at Dandy with wide, wild eyes.

She wants to run, but she's frozen to the spot, and as she stares in horror, more details come into focus.

The man is tied to a chair. His mouth is covered with duct tape, and both of his eyes are blackened. His hair is matted and greasy, and his clothes look filthy, as if he's been here for a long time.

As she gapes at the sight of the man, he begins to make a sound, a kind of muffled, repetitive moan. It takes her a moment to realize that he's saying something through the duct tape.

"Help."

Dandy snaps out of her daze, her eyes quickly scanning the room until she finds a lightbulb hanging next to a chain on the ceiling. She reaches up to pull the cord and a harsh glow fills the space. Without stopping to think, she hurries to the man and begins untying his arms from the chair.

As soon as his first arm is untied, he reaches up with a shaking, trembling hand and begins to tear the duct tape from his mouth. She winces as it rips away, and tiny dots of blood appear from where the adhesive was clinging to the skin, but he doesn't seem to notice. He sucks in giant breaths of air, almost gasping, and tosses the duct tape gag to the floor as she finishes untying his second arm.

"Thank you," he rasps, once he's finally caught his breath.

"What is going on?" she asks. "Who are you?"

His second arm free, he reaches up with both hands and grabs at his face, rubbing his palms against his cheeks, almost as if he's trying to convince himself that he's actually here.

"My name is Peter Barnett," he says. "Mirabel Bellwood was my grandmother."

Blood rushes into Dandy's head, her mind spinning and racing as she takes this in. She doesn't understand. This doesn't make any sense.

"Please," he says. "Untie my legs and I'll explain."

She steps back. "You're not Peter," she says. "I know Peter. He lives here. Mirabel was *his* grandmother."

"That's not Peter," he says, and despite how weak he is, the bitterness in his voice is obvious.

"Who is he, then?" she asks, becoming more frantic with every moment. She becomes aware of a shift in the air. The man's eyes have widened, and he's staring past her now, clearly frightened.

Dandy turns slowly and sees that the man she's known as Peter is standing behind her. He is sweaty and disheveled, and she realizes with horror that his clothes are stained with blood. In his hands, he's holding a hatchet.

"How are you doing, Dandy?" he says with a demonic grin. "I suppose it's about time I introduce myself for real. I'm Ricky. Peter's old roommate."

And then he lunges.

WAIT, YOU'RE WHO?

The thing is, I did go to see my uncle and aunt.

It was Ricky's idea from the start, and if he hadn't given me the nudge, I never would have done it. A bit later, of course, I came to realize that it was all part of his agenda, but even now, even after everything I know about how and why he pulled it all off, I don't regret it. Obviously I wish that it had been under different circumstances, that I'd made that decision on my own, that there hadn't been any fallout, but in the end I got a lot of closure out of that one last trip to Barton.

So I guess I owe the miserable prick that much.

I didn't tell Bryce and Carol I was coming. I just landed on their doorstep, and from the minute I sat at their kitchen table, I wasted no time.

It was like a cork had been pulled out of me. I railed and I screamed, I ranted and I raved. I was angrier, at least on the surface, than I'd ever been. My uncle just sat and took it, pounding beer after beer, waiting for it to be over, accepting his punishment but refusing to the very end to give me the satisfaction of tossing me even one tiny morsel of regret.

My aunt Carol, to her faint credit, shed a lot of tears. After I wore myself out, and Bryce slunk off to bed, she explained that he was a gambler, and by the time I landed on their doorstep, they were in debt up to their eyeballs. Bad debt. The money Mirabel sent them dug them out of a hole that he just kept digging.

"It started early, Peter," she says. "And once it started, it was impossible to stop. I never could look you in the eye because of it. I just couldn't do it. I couldn't be a mother to someone I was stealing from."

It wasn't an excuse, but it was an explanation, and after that there wasn't much left I wanted to talk about. I told her I was going to bed, but she asked me to wait while she retrieved something from another room. It was a letter she'd found on my mother's bedside table after she died. Addressed to Mirabel, sealed and stamped. Ready to be dropped in a mailbox at the first opportunity.

"I wanted to give it to you so many times," Carol said, unable to meet my eyes. "But I worried. I worried about what it might say. What that might mean."

I knew what she meant. There was no point saying anything. I'd already said everything I needed to. I tucked the letter inside the book I was reading. I would share it with Mirabel. We would open it together.

I was gone before they woke up in the morning. I left Barton with peace in my soul.

Ricky was right, I thought as my flight touched down in Nova Scotia. *This is the best thing I have ever done for myself.*

The tie was cut, and for the first time in my life I had some answers.

The plane ticket Mirabel bought for me was dated for a week away, so I spent that time just aimlessly wandering. I'd already quit my job and left my apartment, so I rented a car and drove for a few days, sleeping in parking lots and riding out the clock. This was the flat, whimpering end of everything that came before.

By the time I drove my rental car into the charming little town of Maple Bay, I had put the first half of my life behind me. I was ready to begin the second.

He got me as I walked into Bellwoods for the very first time. There was a note on the door telling me to let myself in, so I did. I stood for a moment in the threshold, taking in the high ceilings, the stately artwork, the magnificent staircase. I heard someone moving up behind me and turned, smiling, expecting to meet my grandmother for the first time. Instead, I came face to face with a man I had never expected to think about again. And then he shoved a Taser into my side.

I woke up in the basement, tied to a chair. Ricky stood over me, grinning. He reached down and yanked the duct tape from my mouth.

"What the hell is going on, Ricky?" I gasped. "Where is my grandmother?"

He gave me a performative frown, pretended to wipe a tear from his eye. "I'm sorry, buddy, I had planned to keep her around long enough to meet you, but things got complicated."

I could feel my heart quicken with fright. "What are you talking about?"

"The old lady is dead, my man. I went to her funeral yesterday. Or I should say, *you* went to her funeral. It's confusing, I know, but these are confusing times, am I right?"

"How did she die, Ricky?" I asked, working to stay calm even though every cell in my body was screaming.

"You saw that staircase, right? A little old lady like that should have been more careful." He grinned sheepishly. "Although I have to admit, I might have helped matters along a little bit. Thing is, I'd *intended* to keep her alive, at least long enough for the two of you to meet. But then she started opening up about her family secrets, and I let myself get greedy, and, well . . . bottom line is, she's dead."

He shrugged then, a big, exaggerated gesture like a circus clown, before reaching out to tighten the bind around my wrists. I stared at him in horror, wondering how I'd missed his true nature.

Or had I?

From the moment I first met Ricky, after answering his online ad for the spare room in his apartment, he'd unsettled me. He was friendly and laid-back on the surface, but there was a cold intensity in his gaze that had made it difficult to look him in the eye and left me with an uneasy feeling in my gut. I was desperate for a place to live, so I ignored it, but even after I moved in, the uneasiness lingered.

Ricky kept a very strange schedule, coming and going at all hours of the night, sometimes disappearing for stretches of a week or more at a time, returning with no explanation. He rarely referred to a personal life, and then only in vague, throwaway terms. In six months living together, he never brought a single person back to the apartment, and I came to suspect that his only acquaintances were the people he connected with online.

The truth is, I didn't want to know what he did with his time, or how he made his money, and so I told myself he was just like the rest of us, scraping together a living in a difficult world. How wrong I was.

He gave me some water, and after reapplying the duct tape, he left me there in the dark with the light off. I spent the entire night like that, tied to a chair in that dark, awful basement, listening to mice and rats scurry around me in the deepest, darkest, blackest space I've ever known.

By the time he came back in the morning, I was already broken. He explained that he needed me alive, but only for a while longer. He had somehow managed to seamlessly pass himself off as me, but he needed me to fill in the final pieces. Passwords and bank accounts, that kind of thing. All the little files tucked away in some giant database, proof of identity.

I made a halfhearted attempt to resist him, to refuse to play along, but it was futile. Unlocking my phone was as simple as holding it up to my face and changing a few settings. Suddenly he had unlimited access to all of my secure information. He placed the phone on a table next to the furnace, and as he turned back to face me, his expression prompted a fear in me beyond anything I'd ever felt in my life. His eyes were wide and glistening with exhilaration, a twitching gash of a smile stretched from ear to ear, and as he advanced, raising a fist, I realized I was staring into the face of evil.

For days he toyed with me, a cat playing with a mouse. I wondered when he would grow tired of his game and finish me.

Then he revealed the next phase of his plan.

He came cheerfully marching into the furnace room, holding a small black book.

"This is the biggest piece of the puzzle," he said. "The greatest gift that Mirabel ever gave me. You. Whatever."

He hadn't taken the tape off, so I just raised an eyebrow as he pulled a chair over to sit across from me. "Your grandmother found this last year," he said, waving the book in the air. "When she had her bedroom moved down to the main floor. It was under a loose floorboard beneath the bed, can you believe that?"

He looked at the book with wonder. "It belonged to her father, your great-grandfather, and it was his diary. Or I suppose you could say it's more like his confession. Either way, juicy stuff. But I'll spare you the details. All you need to know is that this book tells us once and for all where the *Obelisk* Treasure is hidden."

Even through the duct tape and black eyes, I must have registered some level of confusion, because Ricky laughed.

"It's one of the most famous hidden treasures in the world," he says. "Pirates! Can you believe that? And it's hidden on Bellwood property. Or at least, land that *used to be* Bellwood property. Doesn't matter, because I'm the only person who knows. Now I just have to find it."

He didn't elaborate on what was in the book, but he began appearing at odd hours, his clothes caked in dirt, and I began to speculate that he had been digging. By this point, he'd extracted everything he could from me, all the passwords and personal details he needed to take over my identity. He'd made it clear I would never leave this basement, and since he had no other reason to keep me alive, I came to understand that he wanted me to be there if and when he found the treasure. He wanted an audience, a witness to his brilliance.

After that, it was a pretty safe guess what he'd do to me.

A couple of times, I heard other people arrive at Bellwoods. I could hear him speaking to unexpected visitors. My chair was chained to a pipe in the corner of the room, and I would do my best to rattle the chain, hoping to draw attention to my presence.

But he'd always appear with the Taser, and knock me out cold. I'd wake up to silence and a raw, aching hunger. If anyone *did* hear me, nobody ever followed up.

I began to despair.

I had been there in that basement for just over a week, tied to my chair, eating when he decided to feed me, shitting in a box when he bothered to untie me, weakening, fading, wondering when the end would come, when the door flew open and Ricky appeared. He wasn't alone. He shoved another man into the room, and the man fell to the floor in a bloodied, battered heap. He was thin and old, and the lens on one of his glasses was smashed. He stared at me, his face wide with fear.

"Who are you?" he asked, his voice thin and ragged.

I couldn't answer through the duct tape, of course. Ricky grabbed the man by the arm and dragged him across the floor before handcuffing him to the furnace.

"Spill, Doc," he snarled.

"I don't know what you're talking about," said the man.

"You know goddamn well what I'm talking about," spat Ricky. "I saw you with Bill Jinx at the funeral. He told you everything he knew. Don't deny it."

"You've got this all wrong," the old man said. "I don't know a thing. I'm just trying to sell the land. That's where the money is, don't you see that? There's no treasure."

"Bullshit," said Ricky. "Smart man like you spends forty years looking for something you don't think exists? You're holding back on me, Oakley."

I tried to close my eyes once the beating started, but I couldn't look away. Finally Ricky exhausted himself and staggered back to sit on the floor, his back against the wall. The old man lay wheezing and crying on the floor. From my chair I stared, mutely.

"Okay, Oakley," said Ricky finally. His voice was placatory, almost kind. "I might have had things all wrong. You swear you don't know where the treasure is buried? Bill Jinx didn't tell you a thing?"

"I swear," Oakley whispered, his voice a ghostly rasp. "Jinx was a maniac. I am trying to orchestrate a development with Margot Feltzen. You could join us; with this house as part of the package, we could make so much money."

Ricky seemed to consider this. "You mean you'll take me on as partner, and we can forget that this unfortunate encounter ever happened?"

"Yes," said Oakley, somehow managing to lift his head from the floor and nod. "Yes. This is just a misunderstanding."

Ricky laughed. "You must think I was born yesterday, Doc."

Long after Ricky had dragged the man's body away, the echo of his screams stayed with me in the basement, the only thing left to keep me company.

I was halfway asleep, drifting between consciousness and sweet oblivion, when I heard the crash of glass from somewhere upstairs. My ears perked up and I strained to listen. Nothing. Silence.

And then . . . was I imagining it, or was someone speaking? Urgent tones? A girl's voice?

I was pretty sure that Ricky was out somewhere, but even if he wasn't, what did I have to lose? I had played with the chain a million times, and I knew that if I tipped sideways in my chair, I could bring it taut, cause it to make a clanking noise.

I moved as deliberately as I was able, working to maximize the noise.

Clank. Clank. Clank.

Clank. Clank. Clank.

Clank. Clank. Clank.

And then, sweet miracle, she was there. Untying my arms.

"Thank you," I said, after I'd ripped off the duct tape and taken in some deep, full breaths.

"What is going on?" she asked. "Who are you?"

"My name is Peter," I said. "Mirabel Bellwood was my grandmother."

She just stood there, shocked, shaking her head at me.

"Please," I implored. "Please untie my legs and I'll explain."

"You're not Peter," she said. "I know Peter. He lives here. Mirabel was *his* grandmother."

"That's not Peter," I say, my voice dripping with contempt.

"Who is he, then?" the girl asked.

But my heart seemed to shrink in on itself, because Ricky was suddenly standing there in the doorway. I was used to the wild, manic expression on Ricky's face, but today it had morphed into something even more terrifying. His expression was so awful, as if the devil himself had entered the room, that it took me a moment to notice his bloodstained clothes.

It appeared that he knew the girl. "How are you doing, Dandy?" he said. "I suppose it's about time I introduce myself for real. I'm Ricky. Peter's roommate."

He jumped at her, but the girl was quick, and before I knew what she was doing, she'd stepped out from behind the chair and charged at him. He was clearly not expecting this, his eyes widening with surprise as she ducked and threw herself headfirst at his waist, knocking him into the furnace with a loud thud. Then she was out the door and racing down the hallway, and Ricky was chasing her, and I heard their footsteps charging up the rickety wooden steps, and then I was alone once again in this awful space.

OVERBOARD

Cass tries to tell herself that this is just a coincidence, that there must be red notebooks just like this one for sale in every bookshop and drugstore and airport in North America. But as she stands and stares at it, the details come into focus—the coil along the top, the elastic bands, the grimy cover—and she knows without a doubt that this is the notebook that Bill Jinx showed her. The same notebook that he said held all of his evidence and research into the location of the *Obelisk* Treasure.

She hears Bryson moving from the front of the boat back to the cockpit, and without giving herself time to think it over, she grabs the notebook and shoves it down the back of her shorts. As she quietly slides the drawer shut, she spots a Swiss Army Knife in a pencil holder on the desk and reaches for it just as a shadow lands on her. She turns to see Bryson standing in the hatch, one hand on each side of the opening, grinning down at her.

"All good?" he asks.

"You bet!" she says brightly. She slides the corkscrew out of the jackknife and holds it up to show him. "Just needed one of these. Here, will you carry these up for me?" She hands him the baguette and cheese, and when he turns away she reaches back to better adjust the notebook within her waistband. Then she grabs the wine and the glasses and climbs up out of the hatch to join him.

He's propped up a little table in front of the wheel. Cass sits down across from him as he begins to unwrap the cheese.

She is intensely aware of her surroundings. Tied to its mooring, the sailboat drifts lazily in the water, occasionally yanking at its tether when a light wave rolls under the boat. Across the water, Bellwoods stares intensely out at the open ocean, as always. Up on the hill the Trapper house gazes serenely across the bay. At the far end of the inlet, Reg Feltzen's little seaside cottage sinks comfortably back into its perch. And closer than all of them, directly across the water, sits Bill Jinx's shack, the shack he stepped out of the night that he died in the rough nighttime waters just off the mouth of this very inlet.

Cass looks back at Bryson and realizes that he's staring right at her, smiling. Her heart is pounding, and her mouth is dry, but she forces herself to return his smile and then busies herself with trying to open the wine. But her hands are shaking, and she can't seem to twist the corkscrew into the cork.

"Holy shit," says Bryson. "You're shivering. You must be freezing."

She's grateful for the excuse. "Yeah, it's cold now that we've stopped moving."

He reaches for the bottle. "Here, I'll open it. Why don't you grab a blanket from down below."

She nods, unable to find a voice to respond. Wordlessly, she hands him the bottle and turns around. As she lifts her leg to step over the entrance to the hatch, she feels her shirt lift up from the waist of her jeans, and even before she turns around and sees the expression on his face, the wine bottle frozen in his hand, corkscrew half into the cork, she knows with every single fibre of her being that Bryson has seen the notebook.

"Listen," he says, "before you jump to conclusions, let me explain."

He stands and holds out a placatory hand. Instinctively, Cass reaches for the closest thing at hand, the canvas tote bag, and throws it at Bryson's face. Caught by surprise, he bats the tote away with one hand as the wine bottle drops from the other. In that instant, she leaps up onto the edge of the boat and scrambles awkwardly over the lifeline. Bryson takes two broad steps in her direction, but before he can reach her, Cass drops awkwardly off the boat.

The water is about a hundred times colder than she expects. The air is slammed out of her as she cannonballs into the inlet, and when she pushes back through the surface, gasping at the cold and sucking desperately for air, it feels like a million needles are scratching at her skin.

"Cass!" Bryson yells from where he is standing in shock at the edge of the boat. "You have everything wrong!"

"Screw you!" she says, and she turns and begins to paddle toward shore. She has never been a strong swimmer, but in this cold water it's a struggle to even move her limbs. But she has no choice, so she digs deep, and somehow begins to awkwardly splash her way toward shore.

"Cass, you've got to listen to me," he continues. "I found that book in the water, I know it sounds crazy, but I did. I was sailing by the mouth of the inlet, and I saw it bobbing there so I scooped it up. I was going to show it to you today."

He stops talking, and a moment later something splashes into the water in front of her. She gasps, inadvertently sucking in some water. Coughing and spluttering, she tries to catch her breath while remaining afloat.

"Grab it," he yells. "You are going to catch hypothermia."

She can see now that he's thrown a life ring into the water. It bobs just a few feet away from her, a splash of red. She ignores it.

"Come on, Cass!" Bryson yells. "You're acting crazy."

Her blood is pumping now, and her body is adapting to the chill of the water. She realizes with a rush of exhilaration that the shore is actually getting closer. She's making headway.

"I heard you on your phone," she manages to call over her shoulder.

"That was a work call!" he yells. "It's—it's a long story. I swear, Cass. You don't need to be afraid of me!"

She ignores him and fixes her focus on the approaching beach. She might actually pull this off.

She hears another noise behind her and risks a glance over her shoulder. Bryson has climbed down off the sailboat and is stepping into the little rowboat.

"It's not that sinister, Cass!" he pleads. "I promise! I've been doing work for those people you mentioned, the people who are trying to build the development out here, just some coastal surveying and taking photos and stuff. That's why I'm in town! They were super adamant that I keep it all hush-hush, so I didn't mention it to you. But then you started talking about that girl's suspicions, and I called the woman to tell her I don't want to be caught up in any shady business. Her name is Margot Feltzen. She's a real estate agent, you can look her up!"

The rowboat is untied now, and Cass can hear the paddles slapping into the water as he begins to row after her.

Her toe kicks the ground.

Stepping awkwardly, she trudges out of the water and staggers onto the beach, dropping to her knees. Half crying, half laughing, she leans backward and opens her lungs to the fresh, beautiful, dry air. She knows she should get up and run, but she finds herself reaching into her waistband and pulling out the journal.

It's soaked, but when she rips off the rubber bands and opens it, she sees that Bill used a pencil, which means all of the text is still legible.

She flips through the pages, scanning one dated entry after another.

May 19: *Digging. Nothing yet.*

June 7: *Digging. Nothing yet.*

August 22: *Digging. Nothing yet.*

Day after day of the same damn thing. He was a man obsessed.

Cass stands and turns around. The rowboat has covered half the distance between the boat and the shore, and it's moving quickly.

"Come on, Cass," says Bryson. "Do you really think I would kill an old man in cold blood? Do you think I would do that to anyone?"

"I don't know," she calls back to him, and she realizes as the words come out of her mouth that it's true. She doesn't know this guy at all. He might as well be a total stranger.

Maybe he's telling the truth, but right now, alone on this beach, just a few yards from the sad little cottage Bill Jinx lived in, and a few yards from the water he died in, she's not willing to stick around and find out.

She turns and begins to run.

Bryson yells after her but she doesn't even bother to listen. She dashes across the beach and scrambles up the embankment onto the road. To her right is the long driveway up to the Trappers' house. To her left, Bellwoods peeks through the colourful screen of maple trees.

She looks back again and sees that Bryson has hit the beach. He's climbing out of the rowboat and dragging it out of the water.

There's no way she can run up that hill before he catches her. Bellwoods it is.

She begins to sprint in the direction of the mansion, and as she turns into the driveway, heading for the veranda, a noise splits the air.

The bell in the tower is ringing.

THROWING ROCKS

My father was the first person I killed.

When I was a boy, he used to play this game with me. I'd hear him yell, "Ricky!" and I'd jump up from the couch or run out from my bedroom and find him standing in the kitchen with a wild-eyed, shit-eating grin spreading across his face. "Let's go throw rocks," he'd say, already turning on his heel, and I'd follow him through the screen door and out into the backyard, just a postage-stamp scrap of patchy earth and thin grass, weeds pressed up against the chain-link fence that separated us from the rail cut.

He'd kick into the ground with his heel to scrabble up some gravel, then he'd hand me a little bit and take some for himself, and as the train came slicing by, we'd hurl that shit over the fence, screaming like banshees when it hit the side, and laughing like crazy at the shocked faces of the passengers who happened to catch for a split second a glimpse of what we were up to.

I'm telling you the god's honest truth, that's the only quality time my father ever spent with me, and as I stood over his La-Z-Boy, holding a pillow against his face, it was the first thing that came to mind.

"Doesn't take two men to throw rocks at the train, Dad," I told him as he squirmed beneath the pillow. It was barely a struggle. He was a mess of cancer to begin with, and by that time of day he'd been drinking Canadian Club straight from the bottle for hours. Nobody was going to suspect anything, and by the time someone thought to check in on him, he was likely to be well past the expiry date.

I'd made a special trip back to the old trailer just for this. A cousin had managed to track me down through an old email address and passed along the news that my old man was on his way out. I didn't answer her, of course. Didn't want anyone to think I cared or had enough respect for the useless fucker to express anything like disappointment. But I did get on a plane the next morning.

I could have saved myself the money and effort, let nature take its course. But I wanted him to see me. I wanted the son of a bitch to know *I* was responsible for his departure from this mortal coil.

So I did it, and then I walked out the door and didn't look back.

My mother had been dead for years by that point. My older brother had left home before I did, and last I heard he's a meth head and I doubt he even remembers that I exist. Even if he does, I can promise you he isn't about to take a seaside vacation to the East Coast and accidentally bump into me on the boardwalk. That stupid asshole might as well be on Mars.

I'm going to swear this to you right here. I did not plan for things to go this far.

The idea came to me like a lightning bolt that first night when Peter was playing sharesies, letting me read the letter from Mirabel and unloading his feelings on me like a pile of warm baby puke. It isn't every day that you're faced with an opportunity for genuine, dyed-in-the-wool reinvention, but as Peter yammered on and on about his mommy issues, I realized that's exactly what this was. Opportunity. A wealthy grandmother who he'd never met? A big old mansion and all the loot that was sure to be in it? A sad recluse desperate to break ties with his old life? The chance was right there for me to grab. I didn't need a written invitation.

Although, when you get right down to it, I guess I did. Thanks for taking the time to send it, Mirabel.

I convinced Peter he had to go to see his family, leaving me with just enough time to get there and handle things before he arrived. I hacked into his email and carried out an exchange with his grandmother, easily convincing her to send him a plane ticket so I could control the dates and give myself some time.

So at first it was supposed to be just a simple con game. I was working with a week. I intended to show up, play the missing grandson for a few days, squeeze what I could out of the old broad, and then get the hell out of Dodge before the real Peter showed up to help her pick up the pieces. I've got some friends in low places, and I know how to go to ground. I figured granny and grandbaby might kick up a bit of a fuss, maybe call the local police, but by then I'd be hiding out in someone's basement someplace far away where nobody gives a shit about the East Coast, let alone some rich old lady's missing silverware. It was a risk, but in a house that impressive there was bound to be plenty worth stealing, and I had a few tricks up my sleeve.

It turned out to be easier than I ever would have imagined. The old lady bought it, hook, line, and sinker. And if I'd kept my expectations modest, if I'd stuck to the plan, things would have turned out differently. But once I was inside, once I was sleeping in a big, comfortable bed in that big, beautiful house, and seeing how freely Mirabel spent money—on food, on clothes, on upkeep—it became clear to me that there was a lot more for the taking if I was willing to stay a bit longer and work a bit harder.

There was one huge complication, to put it lightly. Peter would be here in just a few days, but I couldn't leave now, not when there was so much money in the bank just itching to be free. But how could I stay when his arrival was imminent?

My mind raced and a new plan emerged. It had been so easy to fool the old lady, hadn't it? She hadn't so much as blinked an eye. Now it was clear that I needed to go the extra mile. I would intercept Peter and deal with him, one way or another. I would get him out of the way and take his place for a while longer.

The job interview was supposed to be my first big step, my opportunity to prove I was serious about staying in Maple Bay, and that I was financially cautious, determined not to take advantage of her. In other words, it was another way to get Mirabel to let down her guard around me. *Oh, Grandma, you're clearly so wise with money. I need to think about how to invest my new income wisely. How do you manage your family accounts?*

What better way to become part of the town than to place myself front and centre, get to know people who would gradually spread the word about Mirabel's lovely, friendly, harmless grandson? I figured I could get her to trust me within a couple of months, after which I'd clean her out and hit the road.

Then Mirabel dropped an ace on the table and changed the game.

A missing treasure. It sounded so crazy that at first I thought the old lady was losing her marbles, getting lost in some fantasy land she'd created after her family all disappeared. But the story she told was convincing. She belonged to an honest-to-shit secret society devoted to unearthing the treasure. She believed her family was somehow involved in the treasure's discovery and disappearance.

Most compelling of all, she had evidence.

A journal, hidden beneath a loose floorboard in her father's bedroom. His detailed account—a confession, really—of what had happened all those years ago, and crucially . . .

"He even explains where the treasure is," she told me, holding the book up and grasping it tight. "Well, in a manner of speaking. He wasn't exactly *specific* about it, but he points in the right direction." She kept talking, but I tuned everything else out. If I'd been clear-headed, on top of my game, I would have paid attention to the story. To the parts involving Mirabel herself. Her family. Her daughter.

Peter.

But I'm sorry, I didn't have time for that touchy-feely bullshit. I was distracted.

He even explains where the treasure is.

I was in a daze as she finished her story, still trying to absorb it as she followed me to the landing with the book in hand. She touched my arm.

"It's a huge relief to my old bones that I have someone to confide in. There are things in this journal that change everything, things I can only trust with family."

"I understand," I said. "There's no way I'd ever consider sharing any of what you just told me."

"Good," she said. "Now go knock 'em dead."

I began to turn away and then paused.

"We'll find that treasure," I said. "You can count on it."

Looking back on the moment now, I wonder what it was that made me slip. Was I so dazzled by the story of the treasure that I got careless, allowing the greed behind my plan to shine through? Whatever the case, her expression changed.

"Did you hear anything I just told you?" she asked me. She was gripping the little black journal and now she rapped on the cover once, like a schoolmarm. "Don't you realize the importance of what's written here? What this means to this family? What this means to *you*? Is the money all you can think about?"

"No!" I said, hastily. "Not at all! I just . . . I think it would be such an adventure to solve this mystery together."

I was too late. Something had been revealed to her. I saw the shift in her eyes as something dawned on her. It was instantaneous, like someone flipping a switch.

"You know," she said, leaning forward ever so slightly to stare at me with narrowed, newly suspicious eyes. "I've been looking for Susan in you—a flash, even a glimpse—but I haven't been able to find her. I wanted so badly for this to be true, but I've been a fool, haven't I? Who are you? Who are you really?"

I had no choice. The jig was up. I kicked out with my leg and hit her right below the knees from the front, and as she threw out her hands to catch her balance, I quickly stepped around to give a light push, just a tap, and then she was out over the top of the staircase.

There was a broken moment when her tumbling, twisting body froze in mid-air and her eyes, wide and frightened and full of awful understanding, caught mine. I grinned at her, and sometimes when I'm feeling bad about what I did, I like to tell myself that at least the last thing she saw was a smile.

* * *

I hadn't killed anyone since my father, and that had been as easy as it gets. This time I had some hoops to jump through, and that's putting it lightly. If I'd had time to figure things out, to make a proper plan, I would have kept her alive a lot longer, at *least* a few months. I would have figured out how to deal with Peter properly, take over his identity and establish myself in the community, and leave no room for anyone to question who I was and where I'd come from. But the old lady left me no choice. Once she'd figured me out, all bets were off.

After the deed was done, I panicked. I even considered getting the fuck out of town before the heat landed on me. But I decided to throw myself into it, because whatever the risk—and it was a big frigging risk—it was dwarfed by the reward. A big, beautiful house. Bank accounts fat with the spoils of strategic, generational investments. *A motherfucking pirate treasure?*

Come. On.

This was the big time. Showtime. Time to dance like my life depended on it and convince the fine folks of Maple Bay that I was the true and rightful heir to the Bellwood fortune.

I expected some pushback, but, to my great surprise, the opposite happened. My alibi wasn't perfect, but it tracked. People came out in droves to pass on their sincere and enthusiastic condolences. Maple Bay didn't have time to be suspicious; they were too busy being nosy. Mirabel's long-lost grandson was more than enough to keep the gossip mill churning, especially since everyone knew the story about her pregnant daughter cutting ties and disappearing with her sketchy new husband all those years ago.

People liked the thought of Mirabel dying *after* being reunited with her long-lost grandson. It softened the blow. So instead of narrowed eyes or whispered insinuations, I got hugs and casseroles and offers to set me up with nephews and grandsons. I hadn't planned on cosplaying as a gay man, but that wasn't difficult. I just played hard to get.

The biggest challenge, of course, was yet to come. It was one thing to impersonate Peter when he was on the other side of the country and a stranger in Maple Bay, but his arrival was imminent and there wasn't room for the two of us in Bellwoods. I'd stayed on top of his travel arrangements, using Mirabel's laptop and email address, so I knew exactly when to expect him. From there it was just a matter of waiting, watching, and whacking him over the head the moment he stepped through the front door.

After that, I had a choice to make: I could kill him on the spot and bury him somewhere on the property, or I could keep him alive for a while and give him a chance to see things play out, show him just how close he'd come to stepping into the beautiful life. And let's be real here, one of those options sounded a lot more fun than the other.

It turned out that keeping Peter around had practical advantages as well. It was laughably easy to unlock his phone and get at his passwords. From there, I was able to cancel his social media accounts, sparse as they were, and take over his banking. Best of all, the stupid fucker had taken all of his worldly possessions with him, including his birth certificate and social insurance card. With those two documents, I was able to apply for a driver's license, which meant I had a government-issued photo ID "proving" my identity. I *was* Peter Bellwood Barnett. Or one of them, anyway. The one who was still living his best life, as opposed to the one tied up in the basement, waiting to be disposed of.

It felt like I'd covered all my bases. Then Cass told me that Bill Jinx was hot on the heels of the treasure, that he *knew* something, and I figured I'd have to deal with him one way or another. But before I had the chance to think it over, the old fool made it easy on me, showed up on my doorstep that very same night, stone-cold drunk and ranting and raving about something he'd discovered. I'm no alpha gym rat, but it wasn't hard to overpower an inebriated ninety-year-old and throw him into the drink. Problem solved.

And it would have been, if Dandy Feltzen hadn't shown up like some weird Gen Z Nancy Drew, asking questions and chasing down hunches. I tried my best to get her off the case—I'm no monster, I don't *want* to go around attacking kids—but she left me with no choice, and to be honest I was feeling pretty good about myself after I threw her down that well. I had it all worked out. A teenage girl obsessed with the treasure. An old man with a questionable internet history (thanks to cheap locks, weak passwords, and me). How hard would it have been to convince the world that Oakley had taken Dandy on some inappropriate adventure?

I'd made sure that Dandy hadn't told anyone about me, and I knew she'd been poking around asking questions about Oakley. I also had a letter of confession, printed on his own computer and signed (under coercion) by Oakley himself, telling about how he'd taken a shine to the young detective, and one thing had led to another . . .

I was sure she was dead. By rights, a headfirst fall from that height onto rocks should have taken out anyone. I'd even heard a loud, dull crack as she landed, and assumed her head had smashed into a rock. So I walked out of that forest feeling pretty solid about my prospects. I knew people would believe Oakley had left town with her, and they'd find the letter when they searched his house. The last big roadblock was out of my way.

Then Bonnie called, and I learned that I should have been suspicious of her from the very beginning. Mirabel, the stupid woman, had filled Bonnie in on everything. Her father's journal. The treasure hidden in the woods. The long-lost grandson.

"I wasn't going to make an issue of it," Bonnie said, standing smugly in front of her little chart with her little pins. "I was going to leave you to it, let you follow your own trail. If Mirabel didn't have the grace to tell me I was being cut out of the investigation, I didn't feel obligated to share my thoughts or research. But then you came to see me at the library that day, and something about you didn't sit right with me. The way you were asking me questions, all eager, as if Mirabel hadn't said a thing to you about the treasure."

"But she did," I told her. "She told me everything."

Bonnie shrugged. "So that part of my hunch was wrong, but I didn't know that, so I did a bit of digging."

"What do you mean?" I asked her, but I could already tell where this was going.

"You aren't Peter Bellwood Barnett," she said. "I don't know who you are, but you aren't Peter."

She had evidence. Yearbook photos. Letters from old school-mates. The woman had done her research, I had to hand it to her. There was enough material there to damn me to hell and back. She could have called the whole thing a day, called the cops and had me locked up by lunchtime, but she didn't, and at the end of the day it was simple.

The bitch got greedy.

316

Bonnie wanted a piece of the action, and she thought that I'd be willing to join forces with her. Poor naive Bonnie. *As if* I'd ever let someone wander the streets with a secret I'd worked so hard to keep under wraps. A secret like this? She'd have been able to dangle it over me for the rest of my life.

Not a chance.

I arrive home from Bonnie's house shaken up, my mind racing. As I walk up the steps and through the front door, I'm trying to figure out how much time I have before someone notices that she's missing and all hell breaks loose. I wonder if there's some way to tie Bonnie's disappearance to Oakley and Dandy.

Maybe, but if anyone is even halfway suspicious, there will be questions, and if there are questions, they'll be bound to investigate her house, and even if I scour the place thoroughly (and honestly, who has the time?), it would be a losing battle.

There was just so much blood . . .

No, I'm going to have to somehow fake a break and enter. Bonnie made it clear that nobody knew she and Mirabel were close, so the chances of anyone drawing a connection to me are slim. The Jaguar could be an issue, but I parked behind her house, and I didn't pass anyone on her road when I left. No, I think that I've got a pretty good—

I freeze. From somewhere deep in the house, I hear something. The murmur of voices.

I turn back to the front door and lock the deadbolt. Moving as quietly as I can, I move to the basement door and descend the stairs.

It was stupid of me to think that the girl would go down easy. She was like a cockroach or a zombie, impossible to get rid of, returning again and again. As I enter the furnace room and find her with Peter, I realize that the jig is up. Forget the treasure, the best I can hope for now is to disappear before the cops come looking for me. If I want to manage that, I have to take care of these last two obstacles.

Peter isn't an issue. I've barely fed or watered the guy since I first tied him up. He's still tied to the chair, barely hanging on. I can come back and finish him off later; for now, Dandy is my focus. But the tricky little gremlin isn't about to go down without a fight.

I lunge for her, and the little bitch ducks and slams into my gut, throwing me against the furnace and slipping past me before I have time to figure out what happened. I pull myself up and go after her, stumbling up the stairs two at a time, snatching desperately at her heels. I make it to the main floor and round the corner just as she makes it to the front door.

She yanks at the doorknob, realizing too late that the door is locked, and as she fumbles for the deadbolt, I cover the ground between us. *This is it*, I think, leaping for a tackle, but somehow she manages a slide and a feint and then she's slipped past me, and she's running in the opposite direction, across the foyer and up the magnificent staircase.

"Good luck with that," I scream after her. "You've trapped yourself now!"

I'm panting, the exertion of the day catching up to me. But the insufferable girl barrels up the staircase without breaking a sweat. I go after her, huffing and puffing as I reach the top just in time to see her bounding up the next set of stairs. Cursing under my breath, I follow, reaching the top floor just in time to see her disappear through the doorway to the tower.

At the bottom of this final, narrow staircase, I stop to catch my breath. I can see her staring down at me through the hatch.

"You're a moron," I call up to her. "You've cornered yourself."

In response, she flips the hatch door shut. A moment later, a loud, resonant clanging comes down at me from up above. She's ringing the bell.

I scramble up the steps and flip the hatch open with ease. As I climb out onto the small open deck of the bell tower, I narrowly miss being hit in the head by the bell, which is swinging wildly back and forth. On the other side of the tower, Dandy reaches out and shoves it as it comes back to her, like someone pushing a little kid on a swing.

As it returns to me, I grab it by the rim, stopping it dead. The clanging escapes down into the inlet, a fading echo that finally disappears, leaving only the sound of the wind behind.

I let the bell drop gently back into place. She stares across at me, her expression a mixture of anger and confusion and resolve.

"Why did you do all this?" she asks.

"Listen, kid," I say. "It's a long story, but I think you can figure out the gist of it."

"The treasure," she says. "Mirabel told you where the treasure is hidden, so you killed her."

"More or less," I say. There's no point pretending now. She's seen what I'm capable of. She knows who I am.

"It was you digging in the woods?" she asks. "Not Bill or Oakley?"

"Bingo!" I smile. "I'll tell you this: when I finally find that treasure, I am never looking at a garden tool again for as long as I live."

"You're not going to find the treasure," she says. "Not now that you've been caught."

I point at her, as if she's hit the nail on the head. "Fair enough," I say. "At this point I'll be happy to get out of town intact. But that's life. Nothing ventured, nothing gained. But I can promise you this, Dandy. You're not going to find that treasure, either."

I take my chance, faking right, then darting left around the bell, snatching at her as she reacts. But she's too quick for me, and manages to slip around to the other side so that we've only changed places. I see her glance down the hatch at her feet and I silently urge her to try it. I know the moment she crouches to climb down is the moment I need to get at her. One hard shove from above is bound to do some serious damage.

She must make the same calculation I do. She steps away from the hatch.

"Why are you covered in blood?" she asks.

I look down at my shirt and mime shock. "Oh my goodness," I say. "I didn't even notice!"

I laugh and she looks suitably horrified.

"You're a psychopath," she says.

I'm getting irritated with this pointless exchange. "You don't need to worry about the blood," I say. "It'll be the last thing on your mind any moment now." I stop and scratch my chin. "When you think about it like that, it might actually *be* the last thing on your mind."

Without warning, I leap around the bell. This time she isn't as prepared and reacts more slowly, and I'm almost able to grab her shoulder, but she drops away from me and rolls underneath the bell, springing back to her feet on the other side.

"You're slippery," I say.

"Just tell me this," she says. "Did you kill Bill Jinx?"

"I did." I shrug. What's the point in lying? It can't hurt to give the kid detective one final revelation before she meets her maker. "I was worried about what he knew. I couldn't take the risk of him getting to the treasure ahead of me. He'd already said more than he should have to Cass, and I figured it was only a matter of time before he blabbed the whole story. I planned to pay him a visit, but he showed up here before I even had the chance. He was drunk as a skunk and screaming nonsense."

Dandy glares at me, shaking her head in disbelief. "And you killed him."

"Hey!" I say with a laugh. "I invited him in for a drink first. That's got to count for something, right? I tried to make nice. Tried to get him to spill the beans. But he was only interested in airing grievances. So I knocked him out, dragged him to his rowboat, and shoved him into the inlet. I knew good old Mother Nature would take care of the rest."

"You're a monster," says Dandy.

"I'm a realist," I say.

She looks thoughtful. "What about the red notebook?" she asks me.

I shake my head. "I thought maybe Frank Oakley had taken it, but he swore up and down that he had no idea what Bill knew. By that time, the guy would have told me anything to be set free—not that I would have, after everything he knew about me—but I have to say I believed him. No, I think Bill must have had that notebook on him when he died, and the great god Neptune has it now."

As I've been talking, I've noticed Dandy let her guard down, just a little bit at a time. She's still staring at me, but I can tell that she's mulling something over in her head, somehow preoccupied. If I'm ever going to catch her off guard, it's now.

"Holy shit!" I say, pointing past her.

She begins to turn her head, distracted for just a fraction of a moment before realizing what I've done, but it's enough. I take her lead from earlier and duck underneath the bell, barrelling into her with full force, pinning her legs to the balcony railing. She yells in pain and tries to pull away from me, but I'm not about to let go now. I grab her sides and pull myself to standing.

I have her pressed against the railing, my hands firmly gripping her shoulders. She struggles, but I've got full control.

Over her shoulder, I look down at the ground, which appears a hundred feet away. It's going to make a rough drop for the poor kid, but that's show business.

"What the hell?"

Instinctively, I turn at the sound of the voice. I only have a split second to realize that Cass is staring at us from the hatch, shocked, because Dandy shifts, slipping out of my grasp and dropping without warning to her knees.

"I'm nothing if I'm not nimble," I hear her say as she propels herself forward, grasping my legs and pulling backward. I scramble to grab onto something, anything, but the railing is low and the momentum of Dandy's movement flips me upside down and over the edge, and then the world is spinning, a kaleidoscope of water and air, the distant silhouette of a town I could have called home, and then I'm coming face to face with the ground, a piece of gravel hitting the side of a train.

THE FRONT DOOR

Dandy climbs the steps slowly, hesitating at the front door before ringing the bell. It's hard to believe that it's only been a week since the wild showdown at Bellwoods. Now she's returned to the old house under completely different circumstances.

The man who opens the door is also different, a different Peter, the *real* Peter, smiling as he invites her in, stepping aside as she crosses the threshold.

She's been inside Bellwoods before, just the once, but again that was different. Now as she enters the grand foyer, she's able to take some time to examine the space. She vaguely remembers the furniture and paintings, and she certainly remembers running up the giant staircase, two at a time, trying to get away from Ricky. She crosses to it and takes a closer look, running a hand over the carved wooden expanse, letting a finger drift along an elegant carved branch and down a curve to where it connects with a limb.

"It's already getting dusty," says Peter, reminding her she's not alone. She turns to him and he smiles. "Apparently Mirabel hired someone to come in to clean and polish it every month. I've still got a lot to learn about this place."

He looks good, much better than when she first met him, tied up to a chair in the basement. The wounds on his face are almost healed, and his skin looks healthier, fuller. He's been eating, she supposes.

They stand there for a moment, smiling uncertainly at each other, and then he claps his hands to break the awkwardness. "How about I make us some tea?"

In the kitchen, they sit in a windowed nook and talk.

"I'm glad to have the chance to thank you," he says.

"You don't need to thank me," she says with a shrug. "I was just in the right place at the right time."

"No," he says firmly, and he holds her gaze. "I'm alive because of you, Danielle. If you hadn't started asking questions, I'd be dead by now. Simple as that."

She considers this.

"I never thought about it like that," she says finally. "You're welcome, I guess."

He laughs at this, and a moment later she joins him.

"It's all kind of crazy," she says. "I mean . . . I kind of *killed* someone."

"In self-defence," he says.

"Oh yeah," she says quickly. "It was his fault, obviously. He was trying to kill *me*. It's just, I don't know, it's nuts. I doubt Grandy expected anything like this when he sent me on that mission."

"Tell me about that," says Peter. "Tell me about him."

Dandy is silent for a long moment. Where is she even supposed to begin?

"Well," she says, finally. "He was the best."

She tells Peter everything. About how Grandy left her his satchel and the letter directing her to the historical society, but also about how much time they spent together, how much he taught her, how he stepped in when her father flew the coop, and how tough it was when he got sick and declined so quickly. She explains to him how important he was to her in so many ways, and she barely notices when tears start to roll down her face. She talks for a long time, telling Peter as much as she can think of about Grandy, as much as she can remember.

Finally, she stops. Peter hands her a box of tissues and she wipes her face.

"Sorry," she says.

He looks at her with genuine kindness. "You don't have anything to be sorry about. It sounds like he was an amazing man. I wish I could have met him."

"He would have liked you," she says. "I mean, he liked everyone, so that's a low bar, but still."

"I wish I'd had the chance to have a relationship with Mirabel," he says. "I didn't know any of my grandparents."

"She was a pretty cool lady," says Dandy. "She and Grandy were good friends when they were younger."

"I know they were," says Peter. "I've been going through her papers and I found a few things that explained quite a bit about how everyone fit together. Did you know that my grandmother owned your grandfather's cottage?"

"What?" Dandy is taken aback.

He nods. "She discussed it with her lawyer before she died. When he got sick, your grandfather discovered the truth as he was getting his affairs in order. He approached Mirabel, who also had no idea, and he asked her if he could buy it, but she said no."

Dandy can't think straight. Grandy didn't own his house? The wording of his will comes back to her as clear as day: *everything I rightfully own, I bequeath to my eldest daughter, Margot Feltzen.* But . . . that didn't include the cottage?

Peter goes on. "She told your grandfather that she would *give him* the cottage. But his illness was progressing very quickly, and he worried he wouldn't have time to make the arrangements before he died. So he asked Mirabel if she would give the cottage to you and your mother once he died."

"Are you serious?" Dandy asks.

Peter nods. "She was only too happy to agree."

It's like all the cogs in Dandy's mind make a quarter turn, and everything suddenly snaps into place. *Of course* Grandy wanted them to have the cottage. *Of course* he would have thought leaving everything else to Margot would have been a fair exchange. He would never have wanted to leave *either* of his daughters out in the cold.

She thinks back to the day of Mirabel's funeral, when she overheard Margot on the phone in Grandy's cottage. Margot referenced Grandy's muddled affairs and some missing paperwork. She must have been talking about the deed to the cottage. A deed, as it turns out, that Grandy never owned in the first place.

One big question remains.

"So why didn't Mirabel do it?" she asks. "Grandy died almost three months before she did. Did she just decide she wanted to keep it?"

"No," he says. "She had every intention of signing over that property. But then she learned that there was more to the story, and she decided to wait for me to arrive. She sent me that letter asking me to come to Maple Bay so she could discuss things with her last remaining family, and decide how best to proceed. You see, it turns out there was a lot more to be arranged than just the cottage."

Dandy remembers her one and only visit to the historical society, when Mirabel asked Dandy to come visit her at Bellwoods. *There's someone I'd like you to meet, and some things to discuss.* She was supposed to meet Peter and discuss the cottage. She looks at the real Peter. "What did she learn?"

"I should probably just show you," he says.

She follows him up the grand staircase and into a study lined with books and with windows looking out at the inlet. Peter sits at a large wooden desk, where a small leather-bound book is neatly centred. He hands it to her.

She opens the front cover and reads aloud. "The confessions of Henry Bellwood, as remembered in October of 1983."

"I believe my grandmother discovered this journal somewhere in this house," he says. "Shortly after your grandfather died, and shortly before she began trying to find me. It doesn't explain everything, but it explains a lot."

"Like what?" asks Dandy.

"You should just read it," he says.

And so she does.

THE CONFESSIONS OF HENRY BELLWOOD

As remembered in October of 1983

My father was aging, and his enterprises
continued to make money, but I couldn't bring
myself to follow in his footsteps. There was
no appeal for me in the dry, airless world
of paper and investments. But the family had
money, and when I approached Father with a
proposal to invest in a new development of
houses, he readily agreed to finance the
project, and my career as a developer began.

I was good at my job. My experiences with
the men who had built Bellwoods came in
handy, and I soon developed a comfortable
rapport with the builders I hired. They
liked me because I valued their opinions
and asked for their advice. It soon became
known locally that Bellwood Developments was
a desirable opportunity for tradespeople and
artisans, and I attracted the best talent.

I was still a young man, and the world was
opening up for me. I had a kind and beautiful wife, a cheerful and intelligent daughter, and my childhood dream of building
things had become a reality. My father lived
with us—or perhaps it's more accurate to say

that we lived with him—and although he was aging quickly, he continued to manage his own affairs, and I often sought his advice and counsel in matters of money and business.

From time to time, I would stroll along the inlet in the early evening and pay a visit to Elmer. His father had died of a heart attack, and Elmer had easily taken over the position of caretaker. He and I would sit in the little glass sunroom, drinking a beer and staring down the inlet. I enjoyed his company, he reminded me of when I was young. Sometimes, he would bring up Junior, but what was there to say? The man was locked up, far away.

We never spoke of the treasure. I knew Elmer had made peace with the thought that we would never see it again, that Archie had somehow taken it away and hidden it some- where else. I could also tell that it didn't bother him. Elmer Feltzen had always been a cheerful, glass half full kind of person, and here in the little house on the inlet, with his friendly wife and their curious, intelligent son, I could tell that he had everything he wanted from life.

I thought about the treasure all the time. After using it to pay off his debts, Father had been true to his word—he hadn't touched another penny of it. Now it sat locked in his safe, as useless and untouched as it had been for all those years at the bottom of the ocean.

It was 1935 and Mirabel was turning six. Her mother decided to take her to Halifax to visit her family and celebrate the spe- cial occasion. The house was quiet without

the little girl's cheerful laughter. After a
simple dinner, Father retired to his study,
and I took my book into the living room to
read by the fire.

It was dark and I had started to nod off,
when the chime of the doorbell rang through
the house. Surprised to have an unexpected
visitor so late, I stood up and walked into
the entrance foyer, unlatching the door and
pulling it open.

Elmer was standing on the veranda. I could
tell right away that something was wrong.
He wasn't smiling, for one thing, and Elmer
always smiled. He didn't wait for me to
invite him inside; he just pushed past me,
and as he did so, I caught a whiff of alcohol and realized that he was unsteady on his
feet.

His words, when he spoke, confirmed that he
was drunk—unusual for Elmer, who rarely had
more than a beer.

"Where's your old man?" he asked.

A chill fluttered over my skin, like the
breeze announcing a storm, but I ignored it
and smiled.

"He's in his study," I said, "but he's probably preparing to retire. Is there something
I can help you with?"

He sneered at me then, a look so out of
place on the face of my old friend that I
felt myself sinking inside.

"Oh, you'll help," he said, contempt dripping from his voice. "The two of you are
going to answer some questions."

Without waiting for me to respond, he stepped around me and into the foyer, his muddy boots leaving tracks on the floor as he stepped to the staircase. Tongue-tied, I followed, hurrying to keep up as he took the steps two at a time. I reached the top as he crossed the landing and threw open the door to Father's study.

"What is the meaning of this?" I heard my father say.

Elmer waited for me to enter the room behind him before speaking. Father was sitting at his desk, a cigar smouldering in an ashtray in front of him, and a crystal tumbler full of whisky close at hand. He looked at me as I stepped into the room, his face wide with shock and anger at the unexpected intrusion.

"Henry, what on earth is going on?" he asked me.

I could only shake my head, although I had a good idea what was coming, this was clearly Elmer's performance. He was never a tall man, but he seemed to grow larger in front of us; he was in full command of the room. He turned back to me and fixed me with a dark gaze before pointing at the chair across from Father's desk.

"Take a seat, Henry," he said.

"How dare you!" my father blustered. "I'll decide who sits and who stands in my own house."

We both ignored him, and meekly I moved to sit.

There was a polished rosewood liquor cabinet against the wall, and Elmer walked

over to it and poured a healthy shot from
a decanter into a glass. His back to us,
he downed it in one go. This time, Father
didn't object. Instead, he looked at me and
I could tell from the frightened expression
on his face that he'd come to the same conclusion I had.

"I ran into an old friend today," Elmer said
finally, slamming the tumbler onto the cabinet and turning to face us. "Red Oakley. You
remember Red, don't you Henry? He was in our
gang, back in the day. He was out with us
in Archie Jinx's dinghy on the day we almost
got into some trouble around the point. You
remember that day, don't you, Henry?"

I managed to nod weakly. From across the
desk, I heard Father clear his throat. A
sharp look from Elmer silenced him. I knew
that as much as he dreaded what was coming,
he wanted to hear it as much as I did.

"Turns out Red—goes by Fred these days—will
be moving back to Maple Bay," Elmer continued. "He's married now, has a son of his
own, and is planning to take over his old
man's practice. I was downtown this afternoon and ran into him. He was quite keen to
see me, asked me to have a drink with him
at the tavern. I was busy, tried to push him
off, but he was quite insistent and I figured, what the hell. No friend like an old
friend, eh, Henry?"

He narrowed his eyes at me and I felt my
hands begin to shake. I grabbed the arms of
the chair to steady myself.

"We got to drinking, and then we got to
talking, and before long we were both deep

into our cups and the stories began to flow. Turned out Red had a lot to say, and one thing in particular stuck out. As a matter of fact, it was a story involving the two of you. A story so interesting that I had to come right here and ask you about it. Now, would either of you care to venture a guess what he told me?"

I had known Elmer for most of my life, and in all that time I had never seen him as anything but cheerful and thoughtful and kind. The man in front of me now was an unfamiliar character. His face was tight and his fists were clenched, and his eyes radi- ated a mixture of anger and indignation and pain, all directed squarely at me.

"How could you have let this happen, Henry?" he asked.

I realized that tears had started to flow down my face. In all of my life, through all of the terrible things that had happened, and all of the awful events yet to come, there was never another moment when I felt as deeply ashamed as I did right then.

"I'm sorry," I whispered.

My father slammed his fist on the table. "Don't say another word, Henry," he demanded, attempting to regain control of the situation.

Elmer whirled on him. "Your day has come, old man. I don't know what you did with the treasure, and I don't care. But you will not sit here for another day, smug in your comfortable house, surrounded by riches, while Junior French rots in a jail cell. The chickens have come home to roost."

My father was breathing heavily, and his face was flushed with anger. He closed his eyes, leaned back in his chair, and managed to catch his breath. For a long, drawn-out moment, Elmer and I watched him, waiting for him to say something. Finally, he opened his eyes and leaned forward, and before either of us knew what was happening, he slid open a desk drawer, pulled out a gun, and shot Elmer straight through the chest.

I stood, my mouth wide with shock, unable to believe what I had just witnessed. On the floor, Elmer let out an anguished gasp and as blood pooled beneath him, his leg twitched violently, and then he was completely still.

I turned to my father, my voice trembling. "In the name of God," I said, "what have you done?"

Father didn't answer. The gun slipped from his hand and fell to the floor, and he dropped back into his chair. He pressed his hand to his chest. At first I thought it was a sign of regret for what he'd done, but then I realized that he was grasping at the buttons of his shirt as if he was trying to rip it open. I watched helplessly as his face turned red, and he began to breathe quickly, in short, small gasps.

"Help," he whispered, his frightened eyes fixed on mine, and then he slumped sideways and fell onto the floor with a heavy thud.

I forced myself to go to him. Kneeling, I managed to push him onto his back. His eyes had rolled back into his head, and there was a waxy pallor to his complexion. I looked

for a pulse, but it was no use, he was
clearly past the point of recovery.

I stood and stared in horror at the scene in
front of me. Both men lay dead on the floor.
How could I possibly explain what had happened here?

I had woven a tangled web, there was
no question. If I called the police and
explained what had happened, there would
be an endless series of questions. Why had
Elmer, known to be one of the kindest, nic-
est men in town, confronted my father in
the first place? What possible argument
or misunderstanding could have led to my
father shooting him in cold blood? I could
play dumb, pretend I hadn't been here, but
that would only pose more questions than it
answered. No matter how I split it, there
was no way around this situation that didn't
result in me revealing everything I knew
about the treasure.

It simply wasn't an option.

To this day, I don't know how I managed
to convince myself to undertake what I did
next. It was as if another man had entered
my body and guided my actions, and I was
simply standing there across the room,
watching myself. I steeled myself, and then
bent to roll Elmer up in the rug. A shameful wave of relief rushed through me when
I realized that most of the blood had been
soaked up by the thick woven wool, and so
the hardwood floor beneath it only needed
a quick wipe. That job completed, I dragged
the awful bundle out of the study and across
the landing. I took my time on the staircase, navigating each step carefully to

avoid inflicting any further indignities on poor Elmer's body.

Finally, once we were down the stairs, across the foyer, and down the veranda steps, I pulled the car around, leaving the headlights off so nobody would happen to notice unusual activity on the road this late at night. Somehow, I hoisted his body into the trunk and got behind the wheel. At the halfway point of Inlet Drive, where the thicket of alders obscures the road from the water, I stopped the car and dragged Elmer's body down through the trees to the shore.

If anyone had chosen this moment to drive along the inlet—teenagers on a date, a police officer killing time until their shift ended—it would have been impossible for me to explain myself. But it was a dark night, and by now the rain was coming down in sheets, and I was the only person around for miles. Indeed it felt, at that terrible hour, as if I were the only person alive in the world.

When I was done, I returned home and retraced my path, clearing up any trace smears of blood from the floor, and then replacing the rug with one from a spare bed-room. I put Father's gun back in the desk drawer, and I knocked his tumbler, still half full of whiskey, onto the floor beside him, then I took the tumbler that Elmer had used and washed and replaced it.

There was one final task to complete. Open-ing Father's safe, I stood and stared for a long moment at the two pine boxes full of gold and silver and jewels, the bulk of what we'd found on that fateful day when we were children. I pulled the boxes out and one last time I ran my hands through the contents, marvelling at the pain and suffering they had brought into the lives of so many people, and cursing the day that we'd found them.

Then I began the process of moving the treasure to my forest hideaway, knowing I would never look at it again.

The sun was beginning to come up as I dragged myself, bone-tired and covered in mud, into the bath. Once I was dry and clothed, I returned to Father's study. Staring down at his body, I used his telephone to call the hospital.

The rest of the day was a blur of activity. The police arrived first, but their questions were routine. There was nothing particularly unusual about the scene in Father's study, and they had no reason to suspect that anything untoward had happened. I had prepared a basic story—I went to bed early, and when Father didn't arrive for breakfast, I checked his study and found him on the floor. It was such a simple, logical, rational explanation that even as the lie slipped through my lips, I could almost believe it myself.

It wasn't until the doctor arrived that my resolve wavered. It was Red Oakley, stepping out of his car and up the veranda steps, looking serious and professional with his doctor's bag.

He confirmed the cause of death quickly
and without much ceremony: a massive heart
attack. Not unusual at his age, especially
considering the shape he was in, and the
alcohol and tobacco present only underscored
the diagnosis. I was grateful when he made
some calls and arranged to have the body
taken away, and we went to stand on the
veranda to wait.

"I suppose this means you'll inherit the
whole lot," he said, and the implication was
clear in his tone.

I'd prepared for this. "It's all gone,
Red," I said. "It didn't last two years. He
gambled some of it and lost the rest in the
stock market."

He nodded, as if he'd expected nothing different. "You'll be better off out from under
the old man's thumb," he said.

I looked at him in surprise. It sounded
as if he had actually developed some
compassion.

"You might be angry to hear this," he said,
"but I told Elmer the whole story. I have
no regrets. He needed to know what happened.
Junior too, I suppose, although that's a
more complicated kettle of fish. The poor
bastard has been rotting in there for the
better part of a decade."

I didn't know what to say to any of this, I
was so shocked by this unexpected tone. He
sounded thoughtful, conciliatory even.

"It wasn't our fault, Henry," he said, putting a hand on my arm. "We were boys. We

338

had no choice in the matter. At the end of
the day, Junior *was* responsible for Archie's
death, so I'm not sure what purpose telling him would serve." He sighed. "I probably
shouldn't have said anything to Elmer, but
we were drunk, and after all these years,
I just wanted to talk to someone about it.
Elmer is an easygoing kind of fellow. I suppose he'll come to see you about it, just to
talk the whole thing through. He mentioned
that you're still his best friend, even
after all these years. Perhaps the three of
us can get together sometime for old times'
sake."

The ambulance arrived then, and he went down
to meet them, leaving me on the veranda to
absorb the rest on my own.

When Elmer didn't return home, his wife
reached out to friends and neighbours to ask
if anyone had seen him. He had never disappeared before, she said, and she was worried.

A couple of days later, one of his boots
washed up onshore. By this time, people had
reported him leaving the tavern and disappearing into the night, drunk and stumbling.
The younger Doctor Oakley was questioned,
and he confirmed the story. By the time he'd
left the tavern to walk home, Elmer had been
in a rough state. Red had offered him the
use of a sofa, but Elmer had insisted on
walking home to clear his head. There was no
mention anywhere of the story Red had told
him. I could only assume that he'd left that
part out of his account.

There were search parties up and down the coast, but after a few days the efforts dwindled. There was an expectation that the body would appear someday. The sea always revealed her secrets.

But in this case, she disappointed.

I went to see Elmer's widow a week or so after he went missing. I took Mirabel with me, and we were greeted at the door by her sister, who ushered us through the house, full of family and friends, and down into the sunroom.

She was sitting in the corner, her little boy on the floor beside her, playing a game.

Reggie looked up and smiled at the sight of Mirabel. As she joined him on the floor, I sat across from his mother.

"We'll be out of here as soon as we can get ourselves sorted out," she said.

I stared at her, taken aback.

"I'm not here to ask you to leave," I said. "On the contrary. I came because I wanted you to know that you should consider this house yours from now forward. And to pay my respects, of course."

She seemed surprised. "I would have expected you'd need a new caretaker," she said. "I can't do that work."

I waved off her concerns. "I'll hire someone to come in and do the work that needs doing. Don't worry about that. This is your home, and someday it will be Reggie's home. I just want you to know that."

She nodded, staring at me thoughtfully.

"What do you think happened to Elmer?" she asked.

I considered my reply carefully, and then I lied to her face.

"I don't think any of us will ever know," I said.

There were more amends to make. I paid a visit to Archie's wife and child, embarrassed at the state of the small shack that Elmer and I had fixed up for her. I promised her that I would help her improve her situation, and I brought together some of my builders and directed them as they built a new house, farther back along the point. It was still a small dwelling, but much nicer and more comfortable, and they moved into it happily. I had the old building removed.

My next task was the most difficult, and I'll admit I put it off for a time. But finally I found the resolve to drive into the city and arrange for a meeting with Junior. He didn't seem surprised to see me, even though I hadn't sent warning. He sat down across the small table and smiled at me.

"It's been a long time, Henry," he said.

"I'm sorry I haven't been here to see you," I told him.

He shook his head. "No need. Nobody wants to come to a place like this."

"Is it that bad?" I asked.

He shrugged. "It's okay. I work in the kitchens. I bake, and I enjoy it. I've been thinking that I might want to continue, once I'm out."

This was the kind of opening I'd been looking for.

"I'll help you," I said.

He raised an eyebrow. "What do you mean?"

"You know my father is dead?" I asked. He nodded. "Well, he owns—owned—a lot of real estate. I can help you find a proper building and you can open a bakery."

He considered this. "In Maple Bay?"

"Yes," I said. "I'll put down the money to help you start the business."

"Why are you doing this, Henry?" he asked.

"You've heard about Elmer?" I asked.

"Yes," he said simply.

"I would like to see someone come out of this with a chance at a new life," I said.

"Out of this," he repeated. "Out of that godforsaken treasure, you mean?"

I nodded.

"None of that is your fault," he said.

I couldn't respond. There was nothing to say.

*　*　*

A shadow had fallen over me, and I was sad all the time. But I drew strength and comfort from my family, and I was grateful for the light they attempted to bring into my life. Sometimes, my wife and I would sit on the veranda with a cup of tea and listen to the sound of Mirabel playing with her friends down on the shore, young Billy Jinx and Reggie Feltzen. Those moments were happy for me, and sometimes I could almost forget what I had done.

Time passed. Junior was released, and I was good to my word, lending him the funds to open a bakery, and selling him one of Father's commercial buildings in town for a small sum. He was a talented baker, and the business was a success. About a year after the business was opened, he married and soon after he and his wife welcomed their first child, a little girl. I knew that Junior could never get those wasted years back, but I found a small measure of satisfaction that he was able to find happiness and fulfillment in his new circumstances.

Mirabel grew up, and the games of adventure she had so enjoyed with the boys came to an end as she began to navigate the world as a young lady. I kept an eye on the young men, giving them work whenever possible, and offering to help them if they ever decided to pursue an education. Neither of them did.

The rhythms of the world are powerful. Even the most chaotic periods drift away with time, and one can be fooled into imagining that balance has been established, and will remain.

I'm grateful that my wife lived long enough to see Mirabel married. Within the year, she was buried, after a courageous battle with cancer. Her passing thrust me into a deep well of depression, and I found myself unable to engage with the world. Mirabel and John did their best to bring me back to the world of the living, but I was broken once again. What had my beautiful, sweet wife done to deserve this early end, when I was standing right there, a guilty man many times over?

The way my wife's fate echoed my mother's was not lost on me, and I began to return once again to the site of the old house in the forest on the other side of the Point. It was gone by now, a pile of rotten lumber and moss-covered stones the only thing left, but time and time again I found my way back to that space in the woods where I had found refuge as a child, and I would sit on the old stone wall, weeping and gnashing my teeth against the injustice of all the things that had come before.

I am sure I would have taken my own life, so dark was the shadow on the valley of my soul, had it not been for Susan. The brightest light of my life, I can say this now—with all credit due to my mother and my wife and my beautiful daughter Mirabel—Susan was the one person who taught me I could perhaps find my way back to a brighter space.

She was a kind girl, intelligent and funny and an exceptional conversationalist. From

the very first days she began to talk, she
would bring her chatter to my study, and
we would spend endless hours speaking of so
many things. She thought of me as a men-
tor of sorts, I suppose, and in my old
age I became her babysitter. Mirabel had
taken over my business, and John was busy
in the pharmacy, and they encouraged our
connection. I found myself waking up smiling again. Instead of dreading each day, I
looked forward to it, and Susan and I aged
together—I into an old man, she into a young
lady. In those days, girls were beginning to
pursue new avenues, and Susan seemed des-
tined for a bright future. I think we all
expected her to become a doctor, or a judge,
or a brilliant writer.

But then she met that boy, and she decided
to point herself in a different direction.
We were all of us shocked when she announced
her pregnancy—Mirabel and John and myself.
We'd barely met Parson, who had only come to
town for a summer of fishing, sailing, and
carousing, but she insisted that he was the
love of her life and they were going to make
a go of things.

Of course, now it's all so obvious to us
that if we'd only shown her the love and
support she clearly craved, we would have
kept her with us, and we could have had a
new generation living in Bellwoods.

But we chose a different route. The screaming fights, the angry words, the painful
accusations thrown through the halls of this
house, were as awful as anything I'd heard
in a generation, since the day I watched
Archie and Junior fighting by the maple

tree. It was her mother who took the lead,
and Mirabel could be a cold woman when she
wanted to be, but even good-natured John had
his part to play, and the house was weighed
down by a dark fog, so heavy that I wondered
if it would ever lift.

I stayed out of the conflict at first, and
I still wonder if perhaps things would have
worked out differently if I had continued
to hold my tongue. But at a certain point,
I decided I needed to intervene. I invited
Susan to the study, and at Father's huge oak
desk, I filled her in on every last detail
of my deepest, darkest secrets.

What was I thinking? If you'd asked me in
the moment, I probably would have said I
was trying to put things in perspective for
Susan. That by telling her in great, grue-
some detail just how much worse things could
be, I could help her recognize that none of
this—the baby, the boyfriend, the change in
plans—was a big deal, that the frenzy would
pass and eventually we all would look back
at this period and laugh at the fuss that
had been made.

But of course that would have been nonsense.
I could have said all of those things, I
could have been a voice of reason and a
shoulder to cry on, without opening Pan-
dora's box. I couldn't admit it to myself at
the time, but I see it now as clear as day.

I was desperate to unburden myself.

So I did. I went all the way back to my
childhood, to my gang of friends, to the
misery we unlocked when we dragged that
chest to shore. I told her every single

thing I did, and every secret I kept, and every evil I facilitated, and as I spoke I felt myself lighten as I released my story into the world. My relief was so great that I failed to notice it was landing on someone else's shoulders.

I was in a trance. I was barely aware of Susan sitting across from me until finally I had come to the end of my confession. I took a deep breath, running my hands over my face, and I think I even smiled, and then I turned to look at my granddaughter, and I knew I had made a terrible, terrible mistake.

Her face was grey, and her mouth was open just a bit, a tiny gap in the flatness of her expression. She blinked several times, quickly, and then she stood up.

"I'm sorry," she said, clutching protectively at her stomach. "I'm—I'm not feeling well. The baby is—"

Without finishing her sentence, she turned and walked out of the room. I knew better than to follow her.

Susan was gone in the morning. She and Parson had packed up quickly and left in the night. It was Mirabel who discovered that they were gone, and there was a long, awful week when she and John tried desperately to track them down—an impossible task: How were they supposed to do that? I knew that Mirabel and John thought she'd left because of them, that their concerns over the baby, her unmarried state, had finally driven her away, but I knew the truth. I knew that once she

arrived on the West Coast, she'd call and
tell them the real reason she'd left: me.

She ended up calling earlier than expected,
from a campsite in Ontario. I only heard
Mirabel's part of the conversation, which
was thin and clipped and, ultimately, short.
Susan had called to tell them she was moving
to be with Parson's family, and she'd be in
touch if and when she felt like it.

My daughter had always been a controlled
person. She rarely raised her voice and
always tried to project a calm exterior.
But something changed in her after that
phone call. A stillness settled within her
that made me wonder if she would ever come
entirely back to us again, the way she had
been. But still I held my tongue. I waited,
allowing myself to believe that Susan would
eventually come to her senses and, if not
forgive me, at least not punish Mirabel for
my actions.

I was willing to take a gamble on whether or
not Susan would eventually tell her mother
what I had confessed to her. But I couldn't
tell that story again. Not to my daughter,
who still loved me.

By the time John had his heart attack and
died at work, and still there was no word
from Susan, it was too late. Mirabel entered
a new phase of her life, and there she
remains, two years later. She is, for all
intents and purposes, a veiled widow. A
stern, martyred person. *A woman left behind.*

And I am now, well and truly, an old man in
my dotage. A great-grandfather, we presume,

although we have heard nothing from Susan, whose child would be a toddler by now.

Doctor Oakley came to see me yesterday. The younger one. Frank, Red's son, although I can't very well call him young. Even five years younger than Mirabel, he's well into middle age himself. He's a shrewd man, like his father. It can be hard to read behind his eyes, but if he ever learned the secrets his father and I shared, he never let on. I'm inclined to think he doesn't know a thing, and that Red took our story to the grave when he passed away some five years back.

Junior is gone too. A year this September. In all the times I spoke with Junior after he was released from prison, he never once mentioned the treasure, and if I was a betting man, I'd gamble he didn't think about it much, either. He left behind a thriving business, a loving family, and the respect of his community—in short, he left the earth on good terms and, I hope, with a peaceful conscience.

I won't be able to say the same when I go, and if Oakley's diagnosis is to be believed, that day is coming soon. Once, we were the Treasure Hunters Club, five boys aglow with the vibrancy of youth. Now I'm an old man, the last of us standing, and I don't have much time left.

I'm too weak, in every sense of the word, to tell Mirabel this story to her face. I've written it down because I expect that once I'm gone, Susan will come home, and she'll fill her mother in on the story. This is my way of corroborating the account and filling

in the details so there's no uncertainty
about what really happened.

Susan knows exactly where the treasure is,
but I will leave it to her to decide if she
wants to unearth it.

So it will sit hidden, awaiting her return.

A LETTER FOR
MIRABEL

Dandy reads the journal perched in a window seat in the corner of Mirabel's study. When she finishes, she stares out the window for a long time, scratching her chin and thinking.

Finally, she turns to me. "Bill wasn't digging in the forest."

"I don't understand," I say.

"Those holes in the forest," she says. "We thought that Bill had dug them, or at least *started* digging them, and then Ricky took over."

I've already considered this. "It makes sense that Ricky was looking in the forest, because Henry says in the journal that's where he hid the treasure, but maybe Bill was digging there first, and Ricky caught up to him."

"No," says Dandy. "Bill never saw this journal. He had no reason to think the treasure was in the woods. But I think he *did* see the chart."

"The chart your grandfather left you when he died," I say, trying to keep track.

"Exactly," she says. "He wanted me to bring it to the society and share it with them. He thought if I brought them a clue, it would convince them to let me join. It showed that a building on the coast abruptly disappeared at some point *after* the treasure went missing, and I offered to check it out."

"But you didn't find anything," I point out.

Dandy nods. "That's right, but I did run into Bill. He told me that I was wasting my time, that I wouldn't find anything there, because there'd never been anything there. He was kind of drunk and talking in riddles, but he sounded really confident, like he knew what he was talking about."

She's thinking hard, working it out as she speaks. "Henry said in his journal that he had a new home built for Archie's wife and child. That would have been Bill and his mother. I think the *old shack* was the one shown on Grandy's chart."

"But Bill would have known about that already, wouldn't he?" I ask.

"Not necessarily," says Dandy. "If the shack was moved when Bill was still too young to remember, he might never have realized that he once lived in a run-down shanty. He also told me that he visited Grandy in the hospital before he died. They were old friends, and I think Grandy would have felt some loyalty to Bill. I think maybe he gave *Bill* a copy of the chart as well."

"I still don't understand what difference it makes," I say. "Bill told you himself, there had never been anything there."

"It was never about the *old* shack," Dandy says, and there's a hint of excitement in her voice. "It was about the *new* shack. Bill told me that he always believed Henry Bellwood knew where the treasure was hidden, but for some reason he'd kept it secret, even from Mirabel, until after he died. When Grandy showed Bill the chart, it tipped him off to something."

"But what?" I ask.

"That the new shack was built shortly after Alexander Bellwood died," she says, growing excited. "Mrs. French told me that old man Bellwood had a reputation as a stingy old bastard. I think Bill put two and two together and figured what we already know from the journal: that at some point Alexander Bellwood intercepted the treasure, and it wasn't until he died that Henry was able to get it back."

"But Bill didn't have the journal," I say as things begin to come into focus. "So he didn't know that Henry hid the treasure in the forest behind Bellwoods."

"Exactly," says Dandy. "After Bill died, I went inside his shack. I noticed digging tools propped in the corner, but I noticed something else, too. There was a strong draft rising up from the floor. I assumed it was just an old, drafty house, but now I think maybe . . ."

"He was digging underneath his own house," I say, finishing the thought.

The shack is small and dark, and just as Dandy promised, there's an aggressive draft coming up from the floorboards.

I help her move the sofa away from the thick old rug in the middle of the floor, and she kneels and begins to roll the rug back, revealing the weathered floorboards beneath.

"They've been pried up," I say, crouching beside her and examining the edges. The boards come up easily, and soon a dark, shallow pit is revealed in the middle of the room.

Dandy unslings her leather pouch and pulls out a heavy-duty old-school flashlight. She shines it into the pit and the beam reflects back to us on a pool of groundwater, but beyond that, the hole appears to be empty.

She hands me the flashlight, and before I can protest, she kicks off her shoes and socks and shimmies to the edge of the hole, dropping herself down feetfirst. The water reaches only to her knees.

I guide the beam as she begins to move around, carefully examining the sides of the pit, but then she stops abruptly and stares down at her feet before plunging her arm into the water. A moment later, she pulls something out.

It's a human skull.

"What the fuck?" I ask, skittering back from the hole.

"Watch the light," she says.

Despite the fact that Dandy is the one in a wet pit, presumably surrounded by bones, she does a much better job of keeping her cool. It isn't until I shine the flashlight back into the hole that I realized she's holding the skull directly in front of her face, and her eyes are wet with tears.

"This was my great-grandfather," she says, her voice thick with emotion. "Grandy spent his whole life feeling like he'd been abandoned by this man's carelessness. I wish he was still here to learn the truth."

"You know the truth," I tell her, reaching down to help her up. "I think that's the next best thing."

We decide to wait until tomorrow to contact the police. We both agree that, after this many years, one more day unreported won't make a whole lot of difference. She carefully places the skull on one of Bill's bookshelves, and after bidding her goodbye, I return to Bellwoods.

There's one more thing I need to do.

I find what I'm looking for slipped into an inside pocket of my backpack, and carry it upstairs to the study. Sitting at the heavy wooden desk, I finally open my mother's final letter to Mirabel.

As I unfold the letter, a photograph falls onto the desk. It's a tiny shot of me as a toddler, dressed in a little plaid outfit in front of a mall photographer's backdrop straight out of the early eighties. I stare at myself for a moment and then reach up to slide the photo into the frame displaying my mother.

My last thought before I begin to read is just how much I look like her.

Mommy—

It's been a while, and I'm sure this letter comes as a surprise to you, but I learned of Grandfather's passing and knew right away that I had to reach out. It's been a long time, and I know I have myself to blame for that. I won't forgive you entirely—not yet—because we need to have a conversation to work through some things before I'm willing to forget how you and Daddy reacted to the news of my pregnancy. But I'm hoping that the photograph I've enclosed of little Peter will help you convince yourself to meet me halfway. I'm willing to meet you there as well.

I feel as if there is much to discuss and a letter isn't the right spot for most of it. I do want you and Daddy to know that I didn't leave because of you. I was furious, of course. But I think we could have found our way through that. The truth is that I left because of Grandfather. He told me some things, Mother . . . I don't know if he told them to you before he died, but whatever the case the things he told me explained a lot about our family, and the truth is . . . after that I couldn't stand the thought of bringing my son up in that home.

But now he's gone, and my opinions have shifted. I believe he unburdened himself to me because he wanted to make amends. I have taken it upon myself to begin that process. You may have received a letter recently from an anonymous sender—it was me. It was my way of trying to point you all toward the truth, but thinking about it now my approach was probably clumsy and confusing. I doubt the five of you have taken the time to come together under such vague pretenses, and so I have decided that I will tell you all what I know when I return to Maple Bay this summer. Maybe then we can all choose to move on together.

It's true! We want to come home, Mommy. Parson's family is not welcoming, and I miss the East Coast. I have a desperate need for you and Daddy to meet my baby. Perhaps, if things go well, there might be room for the three of us at Bellwoods? Parson is a good man, and a hard worker, and he loves us both. Peter is the sweetest little boy you could imagine, and wouldn't it do Bellwoods some good to hold the laughter of a child again? As for me, I miss you both terribly. I miss the inlet and the woods and, yes, even that monstrous old house.

Please say we can come home?

I love you, I love you, I'm sorry, I love you—

Your Susan.

DIRECTION

"So the bones belonged to Elmer Feltzen?" says Falia, who is visiting from New York.

"Yes," says Cass. "The theory is that after old man Bellwood shot and killed Elmer, Henry dragged his body to the shore and couldn't bring himself to throw his old friend into the sea, so he attempted to give him a proper burial instead. Then he had a new shanty built on top of the site, presumably to keep the body from being unearthed."

"But then Archie Jinx found the bones."

"Bill Jinx," Cass corrects. "Archie was Bill's father. *He* died accidentally during a fight with Junior French, who went to prison."

"And evil Ricky-not-Peter killed Bill?"

Cass nods. "After Bill found the bones underneath his shack. He got drunk and went to Bellwoods to confront Ricky, because he thought Ricky was Peter, the last living Bellwood. But Ricky was already suspicious that Bill was honing in on the treasure, and killed him."

Falia thinks about this for a long moment.

"Okay, so, Cass? This is fucking crazy."

Cass laughs. "Right? In the book I'll have a chart explaining who all the key players are, and probably a map of the Point."

Falia reaches out to punch Cass on the arm. "The book!" she screams. "My bestie is writing a book and she's going to make a trillion bucks!"

"Oh, I don't know about that," says Cass.

"I do," says Falia. "This story is a trip, and you have an all-access pass. I told you. What's the mantra?"

"Opportunity," says Cass.

"Opportunity," says Falia, nodding.

In the weeks since Ricky's death, a lot has happened. Much of it isn't public knowledge, not yet, but Cass has been privy to a lot of it. The journal, for instance, is still top secret because the police are using it to help guide them through two very old murder cases, but Cass has had a chance to read a copy, thanks to Dandy Feltzen.

It was Dandy who told Peter about the book Cass was writing, about her friendship with Bill Jinx and how he'd trusted her to tell his story. That was enough for Peter to reach out to Cass, asking her if she'd be willing to continue with the book and offering to help out any way he could.

"Their story deserves to be told," he said when they met for coffee at French's bakery.

Since then, she's had a chance to speak to Mrs. French and Dandy and her mother, and they also agreed to participate, offering to tell her their stories on an exclusive basis. But it was the journal that really iced the cake, shedding light on so much, and filling out this unbelievable story in countless magical ways. Opportunity indeed.

The two women have been chatting nonstop since Cass picked Falia up at the airport, but when they turn into the driveway at Bellwoods, Falia goes completely silent as she stares up at the huge house.

"Fuck me," she says finally, once Cass has parked and they've climbed out of the car. "This place is incredible."

"Hello!" They glance up to see Bree stepping through the front door, cocktail in hand, a silky flowered caftan flowing around her. She comes down the front steps and pulls Falia into an embrace. "Oh my goodness, honey, I feel like I already know you."

"Thank you for taking care of my girl," says Falia.

Bree laughs. "Oh lord. This one doesn't need any help, I think she's proven that she knows how to take care of herself. Peter is in the kitchen, laying out snacks. I told him I'd take care of the main course, just as long as he let me throw a dinner party in this house before he moves out. Now, who wants a cocktail?"

Bree ushers them inside and pours them drinks at the sideboard in the living room and then takes it upon herself to give Falia a tour while Cass continues to the kitchen. Peter greets her with a hug and then continues arranging cheese and charcuterie on a giant wooden board.

"You look at home here," she says as she watches him move around the kitchen with ease. "Are you sure you don't want to keep it?"

He shakes his head. "Are you kidding? It's hard enough sleeping just a couple of floors above the place where I was held captive and tortured, but I am also pretty sure this place is haunted. It's also gigantic. I don't want to clean a house like this for the rest of my life. I'll be happier in the apartment above the bookstore."

In true Bree fashion, she's more or less adopted real-Peter, to borrow a phrase from Dandy, and essentially replaced Ricky—aka fake-Peter—in one clean move. He's going to step into the job at the bookstore and move into the little one-bedroom apartment upstairs. She's already trying to set him up with Officer What-a-waste. Cass is happy for Peter, but mostly she's just selfishly pleased that she won't be the only newcomer who has decided to stay in Maple Bay.

Bellwoods, on the other hand, is going to be taking on a new form. Peter has decided to turn the house into a museum and inter-pretive centre, and he'll use the proceeds to fund the treasure hunt. It will be a collaborative opportunity for academics and amateur treasure hunters to look for Dagger's cache in the wooded acres behind the house, in a noninvasive way.

"Anyone home?" someone calls from the hallway.

"We're down here!" Cass calls, and a moment later Bryson steps into the kitchen, holding two bottles of wine.

"I didn't know if I should go for red or white," he says, placing them on the counter. "So I played it safe." He turns to Cass and pulls her into him, giving her a deep kiss on the mouth as Peter, amused, moves to the fridge to give them some space.

Bryson pulls back and turns to Peter. "Have you got five min-utes to chat? I had a great conversation with a professor in Germany today. He's keen to pull together a team for a month-long dig."

"That can wait," says Cass, taking him by the hand. "You have to meet Falia."

Soon Dandy and her mother arrive with Mrs. French in tow, and after snacks on the veranda, they move to the formal dining room for the main event. Over an elaborate three-course meal cour-tesy of Peter and Bree, the conversation is lively, even as it keeps turning back in the same direction.

"So when does the actual work begin in the backyard?" Falia asks.

"It's not really a backyard," says Bryson. "It's more like fifteen acres of woods and rocks. It'll be a big job, and there are no guarantees that we'll even find anything."

Peter has enlisted Bryson for the big project. He'll be carrying out survey work and coordinating the applications for access to the property. He's extremely excited to be involved so closely in the treasure hunt, but as far as Cass is concerned, the best part is that he'll be settling in Maple Bay more permanently. He's already started looking for an apartment, and although she doesn't want to get ahead of herself, she can't help but think that the Trappers will be home in less than a year, and she'll have to find *somewhere* to live. But there's plenty of time for that to sort itself out.

"So you all really believe that the treasure is still out there somewhere?" Falia asks.

"Absolutely," says Cass, nodding firmly. "One hundred percent. There are so many signs pointing in that direction that it would be more outlandish to think there *isn't* a hidden treasure."

"We won't stop until we've turned over every stone and dug under every root," says Bryson. "We're already speaking to several archaeology programs."

"Obviously it would be a lot quicker to just raze the woods and bulldoze the area," says Peter, "but this will be more in the spirit of what Reggie and Mirabel and Bill and Frank would have wanted."

"Imagine finally digging up that treasure," says Bree. "What an ending for your book, Cass."

"What will happen to the money if you find it?" asks Falia.

Peter doesn't hesitate. "I'll divide it between Rose and the Feltzens," he says. "It's only right, after everything we've learned."

But Mrs. French shakes her head. "I don't care about that money. If you poured it out on my feet, I'd kick it away. If my father's story tells me anything, it's that true satisfaction comes from the life you build, not the life you buy." She turns to Dandy's mother. "Speaking of which, how is Margot handling everything?"

The development is off, obviously. Learning that she didn't own the cottage was a big enough blow, but when Frank Oakley's will was read, it turned out that he had made a last-minute change of heart. He'd decided to pull out of his arrangement with Margot and left all of his land to the Maple Bay Historical Society, which, as it turns out, is an officially registered organization. It also turns out that the only two officers left are Mrs. French and Dandy, who decided without hesitation to donate their inheritance to Peter's project.

"Margot will be fine," says Mary. "She's not one to cry over spilled milk. She'll have another scheme cooked up soon enough. Besides, even my sister realizes that everything else pales in comparison to what we've learned about our family. To think that our father spent his whole life thinking that *his* father got drunk and fell in the inlet, when the truth was so much more complicated."

"My family was responsible for a lot of pain," says Peter. "I feel like I'll spend the rest of my life trying to make up for it."

"None of that is on you, Peter," says Mrs. French. "When my father got out of prison, he was determined to make a new life for himself. He could have let himself become bitter, but he chose the opposite path. He moved on with his life and savoured every moment back on the outside. He didn't have an ounce of malice in his soul, and I truly believe that he would have forgiven Henry

Bellwood, given the chance. I'm sorry to say I don't have the same strength of character, and I will never forgive Henry for what he did, but I don't hold it against you, Peter. The sins of the father should never be visited on the son . . . or the daughter."

"What do you mean by that?" asks Dandy.

"I think it's clear," says Mrs. French. "When Mirabel found the journal, she couldn't very well tell anyone what had happened— here was cold, hard proof, in her father's own hand, that he and her grandfather had carried out terrible atrocities, all in the name of gold. I knew Mirabel for many years, and I can tell you that there was a change in her during the final months of her life. There was a time when she would never have considered letting you join the group, Dandy. I think once she learned all of these terrible things about her family, she became determined to make amends."

She turns to look at Peter again. "I believe that's why she made one final attempt to find you, Peter. I believe she wanted you to come here because she needed someone to help her bear this burden. To help her decide which steps to take next. She needed family."

"To find the treasure?" asks Cass.

"Perhaps," says Mrs. French. "Eventually. But I believe all of it, the treasure, the society . . . it all came second to her real final mission. Atonement. And the real path to atonement is by setting their stories free so their spirits can move on." She reaches across the table and takes Cass's hand in her own. "That's why we're so happy you found us, Cass. You're going to help us bring everything into the light."

"Have you thought of a title yet?" asks Dandy.

"Isn't it obvious?" asks Cass. "I'm going to call it *The Treasure Hunters Club.*"

THE LAST WORD

It feels so good to be back in Grandy's house. Dandy has taken the bedroom under the eaves, with the dormer window that looks down along the inlet. In the evening when her mom gets home from work, they sit in the sunroom chatting until it's gone completely dark, and it feels like they've finally come home.

Dandy's mother tried more than once to convince Peter to accept some kind of payment or rent for the cottage, but he wouldn't hear of it and insisted on signing the entire place over to them. They didn't even have to buy furniture. It all stays, along with the books on the shelves and the pottery in the cabinets, and everything else that was supposed to go to Margot. In a rare moment of graciousness, she told them to keep it all. "It belongs with the house," she said. "And besides, selling it would just be a hassle."

Now they have a home of their own, Dandy and her mother and also, sometimes, the ghost of Grandy. She'll feel him appearing in a doorway behind her, slipping from the corner of her eye just as she turns around. Or she'll catch the scent of him, black tea and old wool, as she steps down the narrow stairwell, and know he's descended just ahead of her.

But it's in the sunroom where she feels him most of all. A warm spot in the seat of his battered old chair, when she flops to read and doze and daydream her way through an afternoon. A shift in the air when she closes her eyes, his presence hovering so close she can almost hear him breathing, feel his face twisting into a gentle smile. When she lies on her back and stares at the ceiling, she can feel him wandering through the yard and down to the water, watching the seasons change, the water lapping against the shore.

He won't stay forever. She knows that. He's here because he has something to tell her. It's not urgent, but it's important, and although she wants to hold off on hearing him out, on recognizing what he means to say, trying to hold back your thoughts is like trying to turn back a clock. They only move in one direction.

And so it comes to Dandy one evening when she's flopped in Grandy's chair in the sunroom, staring out the window at the gleaming full moon. It comes to her all at once, the obvious solution to this most complicated mystery, and as she sits bolt upright in the chair, she suddenly feels Grandy behind her in the corner of the room, leaning against the bookshelf and staring at her.

She can already feel the hot tears filling her eyes, because she knows that this final revelation will mark his final goodbye. That he's been lingering until she figures things out.

"Why are you in such a rush?" she says out loud.

He doesn't answer her, but she can feel his love and sorrow fill the space around her, and she begins to weep, staring out the window until she can hardly bear it any longer, and she forces herself to turn around and look across the room, expecting him to slip from the corner of her vision one last time before disappearing forever.

But he's there. A soft, glowing presence. A radiant face smiling back across the room at her. The moment hardly lasts at all, but it lasts long enough, and then, in a blink, he's gone. She stares at the empty space for a long time before she notices something else. The little green sailboat is back on its shelf, but this time it isn't facing left or right. Its bow is pointing out, straight down the inlet at Bellwoods, a final piece of proof that she's figured it all out.

She slides into her shoes and hoodie, slings the leather bag over her shoulder, and slips out the sunroom door into the night.

The moon glows over the inlet road, and although she doubts she'll see anyone at this time of night, she sticks to the shadows along the edge until she gets to Bill's driveway and follows it down to the shore for the rest of her journey.

She shivers as she passes Bill's little shack, wondering if the ghost of Grandy's father looked like the ghost of Grandy. From Bill's description, the ghost that visited him was angry and vengeful, but maybe that was just because he had more cause to feel wronged.

On the rocky beach below Bellwoods, she stares up at the huge house. Every window is dark. Peter moved out a few weeks ago, and the house has been sitting empty ever since, waiting for its next act.

She climbs up from the beach and slips between the maples onto the property, sliding through the shadows until she's safely concealed at the back of the house. There's cardboard taped over the window in the back door that she broke after getting out of the well. It peels back easily, and she slips her hand down to unlock the deadbolt.

Inside, she pulls the old flashlight from Grandy's satchel and clicks it on. She can feel the house listening as she makes her way down the hallway to the grand entrance hall. She shines the light up at the portraits on the wall, taking a moment to acknowledge the two Bellwood men who were responsible for so much heartache. Then she turns the beam, along with her attention, to the staircase.

The carved panels along the side are beautiful and ornate, but she doesn't waste much time admiring the craftsmanship. She's looking for a natural spot to place the knuckles of two hands, and after she tries several options, taking care to keep them as wide as she imagines a small boy's hands would be, she finds it. Just like the hidden cabinet in Grandy's sunroom, there's a particular way to press, and with a soft *click*, a piece of panelling pops open, revealing the hidden room inside.

It's a small space, but easily big enough for a child to hide out in. A tiny room devised and constructed by craftsmen who were far from home and missing their families, who recognized that a lonely, motherless little boy could use a place of his own, and built him a child-sized hideaway inside their beautifully carved forest.

Dandy's flashlight shines on a few toys, some books, and a moth-eaten quilt and pillow. In the corner, two pine boxes, thick with dust, sit stacked one on top of the other.

It takes Dandy almost two hours to get the boxes onto the dolly she finds in the basement, out the back door, through the woods, and to the rocky rise at the tip of the Point. By the time she stops and sits, the boxes unopened beside her, the sun is beginning its ascent, and the sky is lightening just enough to reveal the crash of waves below her.

For a long moment, she sits there, staring out to sea, aware of Grandy sitting nearby, just out of sight. She thinks about everything he taught her: that wonderful things can be found hidden in misty coves and mountain caves; that everyone has a unique story and they all play out underneath the same huge sky; that the sun can be counted on to break above the horizon every single day, forever and ever.

He taught her that there's more value in a walk together on the beach, in discovering a time-smoothed bottle in the sand, in a good yarn shared with a captive audience, than in all the gold in the world.

Dandy knows her grandfather won't be following her home, but he's here with her now, sitting right behind her shoulder as she opens the first box. Together they watch as the sun rips open the sky, and every time a piece of gold spins through the daybreak and slips back into the sea, it's one more moment they share.

THE END

ACKNOWLEDGMENTS

Thank you to my literary agents, Samantha Haywood and Amy Tompkins at Transatlantic, for their invaluable support and advice at every single step of this process; from their insightful notes on first version of this manuscript—which led to a substantial rewrite and a much stronger book—to their razor-sharp submission strategy that led to the perfect publishing scenario for this novel.

Thank you to my brilliant editors, Joe Brosnan at Grove Atlantic and Adrienne Kerr at Simon & Schuster Canada. The synergy that evolved as our little team of three worked to bring this story across the finish line made this entire experience joyful and fulfilling and endlessly rewarding. I am so grateful to both of you for taking a chance on me and this book.

Likewise, the entire teams at Grove Atlantic and S&S Canada have been an absolute delight to work with. From Dan Rembert and Gretchen Mergenthaler's incredible cover design and packaging, to marketing and sales, and beyond, TTHC has been handled in all regards with tremendous care and attention.

My parents, Beth and Tom Ryan, who always supported and encouraged my pursuit of a career in the arts, were early readers and gave me valuable feedback on an early version of this story. In 2021 my in-laws, Joan and Dan Sargeant, invited me to housesit their beautiful seaside home near Lunenburg, Nova Scotia, during which time the premise and first chapters of this book emerged.

There are so many wonderful people in my corner—friends and family and of course, readers—who've boosted me in so many ways over the years. I am very grateful to everyone who keeps showing up and spreading the word.

Finally, my deepest love and gratitude to Andrew for his unfailing support. Without him, I would never have taken the first step on this wild and wonderful journey.

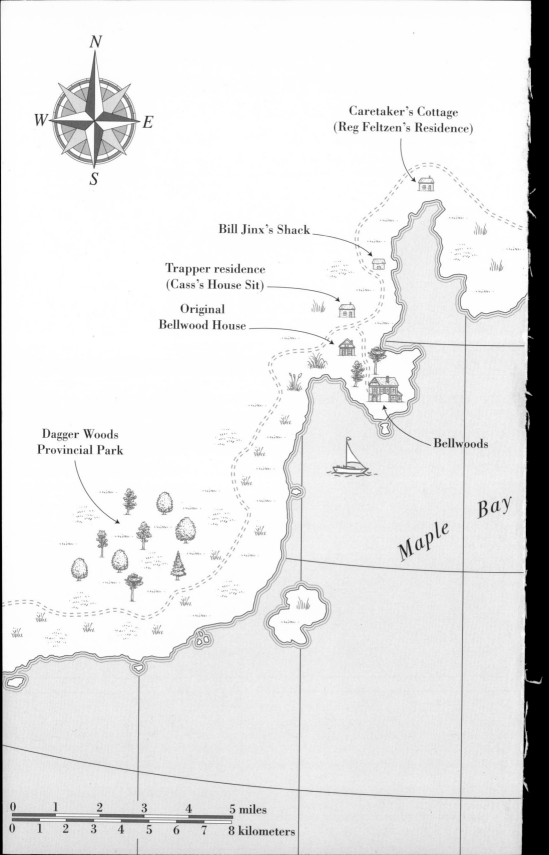